T0381958

A Schooling in Murder

Andrew Taylor is the author of a number of crime novels, including the ground-breaking Roth Trilogy, which was adapted into the acclaimed TV drama *Fallen Angel*, the Marwood and Lovett historical crime series and *The American Boy*, a No.1 *Sunday Times* best-seller and a Richard & Judy Book Club choice. He has won many awards, including an Edgar Scroll from the Mystery Writers of America, the HWA Gold Crown, and the CWA's prestigious Diamond Dagger, awarded for sustained excellence in crime writing. He lives with his wife Caroline in the Forest of Dean.

𝕏 @AndrewJRTaylor
www.andrew-taylor.co.uk

By the same author

A
Schooling
in Murder

ANDREW TAYLOR

HEMLOCK
PRESS

Hemlock Press
An imprint of HarperCollins*Publishers*
1 London Bridge Street,
London SE1 9GF
www.harpercollins.co.uk

HarperCollins*Publishers*
Macken House, 39/40 Mayor Street Upper
Dublin 1, D01 C9W8, Ireland

First published by HarperCollins*Publishers* Ltd 2025
1

A catalogue copy of this book is available from the British Library.

ISBN: 9780008494230 (HB)
ISBN: 9780008494247 (TPB)

This novel is entirely a work of fiction. The names, characters and incidents portrayed
in it are the work of the author's imagination. Any resemblance to actual persons,
living or dead, events or localities is entirely coincidental.

This book is set in Fournier MT Std at HarperCollins*Publishers* India

Printed and Bound in the UK using 100% Renewable
Electricity at CPI Group (UK) Ltd

This book contains FSC™ certified paper and other controlled
sources to ensure responsible forest management.

For more information visit: www.harpercollins.co.uk/green

For Caroline

More wisdom is contained in the best crime fiction than in philosophy.

Ludwig Wittgenstein

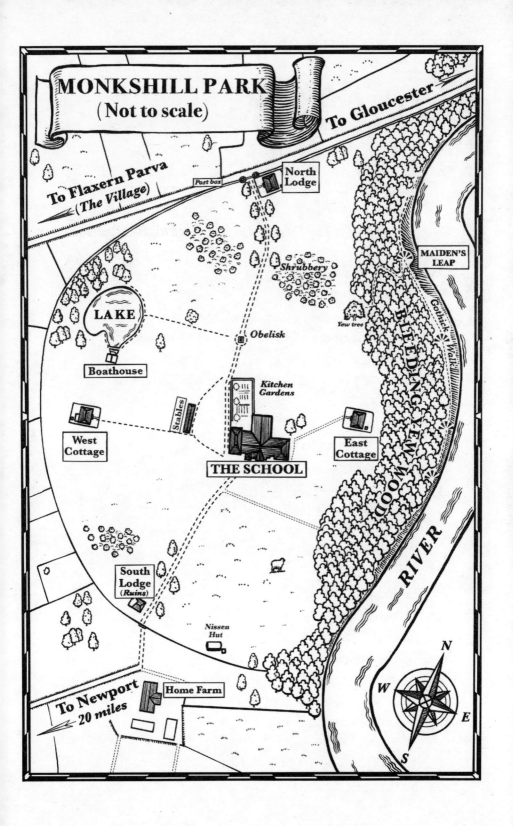

MONKSHILL PARK: THE PEOPLE

The Headmistress and Proprietor – Miss Katherine Pryce-Morgan
Matron and Housekeeper – Miss Pamela Runciman

The Staff
   Miss Enid Archer BA
   Miss Covey
   Miss Vera Hampson
   Mr Alec Shaw BA (Visiting Tutor)
   Miss Maggie Squires
   Miss Annabel Warnock BA

The Girls
   Venetia Canford
   Muriel Fisher
   Priscilla Knecht
   Rosemary Lawson-Smith
   Sylvia Morton
   Miranda and Amanda Twisden

The Servants
Mrs Broadwell, the cook
Stephen Broadwell, her nephew
Mrs Crisp, the cleaner

Others
Tosser
Lady Susan Vauden
Detective Inspector Williamson
PC Fowles

1

‘Murder. It has to be murder.’

I don't mind telling you, his words gave me a shock. For a start, they were a curious echo of my own thoughts, of what I'd been thinking for the past six weeks or so. Besides, you didn't expect a total stranger to blurt out something like that. Particularly when, as far as he knew, there was no one there to hear.

He was a wiry man, not tall, not bad-looking if you liked that sort of thing, with dark hair and a thin face that reminded me of someone – perhaps a boy I'd known when I was young or the sort of nondescript actor who played the hero's best friend in films. I guessed he was about thirty.

He was standing at the start of the drive, with his bicycle leaning against one of the pillars where the gates used to hang. He was wearing a shirt with the sleeves rolled up and baggy flannel trousers secured at the cuffs with bicycle clips.

As I watched, he flexed his fingers and ran them through his hair. There were sweat patches under the arms of his shirt. He stared up the drive, a green tunnel at this time of year because the oaks and limes were bright with new leaves. There wasn't much gravel left underfoot, just ruts and weeds. The drive went into a shallow curve, which made it appear as if it faded into nothing. As if it were a path leading nowhere.

Suddenly he straightened. A column had appeared, marching around the bend of the drive. The two files of green-clad figures almost merged with the greenery on either side. For an instant, they looked like soldiers, ghosts of a recent past, for troops had been stationed at Monkshill at the beginning of the war. Then they resolved themselves into the familiar crocodile of schoolgirls in shapeless green tunics. Beside them marched a tall, slim figure in tweeds with a grey hat like a pudding basin squashed over her head.

My heart lurched at the sight of Enid. I felt the familiar mixture of love and lust. How strange one should still feel such things. I supposed it was a bit like amputees feeling pain in limbs they have lost. Ghost pains.

The man retrieved his bicycle and advanced slowly towards them. He had a slight limp, a way of hitching up his left leg as he walked. I followed. You could tell that everyone had seen him. The chattering stopped, though there was still some furtive whispering going on. For a moment I saw them as they must appear to him: girls of all shapes and sizes, their bodies shrouded in the sack-like tunics, the doughy faces under the felt hats. Half-formed human beings. Works in progress.

As they drew nearer, the man wheeled his bicycle to the side of the drive and waited on the verge for the column to pass him.

Enid gave him a smile. 'Walk on, girls,' she said. 'Wait for me at the bottom of the drive.'

The last girl in the crocodile was Venetia Canford, walking by herself. She was thin and lanky, and her tunic looked as if it

6

had been bought for her when she was much younger. I looked at her with distaste. The first thing you noticed about her was the huge blue eyes. Her mouth was wide, with full lips; too wide and too full for a face that still had puppy fat clinging to its cheeks.

Enid had her back to her. I saw Venetia stick out her tongue at the man. He saw it too. A childish insult. Except it wasn't really childish. Or even an insult. It was something else. Something unsettling.

'Mr Shaw?'

'Yes, that's right. Just arrived.'

'I'm Enid Archer. One of the teachers. Miss Pryce-Morgan said you were due today.' She nodded at the bicycle. 'Did you bike it from Gloucester?'

'Newport,' he said. 'And I wish I hadn't. It must be over twenty miles.'

'Warm work.'

He grinned at her. 'You could say that. Miss Pryce-Morgan has invited me to the house at half-past five. I hope there's time to make myself look respectable.'

'Do you know where to go?'

'Yes – East Cottage. She sent me a sketch map. And with any luck my trunk will be waiting for me.'

Enid pointed up the drive. 'It's not far. The track's about a hundred yards further on. Right-hand side. You can't miss it.' She glanced at the huddle of girls in the gateway. 'I'll see you later. I'd better get back to the Botany Society before they start a riot.'

I always found it bittersweet to be close to Enid. I wanted to be with her, but it sometimes hurt so much it was better to go somewhere else. So I followed Shaw. I was curious about him.

He was an anomaly. The headmistress wasn't keen on having young men in the vicinity of the school, let alone on the staff. But she hadn't had much choice, not at such short notice.

I had heard her discussing the matter with Runty, which was the girls' name for Matron, and not a bad name either. 'It'll only be for the summer term, after all. And we'll call him a visiting tutor rather than a master. We'll keep him away from the house as much as we can.'

'That won't stop half the school falling in love with him,' Runty said. 'But still – as you say, we can guard against that.'

'Beggars can't be choosers,' the head had replied.

So I floated after Shaw, who was wheeling his bicycle, not trusting the surface of the drive. He had a bag strapped to the carrier, along with a folded jacket and what looked like a very small case. He turned onto the rubble track, which skirted the east side of the mansion and ran roughly parallel to the river. The land on either side of the fences was rough grass with a few old trees, some long past their best. It was too rocky to take a crop so it had been given over to sheep.

The ground dipped, and there was the cottage. It was Victorian, I suppose, built for a gamekeeper or gardener. It looked like a decaying dolls' house for a family of large, decayed dolls: four little windows neatly arranged on two floors, with the door between them; the rendered walls cracked and patched with damp and flaking whitewash. The door had a timber porch almost smothered in a tangle of climbing rose and honeysuckle. A barbed wire fence enclosed a narrow strip of garden in front of the cottage. Someone had made a brutal attempt to tidy away the wild garlic and ground elder with a scythe.

Shaw leaned the bicycle against a fence post, pushed open the gate and walked up the cinder path to the porch. He was about to open the door when he swore suddenly and sprang backwards. He touched his hair. I drew nearer and looked up at the porch roof. A dead rabbit was hanging from a nail directly over the doorway. Its back paws had been knotted with twine and looped over a nail knocked into the ridge timber. It was dangling low enough to touch the crown of Shaw's head. Its eyes were dull, and its open mouth was pink and moist.

Wrinkling his nose, he unhooked it and laid it on the ground, which was foolish because the ants would soon find it. Then he went inside. But I stayed behind in the garden. I couldn't bear to go inside. Not now. It was all too raw still. Later perhaps.

Desolation swept over me. It happens sometimes, out of the blue. I never know what will set it off, though I should have been wary about the cottage. When the desolation comes, there's nothing I can do except wait for it to pass.

I went away, following the path that led up to the obelisk. This was supposed to mark the highest spot in the park. From there you could see downstream to the estuary. It looked peaceful today, the sun glinting on impossibly blue waters as if the estuary were pretending to be the Mediterranean. I wondered how many people lay dead among those shifting sandbanks and swirling currents, how many bodies, mine among them, had been washed out to sea.

To distract myself, I thought about the murder. Because it had been murder – there was no other name for it. The first question was, who did it? And the second question was why?

I used to tell my girls there are no new stories, only old ones told in different ways. You don't get much older ones than the story of Cain and Abel. Theirs was a story of murder and so was mine, with me in the role of Abel.

9

Someone had actually wanted me dead and they had taken the steps necessary to achieve this end. Even now, when in a sense it no longer mattered, the very thought made me shiver. Or rather, it would have made me shiver, had I been able to. In my present state, I just had the idea of a shiver, rather than its physical manifestation.

The murder had been almost childishly simple. It happened like this. I was at the Maiden's Leap. The cliff was sheer at this point, and it projected slightly at the top so it overhung the river almost three hundred feet below. Once upon a time there had been a stone wall about eighteen inches high at the front of the platform with a railing running along the top. The wall was now in poor condition and most of the railing had rusted away or been vandalised.

It was the Easter holidays. Many of the girls had gone home to their families, though a substantial minority stayed at school either because their parents were abroad or dead or because they simply didn't want to be bothered with their offspring. Some of the staff stayed at the school to keep an eye on the remaining girls and, in theory, to provide what the head called 'a programme of holiday activities of an educational nature'. Others were there because they had nowhere else to go.

It was a fresh, clear morning. I was standing by the wall and staring at the blues and greens and greys of the distance. I was wondering how many miles I could see and thinking how beautiful it was, and how I must bring Enid here again. A bubble of excitement twitched in my ribcage. Only a few hours more, and we would be together.

Nothing alerted me beforehand. Not a sound. Not a smell. Not a movement of the air. It simply happened.

Someone pushed me hard between the shoulder blades. The

wall trapped my legs below the knee. The rest of me toppled over the edge.

It was all so fast I can't be sure of the order of things after that. A rapid, jolting, scraping fall. There was a blow to my head – perhaps I hit a rock – and all the air seemed to leave my body. Or was it the other way round? There was pain, exquisite, overwhelming, mind-numbing pain.

And then there was nothing at all. Blessed, bloody nothing.

After a while, I felt better and went back to the cottage. Shaw was in the back garden, which was largely the domain of brambles. He had succeeded in pumping up some water from the well in the back porch. Now he was inspecting the earth closet and the ruined pig cot.

I saw Stephen approaching before he did. Stephen was the cook-housekeeper's twelve-year-old nephew. According to staffroom gossip, his father was dead and his mother had run off with another man. As a special favour, he was allowed to live with his aunt – it was either that or an orphanage – and even attend some of the girls' lessons on condition that he sat at the back and didn't talk to anyone. This wasn't evidence of Miss Pryce-Morgan's benevolent nature, more of her fear that Stephen's aunt would hand in her notice if he wasn't allowed to stay.

The boy hovered by the back gate, his cheeks pink with exercise or embarrassment. Shaw must have heard something. He looked up.

'Hello.'

Stephen cleared his throat and said in a rush: 'It's up at the house.'

'What is?'

'Your trunk. The one the carrier brought.'

'That's one mystery solved. I was wondering where it had got to.'

Stephen rubbed his hand down his khaki shorts. He was small for his age. He always had a slight frown, as if he found the world permanently mysterious, a puzzle he needed to solve. 'The man brought it up yesterday.' His shyness was beginning to dissipate. 'Auntie told him to put it in the old dairy.'

'Can you show me where that is?'

'All right.'

'And who are you when you're at home?'

'Stephen.'

Shaw glanced at the sky. 'Hang on. I'll put my bike under cover in case it rains.'

He walked down the path at the side of the cottage. Stephen followed, watching Shaw intently, as if determined to commit every detail to memory.

'Someone left a dead rabbit by the front door,' Shaw said, pausing at the corner of the house. 'Any idea who?'

'Could be Tosser.'

'Is that a real name?'

'It's what everyone calls him.'

'But why would he leave a rabbit there?'

'I expect he wants you to buy it.'

Shaw shrugged. He moved the bicycle under the branches of a walnut tree beside the fence. He unstrapped the luggage on the carrier and put it on the table in the living room. He shook out his tweed jacket and put it on.

Stephen pursued him like a small, watchful dog. 'Is that a typewriter?' he asked, pointing at the small case beside Shaw's bag.

'Yes.'

'Why?'

'Why what?'

'Why do you need it?'

Shaw sighed. 'I'm thinking of writing a novel.'

'Is it hard?'

'Writing a novel? I don't know. But it can't be that difficult, can it? Just one word after another.'

'What sort will it be?'

'A murder mystery, a whodunnit. I decided that on the way here today. I'm going to give Agatha Christie a run for her money.'

What about my murder mystery? I wanted to ask. *Why don't you solve that instead?*

'Will it make you rich?' the boy said.

'I certainly hope so. Why do you ask so many questions? That's enough for now.'

Stephen set off at a brisk pace, his thin shoulder blades pumping up and down like angular pistons beneath the faded Aertex shirt. The path wound up to the wider track, overgrown and rutted, which climbed up to the obelisk, where several paths met.

'Is it much further?' Shaw asked.

The boy glanced over his shoulder. 'No.'

He marched on, with Shaw limping behind him. The path ran along the line of a long high brick wall, above which were the unpruned tips of fruit trees. On the right, on the lower ground to the west, close to the north drive, was a quadrangle of buildings with sagging slate roofs and broken windows: what was left of the stables.

Then the house came into sight. The headmistress always

referred to it as 'the mansion' to make it sound more impressive. But from this angle it was just a cluster of ill-matched gables and irregular walls, with windows scattered about without any attempt at harmony, a place of peeling paint and leaking gutters.

On the right of the path were the dark, dusty leaves of the overgrown shrubbery. Stephen increased his pace as if anxious to pass it.

There were muffled giggles in the depths of the bushes. Shaw turned his head towards the sound. Four or five white faces floated among the leaves like fat white moons. At least three-quarters of the girls of Monkshill Park were overcome with an irresistible urge to giggle whenever they saw a man. Better that, of course, than behaving like Venetia Canford when someone in trousers appeared.

The trunk was on one of the marble shelves in the dairy. It was cold in there, and Stephen shivered.

Shaw glanced at him. 'I can't carry that by myself. Will you give me a hand?'

'We could borrow a barrow. Tosser's got one.'

'OK. Let's go and ask him.'

'It'll cost you, mind. One way or another.'

They found the old man in the kitchen garden. He was sitting in the largest of the three greenhouses and smoking his foul pipe stuffed with his horrible homegrown tobacco. He didn't move as they approached.

'Hello,' Shaw said. 'Stephen tells me you might be able to lend me a barrow for half an hour.'

'Oh aye?'

'I'll be staying at East Cottage for a while, but the carrier left my trunk up at the house.'

'Help yourself.' Tosser jerked his thumb towards the shed at the end of the greenhouse. 'The boy will show you.'

'My name's Shaw, by the way. Alec Shaw.'

Tosser nodded but didn't vouchsafe his own name.

'I'll bring the barrow back right away.' Shaw gestured at the garden. 'I must say you keep this place pretty trim. Can't be easy. Do you have help?'

'If you can call it that,' Tosser said.

Which meant something or nothing. Mainly the latter. Tosser had never worked as a gardener. Besides, since the beginning of the war, the walled garden had been the province of Mr Lewis at Home Farm, as had much of the park. Tosser used the garden more as an amenity, a resource – a place to sit and smoke in the sun, a source of stolen vegetables, fruit or garden tools; a place to conduct business. As now.

He cleared his throat, a rich gurgling sound. 'I'll drop by about the rabbit.'

'What?'

'The rabbit. Tasty little doe.'

'Oh. Yes, I see. Actually I—'

'You'll want to be getting along now. It'll keep till later.'

Tosser closed his eyes, closing the conversation as well.

I stared at him. God, he was such a nasty little man. Could it have been him? Maybe. He had reason enough.

2

I didn't need sleep now, not as such. But I did have periods of absence. I thought of them as states of non-being. Vacancies. It was as if someone had switched off the current. One day, perhaps, the current wouldn't come on again, and that would be that. Like a torch battery, I would be all used up, and then there would be nothing left except nothing.

When I came back to myself, I could tell by the sun that it was an hour or so later. I went up to the house. I was hoping to find Enid. The Christians had one thing right: love didn't die with the body, or at least not right away.

I was also curious to see how Shaw would fare with PM and Runty. And vice versa – I had noticed that men made them uncomfortable; they treated even the vicar with caution as if he were a semi-domesticated animal who could not be trusted to ignore an unexpected call of the wild.

The headmistress's study was a large room with a very pretty bow window. Most of the other rooms at Monkshill were bleak and sparsely furnished. But PM had installed her own bits and pieces in the study, including portraits of alleged ancestors, partly for her own comfort and partly in the hope of impressing visiting parents.

By the time I turned up, Shaw hadn't arrived, but the welcoming committee was already assembled. Most of the teaching staff were there, and of course Miss Runciman. Technically Runty was only the school matron, but her real position was akin to that of a wily grand vizier serving an ineffectual sultan.

I looked first for Enid, who was standing by the fireplace and looking pale and tired. Maggie Squires was addressing her as though she were a public meeting. Maggie had a moustache and wore heavy tweeds whatever the weather. She taught deportment and dancing, a cruel joke perpetrated on her by fate and the headmistress, as well as PT and arithmetic.

Runty sidled up to them. 'I hope you aren't finding Miss Warnock's absence too much of a problem.' She glanced at Enid. 'Especially you, of course.'

'No.' Enid looked flustered. 'Why should I?'

'You must have had to shoulder a lot of her teaching responsibilities, as well as her prep rota and so forth.'

'Well, yes, but now Mr Shaw is here, I expect—'

'And you and she seemed such great chums. You went about together a good deal, didn't you?' Runty patted Enid's arm. 'Her departure was quite a shock.'

Enid's face looked as if she were trying not to cry. 'I suppose we were all surprised.'

Runty lowered her voice. 'Between ourselves, it isn't the first time Miss Warnock's left a school in the lurch. I happen to know that she had to leave Worcester at very short notice.'

Bitch, I thought, *you bitch*. How much had she known about that? How much did she suspect?

Enid bit her lip and looked away, searching for a diversion.

Fortunately one turned up. There was a tap on the door, and Shaw came in. Miss Pryce-Morgan abandoned little Miss Covey (needlework, art, Bible study and more or less everything else for the little ones) in mid flow and plunged towards him.

Shaw had tried to smarten himself up. He had splashed cold water on his face, changed his shirt, put on a tie and combed his hair. But PM wouldn't approve of his shoes, which were in need of a polish, and the cuffs of his trousers were speckled with dried mud.

Still, she put a brave face on it and towed him around the room like a recently captured barbarian, introducing him to his new colleagues. 'Mr Shaw – our temporary visiting tutor. He'll be joining Miss Archer to teach the School Certificate set and helping out elsewhere as needed.'

When they came to Enid, Shaw's face brightened. 'Hello again – find any good specimens?'

The head frowned. Enid said quickly, 'We met on the drive this afternoon. Mr Shaw arrived when I was taking the Botany Society to Home Farm.'

PM nodded and steered Shaw towards Miss Covey. He grinned at Enid as he moved away, and she smiled back with more warmth than I considered altogether appropriate.

Meanwhile, Runty was pouring the sherry. The glasses, which were as small as a sherry glass could possibly be, had already been set out on a tray. As usual, the sherry had been decanted. I had always suspected that the sweetish stuff they occasionally gave us was watered down, and now I knew it for a fact. I had watched Runty diluting it yesterday evening, while PM droned on about the extra expense of renting East Cottage for the new tutor.

Cradling her glass, Miss Covey sidled closer to Maggie Squires. 'I was wondering . . .' she said in a whisper.

'Wondering what?' Maggie said in a voice that could be heard on the other side of the room.

Miss Covey cleared her throat. Everything about her was grey – her clothes, her face, her hair. She edged closer, bringing her mouth within a few inches of Maggie's ears. 'What will Mr Shaw do when he needs . . . ?'

'Needs what?'

Little Covey brought her mouth even closer. 'The lavatory.'

'Use the staff one, I imagine. Same as everyone else.'

The staff lavatory was off the side hall. It was a splendidly ornate Victorian affair set upon a wooden dais that gave one the not unpleasant feeling of sitting on a throne.

'Oh. I do hope it won't cause any awkwardness.'

'No. Why should it?'

'He's – you know – a *man*.'

Maggie patted Miss Covey on the back, causing her to spill some of her sherry on her grey cardigan. 'Don't you worry. I'm sure your virtue will be safe with him.'

The party, if that's the right term, didn't last long, partly to avoid the danger of having to pour everyone another glass of sherry and partly because it was time for the rest of the staff to supervise the girls' supper, which they called 'tea', and their evening prep.

I lingered behind, when the head and Runty had got rid of everyone. PM unlocked the cupboard below her desk and took out the gin and the Italian vermouth. Since my death I had discovered that they had at least one glass apiece every evening to whet their appetite for supper.

PM took a sip and lit a cigarette. 'Inspector Williamson phoned.'

Runty sat up sharply. 'About Miss Warnock?'

'It's good news, thank God. They think that she almost certainly left of her own free will.'

'Perhaps it's for the best.'

'But they're still puzzled about where she went after she left here.'

'She must have caught a bus.'

'Perhaps.' PM rolled her shoulders. 'Though apparently none of the drivers remembers her. Not that that means much necessarily. They're always gossiping with their friends and they wouldn't notice if a bomb dropped on them.'

'She might have had a car pick her up.'

'Yes. Or even walked. Then she needn't have gone through the village at all.'

'Is that what Williamson thinks?'

'He says he's keeping an open mind. But it hardly matters, does it? He said it all seemed pretty conclusive to him. She took her handbag and her ration book and so forth. Her jewellery, even, such as it was. And her letters, diaries, private things like that. All she left behind were a few clothes and books and things. He says that could be because she thought they weren't worth the effort of taking. And she'd just been paid for last term so she's not short of money.'

'What about her bank account? Did the police check that?'

'I gather that the one we use for her salary hasn't been touched, not yet.'

'I expect she has other accounts.'

PM shrugged. 'The important thing is that Williamson says there's really nothing for them to investigate. People are perfectly at liberty to go off if they want. It's not a crime.'

'Then we can draw a line under the whole business. Especially now we've found a temporary replacement.'

'I think this deserves a toast, don't you?'

Runty smiled and picked up her glass. 'And perhaps it's a blessing in disguise. When you think of those rumours. After all, we never got to the bottom of what happened in Worcester.'

The two women looked at each other over the rims of their glasses.

PM cleared her throat. 'Least said, soonest mended.'

Was it you who killed me, I wondered, *or your creature? Or someone else?*

Later that evening I found Enid in the staffroom, playing yet another game of German Whist with Maggie Squires. The news was on in the background, though neither of them was paying full attention to it. Churchill, Truman and Stalin were planning to meet in Germany. It had been decided that Hitler's successor, Grand Admiral Dönitz, was to be treated as a war criminal.

Maggie lifted her head and said, 'Serves him right.' She turned over the topmost card of the stack. 'Hearts are trumps. Oh dear.'

Enid was sorting her cards into suits. 'I just wish the horrid thing was over.'

Maggie grunted agreement. Enid put down her first card. The excitement of the Victory in Europe celebrations had left many people with a sense of anticlimax. Japan had still not surrendered. Most wartime restrictions remained in place, and peace and plenty seemed almost as distant as ever. Maggie and at least a dozen girls were still waiting for news of loved ones, living from day to day with the dull ache of uncertainty.

After listening to the headlines, I left them to their game and went upstairs. One of the few advantages of my situation was that I could snoop to my heart's content and go wherever

I wished – as long as I had been there during life. A closed door was not a barrier if my living self had ever been through the doorway. Nor were people – I could pass through them easily enough – though the experience was unpleasant, as if the essences of the living and the dead mingled with each other only under protest.

On the other hand, rooms I had never entered were blocked to me, and so were places outside the house where I had never been. Nor could I go where I had not walked. I discovered this early on when I tried to board a bus to Gloucester. An invisible barrier had prevented me. This effectively meant I was a prisoner, with my movements restricted to parts of Monkshill Park, Home Farm and the village.

When I reached the landing I went along to the back of the house, which in the old days had been the servants' part of the building. Most of the dormitories were there. They had grubby wallpaper and drab, scuffed paintwork. They smelled of unhappiness, damp and secrets.

Each dormitory was identically furnished with narrow iron bedsteads, horsehair mattresses and bedside cupboards. Each had a row of hooks with a line of chairs below, with the girls' names above the hooks.

Some of the dormitories had been named after trees – Oak, Elm, Ash and so on. Birch was one of the smaller ones. It had only six beds. One of them was occupied by Venetia Canford, who ruled the roost with manic unpredictability. Another was Sylvia Morton's.

If I had a favourite among the girls, it was Sylvia. She was fourteen, a dark-haired girl with a square face. There was a determination about her, an obstinacy, which I knew would either be a curse or a blessing for her in later life, perhaps both.

22

She reminded me a little of a girl I taught at my last school. Alice had possessed a similar single-mindedness and, like Sylvia, had greedily devoured whatever her teachers laid before her.

Sylvia had had the misfortune to be at the school since 1939, during the holidays as well as in termtime. Her mother was dead, and her father was somewhere on active service with the Royal Navy. Her fees were paid promptly by a lawyer in London and her well-being was left in the hands of Miss Pryce-Morgan. No one came to see her. On Sundays, during Letter Prep, she wrote to her father's lawyer, brief, factual reports of the week's activities, and sometimes she would request an article of clothing or a Postal Order. The school was her world, and not much of a world at that. But she was a fighter. She wanted to make her own life, and I had tried to help her.

When I came into the room, the first thing I heard were muffled sobs. Prissy Knecht was crouching in the corner by the window. She was already in her nightdress. She had her arms wrapped around her knees and was staring in terror at Venetia Canford.

'You poor little thing,' Venetia was saying to her. 'Three slugs! What rotten bad luck they should all be on your pillow.'

'Take them away,' Prissy muttered. 'Please. Please.'

'On the other hand, they've come all this way to see you. You wouldn't want to hurt their feelings, would you?'

Sylvia was already in bed and trying to read.

'Shall I bring the orange one over? It looks particularly keen on you. I think it's making a cross on your pillow. A slime kiss. How jolly.'

Sylvia put down her book and got out of bed. She padded across the floor to the window and opened it. Venetia watched in silence. Sylvia picked up Prissy's pillow and shook it outside.

One slug remained. She flicked it away with her forefinger, stripped off the pillow case and dropped the pillow back on the bed.

'How lovely,' Venetia drawled. 'True friendship.'

Sylvia was wise enough to say nothing. She got back into bed and picked up her book.

'Or are you more than friends? Are you lizzies? Did Warnie teach you how lizzies do it to each other? Do tell!'

That shocked even me – both that Venetia had some idea what a lesbian was, and that she had somehow learned or at least suspected that the label fitted me. But Sylvia and Prissy were looking completely blank. I doubted they even knew the facts of life.

Venetia approached Sylvia's bed. 'Is that a lizzie book? Let me see!'

As she was speaking, there were heavy footsteps on the landing. The door burst open and knocked into a chair. Maggie Squires marched in.

'Why aren't you girls in bed?' she demanded. 'Quick march! Time for lights out.'

When everyone had settled down, she flipped off the light and shut the door with a bang. The dormitory was almost in darkness. The blackout was down, and soft evening light filtered around the edges of the curtains. The only sounds were Maggie's retreating footsteps and Prissy's muffled sobs.

For the moment, Venetia lay quiet and still. Then she whispered, 'Lizzies.'

I stayed in the house until Enid went to bed. I went with her up the backstairs to the second floor and along the landing to the main house. There were five bedrooms up here, together with

24

a bathroom. One of the rooms was Enid's, and another had been mine.

The light was dim – the entire landing was lit by a single low-wattage bulb. Enid hesitated and looked about her. Maggie Squires was still downstairs in the staffroom. Little Covey was snoring – for such a small woman, she made an astonishing amount of noise. The fifth bedroom belonged to Vera Hampson (Religious Education for Senior Classes, English, geography), a misleadingly severe-looking woman who, PM said, had the misfortune to be Irish but was otherwise quite presentable. She was downstairs in the kitchen, making cocoa for herself and Maggie. All clear.

I had asked the headmistress for a key to my door when I first came here, but she told me that wasn't possible. It was school policy that members of staff should not lock their doors. 'In case of a bombing raid,' she added vaguely, 'or a fire. Besides, so many of our keys are missing. And Mrs Crisp needs to come in and clean.' (Mrs Crisp was the charwoman, though she was rarely sighted on the second floor.) Enid and I thought that the real reason was to allow Runty free range for snooping.

When I was reported missing, however, my key had rapidly been found. (I now knew that PM kept all the keys in a box on the bottom shelf of the green safe that squatted in the closet off her study.) PM and Runty searched my room, tutting over the unemptied ashtray and the books on my shelves. ('Virginia Woolf! Oh dear, oh dear!') Afterwards they locked the door behind them, and the key went back in the safe.

But Enid hadn't given up hope. Tonight she tiptoed over to the door, turned the knob and pushed. But it was still locked. I knew why she was so desperate to get in there. The reason no longer mattered to me, but it did to her. Afterwards she went into her own room and began the ritual of going to bed.

For once I didn't want to linger with her. I was in a foul mood. To be honest – and there was no point in being anything else now – I didn't think I was a very nice person. I was all sharp edges and dark corners. (That was one of the sweetest things about Enid. She seemed not to mind all that. She had just accepted me as I was.)

When I left the house that night, I wandered up to the obelisk. Eventually I would slip away to the Maiden's Leap, the place where I had last been alive and where, usually, I was drawn to roost during the small hours of the night. Like so many aspects of my existence at present, I didn't understand why that should be, but it was, and that was that.

There was still light in the sky, which was now a panoply of darkening blue with stripes of fire at the horizon. A vast horse chestnut reared up on the slope down to the lake. Pale flower cones glimmered like candles in the mist among the densely packed leaves, turning it into a bloated Christmas tree. I like the dusk, the in-between time. It's neither one thing nor the other, like me.

The unanswerable questions invaded my mind in a rush. Who killed me? Why? Would my murderer ever pay the price for what she or he had done? What would Enid do now that I wasn't here to take care of her?

And what about Sylvia Morton, desperate for Oxford, for a chance to build a different life? She needed me, or someone like me, to help her. So did Prissy Knecht, the stranger in our midst, yearning for security, for acceptance. They all needed me. How would they manage?

But probably they would all do perfectly well without me.

We all exaggerate our own importance in other people's lives. Perhaps I hadn't really mattered to them, or to anyone else—

A barn owl flew past. I saw it, a white, silent blur. It was very close to me indeed, but I didn't feel the air displaced by its wings on my skin – only an uncomfortable tingle, like a mild electrical shock. An instant later I realised that the owl hadn't flown *by* me. It had flown *through* me, leaving only that tingle to mark its passage. As far as the owl was concerned, I suspected, I was nothing, nothing at all. Not even a tingle.

It was hard to accept the fact of death, while this partial consciousness remained. But now, for a moment, the terrible reality of my condition was forced upon me. I wanted to weep. But I had no eyes to weep with, no tears to fall.

I had nothing. I was nothing.

3

Chapter One

The shadows of evening were falling when the Daimler purred past the lodge gates and into the drive. The woman at the wheel stared straight ahead, ignoring the lodge keeper's wife, who was curtsying respectfully by the gate she just opened. The car accelerated, took the bridge at the southern end of the lake without checking its pace and went into the long bend fringed by rhododendrons. Finally it surged into the gravel sweep outside Abbotsfield Court and came abruptly to a halt with a spray of gravel below the portico of the mansion.

Leaving the engine running, the driver opened her door. A slim, silk-stockinged leg was the first of her to emerge. Simultaneously, two footmen run down the steps towards her. They were followed by a gentleman in evening dress, who . . .

Alec Shaw stood up and stretched. He went into the kitchen, where the kettle had been boiling on the Primus stove for at least a minute.

He doesn't mean *run down the steps*, I thought, as I stared at the sheet of paper rearing up from the platen of the typewriter. He means *ran*. The error irritated the teacher in me, and to a quite absurd degree. It was unforgivably careless. And wasn't a curtsy by its very nature respectful? As for the purring Daimler, if that wasn't a cliché, I didn't know what was. I yearned for a red pencil.

It was Sunday morning. I had returned to myself with the resolution to be more positive, to make the most of what I had. To that end, I told myself not to be foolishly sentimental about East Cottage. I had slipped inside and found Shaw at work on his novel. To give the man his due, he hadn't wasted much time before starting it.

I glanced into the kitchen, where he was now pouring his tea. He added milk and brought the cup back to the table in the living room. He sat down, lit a cigarette and reread what he had written. I willed him to exercise his critical faculty. If he had one.

He wound back the platen, returning to the top of the page. He put a line of xxxs through *respectfully*. My opinion of him improved. He blew out a lungful of smoke and whistled tunelessly through his teeth while he changed *run* into *ran*. Then, increasingly bemused, I watched him uncap his pen and put a line through *purred*. After a moment's thought and a sip of tea, he wrote above the deletion the word *shot*. He frowned at it and then added a question-mark in the left-hand margin. He put the cigarette in the corner of his mouth and went back to work. He was a three-fingered typist, and reasonably fast.

29

. . . was smoking a cigarette in an ivory holder.

One footman turned off the engine while the other opened the boot and removed a quantity of white-leather luggage embossed with the monogram C.M.Q. Meanwhile, the . . .

But I wasn't interested in what he was writing. I was interested in his corrections. In *my* corrections.

Was it merely chance, I wondered, that he had immediately made the three changes that had occurred to me? Could he somehow hear me? Or, rather, sense my thoughts if I had directed them at him?

I put the matter to the test. I stared at him, focusing on the cigarette, and thought as hard as I could: *Tap the ash into the ash tray now.*

But he continued to type. I watched the coil of ash expand. It crumpled and then fell onto the keyboard of the typewriter.

He swore, took the cigarette from his mouth and blew vigorously at the keyboard, sending a shower of ash into his tea and over the surrounding table. He swore again, this time more loudly.

I felt depressed. Just for a moment I had thought that someone alive, someone still of flesh and blood, had heard me; that I wasn't entirely divorced from the world of the living after all; that perhaps someone might be able to help me. *Help me. Help me.*

There was a burst of typing, short and staccato like a burst of machine-gun fire. I glanced down at the paper to see what he had written now.

Help me. Help me.

He frowned at the words, as if quite reasonably wondering

where they had come from. Then he nodded and added: *she murmured to the footman with her suitcases.*

I felt suddenly weary, as though I had just finished a three-hour exam. But excitement buoyed me up. Perhaps that's it, I thought, I can't get through directly. I gathered all my strength and tried again to reach him; or if not him, then his typewriter, his novel.

Maiden's Leap, I said. *Maiden's Leap.*

I watched the keys move under his fingers, at first quickly, but slowing towards the end. Four words. Two plus two.

Maiden's Leap. Maiden's Leap.

* * *

The School is conducted according to strict Christian Principles. Religious instruction is overseen by the Rector of Flaxern Parva, the village at the North Lodge of the Park. On weekdays, all girls attend Morning and Evening Prayers at School. Sunday services are usually held at the mansion. At least once a month, however, the whole School attends Divine Service at Church, weather permitting, for Holy Eucharist. Please write to the Headmistress if your daughter wishes to attend Confirmation Classes.

Monkshill Park: School Prospectus

The sky was dense with clouds, but it was still dry, so the school went to church. Everyone went, apart from the servants and the boy, Stephen.

As usual, everyone gathered in the hall, the only place in the house large enough to accommodate the whole school, staff included. 'Hall' is an inadequate word: it was a long, lofty room shaped like an elongated octagon; a space designed for show. It had a grand, cantilevered staircase opposite the front door and a marble fireplace at either end.

The girls were in their Sunday dresses, paler in colour than their everyday tunics. The girls called them their slime-greens. Miss Runciman distributed order marks for a missing button, a torn glove or an inadequately shined shoe.

The walk to church was about a mile – first to the obelisk and then onto a gravelled footpath that branched away from the north drive. I went with the school, not from religious feeling – in life I had been an atheist, which made my current situation particularly galling – but to be with Enid, to watch her. She was walking with Prissy, who tended to be left on her own.

I liked to see as much as I could of Enid, to hear her voice, simply to be with her. It was as if I needed to imprint as much as I could of her on my memory before it was too late. She wasn't pretty in a conventional way. She had close-cropped hair and a narrow face. Her features were delicate and regular, and I particularly liked her ears. Her voice was gentle and well-modulated though she could make herself heard if she wanted. I thought she was beautiful.

These were just words. They couldn't hold the essence of Enid Archer any more than a net can hold water.

The school marched through Flaxern Parva. The village had a bedraggled air. The green and the main street were still decorated with drooping Union Jacks and sodden bunting from the Victory in Europe celebrations.

The girls filed into the church a good ten minutes before the start of the ten thirty Holy Eucharist. Once they were seated, Runty glanced over her shoulder and then murmured something to PM. I guessed she was commenting on Alec Shaw's absence. PM had made it clear to him that his attendance was compulsory.

He came in during the first hymn, clearly out of breath. Enid turned her head at the clack of the church door and beckoned him over to the pews where the staff sat. He squeezed in beside her. He had cut himself shaving.

PM frowned at him. Enid didn't say anything. She just smiled. And I felt stupidly, pointlessly jealous.

Afterwards Enid and Shaw walked back together, with Prissy in tow like a small cargo ship under the protection of two destroyers. Little Covey went with them, occasionally contributing a comment about the sermon or the weather or anything else that popped into her mind.

'Do you have some spare time this afternoon, Mr Shaw?' Enid said. 'The head suggested we go over the timetable and discuss how we divide the work. And you might find it useful to see the classrooms and the textbooks we have. Such as they are.'

'Yes, please.' He smiled at her. 'Do call me Alec, by the way.'

'All right – and I'm Enid. Have you come far?'

'Hertfordshire – near Hitchin. I was teaching at a prep school there, but I had rather a bad dose of pneumonia during the winter, and I had to resign.'

I wondered if that were true. I have a suspicious nature. He looked healthy enough to me. And why hadn't he been doing something useful for the war effort? He wasn't old. He looked about thirty.

'That's bad luck. Are you all right now?'

'Yes – fine. As long as I don't push myself too hard. This job came along at just the right time. Gives me a breathing space, while I look about for a permanent post.'

'I warn you,' Enid said. 'All the girls will fall in love with you. Mind you, they fall in love with anything, given half a chance.'

I wondered if Prissy had overheard that. She was walking a little behind the teachers, but she had gradually drawn closer to them. If they had any sense they would turn the volume down.

'At my school,' Miss Covey put in, 'we were all in love with Jesus.'

'How nice,' Shaw said. 'And . . . and suitable, of course.'

'Some of our own girls are very religious too,' Enid said tactfully. 'Which reminds me, did you know we have some monastic ruins in the park?'

'Hence Monkshill?'

'I suppose so. Ann— Someone told me it was once a grange of Flaxern Abbey.'

Someone? Is that all I was to Enid now? *Someone*.

'A grange?' Shaw said.

'I think it means a sort of outlying monastery farm. To tell the truth, the ruins aren't up to much, and they were messed about by the Victorians. But it doesn't stop the girls seeing the ghosts of the monks there.'

'I think that's probably indigestion,' Little Covey said. 'Some of them eat biscuits before bedtime, or even after lights out. They will do it, and it always leads to trouble. They sometimes say they see the hermit too.'

Shaw was looking confused, which was often the effect of Miss Covey's conversation. Once again, Enid came to the rescue.

'The hermit's nothing to do with the monks. One of the estate's owners laid out a Gothick Walk along the river in the eighteenth century. As a sort of aristocratic tourist attraction, I suppose. It included a feature called Hermit's Cave. But as far as I know it's never contained a hermit.'

It seemed to me that Shaw's attention had sharpened. He said, 'I must go and have a look at it.'

'I believe it's awfully overgrown, and very dangerous in places.' Enid sounded flustered, as well she might be. 'The army fenced it off when they were here. It's out of bounds to everyone, even the staff.'

'What are the features of the walk?'

'I'm sure most of them have crumbled away by now. I believe it had the usual stuff. A shell grotto, a rock pool with a statue, a viewpoint . . .'

'Don't forget the Maiden's Leap,' Miss Covey said. 'I distinctly remember Miss Warnock telling us about the Maiden's Leap. A poor girl had been abandoned by her heartless lover, and in her despair she leapt to her death. Naturally it wasn't true. It was just a made-up story.'

'Oh yes,' Enid said. 'That's another one.'

'At least, I hope it was,' Covey said. 'Made-up, I mean.'

4

These were the circumstances that led up to my murder.

Enid and I had arranged to go away together during the Easter holidays. I had booked us into a pub in Old Radnor, just over the Welsh border. The room had a double bed, the landlady said in her letter. Would that be all right for two ladies to share? 'Dear God, it would,' I said to Enid, and she looked up at me through her lashes and said nothing.

We were going to walk and read and – well – enjoy each other's company without having to worry about other people. It was hard to find somewhere to be together in private at school. I had visited Enid's bedroom once or twice but that was risky. East Cottage had been safer, but in March and early April it had also been cold, damp and irredeemably squalid.

'Anyway I don't want to do it at school,' Enid said, 'with us always looking over our shoulders. Especially not the first time.' She touched my cheek. 'You understand?'

I said of course I understood. If she'd asked me to, I would have understood that the moon was green. As far as I was concerned, the only important thing was that I loved her. I longed for us to be in that double bed in the pub bedroom with the door locked against the rest of the world. That room, that bed, would be world enough for me and, I hoped, for her.

We planned the holiday carefully. In order to avoid gossip, Enid suggested, we should leave separately. She was to leave Monkshill first, taking the bus to Newport where she was to spend the night and then go on to Gloucester by train. On the following morning, I was to catch the midday bus that went in the other direction — to Gloucester, where Enid would be waiting. Enid had a rucksack and so did I. We wouldn't need much. It wasn't as if we'd have to dress for dinner.

'You don't think I'm being silly?' she asked. 'I'm terrified of people gossiping about us.'

I squeezed her hand. 'It's fine. I understand. Actually it could work quite well. I need to check a few things for the article. I can go down to the Maiden's Leap on my way to catch the bus.'

'You'll let me read it soon?'

'You'll be my very first reader. I promise.'

The elaborate precautions were important because if PM and Runty had found out we were going on holiday together, there would almost certainly have been trouble. They were already looking askance at us because we spent so much time in each other's company. Once she and PM got a hint that we might be more than friends, I was pretty sure that I would be sacked, turned off without a reference like an unsatisfactory housemaid. I had form, as they say. Rumours had followed me here from my old school. I suspected that Runty in particular was looking for a way to get rid of me. She had her own reasons for that.

Back to the murder. On the day it happened, I left the house immediately after breakfast. I had told everyone I was going to stay with my cousin.

I was early but I was too excited to stay still, like a child on the day before her birthday, full to the brim with surplus energy. I needed to be up and doing. I planned to go to the Maiden's Leap on my way to the village and finish some research.

I said goodbye to Maggie and Little Covey and went off. On my way out Mrs Crisp asked if she should turn out my room while I was gone, but I told her to leave it – I would only be away for a few nights. As I was leaving the house I had a quick word with Sylvia Morton about the Latin holiday task I had set her.

I wanted to make a note of the exercise. My fountain pen was buried in my rucksack so Sylvia gave me a pencil. I had my Gothick Walk exercise book in my pocket, and I made a note about the holiday prep inside the back cover. Afterwards I offered the pencil back to her, but she said it wasn't hers – she'd just found it on the floor.

'It's Rosemary Lawson-Smith's,' she said. 'Look – it's got her name on it.'

The younger girls were possessive little beasts and they liked to name everything. They would slice a half-inch strip from the unsharpened end of their pencil and write their name on it.

'She's gone home, hasn't she?' I said. 'I'll hang on to it for now.'

I remember thinking the pencil would come in handy. It would save me having to dig out my pen at the Maiden's Leap. I put it in the pocket of my coat, along with the exercise book.

Sylvia was the last person I talked to in my life, and indeed the last person I saw.

It was a pleasant morning, crisp and bright. I went up to the obelisk. At a brisk walk, it would take me less than twenty minutes from there to reach the bus stop in the village. I had well over an hour to kill. (There's an ironic phrase. An hour to death, more like.) There was plenty of time to go down to the Gothick Walk.

The Walk ran high above the river for about a mile. It had been left to rot since the second half of Queen Victoria's reign, when the fortunes of Monkshill Park had gone into a decline. A dense belt of trees and saplings and bushes had grown up along the top of the cliff. It sloped steeply down to the precipice above the river, almost completely masking the path and its features.

At some point, an iron fence had been erected along the boundary of this accidental wood, presumably to prevent stock from wandering into it and falling into the river. Then the army, during its brief occupation of the grounds at the beginning of the war, had strengthened the fence still further with a formidable tangle of barbed wire, citing reasons of national security. This new barrier was further protected with menacing hand-painted notices saying DANGER and KEEP OUT.

I had heard about the Walk because it had been briefly mentioned in a *Country Life* article about the house before the war. My degree had been in history, and in another life I should have liked to be an academic. I thought it might be fun to see what was left of the Walk and try to write an article about it. Perhaps *Notes & Queries* would publish it.

To tell the truth, Monkshill was such an intellectual desert that I needed to find something to occupy my mind. I went into Gloucester one Saturday in February, where I had the good fortune to find a booklet about Monkshill's pleasure grounds in a second-hand bookshop. It had been published locally in 1799; it devoted several pages to the Walk, then the height of tourist fashion, and listed its attractions.

39

I stole an exercise book from the stationery cupboard when Runty accidentally left it unlocked for a couple of hours. I was using the front of it for my notes, and I intended to draft the article in the back.

It hadn't been easy to find a way into the wood. Whoever had constructed the fence had made a serious job of it, extending it over the edge of the precipice at either end, to prevent people scrambling around it. I followed its line, checking every yard. Eventually I found a way in beyond the obelisk and well out of sight of the house and main paths of the park.

At this point, the original iron fence had been gradually swallowed by a bramble bush. Whoever had installed the barbed wire had clearly decided that the brambles were enough of a barrier and no reinforcement was required. In the middle of the bush was a large yew tree that was almost certainly several centuries older than the house.

This was a special tree – a bleeding yew, its branches twisted into strange shapes and its trunk hollowed out by time. The bark oozed a blood-red sap that glowed the colour of rubies when the sun caught it at the right angle. That's what had originally attracted my attention to it. When I was a girl, my grandmother had shown me a bleeding yew in a churchyard. It was a tree that accreted legends and ghost stories.

When I looked more closely at the Monkshill yew, I discovered that if you wriggled around it there was a path of sorts through the brambles, which dropped sharply as the land fell away. It led down to the iron fence. There was a gap almost three feet high below the bottom of the fence. It was wide enough for an agile adult to scramble through.

There were signs that this hole had been intentionally enlarged. I suspected that someone had been before me and was trying to conceal the fact. Fallen branches had been dragged across the path to make it harder to see. A poacher, I guessed – perhaps Tosser, who was remarkably agile, despite his appearance of decrepitude.

Once I was past the fence, my problems weren't over. Unlike the woodland in the rest of the park, this patch hadn't been managed for the better part of a century. It was packed with trees, saplings, bushes and weeds. In my mind I gave it the name of Bleeding Yew Wood, which seemed to have a suitably Gothick flavour.

There must have been a network of paths when the Walk was laid out a hundred and fifty years earlier. I knew that the Walk itself, if it still existed, would run along the precipice, or very close to it. I struggled down there with the help of a billhook stolen from the shed in the kitchen garden. More by luck than good judgement, I found the remains of what I knew must be the Maiden's Leap, a stone platform that projected from the rock face.

That's where I went on the last day of my life. I put the rucksack on the stone bench and checked the dimensions of the paved platform. I also examined what was left of the delicate wrought-iron railings that ran on top of a low wall along the edge of the precipice. I'm no artist but I made a rough sketch in my notebook. If I could get hold of a camera and some film, I remember thinking, I would take a photograph of it before it was lost forever.

After I had done that, I glanced at my watch. I still had plenty of time before the bus. I stood for a moment admiring the view, the brown river winding like a great serpent immediately below me, the blues of the estuary beyond, and the broad, flat meadows on the other side.

The river was turbulent, swollen by the storms of spring. It had flooded the meadows on the further bank. The tide was on the ebb, the water rushing towards the estuary and the sea beyond, sweeping along the branches and other debris it had gathered upstream.

I was happy. Soon I would be with Enid. Soon there would be the double bed.

There was a bird hovering over the river, and I remember wondering whether it was a buzzard.

I have told you the rest.

I daresay there might have been more questions asked about my disappearance if my family had made a fuss about it. But I was ill-equipped in that respect.

My father had owned a small department store in Calcutta. The store had been founded by his father, who had originally come to India as an engineer on the railways. I was my parents' first child. Apparently my mother was a great reader of poetry, and she chose to have me christened Annabel after 'Annabel Lee', the gloomy poem about a dead lover by Edgar Allan Poe. Having done this, she died, leaving me motherless at three weeks old.

When I was a toddler, my father sent me home to live with Granny, my mother's mother. Granny liked me, and I liked Granny, so we got on well enough. Money arrived regularly to pay for my upkeep and education. Shortly after I left India, my father married his secretary and started a second family. He never came back to England. I've no memory of him, and I doubt he had much memory of me.

At the age of nine, I was sent to boarding school. This was when I learned to hate my name. No one else was called Annabel. It had an old-fashioned, romantic air about it that attracted mockery as naturally as a dog attracted fleas. It wasn't until I was sixteen or seventeen that I learned to like it again. By that time it had become a badge of difference, of distinction; a matter of pride, rather than shame. I allowed no one to shorten it. 'Anna' or 'Bel' were ordinary names. 'Annabel' was me, and me alone.

It was around that time that my father stopped sending me presents at Christmas and on my birthday. But the payments continued. After school, I went to Bristol University to read history, which was where I made the thrilling discovery that I preferred women to men.

The payments from India came to an end when I left Bristol. I would have liked to stay at university and do a research degree but there was no money for that. I wrote to my father, but he did not reply. Six months later I had a letter from his second wife announcing that he had died of a heart attack the previous year and sending, perhaps as corroborating evidence, a snapshot of his tombstone. The news had no effect on me beyond mild irritation that he hadn't left me anything. My reaction was very different the following year, when Granny died. Then I was bereft.

By then I was teaching at a girls' day school in North London. After a few years there I went to Worcester Ladies' College, where I thrived. Teaching was a reserved occupation so I stayed there when war broke out. Until the disaster happened, that is. It wasn't my fault, but I understood that the school needed a scapegoat. I just wish it hadn't been me.

During those years after university, I made plenty of friends and had half a dozen lovers. But none of them was like Enid. The irony is, I wouldn't have met her at all if I hadn't come to Monkshill. So I suppose you could say that Enid was the silver lining for what happened at Worcester . . .

43

5

After church, I followed Shaw back to East Cottage, leaving Enid to take Letter Prep, which involved watching the younger children as they ground out their weekly letters to their parents, full of dutiful reports of marks gained and anguished pleas for sweets.

He lit the Primus stove, filled the kettle and put it on to boil. Afterwards he sat down at his typewriter and took out a cigarette. I waited at his shoulder. I wanted to try to communicate with him again. Or if not with him, then with his typewriter, his novel. He had obviously registered Miss Covey's mention of the Maiden's Leap.

He reread the first page of his typescript. It might be rubbish but you couldn't fault him for lack of trying. But before he had time to write a word, there was a knock at the door. It opened without invitation, revealing Tosser in the porch. He had probably been on the watch for Shaw's return. Tortoise-like, he poked his head over the threshold.

'I come about the rabbit.'

'Look, I don't actually want it.'

'What you done with it?'

Shaw pointed to a bucket on the ground. 'It's in there.'

The old man took up the corpse and dangled it enticingly in front of Shaw's face.

'It's a young 'un, look. Meat's so tender it melts in your mouth.'

'I'm sorry – I don't want it.' Shaw waved his hand towards the kitchen. 'Besides I couldn't cook it in there.'

Tosser swung the rabbit to and fro like a pendulum. A few drops of liquid – blood? urine? – fell to the flagged floor.

'Tell you what. I'll do it for you.'

'Cook it?'

'Yes – and skin it and gut it. Make a stew. Lovely fresh veg. All I need from you is four bob and a saucepan to cook it in. You'll get two dinners out of it at least. Maybe three if you don't make a pig of yourself.'

'No,' Shaw said, his irritation mounting. 'I don't want it. Anyway, I don't much care for rabbit. All those little bones. And I haven't got four shillings to spare.'

'All right. Three shillings. I must be going soft in the head.'

'No.'

Tosser sniffed. 'No accounting for taste.'

Rabbit in hand, he left the cottage. Shaw watched him walking down to the path. Tosser paused at the gate. Next to it, Shaw's bicycle was leaning against the fence. Tosser looked at it in a brooding sort of way. He turned and stared at Shaw.

'Nice machine you got there.'

He spat on the ground, just missing the bicycle. After that he walked slowly away. Shaw went back inside and shut the door.

'I hope you don't regret that,' I said, though of course he couldn't hear me. 'You've made an enemy.'

45

***

Above all, our girls are encouraged to act as young ladies at all times, and to treat everyone they meet, high or low, with the same easy courtesy . . .

Monkshill Park: School Prospectus

The bell rang for lunch. It was a handbell, and it dominated and punctuated the life of the school from morning to night. It was a point of honour among the bell monitors to ring the beastly thing as loudly as possible as they marched along the uncarpeted halls and stone-flagged passages of Monkshill.

The school was divided into three houses, each of twenty to thirty girls of varying ages. Though there was only one kitchen at Monkshill, each house ate separately from the others because none of the rooms was large enough for everyone to sit down at once. The houses were called by the family names of England's grander ducal families to give them a suitably aristocratic aura.

The teaching staff ate with the girls and sat at the head of tables. The meals were intended to be educational as well as nourishing, so the girls were obliged to take it in turns to sit on either side of the teacher at the head of their table and make conversation with them. This was a skill, Miss Pryce-Morgan told them, that would prove invaluable in later life. Imagine, she often said as she warmed to her theme, how awful it would be if you found yourself tongue-tied when you and your husband were lunching at Buckingham Palace. Fortunately such a catastrophe wouldn't happen to them. Monkshill girls would always find the right thing to say.

Cavendish House ate their meals in the former servants' hall. I joined them at lunch in my present state as a disembodied observer, which was infinitely preferable to having to eat the

46

food and make conversation. Sylvia, Prissy and Venetia were all in Cavendish, and Enid was their housemistress; but that wasn't my main reason for going. I wanted to see how Alec Shaw coped.

It had been agreed that he should eat his lunches at school and take a table, like the rest of the staff. When he came into the room, the girls stared at him as though he were an apparition. There was the usual outbreak of whispering, and Maggie Squires had to bellow for silence. She sat at the other end of his table to make sure everyone behaved.

'Please, sir,' said a little second former called Rosemary Lawson-Smith, who was sitting on Shaw's right, 'do you know Miss Warnock?'

He glanced at her. 'No, I don't.'

'Is she coming back?'

He was concentrating on filling a plate with stew – small pieces of vein-streaked offal floating in grey, watery gravy and adorned with numerous potatoes and the occasional carrot. 'I'm not sure. I rather doubt it.'

'Good.'

Shaw looked startled. 'Why?'

'I didn't like her.'

Little beast, I thought. *I didn't like you, either.*

'Shall I tell you why?'

'No thanks,' Shaw said. 'Pass the plate along, please.'

'But don't you want to know, sir?'

'Not particularly. Besides, it's not nice to speak about other people behind their backs.'

There was a pause. My opinion of Shaw was improving. He put a little stew on his own plate and looked dubiously at it. 'Would you pass me the salt, please?'

47

'Please, sir, Miss Pryce-Morgan says, when you want the salt, you should ask your neighbour if they want some, and then if they're nice well-brought-up people, they ask if they can pass the salt to you.'

'Really? Just pass the salt, will you? And don't be cheeky.'

Rosemary flushed, and their conversation lapsed. Another girl asked Shaw if he would be going somewhere pleasant for his holidays, and he said no, probably not as far as he knew. She told him at length how she and her mother were going to stay at a boarding house in Torquay and what they planned to do. He looked bored. Then came pudding, which was Dead Man's Leg. That was the girls' name for a dense sponge pudding with very little jam in it. They were having it warm for lunch, and they would have it cold in the evening.

'Please, sir,' said Rosemary Lawson-Smith when she had finished.

Shaw looked warily at her. 'What is it?'

'Why aren't you in the army or something?'

'I was.'

'What did you do after that?' Rosemary asked.

Shaw didn't answer because his mouth was full. Then Enid stood up, and that was the end of the interrogation. Cavendish House shuffled to its feet and listened to their housemistress saying grace. Somehow, though, the conversation with Rosemary Lawson-Smith was the start of the rumour among the girls that in his previous career Mr Shaw had been a spy.

'Do you know what a lizzie is?' Sylvia Morton said. She had a small and battered book under her arm.

Stephen looked up from whittling a stick with his penknife. 'Why?'

'Someone said it the other day. I looked it up but it isn't in the dictionary.'

Good girl, I thought. *You looked it up.*

'But I don't think it can be very nice.'

Stephen shrugged. He was a year or two younger than Sylvia, and a child in many ways. His world had narrower horizons than hers. He was no fool, though, and wasted at Monkshill. Before my death I had been hoping to find a place for him at the nearest grammar school, which was in one of the towns on the way to Gloucester.

The two of them were at the boathouse on the south bank. Officially, the lake was out of bounds. Venetia Canford said that was because a housemaid had drowned in it a few years ago, and her ghost still walked at night, trying to get back to the house. Sometimes she succeeded. Venetia said her uncle, who lived nearby when there wasn't a war on, had told her all about it. She made a point of telling this story to new girls, leading to a gratifying number of nightmares and even the occasional case of bedwetting.

The lake was a weed-strewn expanse of murky water set in a depression surrounded by woodland. The ghost story was probably more effective than school rules at keeping people away. There were always exceptions, however, and among them Sylvia. And indeed me. I'd taken Enid to the boathouse once but it hadn't been much fun. Soon after that, I had found a key for East Cottage.

The boathouse had a rotten wooden jetty beside it, to which a half-submerged punt was still moored. There was a verandah with a room behind. You had to watch your step on both the verandah and the jetty – several of the planks were rotten, and in places they had fallen away completely. The glazed doors of

49

the room had long since gone, apart from a few fragments of glass among the dead leaves. But its roof was still more or less weathertight.

Sylvia and Stephen sometimes met there on a Sunday afternoon. From the doorway you had a clear view of the paths through the trees which were still useable, and there was a back door, which meant you could retreat into the undergrowth behind.

He closed the penknife and slipped it into the pocket of his shorts. 'What you got this time?'

'It's called *Peril at End House*. It's really good. A Poirot.'

She gave him the book. The girls had found over a hundred detective novels in one of the attics. They had been abandoned by the people who lived at Monkshill before the war, when it was still a private house. The books were passed around like contraband among the older girls, the ones that actually read for pleasure. Miss Pryce-Morgan did not approve of detective fiction, which gave it the allure of forbidden fruit.

Before I died, I hadn't known that Sylvia sometimes lent Stephen books, or even that they were friends, and that he lent her books in return. There was so much I hadn't known then. If nothing else, death had been educational.

'Have you got me anything?' she asked.

'No. She stayed at home on her afternoon off.'

That was another thing I had discovered recently. On his aunt's afternoons off, she often caught the bus into town and took her nephew with her. Mrs Broadwell parked Stephen in the library and allowed him to use her tickets, while she went shopping and had tea with her friends. He pretended he was choosing books for her. Fortunately his aunt was not a reader.

'You will look next time you go, won't you?' Sylvia said. 'You promise?'

'All right.' He shifted, and the floorboards creaked ominously beneath his weight. 'If I can.'

'You still remember the title of the one I want?'

'*Busman's Something*. By Dorothy Sayers.'

'*Busman's Honeymoon*. By Dorothy L. Sayers.'

'It doesn't sound like much of a murder mystery,' Stephen said.

'Well it is. It comes after *Gaudy Night*. Miss Warnock said it's not as good. But *Gaudy Night* is the best detective story there is. Not for everyone, she said, but for me.'

'Why?'

'Because it's about the women at an Oxford college. It's why I want to go to Oxford.'

Bless the child, I thought, and I hope you do. Sylvia turned pink with embarrassment at having revealed something so close to her heart, so private. Poor kid. My own copy of *Gaudy Night* was at present locked away in my room on the second floor, along with everything else.

Stephen shrugged again. If he had ambitions, they lay in other directions. 'I say,' he said. 'There's a new man living in East Cottage.'

'I know. He came into lunch today. He's going to be teaching me. Latin and stuff like that.'

'Yes, but I talked to him too. Auntie sent me – the carrier left his trunk up at the house, and I had to help him get it on Tosser's barrow.'

'What's he like?'

'He's OK – he gave me sixpence for helping him. And I found out something. He's writing a detective story.'

Sylvia stared at him. 'What? Really? Truly? A proper one?'

'Yes. Like Agatha Christie.'

'What's it about?'

'He didn't say. But you must have to be really clever to write a story like that. Sort of like a detective yourself.'

'Yes,' Sylvia said. And then in a different voice, 'Yes, you're right. I wonder.'

'What?'

'If he could help find out what happened to Miss Warnock.'

'But she just went away, didn't she?'

That was how most of the children had responded to my disappearance. I had been there with them. And then suddenly I wasn't. As far as they were concerned, that was all there was to it. There was nothing intrinsically strange about that because I was an adult, and adults did unaccountable, unpredictable things. Adults were an alien species.

Sylvia said, 'She gave me some holiday prep – Latin prose. She said she'd go through it with me when she got back. Before term started.'

'Perhaps she changed her mind?'

Sylvia shook her head violently. 'But she wouldn't. Not about something like that. Besides, she only told me on the morning she left, just as she was leaving the house for the bus.'

Stephen had opened *Peril At End House* and was looking at the first page. He looked up. 'Bus?'

'Yes. That's what she said. She was off to catch the bus.'

'From the village? The one just after eleven?'

'Yes. So that means she—'

'She didn't catch that bus,' Stephen said.

'How do you know?'

'I'd have seen her,' he said. 'I was playing on the green with Jack. We were watching to see who got on.'

Sylvia raised her eyebrows. 'Who's Jack?'

'Friend of mine. His ma has the greengrocer's by the church.'

'But why were you watching who got on the bus?'

Stephen looked shifty. 'To see if his sister did. She said she might go to Gloucester but she wasn't sure.'

'But why . . . ?'

Stephen shrugged. I guessed they had been after the sister's sweet ration or cigarettes. Or furtively curious about her private belongings. He went on, 'She must have walked somewhere. Or got a lift. Or went by South Lodge and got the bus to Newport.'

'I thought she was going to catch the bus at Flaxern Parva.'

Typical of the police, I thought, and typical of bloody Pryce-Morgan: neither of them had thought to ask the girls who were still at Monkshill, let alone the cook's nephew, if they had seen anything of me on the day I disappeared. PM had probably been terrified that the girls might let slip something when they wrote to their parents.

'Anyway,' Stephen said, 'there's nothing we can do about it, is there?'

'Why not?' Sylvia demanded.

'Because we're just kids. They wouldn't listen to me, anyway.'

'Oh blow it!' Sylvia said.

She pointed a finger in the direction of the lake. Venetia Canford was coming down the path. Alec Shaw was walking beside her.

Venetia hated me. And it would not have bent the truth too far to say that I returned the favour. I was twenty years older than she was. I had been her teacher, she had been my pupil. All that was irrelevant. On a level that was beyond words, we had each other's number. She knew she couldn't fool me, and I sometimes worried that I couldn't fool her either. I also had a good reason to suspect that her hatred of me had intensified a few days before my death.

I left Sylvia and Stephen retreating from the boathouse through the wood that sloped upwards from the lake. I went to eavesdrop on Venetia and Shaw, who had reached the opposite bank of the lake.

'. . . it's not very nice, is it?' Venetia was saying. 'They say it's full of dead bodies. I expect it is.'

'It's a bit gloomy,' Shaw conceded. 'Anyway, thanks for showing it me.'

'There used to be an old icehouse over there, but the roof fell in and it's just a pile of rubble now.'

'And what's that over there?'

'A boathouse. I go there sometimes. To be alone. To be private.'

She turned her head and stared up at him, as if she wanted him to understand that the words meant more than they said on the surface. I'm not sure they actually did. She was a child practising with grown-up weapons to see what effect they had. Not knowing what they could do if she practised on the wrong person.

Shaw patted his pocket and took out a packet of cigarettes. 'I thought you said the lake was out of bounds to the school.'

She shrugged. She had a sinuous way of shrugging that made me want to slap her. 'Someone was saying you used to be a spy.'

'Then someone was talking nonsense.'

'But you would say that, wouldn't you, sir? If you were a spy.'

Shaw didn't reply. He struck a match and cupped his hands around the flame as he lit the cigarette.

'Can I have one?'

'What? Of course you can't.'

'I smoke all the time.'

'Then you're very foolish. You're far too young. Besides, it's against the school rules.'

She said nothing, just fixed him with those blue eyes like twin searchlights.

'I'm not going to report you this time,' he said sternly. 'But I want no more of this foolishness.'

'But I want a cigarette,' she said, pushing out her lower lip. 'If you don't give me one, I'll say you tried to kiss me.'

'Don't be ridiculous.'

They stared at each other. *Good for you,* I thought, *if you'd given her what she wanted, she'd make you her creature for ever.* Venetia moistened her wide lips. He turned away from her and

55

walked quickly up the track, away from the lake. She watched him go.

That was how Venetia operated: she would lead you one way and then suddenly attack from an unexpected direction. Also, she gave the impression that she didn't care about anything, which was a very powerful weapon, and one she used again and again.

If she was ever afraid of anyone, she had been afraid of me because I wouldn't let her bully me. I was as ruthless as she was. And perhaps Shaw was as well.

At four o'clock, Enid and Shaw met for tea in the staffroom. They were alone in there. Most teachers either went out on Sunday afternoons or stayed in their own rooms.

Enid put the kettle on the ring. 'The trouble is,' she said, 'we don't usually put girls in for School Certificate. It's only since the war that a few of the parents have started asking for it. I suppose it's because more and more girls are looking for jobs these days, and they need qualifications for that. So we're having to make it up as we go along. Of course Annabel knew all about it as she'd taught at Worcester Ladies', but they've always been an academic school, and they have all the resources in the world . . .'

She broke off and turned away to spoon tea into the pot.

'Annabel?' Shaw said.

'Annabel Warnock,' Enid said, her back still turned to him. 'The one whose place you're filling.'

'As well as I can,' Shaw said. 'I was teaching thirteen-year-olds for Common Entrance.'

'Yes, but I'm sure the standard for that is pretty high in a decent prep school. Not that far removed from School Cert.'

They talked for half an hour. I soon grew bored with their conversation, which was all about syllabuses and classrooms and which of them was best equipped to take my senior French class. After a while I withdrew into myself. When I came back, Shaw had left the house and Enid had gone up to her room to finish her marking. (I had tried to stop her working so hard. She was far too conscientious for a school like Monkshill Park. It was partly because this was her first teaching job, and she hadn't had time to develop a protective coating of cynicism.)

I went over to the cottage to see what Shaw was up to now. I was relieved to find him at work on his novel. After our experience before church, I was afraid I might have frightened him off. That would have been a tragedy, at least for me. I wanted to find out if I could repeat the experiment. Could I somehow communicate with a living human being? That was a heartrendingly exciting prospect in itself. But there was another aspect to this. If I couldn't investigate my own murder, then someone else had to. Shaw was my only hope.

I heard the sound of the typewriter through the open window. Inside the cottage, I discovered that the story had moved on since I had last seen it – he had finished the first page and begun the second.

. . . are you doing here?' Roderick demanded. 'I'm surprised you dare show your face after what happened.'

'Nanny wired me,' Cynthia said. 'She said Uncle George is dying.'

'Balderdash. Nanny's a silly old woman. It's probably just something he ate. He . . .

I needed to focus on the hands, on the typewriter, on the page he was writing. I stared hard, trying to concentrate my mind on the sheet of paper in the typewriter, as children use a magnifying glass to concentrate the sun's rays into a golden, burning spot, a miniature sun.

Gothick Walk. Look there.

The result was gratifying. Shaw's fingers thumped on the keys. *Gothick Walk. Look there.* Automatically he slammed the carriage return leaver; the roller rotated; the paper slid up a line; and the typewriter's bell went *Ping*.

Simultaneously he reared away from the machine as if it was suddenly red hot. He ran his hands through his hair, reducing it to a tangle of greasy spikes. He stood up. The chair toppled behind him. He ignored it. He rubbed his eyes as though trying to erase out what they had seen. Then, hesitantly, he looked again at the words he had typed.

Gothick Walk. Look there.

He stood up and went over to the empty fireplace, where he lit a cigarette. He drew in the smoke with desperate energy. Suck, suck, suck, like a greedy baby. But his eyes never left the typewriter. Perhaps he feared it might start vomiting a stream of words of its own volition.

He flicked the butt into the grate, though it was only half-smoked. He crossed the room in three strides and ripped the paper from the typewriter. He took it to the fireplace, holding it away from him between finger and thumb as though it was infectious, and dropped it into the grate. He struck a match on the hearthstone, lit one corner of the page and sat back on his heels to watch it burn. As the paper flared and curled, turned golden then dark, individual words leapt briefly into life.

George is dying . . . Gothick . . . look . . .

'Christ,' he muttered. 'Oh Christ.'

He ground the ashes to dust with vicious stabs of the poker. He fetched a glass of water, which he drank standing at the open window. Back at the table, he rolled a clean sheet into the platen and typed: *1. Give the Present Indicative Act of fero and the Present Indicative Passive of capio in full.* Ping.

I focused on his hands and the typewriter again: *Go to Maiden's Leap.*

He typed: *2. Give the Ablative Singular and meaning of vis, vir, virus, supellex, meridies.* Ping.

I felt myself slump – whatever my*self* now meant. The tiredness was worse than this morning's. The power had gone from me, the energy had drained away.

I hadn't reached him this time. Which reinforced the theory that he was only accessible to me when he was at work on his story. His stupid attempt to write a novel was apparently my only means of having any effect on the life I had left behind. Why should that be? Was it something to do with the fact that he was a writer, trying to conjure something out of nothing just as I had tried in a very different way with my essay on the Gothick Walk?

He stopped typing and reached for the cigarettes again. 'Christ,' he said again. 'I'm going mad.'

There are worse things in life, I wanted to tell him, than a little temporary madness or a flying visit from the inexplicable. Death, for example.

Eventually I dragged myself away from all the excitement at East Cottage and went back to Bleeding Yew Wood and the Maiden's Leap.

I stayed there for the rest of the afternoon and evening,

listening to the noises and watching the creatures that came and went. Rabbits, a fox, an old badger and a variety of smaller animals followed their own lives, seemingly oblivious to the dead thing that was eavesdropping on them. Gradually they faded away. As twilight darkened towards night, the birds fell silent one by one, apart from the hoots of a pair of owls in the distance.

I had somehow made Shaw type the words I wanted him to type.

Only, it seemed, when certain conditions were satisfied, but even so it was possible for me to communicate one-way with someone who was alive, albeit in a limited way. I only had the strength to project (if that's the word) a short phrase at a time. There was also the risk that if I interfered with Shaw's novel too much and too often, he would think he was going mad and abandon his book. That wouldn't help anyone. But if I could pique his curiosity enough to investigate the Gothick Walk, there was just a possibility he might find a trace of what had happened to me . . .

If I could also find a way to communicate with Enid by the same method, a range of new possibilities would open up. For a start, I could tell her that I had been murdered. I hated the thought that she might think I had panicked just before our holiday together and abandoned her. Or, worse still, that I hadn't really cared for her, that I had toyed with her affections like the seducer in a Victorian novel and then abruptly disappeared from her life.

Gradually my mind quietened. I was so tired. The sounds of the wood took the place of thoughts. Trees are never silent. Even when the air is still, they find mysterious ways to move, to talk to each other with the rustle of leaves and the creak of branches and the entangling of roots beneath the ground.

I listened to them while I was sliding towards that absence which was the nearest thing I now had to sleep. It was a gradual process, difficult to put into words: the sight and sounds of the living world gradually became thin and gauze-like until they and I faded to nothing, like an unfixed photograph left in the sunshine.

I was nearly there, nearly nothing, when I heard footsteps somewhere far away. At first I thought it was Tosser, though he tended to do his poaching in West Cover, where the going was easier. Anyway, the rhythm of the footsteps was different from his – faster, more assured in the almost dark of a night in May. I could hardly hear them.

I already knew that somebody else must come here, or at least that somebody had done in the recent past. Somebody must have made the camouflaged gap under the fence which I had found so convenient in life. And somebody must be still using it, for otherwise the gap would have soon become choked with bramble suckers and nettles.

It was too late to investigate now. I was slipping away, and I could no more resist it than the tug of the ebbing tide on the day I died.

7

When I came back to myself on Monday morning, the sun was still low in the sky, and the world was fresh and beautiful.

I didn't know how long I would remain aware of this living world. But while I was, I wanted to discover who had killed me – and, as well, to keep Enid safe. Quite apart from the time-bomb waiting to be discovered behind my locked door on the second floor, I couldn't be sure that the murderer had finished his or her work. For all I knew, Enid might be the second victim.

The sun climbed higher. Colours brightened. The air filled with noises. I began to make a list of those who might have wanted me dead. Tosser had had good reason to dislike me. So had PM and Runty. Or even Venetia Canford. I was not a large woman, after all, or rather I hadn't been. Any of those could have pushed me. For all I knew there were others. The thing about a boarding school is that it's an enclosed world. It's an emotional hothouse where an insignificant offence can assume the proportions of an unforgivable injury.

It was time to make a move. By now, I guessed, the school

was having breakfast. I followed the familiar path among the trees and came to the vast bramble bush, the bleeding yew and the gap beneath the fence.

That was when I saw the button lying on the ground. It was brown, and about the diameter of a shilling. It still had two or three strands of thread attached to it. I was absolutely certain that it hadn't been there yesterday. I remembered the footsteps in the night and now I knew for sure that I hadn't been alone in the wood.

A button. The sort of clue that popped up in dozens of detective stories. Life was such a cliché sometimes.

After breakfast, there was half an hour before the morning assembly. During this time, many of the girls were occupied with their duty rotas.

The rotas were Runty's solution to the omnipresent servant problem. Since the war started, the problem had grown particularly acute at Monkshill. (That was why Mrs Broadwell, the cook, was paid so well and why she was given such extraordinary latitude, including permission for her nephew, Stephen, to live at the school.) Mrs Crisp, a widow who lived in the North Lodge, came in to do the cleaning five and a half days a week. Two unreliable women came up from the village to help her, but only for three or four mornings a week at best. Everything else was done by the girls, under the direction of Miss Runciman and Mrs Broadwell. Credit where credit was due: Runty had a genius for delegating work and organising others.

The girls made their own beds; they dusted the dormitories, classrooms and public rooms of the house; they cleaned the downstairs windows and washed the chequered marble floor in the hall; they polished the furniture and cleared the tables;

they served tea for the staffroom and headmistress's study and afterwards they washed up the cups and saucers. In effect, they acted as a small army of part-time maids. They were led to believe that this was an important part of their education, both moral and practical.

'When you have a house of your own,' Miss Pryce-Morgan would tell her captive audience at least once a term, 'you will know what to expect from your servants because you have done it yourself, and you will have done it to a standard fit for any gentleman's home in the kingdom.'

On Monday morning, I found Sylvia Morton polishing the hall table. She had violet shadows under her eyes and a tendency to yawn. She had probably been reading under the bedclothes again. The table was a few paces from the door to the library, which was used as the fourth form classroom but retained the name it had before the war. The door was ajar. The library window faced east. A stripe of sunlight slipped between door and jamb and stretched across the hall floor.

I heard slow footsteps in the library. Someone was humming a tune, slow and peaceful like a lullaby; not one I recognised. Everyone grumbled about the cleaning rotas, but in fact it was not unpleasant to escape the noisy company of eighty-three girls, especially in the warmer months.

Suddenly there was a sharp intake of breath, and the sound of something falling to the floor. Footsteps clumped across the bare boards and Prissy appeared in the doorway.

'Sylvie,' she whispered, her eyes wide with fear. 'There's a mouse!'

'Where?'

'On the shelf by the blackboard.' Fear made Prissy's accent more Teutonic than usual. 'With the Bibles.'

'Don't worry. It's more scared than you are. It'll soon run off.'

'But it can't run anywhere.' The thin voice rose to a wail. 'It's dead.'

'Hush.' Girls on cleaning duty in the main house were strictly forbidden to talk to each other. 'Then it can't hurt you, can it?'

'But what shall I do? I can't *touch* it. And if I leave it, Runty will see.'

'I'll deal with it,' Sylvia said.

I watched Prissy's face light up with gratitude. It was the slugs all over again. This was one reason I liked Sylvia. She had guts and she also had a brusque kindness. All the more so in this case because I knew she disliked mice intensely. Rats were even worse. She was terrified of them.

Prissy glanced over her shoulder at the closed door of RM's study. 'What if they catch you?'

'I don't care. Where is it?'

Sylvia swallowed. She was a sensible girl so she was afraid of PM and Runty. I guessed that her resolution was already ebbing away. She picked up her dustpan and brush and marched into the library. Prissy hovered in the doorway, tugging at bony, ink-stained fingers.

The library was a long room with rows of scarred desks facing the blackboard. The mistress had a tall desk of her own, which stood beside the single window at the far end. To left and right, handsome oak bookcases ran along walls and stretched to the moulded plaster ceiling, now reduced to a dirty yellow expanse stained with damp. It made me think of the rotting icing on Miss Havisham's wedding cake.

The previous occupants of the house had packed up the contents of the library with the rest of their belongings when they decamped to Canada at the beginning of the war. There were only Bibles and textbooks on the shelves now, as well as the meagre school library. The latter consisted of a few battered classics, some volumes of poetry and a dozen Edwardian novels of school life.

The mouse was lying on its side on a shelf near the blackboard, its back nestling as if for spiritual protection against the spine of a Bible. Sylvia swept the little corpse into the dustpan, along with a piece of string that was somehow attached to it. She glanced up at the window, probably wondering if she could throw it outside. But the window was a huge Georgian sash that stretched almost to the ceiling. The lower window had been screwed shut because the sash cords had rotted. Only the upper part could be opened, and that was out of reach.

Sylvia walked back to the door, holding the dustpan at arm's length before her as if the mouse's body might be infectious. She avoided looking directly at it.

'Are you sure it's dead?' Prissy said in a sibilant whisper. 'Really sure?'

Sylvia glanced at the mouse. 'Of course it's dead. Look.'

It was on its back, its legs pointing stiffly upwards. The head was at an angle to the body. The mouth was open, revealing sharp white teeth. The eyes were suffused with blood.

Prissy shied away. 'How do you think it died?'

'Can't you see?'

Prissy and I gathered around and looked. The piece of string encircled the mouse's neck. It had been pulled so tight it was almost buried in the fur. Drawn a little tighter, the mouse would have lost its head.

Prissy gave a shriek, instantly hushed. 'I don't understand.'

'This wasn't an accident, was it? Someone strangled it.'

'What are you saying? It was . . . ?'

Sylvia said, half seriously, half attempting a joke, 'It looks like murder to me.'

Alec Shaw had bags under his eyes, which wasn't altogether surprising. He had cut himself shaving again too. But he was in good time for morning prayers in the hall, after which PM harangued the school about the importance of well-trimmed nails and the abomination that was coloured nail varnish.

I had come almost to admire the headmistress's daily homilies. They were extempore, and you could rarely predict what the daily subject would be. Shaw kept a straight face, though he did glance at Enid to see how she was taking it.

I grew bored and wandered off to the kitchen, where Mrs Broadwell was having a cup of tea and a cigarette with Mrs Crisp. The room was cavernous and high-ceilinged with an enormous iron cooking range flaking with rust, which was fortunately no longer used.

Mrs Crisp was a tall woman who in happier times might well have been plump. Now the skin hung like a discarded dust-sheet over her heavy bones. She had slab-like hands, raw and wrinkled with endless washing and scrubbing.

'No please-and-thank-you,' she was saying, 'or would it be convenient? Just do for him once a week, Mrs Hitler said, Wednesday afternoon would be best. And parcel up his laundry and bring it back to the house. So I'll have to come all the way back here before I go home.'

'His laundry's going separate,' Mrs Broadwell said. 'That's what she told me.'

'Why?'

'Search me. Because of the stains? You know what men are

like. Mind you, I'd rather have a man to deal with than Mrs Hitler.' Mrs Broadwell jerked her head in the direction of the front of the house, towards Miss Runciman. 'Less trouble.' She tapped the ash from her cigarette with elaborate care and said, in a lower voice, 'Talking of men: any news?'

Mrs Crisp seemed to shrink into herself. She said, with obvious reluctance, 'Jim Fowles come round on Saturday night. No warning. Just turned up on the doorstep when I was cooking my tea.'

'Born nosy, that one. Just because he's a policeman, thinks he can poke his nose in anywhere.'

'He asked if I'd heard anything from Sam. He had a good look around while he was there, of course.'

'It's not right,' Mrs Broadwell said absently. She glanced at the shopping list on the table.

'He's not as bad as them bloody Redcaps,' Mrs Crisp said, as she had said so often before. 'They're worse than the Gestapo.'

There was a lull in the conversation. The visits from the Military Police were old news. Mrs Broadwell was no longer interested in their behaviour. She picked up her pencil and wrote *Carrots?* on her list. Mrs Crisp finished her tea and looked hopefully at the teapot.

Mrs Broadwell looked up. 'I wonder where he is though. Your Sam, I mean. Must be somewhere.'

'I told you, I reckon he went to Ireland. His dad was Irish, you know.' Mrs Crisp shifted in her seat and I guessed she didn't want to talk about her son. On that subject, perhaps she had used up all the words at her disposal long ago. She said abruptly, 'Have you met him, by the way? The new chap?'

'Not to speak to.' Mrs Broadwell stood up and carried the teapot to the sink. 'He came into dinner after church,' she said over her shoulder. 'They stared at him like he was something out of a zoo.' She scooped the tea leaves with her hand and flung them into the bucket, which meant they had already been reused once. 'Our Steve helped him down to the cottage with his trunk on Saturday. He's got a typewriter down there. Steve says he's writing a book.'

'Why would he want to do that?' Mrs Crisp said. 'Hasn't he got better things to do?'

8

I couldn't resist seeing how Shaw managed what PM now referred to as 'our School Certificate class' when she was trying to impress a parent. She hadn't been keen on it originally. She didn't like the idea of her girls taking exams. But times had changed, and even she now recognised that there might be advantages in it for the school.

No one could remember a Monkshill girl taking the School Certificate exams, let alone matriculating. The only reason that the school had a class now was because Enid and I had fought for it. And – credit where credit was due – we wouldn't have done that if it hadn't been for Sylvia Morton with her unheard-of desire to go to Oxford and get a degree.

The girl had been inspired by reading *Gaudy Night*, by Dorothy L. Sayers. The novel's toe-curling romance and rampant snobbery had passed her by. But something about the notion of scholarly truth had fired her imagination: in particular, perhaps, the novel's insistence that the pursuit of truth for its own sake was as worthwhile for a woman as for a man.

Both Enid and I enjoyed teaching – proper teaching, I mean,

when you managed to spark something in your pupils, and led them to find something inside themselves that they didn't know they had, or helped them understand what they thought would always be incomprehensible; when you encouraged them to explore on their own, rather than merely sit back while we stuffed their heads with dreary facts and absurd notions about how nicely-brought-up young ladies should behave in a world that no longer existed.

So when Sylvia came to me and asked about School Certificate, we were keen to help. She had already drummed up support from Prissy and a few other girls. Enid and I sent away for copies of the syllabus and past examination papers. In order to matriculate, you had to pass five subjects at the same time. These had to include English, Maths and a foreign language. We worked on the headmistress until at last she allowed us to establish a special School Certificate set. She frowned on science subjects, however, and on no account were we allowed to teach biology.

At present there were four other girls in the class. Two of them were twins, Miranda and Amanda Twisden, who loved accumulating badges, qualifications and certificates of any sort; they had no academic ambitions as such, but they welcomed any chance to compete against each other, which they did with vicious determination. Then there was Muriel Fisher, a tall, silent girl who liked to do number puzzles in her spare time in the intervals of grappling with theological questions. Finally, Priscilla Knecht had joined the class because it gave her a chance to see more of Sylvia. Not that she was a fool. Far from it.

The absurd truth was that if Sylvia or anyone else wanted to get into Oxford, she would need a School Certificate pass in Latin. That held true whatever subject she applied to read at university. Teaching Latin had been my particular responsibility.

71

Starting from scratch, the class had made good progress in the last two terms, but they still had a very long way to go.

PM and Runty had now come to see the School Certificate class as an asset – not as important as dancing lessons, of course, but certainly on a par with rounders and head and shoulders above the Botany Society. As a result, my sudden disappearance from the scene had been even more of an inconvenience than it would otherwise have been, particularly because of Enid's lack of experience. Which was why they had been obliged to bring in Alec Shaw at such short notice, not only as a temporary cover for my routine teaching, but also to deal with Latin for the School Certificate class.

I found the class in a drably utilitarian room beyond the library. According to the label on the row of bells in the kitchen passage, this had once been the estate office. Shaw and the girls were sitting around the big table. The only sounds were the faint scratch of pencil on paper and the rasp of Prissy's breathing.

On the blackboard, Shaw had written the day's date, 14 May 1945, and the test questions which I had watched him typing yesterday evening. He was doing what I would have done with a new class: testing them to find out what they already knew.

Meanwhile he lounged in his chair and pored over the crossword in Saturday's edition of *The Times*. Half the paper was lying beside his chair in an untidy heap on the floor. Random headlines leapt out at me:

SUICIDE OF GERMAN S.S. CHIEF
OCCUPATION OF GERMANY
U.S. ARMIES ON THE MOVE

PM would be furious if she found Shaw desecrating *The Times*. It arrived at Monkshill in the afternoon. After PM had read the day's paper, it went as a great favour into the staffroom, though not for long. Removing the newspaper from the staffroom was strictly forbidden, as was mutilating it in any way. Runty would collect it and return it to PM, who kept piles of old *Times* in the study closet. I had never worked out why she hoarded the paper so religiously. It was a question for a psychiatrist.

I hovered by the blackboard and scanned the questions.

1. Give the Present Indicative Act of fero and the Present Indicative Passive of capio in full.
2. Give the Ablative Singular and meaning of vis, vir, virus, supellex, meridies.
3. Translate into Latin: The allies will fight bravely lest the city of Athens should be attacked by the enemy.

The poor man was in for a shock. He was presumably used to the standard of a decent boys' prep school, not to an intellectual desert like Monkshill Park. I made my way around the table to monitor the progress of his new pupils. Miranda and Amanda were scowling ferociously at their exercise books. Muriel had filled in some of the answers, mostly wrongly, and was picking at one of her spots. Prissy was looking even more miserable than usual but she had done a little better than Muriel. Sylvia was frowning. She had answered more of the questions than anyone else, if not always correctly.

Shaw looked up from the crossword, his pencil hovering over 13 Down (*The mail seems late [4, 6,]*) to see how the girls were doing.

'Five minutes more,' he said.

Dead letter, I thought.

But he sighed and moved on to 14 Across.

73

I usually enjoyed the kitchen garden, and May was a good time to be there. It was a place to think, and a place merely to be. I went there about midday. The sun was out. Though I couldn't feel its warmth, I knew it must be there: I could remember the sensation of it on my skin.

I hovered around a bench near the south wall, where in the world of the living the old bricks would be bouncing the heat into the garden. The only person in sight was Tosser, who was sprawling on another bench by the shed where the tools were kept. He had a pipe in his mouth and was studying a newspaper.

I hoped the garden would cheer me up. I was feeling depressed and envious. You might think that in my current state I could have risen above such emotions, but you'd be wrong. Watching Shaw with my School Cert class had upset me unexpectedly. I had liked teaching them. They had been my girls. And now they were Shaw's. What made it worse was that even with my limited knowledge of his professional skills, I had seen enough of him today to sense that he would be good at the job.

Better than me, perhaps? It was absurd that I should care in my present situation. But feelings were absurd, weren't they? You couldn't argue with them. You just had to put up with them or pretend they weren't there.

I heard the creak of the gate opening. It was Stephen with a basket on his arm. He walked briskly up the path and into the shed. He passed close to Tosser on his bench, but the old man ignored him.

Curious, I drew nearer. The boy was only a moment inside. When he came out, the basket was full of new potatoes, spring greens and radishes, with a bunch of early sweet peas on top.

I wasn't the only one who was curious. Tosser rose to his feet and stared at him. Stephen swerved to avoid him, but Tosser changed direction at the same time and they ended up colliding. His pipe fell to the ground, spilling its smouldering contents.

'What the fuck do you think you're doing? You're always in the bloody way.'

'Sorry,' Stephen mumbled. 'I didn't mean to. I—'

'What you got there anyway?'

'Just some veg.'

'You stealing them, boy?'

'No, Luigi left them for Auntie. Honest.'

Tosser feigned ignorance. 'Who?'

'Mr Lewis's Italian.'

The kitchen garden was in Mr Lewis's hands, but much of the work in it was done by Luigi. He was an obliging man in his late thirties, who seemed happy to be growing things rather than shooting at people or kicking his heels in a prisoner-of-war camp.

'That bloody Eyetie? Who's he to be giving away vegetables that belong to other people? Eh? That's stealing, that is.'

'But Auntie said he wanted us to have them. He—'

'Ah . . .' Tosser's eyes narrowed. 'So that's the way the wind blows, eh?'

He made a lunge for the basket, but Stephen avoided him. 'What do you mean?'

'I mean your aunt's no better than she should be. Your aunt and that little fascist monkey? It's a fucking joke, ain't it?'

But Stephen was already walking quickly away, the basket clutched to his narrow chest, ready to break into a run at any moment.

'Bugger off, you little bastard,' Tosser called after him. 'That's what you are, ain't you? Don't think I don't know. Bloody bastard.'

9

After lunch, Sylvia and Prissy buried the mouse in the shrubbery. They had wrapped the body in an ink-stained handkerchief. Prissy dug the shallow grave with a stick. The earth was damp and her hands and knees were soon filthy, which would lead to trouble later if Runty saw them in that state. Runty didn't like Prissy at the best of times and was always looking for an excuse to punish her. This was partly because Prissy was poor, a charity case whose fees were paid by her host family, and partly because she was a German refugee; but mostly, I suspected, because Prissy was Jewish.

Sylvia pushed the body into the grave, using a twig to avoid touching it. Prissy covered it with earth, which she firmed down with the palms of her hands. She looked up at Sylvia. 'Should we say something?'

'What?'

'I don't know. Like a psalm.'

'It's only a mouse.'

'But even so . . .'

'Don't be silly.'

Prissy recoiled as if Sylvia had slapped her.

'It's all right,' Sylvia said, sounding both awkward and irritated. 'But just – you know – it's a mouse, not a person. It hasn't got a soul.'

'Do you really think it was murdered?'

Sylvia shrugged. 'I suppose so.' She sounded more uncertain about it than she had this morning. 'If you can murder a mouse.'

Leaves rustled behind them. I had the uncomfortable sense that a living thing had passed through the left-hand side of my body.

'What on earth are you doing?'

The two girls wheeled around and scrambled awkwardly to their feet. Venetia Canford stared contemptuously at them.

'Nothing,' Sylvia said. 'Just . . . just playing.'

'At what? Making mud pies? God, how old are you? Three?'

The bell for lessons clanged inside the house.

Venetia glanced at Prissy. 'You're filthy. You'll catch it if Runty sees you like that.'

She turned on her heel and strolled away.

'Well?' Enid said. 'How was your first day?'

'Do they always giggle and whisper like that?' Shaw said.

'They will when you're teaching them, I'm afraid. But I'm sure it will get better as they get used to you.'

'As for the teaching . . . it's not exactly demanding, is it? For the teacher, I mean.'

Enid smiled. 'It's more a matter of keeping them busy and reasonably quiet. But what about the School Cert class?'

'Keen,' Shaw said. 'I'll say that for them. Really keen. Not like boys.'

'And academically?'

77

'Well . . .'

He stopped to light his pipe. He and Enid were strolling in front of the house, which was very different from the back. It had been faced with limestone. The main facade was chastely beautiful. There were ornately decorated single-storey pavilions attached to the ends, linked to the central block with glazed colonnades. If you ignored the peeling paintwork and the odd windowpane patched with plywood, you could imagine the place in a Jane Austen novel. There had once been a lawn and flowerbeds in front of the house, but now the grass was long. After a month or so it would be cut and baled by Mr Lewis and his men; fodder for the winter months.

In a quarter of an hour, the bell would ring for roll call and then, ten minutes later, the girls would have their tea, the last meal of their day. It was strange and even a little humiliating to realise that the school routine continued without me. It was as if I had never existed.

'I don't think there will be a problem with history,' Shaw went on. 'Nothing I can't handle as long as they will put in the work. But they still have a lot of ground to cover with Latin if they want to reach School Cert standard.'

'That's what Annabel said. Your . . . your predecessor.'

'What about your subjects?'

'We are getting there. It's a slow business.' Enid taught Maths and French; she and I used to share the English.

'If Sylvia really wants to go to university, she'll need to get her Higher School Certificate as well.'

'She won't be able to do them here,' Enid said. 'Her best bet would be a grammar school or somewhere like Cheltenham or Worcester, if there's the money for that. Her mother's dead, so it all depends on what the father wants for her. She hasn't seen him since 1939, and she hasn't had a letter for more than three years.'

'He's still alive?'

'She doesn't know. He was at the Fall of Singapore, and she hasn't heard from him since then. No one has actually told her he's dead.'

'Poor kid.'

'A brave one too,' Enid said.

She turned towards him, and her forehead creased in that way she had when she was talking about something she really cared about. I remembered her looking like that when we were at the lake one Sunday, the time she put her hand on my arm and said without any preamble, *I think I'm falling in love with you.* It was she who had said it first, before anything had happened between us. I don't think I've ever been happier.

This time, with the same creases in her forehead, the same look in her face, she said to Shaw: 'She needs to go to university. Annabel and I agreed about that. Not necessarily Oxford, but somewhere. And I'll do anything I can to help. It's the one thing in her life that makes any sense to her.'

They walked in silence for a moment. I always was a jealous cow and I didn't like seeing her tête-à-tête with Shaw.

'Where did you teach before you came here?' he asked.

'Nowhere. I used to work in a library, but I wanted a change. I've got a degree so I had something to offer. I saw the job here and I thought it was worth a try. I rather liked the idea of living in the country. PM interviewed me and offered it to me on the spot.'

'I imagine people weren't exactly queuing up for it.' Shaw tapped his forehead in mock apology. 'Sorry – that was crass. I'm sure you'd have got it even if they had been.'

79

There was another pause. I hoped he had mortally offended her.

'And how are you getting on at East Cottage?' Enid asked in a bright voice like a determined hostess making conversation with a shy guest.

She and I had gone to East Cottage on two occasions – once downstairs, when we had first kissed properly, and once upstairs when we'd sat on the cold, bare mattress and I'd failed to persuade her that we should do more than kissing. I hated to think of Shaw sleeping on that same mattress.

'It's fine – a bit primitive,' he said. 'I've had worse digs.'

'There's a rumour going about the school that you're an author. That you're writing a book there.'

'Yes. Actually I am. Writing a book, I mean.' Shaw looked embarrassed, as if caught out doing something mildly shameful. 'But I wouldn't call myself an author. Anyway, how on earth do they know?'

'I've no idea. But they find out everything sooner or later.'

'Come to think of it, I told what's his name – Stephen? – on my first day. He was asking about my typewriter.'

'There you are then. What sort of a book is it?'

'A detective story.' He cleared his throat. 'It's something to do in the evenings. To amuse myself.'

'How exciting.'

'I've only just started. Awful rubbish, of course.' He glanced at her. 'Which reminds me. You remember the Gothick Walk you mentioned yesterday? I wondered if I could work it into my novel somehow.'

'How? By having a murder there?'

'Why not?'

The bell rang. Enid glanced at her watch. She was one of

the teachers on duty this evening. She said goodbye to him and went off to the side door.

Shaw watched her for a moment, his hands deep in his flannel bags and the pipe stuck in the corner of his mouth. As visiting tutor, he had no duties other than teaching and the preparation and marking that went with it; and he was also supposed to join the rest of the teaching staff for the Sunday service, morning prayers, the daily assembly and lunch. Otherwise he was free to use his time as he wished.

After a moment he sauntered off to East Cottage, with me trailing behind. I followed him inside. He had been there for forty-eight hours, but he had made little effort to make the place homely. His belongings were strewn about the living room; the ashtray had overflowed on the table; the kitchen door was open, revealing a pile of unwashed crockery in the sink. It was the same story in the bedroom. His trunk was still on the floor with its lid up. He had unpacked only half his belongings so far, including a bottle of whisky that was standing on the chair by the bed. All in all, he was an untidy beast with little talent for domesticity.

He draped his jacket over the back of his chair. On his way to the kitchen, he paused and sniffed. He frowned and sniffed again. I guessed by the expression on his face that he could smell something unpleasant.

He went into the kitchen, where he lit the Primus stove and put the kettle on to boil. In the living room, he sat at the table and relit his pipe. I perched, metaphorically speaking, on his shoulder. For a moment he leafed through the three completed pages of his novel, making the occasional alteration with a pencil. Then he turned to the sheet of paper already in the typewriter:

. . . a shadow of his usual hearty self. Propped up against the pillows of the fourposter, he moved his head from side to side, moaning softly. His face was grey.

'Look who's here to see you,' Nanny said brightly, patting his hand.

'Uncle George? It's me, Cynthia.'

His bleary eyes tried to focus on his niece's face. He licked dry lips. Nanny held a glass of water to his mouth. A dribble of water ran down his chin.

Shaw scowled at the tosh he had written, as well he might. If he wanted to emulate Agatha Christie, he had a long way to go. He sighed and began to type. I focused all my concentration on the page, on his fingers.

'Nanny wired me, darling. I came as soon as I could.'

The old man's claw-like hand crawled slowly across the counterpane towards her. Cynthia put her own hand on his. His lips moved, but Cynthia couldn't hear what he was saying. She leaned closer, bringing her ear within an inch of his lips.

'Look in the Red Room,' he murmured. 'The rucksack, the exercise book . . .

Ping went the bell of the carriage return. Shaw sat up abruptly as if someone had jabbed him with a pin. In his agitation, the pipe fell from his mouth and landed partly on the typewriter and partly on the table. 'Christ!'

The rucksack, the exercise book . . . I had made him type those words. I felt more exhausted than before. The emptiness tugged me, trying to drag me into the place where I was no longer anything at all.

He ripped the page from the typewriter. He blew vigorously into the machine, sending flakes of smouldering ash over the pages of his manuscript. As he was swatting them with the palm of his hand, the kettle began to whistle. The sound rose rapidly to a sustained and piercing crescendo, as piercingly imperious as an air-raid siren.

'Bugger,' he muttered as he ran into the kitchen. 'Bugger, bugger, bugger.'

While the tea was brewing, he made an ineffectual effort to tidy the living room. He straightened the chair, opened the window and gathered the pages of his manuscript together. He carried the ashtray to the fireplace and emptied it into the ash bucket.

That was when we both saw the sturdy brown spiral on the brick-red tiles in front of the fire basket. It was partly concealed by the low fender around the hearth.

The turd was almost perfect in its way, like a short but perfectly proportioned snake. It had a pointed head that was elegantly poised as if to bite someone.

10

The teaching staff usually had their suppers between seven and eight, unless they were on duty. We foraged for ourselves in the evenings – everyone had their own jealously guarded supplies, which led to a certain amount of friction. Runty prepared something for herself and PM, which they ate on trays in the study. Everyone else ate in the kitchen. Mrs Broadwell disliked sharing her kitchen with the teachers and was always looking for grounds for complaint to superior authority in the form of Mrs Hitler.

On this Monday evening, I watched Enid boiling herself an egg. (Mr Lewis had a profitable sideline in selling them to the staff.) The kitchen was less gloomy now the blackout was down and the days were lengthening. Afterwards we went upstairs to her bedroom.

For me, being in that room was part pleasure, part pain. Enid had a small table by the window, which had a glorious view of the estuary from the front of the house. She sat there for twenty minutes, marking a pile of exercise books. As she worked, she sprawled in her chair, all long legs and long arms. She reminded me of a greyhound puppy with impossibly long limbs still learning the skill of coordination.

The memories flooded back, reminding me of everything I had lost. I watched her, trying to memorise the perfect curve of her forearm and the way her neck glided so sweetly into her shoulders. The neck of her blouse was unbuttoned and I could see the hollows above the collarbones, where I used to kiss the soft skin and smell its sweetness.

All gone now.

Enid finished the marking. She unzipped her black leather letter case. She had already begun a letter to a friend from university who was now working as an interpreter somewhere with the army in Germany. I drew closer. The nib of her pen was poised over the pad for a moment. She began to write.

Great excitement here. Our new teacher has arrived - and he's a man!! The girls are all agog! PM couldn't find a replacement mistress at such short notice, so she had to settle for Mr Shaw, though only on a temporary basis. In theory he's not on the staff at all - we have to call him a 'visiting tutor', not a master, because PM thinks it wouldn't be proper in a girls' school, and above all the parents wouldn't like it.

It's good news for me, though. He's going to help with the School Cert lot, and also take over most of my friend's . . .

I focused all my concentration, all my energy on the pen, the paper, the moving hand. *Enid, it's Annabel. I'm here.*

. . . teaching. Still no news of her, by the way - it's a real mystery. I rather miss her. It was lovely having someone to chat to. The new chap has to live in a cottage in the grounds. So far he seems quite pleasant, though of course it's . . .

Once again: *Enid, it's Annabel.*

. . . early days yet. He has a bit of a limp. I wonder if he was wounded. He's not exactly handsome, but he's already become what the girls call a pash-magnet. I'm sure your work is much more . . .

I fell back, exhausted. It was depressing to find that I merited little more than a passing mention in Enid's letter. Shaw was clearly a far more interesting subject. But it was even more depressing that I hadn't been able to reach her when she was writing. It seemed that the only person I could reach in the living world was Shaw, and even then only if he was writing his wretched novel.

She capped the fountain pen and put the letter case away. I stayed with her while she got ready for bed. Once she was under the covers, she picked up her book from the bedside table. It was *Peter Abelard* by Helen Waddell, which made me smile – it's an impeccably romantic historical novel in which the chap ends up castrated.

She had been using an old envelope as a marker. Rather than read the book, however, she removed something from inside the envelope. It was a scrap of muslin, folded in a packet. She opened it with great care. There was a lock of fair hair inside, tied together with a scrap of white ribbon.

86

I stopped smiling. Enid's face was intent and brooding. She raised the lock to her lips. Then she returned the muslin packet to the envelope and took up the book.

Whose hair was it? My jealousy was as instinctive as it was irrational. By unspoken agreement, we had never talked about old lovers. I'd gathered that she had gone out with one or two men in her past life, but never with a woman. I knew nothing more than that, not even if she'd been to bed with them. I'd been similarly reticent. What mattered now, I had felt, was us. What mattered was our present and our future, not the past.

Yes, it was absurd to be jealous, and on such slender evidence. Anyway, the hair looked too fine to be a man's. Perhaps it had come from a girlfriend or a child.

I had no way of knowing. But I couldn't help wishing that Enid had thrown it away once she'd met me. But she hadn't. She'd cherished it instead. And now she was kissing it.

At the Maiden's Leap that night, I lectured myself about the folly of wanting to change something that could not be changed, only endured. I tried not to think about the lock of hair or about the fact I couldn't reach Enid when she was writing, as I had with Shaw.

As the light faded, the wood settled around me. Somewhere below, the invisible river slid towards the sea, towards whatever was left of my physical remains.

I thought about the turd, which had taken me by surprise and, to be honest, amused me. I wondered whether Shaw would ever find out who had left it for him to find. I could think of two obvious suspects, and that was just a start.

One was Tosser. The other was Venetia.

Venetia was still more or less a child. But that didn't matter.

It was never wise to underestimate how nasty children could be to each another and to anyone else. Just before my death, I had given Venetia what appeared to be a very good reason to want me out of the way.

I was sliding towards my nightly absence. The last thing I thought about before I faded away with the light was the button I had found this morning. I had forgotten to check if it was still lying in the hole under the fence.

In the morning, however, I discovered that the button was gone.

I was later than usual. Judging by the sky, it was getting on for eight o'clock. At the house, they would be preparing for the morning roll call before breakfast. I wandered aimlessly up the drive towards North Lodge, the park's entrance if you approached it from the Gloucester Road.

The keeper's cottage was closely shrouded with overgrown trees. At one time the external walls had been painted white, but now they were stained with damp. Some of the rendering had fallen off, revealing the soft, gently crumbling stonework beneath.

A stiff breeze was blowing from the east, making the branches sway and rustle. One of the trees was a tall, ragged Douglas fir, which by some quirk of its growth had a particularly long, crooked branch that pointed downwards towards the slate roof. The girls called it the witch's finger and credited Mrs Crisp with sinister occult powers.

When I was alive I had never been inside the house, so I was unable to go there now. Instead I stood beside the gateway and watched the traffic, such as it was, for twenty minutes. Anything for a bit of novelty. The postman went past on his bicycle. Three children, a boy and two girls, ambled towards the village school nearly a mile away, trying to hit each other with their satchels on the way. A tractor with a trailer turned into the drive. Luigi, the Italian POW working for Mr Lewis, was at the wheel.

Mrs Crisp came out of the lodge, locking the door behind her. She had crammed a beret on her head. Below it was a ragged fringe of lank grey hair, reminding me that, with characteristic cruelty, Venetia Canford had nicknamed her the Floor Mop.

She hurried down the path and let herself out of the garden. She was running late for work, and if Runty saw her, there would be trouble. She turned to latch the gate behind her. As she did so, she glanced up at the blank windows of her home.

So did I. I thought a curtain moved in the upstairs room at the back. But the window was open a crack and there was a stiff breeze.

11

The School provides many outside leisure activities in season, including Lacrosse, Nature Walks, Tennis, Swimming, etc., etc. Senior girls may be permitted to keep a bicycle at school. It is a privilege that a girl must earn. In the first instance, parents or guardians should apply to the Headmistress.

Monkshill Park: School Prospectus

PM told prospective parents that Monkshill girls were never idle. The devil, she explained to them, soon found work for idle hands. It was one of her favourite sayings – one of a selection culled from her late-Victorian upbringing. In practice, though, the girls had more time to fill than at any other school I had known. Most of them didn't know what to do with it. The poor kids were bored.

In theory, at least two hours every afternoon were set aside for games. But there were no neatly mown lawns for tennis or lacrosse, even if the school had had the appropriate equipment for the girls to use. The dark, haunted waters of the lake were strictly out of bounds, even if anyone had wanted to swim in them.

The largely compulsory excursions of the Botany Society might be classed as nature walks if you were feeling generous, though Enid and I used the society as a form of punishment and referred to it between ourselves as Botany Bay, the penal colony in Australia. One or two older girls kept bicycles at the school, though they were forbidden to leave the park unless accompanied by a mistress. The bicycles were a mark of status, a sign of seniority, rather than a serious means of transport or exercise.

I wandered into PM's study during morning break. I found her in the closet. The room was about three yards square and lit by a small window protected with bars. She was alone and the safe was open. I would have liked to see what she was looking at, but I couldn't go into the closet because I'd never been inside it when I was alive.

I included the headmistress among my suspects, either alone or in concert with Runty. I remembered what she'd said to Runty after Saturday's sherry party. *Least said, soonest mended.* They had had good reason to be afraid of me, or so they believed. I could easily imagine Runty in particular following me down to the Maiden's Leap on my last morning – she was a sturdy, vigorous person much like a malignant troll, and quite capable of giving me a forceful shove. She had never liked me.

At first sight, it was harder to envisage PM in the role of First Murderer. She was a large, stately woman in her fifties, a good twenty years older than Runty; she was also physically less active. But people do surprising things when they are desperate.

There was a knock at the study door. PM made a *tsk* of annoyance. She closed the safe and scuttled out of the closet with undignified haste. She straightened her blouse, patted her steel-grey hair and called, 'Come!'

Venetia Canford entered the room. She looked uncharacteristically tidy. 'Excuse me, Miss Pryce-Morgan.'

'Venetia, my dear. Come in and close the door. What is it?'

The girl stood there demurely, head bowed, hands clasped. 'I wondered if I might have my bicycle here.'

'Your bicycle?' PM looked grave. 'As you know, that's a privilege for the older girls. Perhaps you should wait until you're sixteen, and then ask your uncle or aunt to write to me.'

Venetia raised her head and trained the full force of her twin blue searchlights on PM. 'But Aunt Susan's awfully busy in London with her committees, and Uncle Tom's abroad. I don't really like to bother them with something like that. The thing is, when I saw Dr Haines at Easter, he said exercise would be good for me. Like cycling, that's what he said. Because I'm growing so fast.'

Don't let her, you silly woman, I thought. *She's just trying it on.*

'Oh . . . well, that does put a different complexion on things, if there are medical reasons.' Miss Pryce-Morgan wavered and was lost. 'And I quite understand your not wanting to bother Lady Susan – it's considerate of you. And isn't Major Vauden in Washington at present? But we can't produce your bicycle from nowhere, I'm afraid.'

Venetia smiled sweetly. 'Oh that would be all right. They'll bring mine over from Fontenoy if I send them a postcard. Thanks *awfully*, Miss Pryce-Morgan.'

'Please, sir,' Sylvia said to Shaw after the end of the second lesson.

He paused. He was carrying a pile of exercise books. 'What

is it?' He was in a hurry, as all the teachers were at this time, hoping they would be able to fit in a cup of tea and a cigarette during morning break.

'What about my holiday prep?'

'What about it?'

I wanted to kick the man. His voice was downright unfriendly.

Sylvia went pink but she held her ground. 'Miss Warnock gave me some before she left. Could you mark it for me? Please.'

Something about her manner must have softened him. He nodded. 'Yes of course. Where is it?'

'In my exercise book. She said to do it at the back, as it was a holiday prep.'

He hefted the pile on his arm. 'In that case I already have it. I'll look at it this evening.'

'Thank you, sir,' she said, ever so humbly.

You shouldn't have to be humble, I thought. *Not when you're trying to learn.*

Shaw went into the staffroom, and Sylvia joined the queue for milk in the old servants' hall.

Prissy materialised beside her. 'I got yours for you.'

Sylvia took the glass ungraciously. She wandered over to the window overlooking the kitchen yard. Stephen was there, chopping wood for the autumn. Runty wanted to build up a good supply because coal and coke were so scarce and expensive.

Prissy followed her. Her eyes were on Sylvia, not Stephen. 'Have you found out anything new?'

'About what?' Sylvia said, wilfully obtuse.

'About who killed the mouse.'

Sylvia stared at Prissy, her face expressionless. I willed her to say something nice, because if she didn't say something nice to Prissy, no one else would. Besides, I wanted Sylvia to be kind

93

as well as clever. Because that was what I regretted most now that I was dead. Not the missed opportunities, nor the roads I hadn't taken. Not my failure to find a job at some halfway decent university and make a name for myself as a historian. Not even my lack of courage. What I regretted most was that I hadn't been nicer to people during my life. I hadn't realised that being unkind to someone else was also, in the long run, being unkind to yourself.

Sylvia nodded. 'No. So we must use our little grey cells, like Monsieur Poirot says. See where that leads us. First things first. Means. Motive. Opportunity.'

Good girl.

Prissy's eyes shone behind her glasses. 'How do we start?'

'By asking questions. Let's look at opportunity. Who could get into the library between the end of classes on Saturday and Monday morning? Where did the mouse come from? How did it die?'

'But isn't that means, not opportunity?'

Sylvia waved the question away. 'Yes. We're doing means now. Keep up.'

'It was killed because it was strangled with that bit of string,' Prissy said. 'Obviously.'

'Not necessarily. I'd've thought it would be quite hard to hold a live mouse and strangle it with a bit of string at the same time.'

'Mrs Broadwell puts mousetraps in the kitchen and the larder. Perhaps it came from one of those.'

'Yes.' Sylvia looked slightly put out that she hadn't come up with this idea herself. But she swiftly regained the initiative: 'So here's a theory: if the killer got up early on Sunday and sneaked downstairs, she could have found a dead mouse in one of the traps before anyone was up. If that's right, then it's probably someone at the school, not an outsider. Particularly as you can't open the library window.'

Both girls wrinkled their noses at the thought of someone they knew creeping into the kitchen in search of a dead mouse.

'And after that they'd have had all day to put it in the library,' Sylvia went on. 'Because there's no teaching on Sunday. That's the means. *And* the opportunity.'

'But why did they do it?'

'That's the motive part,' Sylvia informed her. 'Once we've worked that out, we can almost certainly work out the killer.'

Prissy cleared her throat and said hesitantly, 'But if the mouse was in a trap in the kitchen, doesn't that mean Mrs Broadwell killed it? Because she probably set the trap?'

'Well yes.' Sylvia did not look best pleased at the correction. 'But that's not important, is it? We want to find out who tied the string round its neck and put it in the library.'

At this interesting moment, the bell rang, signalling the end of break. Prissy turned to leave. Sylvia hesitated, glancing out of the window.

Stephen was still in the yard but he was no longer chopping wood. He was looking up at her.

Even as late as the 1930s, a house and gardens the size of Monkshill Park probably had ten or twelve indoor and outdoor servants to keep the place going.

Now, as I mentioned earlier, we had only Mrs Broadwell in the kitchen as a sort of sergeant-major under the notional command of Runty (or – as I now thought of her – Mrs Hitler), together with Mrs Crisp, the unreliable charwomen and the unskilled labour force of schoolgirls.

Finally there was Stephen, Mrs Broadwell's nephew. He was technically on the roll of the church school in the village but his attendance there was sporadic. He had come to Monkshill with his aunt in 1941. He was such a familiar sight about the place that people barely noticed him, despite the fact he was a boy.

In return for his keep, he helped out wherever help was needed – taking an urgent letter to the postbox for Runty, for example, cleaning the silver in PM's cutlery canteen, weeding in the kitchen garden or sweeping leaves. Or chopping firewood, as he had been doing this morning. As far as PM and Runty were concerned, he was effectively another unpaid servant, useful in that he could be set to do the dirtier work that would have been inappropriate for the girls.

It was such a waste. He was a bright boy, literate enough to read and understand complex detective novels and (as I'd learned only lately) sufficiently numerate to help his aunt with the kitchen accounts. At the end of last term, I'd had a word with Mrs Broadwell and persuaded her to let me mention him to the headmaster of the local grammar school, six miles away by bus.

The head was an old acquaintance of mine – I had known him slightly at university – and he'd agreed as a favour to overlook Stephen's lack of formal education and interview him over the holidays to see if something might be done to help him. But the appointment had been arranged for the Saturday after my return from holiday. And, without me, the whole project had fallen by the wayside.

Now I was dead, now I was invisible, I saw people in different ways, and in the private moments of their lives because I was able to move invisibly among them. The domestic staff had swum into focus in a way that they had never done in my life.

What I learned only reinforced my opinion about Stephen: he was too intelligent to be left to rot in the kitchen at Runty's beck and call. It was significant that he and Sylvia had become friends, despite the social gulf between them. In my judgement they were the two children at Monkshill who most needed the sort of education that Miss Pryce-Morgan's school conspicuously failed to provide.

On that Tuesday morning, after Prissy and Sylvia's discussion about the mouse murder, I learned that Stephen and Sylvia had their own system of communication. As the bell rang to signal the end of morning break, as Prissy joined the stream of girls leaving the old servants' hall, Sylvia hung back and glanced down from the window at Stephen.

He was still looking up at the window. He pointed his left forefinger towards the sky, and put his right forefinger across the top of it.

Sylvia, shielding her hand with her body from the sight of girls milling about behind her, made a thumbs-up in reply. Clearly she understood what he meant. I didn't. Not then.

12

I followed Stephen. He slipped out of the yard and turned sharp right. He followed the line of the garden wall at first and then cut through the shrubbery, jumped into the ditch below the ha-ha and skirted Mr Lewis's wheat field beyond. The tractor and trailer I had seen this morning were parked near the gate. The POW was mending a fence nearby.

Stephen's face gave nothing away. He was frowning slightly, as he so often did, and walking quickly with his shoulders hunched. He took the path leading past the old stables and down to the lake, as Venetia and Shaw had done on Sunday. When he got there, he continued around the bank. I assumed his destination was the boathouse. But instead he crossed the decaying jetty and walked up the path that led into West Cover. The boundary of the park was on the far side of this patch of woodland.

Before you got to the wood, however, there was a cottage which was almost a twin of Alec Shaw's. It had probably been built to house a gamekeeper.

Why was Stephen coming here? Could it be that Sylvia

98

had succeeded in persuading him that there was something they could do about investigating my disappearance, despite his reluctance on Sunday? As he drew nearer the cottage, he became increasingly wary, crouching down and using every available cover. The sign he had given Sylvia in the kitchen yard this morning now made sense: the letter T – T for Tosser. The disgusting old man lived here.

I had visited the place only once when I was alive. It was shortly before my death and near the end of the Lent term. I went down there in the gap between afternoon school and the roll call before the girls' tea, their last meal of the day. The smoke rising from the kitchen chimney had been fresh and thick, as if Tosser had recently put more wood into the stove. I didn't want to be there, but I had to come.

There was a board by the gate, to which Tosser nailed or strung up the corpses of animals he had caught in gin traps or snares. The crow family treated the board as a larder. When I visited there had been a stoat, a fox cub, a rabbit too old for the pot, a goshawk, and even what was left of a cat that looked suspiciously like Mrs Crisp's, which had gone missing about three weeks earlier. Some of the kills were recent, others had been reduced to little more than bleached bone and scraps of fur. As I drew near, I disturbed two magpies, who rose reluctantly into the air.

I wasn't sure why the board of death was there, or why Tosser killed these creatures, unless it was for the pure pleasure it gave him. There was no longer any game on the estate to preserve from predators, and he was no longer a gamekeeper, if he ever had been.

Enid had heard a story in the village that the old man had grown up in the cottage with his parents, both of whom had

99

worked at Monkshill before the Great War, and that when they had died he had simply stayed on, and no one had bothered to turn him out. He lived alone now. He used to have a dog, a vicious border collie with one brown eye, one blue. But it died, much to the relief of everyone except its owner.

We used to speculate about how Tosser managed for money. His only official source of income was the school – he was paid a few shillings a week to feed the boiler that heated the water. The boiler was in an outhouse in the kitchen yard. Twice a day, early morning and early evening, he shovelled coke into it, and in the morning he also dug out the previous day's ashes. But the money he earned by that would hardly keep him in tea and bread, let alone allow him to drink in the Ruispidge Arms four or five nights a week.

I had opened the gate and walked up the path. The cottage door had been ajar. It opened directly into a living room with a flagged floor and a few scraps of carpet, on which a jumble of dark-stained furniture was arrayed in no particular order.

It was an unseasonably warm afternoon, and the smell inside the living room hovered in diluted form around the doorway: unwashed bodies, unwashed clothes, stale tobacco, embedded dirt and the sweet, sickly decay of rot.

I banged on the door and retreated a step or two to lessen the smell. I waited but nothing happened. I was wondering whether to knock again when I heard a sound to my left. I turned my head. Tosser had emerged from a wooden lean-to shed at the end of the cottage. He was carrying an armful of logs.

'What you doing?' he'd said, which came out in a slushy mumble because he rarely bothered to put his teeth in.

'I want a word with you,' I said.

'I'm busy.' He jerked his head towards the gate, motioning me to leave. 'I'll be up in the kitchen garden tomorrow. Maybe.'

'This won't wait.'

He advanced slowly towards me. I'd felt a twinge of fear, though he barely came up to my shoulder. I held my ground.

'Two girls saw you this afternoon,' I said. 'Where you shouldn't have been.'

He stopped. 'Don't know what you mean.'

'I'll tell you then. You were outside the girls' showers.'

'It's a free country.'

'Not there it isn't.'

'Happened to be passing. That's all.'

'You're not meant to be near the school. Just the kitchen garden and the boiler house.'

'Mr Lewis says—'

'I don't care what Mr Lewis says.' I hoped I sounded braver than I felt. 'You shouldn't be near the school. You definitely shouldn't be peeping at schoolgirls in the shower block.'

'Must have been someone else.'

'You were standing on a bucket and looking in. The window was open.'

'No. Not me. Can't have been.'

'You should be ashamed of yourself. If I see you anywhere near the house, anywhere near the girls, I'll make sure you're turned out of this cottage. And I'll also tell the police what I saw. Who do you think they're going to believe? You or me?'

I turned and walked swiftly away. I heard nothing behind me. My muscles were tense, waiting for an attack. I knew he was watching. Perhaps it was my imagination, but I felt his hatred flowing towards me.

The threat of losing your home and your job? Of being

labelled a Peeping Tom before all the world? Of police involvement? If that didn't add up to a motive for murder, I didn't know what would.

To return to Stephen on that Tuesday morning.

Once he reached the cottage, he behaved less warily. Without even a glance at the board of death, he marched up to the door and tried the handle. It didn't open. He tried again, putting his shoulder to the door in case it was stuck, with the same result.

He backed away and made a circuit of the cottage. I couldn't follow him because the front of the house was all I had seen of it in life. He was gone a good ten minutes, which suggested that he was being thorough in his reconnaissance. But I had no idea what he was looking for or indeed why he was here.

He reappeared by the lean-to shed. Glancing over his shoulder, he tried the door. It wasn't locked, and he went inside. I wasn't able to see much of the interior – only part of a workbench and the corner of the log pile – and Stephen himself was screened by the open door. When he came out he glanced about him again. Still frowning, he walked quickly out of the garden and broke into a run towards the lake and the mansion beyond.

I used to think that if human consciousness survived death, the one advantage would be that you would probably understand everything at last, including your own place in the world. Now I know that had been a naive and inaccurate assumption. After death – after my death, at least – there were more mysteries, not fewer.

13

After lunch, Miss Runciman carried a tray of coffee into the head's study.

Somehow she had got hold of real coffee — black market obviously, probably American in origin and extortionately expensive. They kept it under lock and key in the closet, along with the grinder. Each day, Runty would carefully measure out a handful of beans and grind it with her own fair hand. She would carry the coffee to the kitchen, make a pot, set a tray with two cups and saucers, milk and sugar and bring it back to Miss Pryce-Morgan.

'I could kill for a cup of proper coffee,' Enid said to me once. 'Truly I could.'

I no longer had a sense of smell — I had lost it when I died, along with taste and touch, though I could still see and hear. But my memory was intact. I could remember the smells of coffee and frying bacon. And for that matter the smell of sex.

I followed Runty into the study.

'You're a darling,' PM said as Runty placed the tray on the

table between two armchairs. 'I don't know what I'd do without you.'

Runty patted the headmistress's arm. 'I'm not going anywhere.'

They took cigarettes, which Runty lit, using the engraved silver lighter that PM had given her as a birthday present.

'Well,' she said. 'How do you think he's shaping up? Our man, I mean.'

PM flapped her hand, batting the smoke away from her narrowed eyes. 'I've had no complaints.'

'That's a relief.'

'It's early days.'

'The saving grace is that he probably won't be here long,' Runty pointed out. 'I'm sure there'll soon be bags of suitable women looking for jobs.'

'We must draft the advertisement.' PM paused and then produced one of her pearls of wisdom. 'The early bird catches the worm.'

'Would you like me to have Miss Warnock's room cleared?' Runty asked. 'She's obviously not coming back. We'll need it for the new teacher.'

'Yes, dear.'

'Also, it's a bit of a pigsty as it is. Mrs Crisp needs to give it a really thorough clean.'

A pigsty? I thought. *How dare you?*

PM nodded. 'I'll write to the cousin again. Just in case she's heard something. Has she any other relations?'

'Not that I know of,' Runty said. 'I asked Miss Archer but she hadn't heard of any.'

'But at least we have the cousin's address. We can send her things there. I wonder if she would reimburse us for the cost?'

'I doubt it. When would you like me to make a start?'

'Whenever you like. When you have a moment.'

The thought of Runty fingering my clothes, my books, my ornaments filled me with disgust. But clearing my bedroom had to happen sooner or later, and there was nothing I could do about it. What really worried me was whether Runty or Mrs Crisp would find what Enid and I had hidden under the floor.

Before our abortive holiday, Enid and I had discussed what to do with our valuables – the small things that mattered to us, but that we hadn't wanted to lug around in our rucksacks. I had come up with a solution. My bedroom was uncarpeted, apart from a pair of large threadbare rugs. One of these was in front of the washstand. One evening, standing there in bare feet, I'd discovered a rectangular indentation. It wobbled slightly. When I lifted the rug, I found that the floor beneath had been repaired. A small section had been cut away from the original oak board and replaced with pine. It was a botched job. The pine was not as thick as the old board and it was also too narrow for the gap. To make matters worse, it had been fixed to the joist below with two short nails. One of them had buckled when it was nailed down, and the other wasn't enough to make the inserted board secure.

It wasn't hard to lever up the board. Underneath was the usual gritty cavity between the joists. It stretched into the darkness at either end. There was something mysterious about it, like all the secret places of a house that its human occupants never see.

It was the perfect hiding place. On our last evening together at Monkshill, Enid and I assembled our valuables on top of my bed. Her pile included some jewellery, among them a brooch I had given her, and one or two indiscreet notes I'd written to her. Mine had letters, diaries and a few photographs, together with other odds and ends. She put her belongings into a cotton bag that had once held shoes. I shovelled mine into a large brown envelope. We concealed them between the joists.

Anyone reading my current diary would have been left in no doubt about our relationship and my feelings for Enid. They would also learn a good deal about my past lovers, some of whom had taken pleasure in being shockingly, dangerously indiscreet on the page.

My reputation didn't matter any more. But Enid's did.

After school, Shaw went back to his cottage, pipe in mouth, strolling along as if he hadn't a care in the world. He had locked the door in his absence, presumably as a consequence of yesterday's discovery in the fireplace.

Once inside, he followed the familiar ritual of setting the kettle on to boil and taking his machine out of its case. I had to give the man credit: despite the pressures on his time, and despite the alarm that my interpolations must have caused him, he was carrying on with his detective story. I moved closer to help him.

... drained his glass and beckoned the butler. 'Look here, Frampton, you'd better bring up another bottle of the '04. You should have known we'd need two, now Miss Cynthia's deigned to join us.'

'Haven't you had enough, Roddy?'

'No,' he said bluntly.

Cynthia pursed her lips. When Frampton had left the room, she spoke again. 'You know that Uncle George keeps the '04 for special occasions.'

'Don't nag, darling. Anyway this is a special occasion. Find the bleeding yew.

This time Shaw's reaction to my contribution was different. It was almost as if he had been expecting it. He stopped typing, leaned back in his chair and relit the pipe. For a few seconds, he stared at the words on the page. He sat up with a grunt, expelling a gush of tobacco smoke. He hunched over the typewriter and tapped the backspace key until he reached the end of *occasion*. Slowly and deliberately, he put a row of xxxs through *Find the bleeding yew*. He sucked hard on the pipe and began to type once more.

. . . It's not every day that my uncle has someone here to drink his health. Let's face, Cyn, he needs all the health he can get at present.'
    'Don't be such a beast.'
    The door opened and the yew . . .

Shaw broke off again. He wrenched the paper from the typewriter and rolled a fresh sheet around the platen. Word by word, he retyped all the messages I had sent him:

Help me. Help me.
Maiden's Leap. Maiden's Leap.
Gothick Walk. Look there.
The rucksack, the exercise book.
Find the bleeding yew.
The yew.

I tried to make him add *in the fence* but it didn't work. I could only reach him, or rather reach his fingers, when he was writing his novel. In other words, when he was making things up.

He removed the page and studied it. Then he dropped the paper and pushed the typewriter aside. He unstrapped his briefcase and emptied its contents on to the table. There were exercise books for marking and mimeographs of old test-papers that he had probably brought from his previous school.

For a few minutes, I watched him marking the third form's history prep. He was trying to distract himself.

Panic nibbled my mind like a mouse. My thoughts were ragged and full of holes. The old fear came back. What if my ability to reach Shaw in this way would not go on indefinitely? Perhaps when it ended, then so would I.

His kettle began to squeal, and I wanted to squeal with it.

Enid was on duty after evening prep. I went with her as she toured the dormitories. I found it unsettling that everything was going on just as usual without me – all the old faces, all the old routines, all the old sights and sounds. It hadn't taken long for the waters to close over my head. I might never have existed at all.

In Birch, Venetia was boasting about how she had persuaded the headmistress to allow her to have her bicycle at school.

'It won't take me ten minutes to get to the shop in the village.' She lowered her voice and whispered in Sylvia's ear, 'And the pub.'

'They won't serve you,' Sylvia said, and turned the page of her book.

'That's all you know. I have my methods.'

'Like Sherlock Holmes.'

'What? What's he got to do with it?'

Sylvia shrugged. 'It doesn't matter.'

'You're such a bore, Sylvia,' Venetia said, still in a whisper. 'You do know that, don't you?'

'Yes.'

'And a swot. Always with your nose in a book. You never have any fun, do you? You'll be one of those women people laugh at.'

Meanwhile Enid was at the other end of the room, helping Prissy brush her lank black hair, which always seemed to acquire more knots and tangles than anyone else's. One of the things I loved about Enid was her gentleness. There was nothing weak about it. Usually, if the girls thought you were soft, they ragged you mercilessly. But they didn't with her. Instead they became softer themselves.

Afterwards, Prissy climbed into bed. While Venetia was telling Enid about her bicycle, Prissy leaned across the divide between her bed and Sylvia's.

'Syl?'

Sylvia frowned and laid down her book. She was reading *The Murder of Roger Ackroyd* again. 'Don't call me that. What is it?'

'You know *The Body in the Library*? The Agatha Christie book?'

'Of course I do. I lent it to you.'

'But isn't that what we've got?'

'What *are* you talking about?'

'The mouse,' Prissy hissed. 'In the library. It had string round its neck as if it had been strangled. Just like in the book when they find the body in the library.'

'What?' Sylvia said.

'Our mouse – it's just like the book.'

'But that's . . .'

'Put your books away, girls, and settle down.'

Thirty seconds later, Enid flipped the switch and darkness settled on the dormitory.

I trailed after Enid for the rest of the evening because I couldn't drag myself away. Talk about hopeless love. Before I met Enid, I'd seen myself as a ruthless philanderer, flitting from flower to flower. More fool me.

After lights out, she went to bed herself, early though it was. In the bedroom, I watched her undressing and washing. I even followed her into the bathroom when she did her teeth. I was like a needy puppy. The living Annabel Warnock would have despised the dead one.

Later, when Enid was in bed, when the light was out, I heard her stealthy movements and her ragged breathing. I knew what she was doing, and I wished I could be doing it to her, giving her pleasure even if I could have none myself.

What was she thinking as she lay there, with her hand moving faster and faster? It was a mystery what went through other people's minds when they abandoned themselves to their little deaths. I hoped there was some memory of me in Enid's head, an echo, a resonance – anything really, anything that meant she remembered me.

The fact that I couldn't be with her, not in the way I wanted, became so painful that I left her to it and returned to the Maiden's Leap. I was tired by then anyway, and my grip on the world was slackening. When I settled myself, I expected to drift swiftly into nothingness. But the evening had one more event in store.

I was at the exact spot where I had been pushed. It was cloudy but somewhere there was a moon. Two invisible planes were flying overhead, one after the other, following the river into the borderlands between England and Wales. As the whirr of their propellers faded, I heard another, nearer sound.

Footsteps.

Three or four, perhaps, followed by the familiar silence, or rather by the usual subdued noises of this wood at night. And 'footsteps' wasn't quite the right word for what I heard. It was more a distant and irregular rustle of leaves, a crackling of small twigs underfoot.

I was suddenly alert, as if someone had given me a shot of adrenaline. My tiredness dropped away. I stared in the general direction of the sounds. I listened. It seemed to me that the movements had come further along the line of the Gothick Walk.

There came the faint but unmistakable rasp of a match. A tiny flame flared against the darkness. Only for an instant. In that instant I saw a heavy hunched silhouette like a bear's in a child's picture book. Then it was gone.

14

When I came to myself (the phrase now seemed particularly apt) on Wednesday morning, the first thing to cross my mind wasn't the bear. It was Enid. In fact it was almost always Enid. Every morning.

Why I had fallen so hard for her was a mystery to me. She was nothing like the other lovers. She wasn't exceptionally beautiful, not as the world would see it. Nor was she witty or particularly lively. But it must have taken so much courage for her to make the first move when she didn't even know for sure that I liked women, for her to say those words to me by the lake.

I think I'm falling in love with you.

I went up to the house to see what Enid was doing. The quickest route was into the kitchen yard and through the back door. In the kitchen, two vast pans of porridge stood on each of the stoves. Monkshill porridge was universally hated. It had the appearance and the consistency of warm, wet concrete. Sometimes the girls had to eat it cold. I had seen them smuggle it into handkerchiefs or push it down between floorboards. I had seen it make them vomit.

The only person in the room was Mrs Crisp, the Floor Mop. She had replaced the beret with a headscarf knotted at the front, strands of grey hair escaping under the edges. The door to the cellars was open. Noises below suggested that Mrs Broadwell was moving bottles or jars about. Along the passage, Runty was giving someone a hard time against the distant background chatter and clatter of the girls assembling for breakfast.

I had intended merely to pass through the kitchen on my way to the rest of the house. But Mrs Crisp's behaviour gave me pause.

She was hovering over the tea caddy and spooning tea into a small brown paper bag, which she then stuffed into the pocket of her pinafore. It was a wide, deep pocket, which was just as well, because after the tea, she moved onto the sugar with another paper bag.

Next came the substantial tub where Mrs Broadwell kept the solidified piebald grease that went under the name of butter at Monkshill. The girls were obliged to hand over their weekly rations, which included two ounces apiece of butter and margarine, each in its little pot. These were mixed together but not thoroughly enough to blend the two materials.

The result of this process was a slippery grey substance, within which were trapped yellow islands of butter, though not a great many of them. (Runty took a preliminary helping of butter for herself and PM, which they kept in a tin box on the floor of the study closet. Mrs Broadwell also removed a tithe for herself and Stephen.)

Mrs Crisp scraped a knife over the grey surface and smeared the contents of the blade onto a worn piece of greaseproof paper, which joined the rest of the booty in her pocket. With a glance towards the cellar door, she darted into the scullery and transferred the booty into her bag, which was hanging on the door. Finally she lifted the lid of the bucket of scraps destined for the pig bin. A crust from a stale loaf was resting on top. It joined the other items in her bag.

You could hardly blame her for helping herself. The school paid her a pittance, and Mrs Broadwell's generosity was limited and strictly conditional on Mrs Crisp's subservience. Now, looking at her tired, harassed face, I thought she needed all the nourishment she could get.

On my way along the passage I passed the boot room. The door was open. Runty was inside, tearing a strip off the unfortunate Stephen. She wasn't much taller than him so they looked like a pair of children, a bully and her victim.

'What do you mean, you forgot?' she demanded, with the weary cruelty of a bosun giving a cabin boy another fifty lashes. 'Do you call that an excuse? Look!' She held up a pair of brogues that belonged to Miss Pryce-Morgan. 'You can't tell me those have been cleaned.'

Stephen's face flamed with embarrassment and the irrational shame of the wrongly accused. 'Sorry, miss. I forgot to—'

'No, they are *not* clean! Look at them. Look, boy! Tell me what that is.' Runty stabbed the leather with her finger. 'There. And there.'

'It's mud, miss.'

'You got that right at least. And the mud shouldn't be there, should it?'

'No, miss. Sorry.'

Every night, Runty and PM put shoes which needed cleaning outside their bedroom doors. Stephen was meant to clean them before they got up, and before the girls came downstairs.

'It was the alarm,' he explained. 'It didn't go off. And when I got up, Auntie said it was too late to get the shoes and—'

'Don't try and hide behind your aunt. I expect Mrs Broadwell is ashamed of you for being so lazy and foolish. And also *ungrateful*. Is this how you repay us for giving you a roof over your head and three square meals a day?' She picked up her own black lace-ups and thrust both pairs of shoes at him. 'Go on – do them now. Take the polish and brushes out to the yard and clean them there. Afterwards you can give them to Mrs Crisp and tell her to take them up to our rooms when she makes the beds.'

Runty bustled away to make someone else's life a misery. Stephen's shoulders were shaking. His breathing was ragged. There were tears in his eyes – tears of rage, tears of shame.

I went away. Like Mrs Crisp, the poor kid deserved a bit of privacy.

I found Enid in the staffroom. She had been waylaid by Little Covey, who was knitting socks for our gallant sailors. This was her chief contribution to the war effort but, despite nearly six years of practice, she was not a skilful knitter. Enid was helping her untangle her current mixture of muddy, recycled wool, while Miss Covey was describing in wearisome detail the spring planting in her little garden at the side of the house.

Meanwhile Miss Hampson was marking the second form's geography homework and muttering under her breath. 'Dear heaven, would you look at this, Archer? I ask the brainless child to do me a map of Ireland. Instead she's drawn me what looks like a sack of potatoes with the word Dublin in the middle.'

Shaw turned up just before the bell rang for morning prayers. He looked seedy, and I wondered if he had turned to the whisky bottle after I had left him. It was possible that the accumulated force of my insertions had finally forced him to face up to the fact that someone was trying to communicate with him.

Either that or he would be forced to conclude that he was at the mercy of brief seizures in which he developed the symptoms of a split personality. So the poor man had a choice: paranormal communications with A. N. Other or purely homegrown delusions. If I had been faced with those alternatives, I would have turned to drink too.

The four of them filed out of the staffroom and made their way to the hall, where the girls were already gathered. They lined up with the other teachers on the lower steps of the staircase. Shaw managed to position himself next to Enid. I watched them carefully to make sure he didn't contrive to brush her arm with his. Not for the first time I thought how odd and inconvenient it was that jealousy should survive death.

PM and Runty made their grand entrance from above, descending like divine beings from the heaven of the first-floor landing. We had prayers. We had the hymn, 'Onward, Christian Soldiers', sung to Miss Hampson's thumping accompaniment on the out-of-tune piano under the stairs. Finally, Miss Pryce-Morgan addressed the school on the subject of trousers, specifically on the awfulness of women wearing them. This deplorable modern habit not only made a laughing stock of the fair sex but was repugnant to God and man.

She broke off in mid flow. 'Priscilla! Priscilla Knecht!'

Prissy turned an unhealthy pink and stared at her feet. 'Yes, Miss . . . Miss Pryce-Morgan.'

'Don't slouch. It's not respectful, it's not graceful, and it's simply not how we do things in this country. We stand up straight and we look each other in the eye. We don't mumble either.' She ran her eyes down the unfortunate child. 'And we pull up our socks.'

Rosemary Lawson-Smith tittered. Prissy bent down to straighten her socks. A tear slipped beneath the rim of her glasses and fell onto the toe of her left shoe, where it glistened like a dark pearl.

'Above all,' PM said, returning to this morning's theme, 'trousers are unwomanly. When you are grown-up, you will find that no decent man will look twice at a girl in trousers. If you learn nothing else here, Priscilla, I hope you never wear trousers.'

At that point I left them to it. PM's prejudices were usually absurd but sometimes they turned sour, and I could not bear it when she began to pick victims. Like Runty, she had a streak of cruelty.

I went back to Bleeding Yew Wood. It was time to face up to what I had seen. It wasn't just the flaring match and the brief glimpse of a bulky silhouette. There had also been the footsteps the other night.

Moreover, some of the narrow zigzag paths I had followed among the anarchic network of trees, weeds, saplings and bushes were still clearly visible – and this at a time of year when all nature was throwing out branches and suckers and weeds. Someone was still using them. Finally, there was the brown button that had appeared and then disappeared from the hole under the fence.

The Bear. That's what I called the shape I had seen. It was alive. It was human. And it was in my wood.

When I was alive, I had succeeded in identifying some features from the Gothick Walk.

Immediately to the north of the Maiden's Leap, the Monks' Arches consisted of three irregular arches blasted through spurs of rock. The path passed underneath them to the features upstream. The Cold Bath, fed by an underground stream alleged to have therapeutic qualities, had vanished but, further along, the Stone Throne was still there, though it had lost its Gothick Canopy and one of its arms.

The Hermit's Cave and the Abbot's Postern should have come next but I had found no trace of either. The next one I had identified for certain was a former viewpoint called the Eagle's Nest, now shrouded in trees. The Druids' Temple, an amphitheatre set into the slope of the hill, was still discernible, though it had been reduced to fragments of stonework gradually crumbling to dust under the onslaught of nature.

Most of my historical information came from a book I had found in Gloucester: *Some Observations on the Pleasure Grounds of Monkshill Park* (1810), by the Rev. Jeffrey Youlgreave, AM. But Youlgreave had been concerned with the Gothick Walk itself, not with what he called the 'bosky copses, sun-dappled glades and faëry dells' that lay immediately behind it. His copses, glades and dells were now a jungle of nettles, ivy, brambles, lanky oaks, sweet chestnut shoots, birch, hazel and white beam; and there wasn't a faëry in sight, unless faëries are really dead souls, in which case I suppose I would qualify.

To make matters worse, Bleeding Yew Wood covered a surprisingly large area as it straggled along the side of the river and up the slope to the parkland. In its prime, the Walk had extended for nearly two miles along the cliffs. Below it, the river made the shape of an S, and the Walk's designers had taken advantage of this to build viewpoints looking north and south as well as east. During my life I had been able to explore only the narrow strip next to the river where the Gothick Walk was. A troop of Boy Scouts could have hidden in the rest of the wood without my being any the wiser.

The more I considered the possibility that Tosser was coming here by night, the less likely it seemed. He was an old man, after all, and no longer as spry as he had been. Finding his way in this densely packed wood at night wouldn't be easy even in broad daylight. A poacher could find much easier pickings elsewhere.

My first task now was to search the area around the Monks' Arches in the hope of finding a match, a cigarette end or some cigarette ash. That proved a waste of time. Afterwards I followed the line of the Walk upstream.

So far I had found nothing, not the slightest trace of a nocturnal visitor. I wondered whether the very fact I had found nothing could be in itself significant. Could I infer that my Bear had been very careful not to leave traces behind, though he – or she – could not have known I was watching? Did that suggest that the Bear was habitually cautious? But that would be pushing logic over the edge into absurdity.

After a few hours, I'd had enough. I returned to the Maiden's Leap. The Walk continued downstream, taking in an Iron Age fort and a shell-encrusted grotto, but I'd leave those for later.

As I was leaving, I noticed a bramble sucker had extended itself across the path downstream. *Must get the billhook to that.* The thought was both automatic and absurd, because of course bramble suckers were no longer an obstacle to me and I could hardly use a billhook in my present state.

The billhook? Was it still there?

I used to tuck it behind the stone bench when I wasn't using it because I hadn't wanted to lug it back to the house every time I came here. Besides if I had met Tosser or Mr Lewis on the way, it might have been a little awkward if they caught me carrying stolen goods.

I looked behind the bench. The billhook had gone.

15

As I was passing the shrubbery on my way back to school, a very small girl shot out of the bushes. Her knees were dirty and her face was stained with tears. Behind her, in hot pursuit, was Rosemary Lawson-Smith. She was holding a bundle of nettles in her gloved hand and swishing them at the unprotected calves of her victim. Behind her came two other girls, similarly equipped.

Rosemary was the one who had gratuitously confided to Shaw at Sunday lunch that she hadn't liked me. She was a fundamentally nasty child, and probably had been ever since the womb. She had a habit of marking out someone weaker and more vulnerable than herself, and then recruiting assistants to make the victim's life a living hell. Venetia Canford could be nasty too, as poor Prissy knew to her cost, but Venetia was a loner and a creature of impulse, whereas Rosemary's malice was calculated.

This was one of the most frustrating things about my present state, neither one thing nor the other. When I had been alive, I could do something about people like Rosemary. I could comfort the weeping victims and punish the bullies. But now I was helpless. I could only watch and listen.

Fortunately the duty monitor rang the five-minute bell for the start of afternoon school, and the little girls scampered in front of me into the house. In the hall, the fourth form was making its way in twos and threes into what had been the dining room.

This was at the front of the house and next to the former library. Most of the furniture had gone. The carpet had been taken up, and pale rectangles on the walls showed where there had been pictures. The mantelpiece was gone, leaving a blackened hole behind; it was rumoured that one of the soldiers had taken a fancy to it during the army's brief occupation.

A gramophone stood on the table by the window, and Prissy was winding it up with a world-weary expression on her face. (The younger girls competed for this job but the fourth form and above considered it far beneath their dignity.) The twins, Amanda and Miranda Twisden, were arguing quietly and fiercely about which of them should be the lady this time.

'It's your turn to be the gentleman,' Miranda was whispering. 'Don't be mean. I was last time. I *hate* being the gentleman.'

Maggie Squires was already there. Breathing heavily, she was copying a diagram from the book she held in her hand onto the blackboard. The book was Victor Silvester's *Modern Ballroom Dancing*. Last year, a parent had presented it to the school, along with the gramophone and a set of records by Mr Silvester and his Ballroom Orchestra.

Sylvia came in late, and Prissy's eyes turned like an anxious dog's towards her. She gave a little wave with her free hand, but Sylvia didn't see her. Last of all came Venetia, who slouched into the room, glanced about her and yawned. Somehow she made every other girl in the room look juvenile and half-formed by comparison.

'Be quiet, girls,' roared Maggie. 'Close the door please, Venetia. Quietly. Right. The quickstep. Priscilla, put the record on the gramophone. We're learning the natural pivot turn. Amanda, stop talking, and you might learn something useful. Now look carefully: the top diagram on the board, that shows the man's steps. And the bottom one is the lady's. Got that? Gentleman on top, lady below.'

Venetia smirked.

'Find a partner.'

'Sylvia?' Prissy said. 'Would you—?'

'No dear, I want you on the gramophone,' Maggie said. 'Except when you're helping me demonstrate.'

Prissy blushed a deep, unlovely red.

'Sylvia, you and Venetia can be partners.'

The two girls sidled together without looking at each other.

'I'm the lady,' Venetia muttered. 'I can never remember what the man's steps are.'

'All right.'

'Look at the board, girls. The man steps forward with his right foot, turning on it to the right. And then he steps to the side – quick, like so – with the left foot and – position three, also quick – closes the right foot up to the left. Meanwhile the lady . . .'

When the preamble was over, and the record was playing, Maggie seized Prissy's hand and proceeded to give a demonstration. The girls watched. Some sniggered discreetly. When at last the spectacle came to an end, Maggie was sweating heavily and Prissy looked even more shell-shocked than usual.

'Put the record on again, dear,' Maggie said breathlessly. 'Now, girls, your turn.'

The room filled with the ill-matched sounds of jaunty music and the irregular slaps and thumps of leather soles on bare oak boards.

'Ow!' cried Venetia in a voice loud enough to be heard over the racket. Everyone stopped dancing. The quickstep music rattled on.

'What is it now?' Maggie demanded.

Venetia was clutching her right ankle. She turned an agonised face towards Maggie. 'I've twisted it, Miss Squires. It's agony . . . Could I go and find Matron? Please – it might even be a sprain.'

If I had been Maggie, I'd have told Venetia to sit down for the rest of the lesson and watch; she could go to Matron during afternoon break. But beneath her brusque manner, Maggie was as soft as they came. She told Venetia to go and find Miss Runciman. Venetia declined the offer of an arm to lean on and limped slowly and pathetically from the room. Sylvia opened and closed the door for her. As she passed into the hall, Venetia gave her an evil grin.

I wasn't unduly surprised when Venetia's limp vanished as soon as she was through the baize door that led to the back of the house. Rather than look for Runty in the housekeeper's room or upstairs in the San, she went along to the kitchen.

Stephen was in there, reading *Peril at End House* at the table. He looked up at her, and his frown deepened. Girls were not allowed in the kitchen except when helping to serve or clear up meals. There was no sign of his aunt, who generally had a nap after lunch.

'Where's the Floor Mop?' Venetia said without preamble.

He nodded towards the scullery door, which was closed.

Venetia and I went through. Mrs Crisp was standing at the draining board and scrubbing the tarnish on Miss Pryce-Morgan's silver candlesticks with an old toothbrush.

Venetia closed the door behind her. Mrs Crisp stared at her and said nothing.

'I want you to get some more cigarettes,' Venetia said. 'And some chocolate or sweets. Anything sweet. And half a bottle of gin.'

'I can't. Not gin. And after last time even cigarettes . . .'

'Why not?'

'Because people were talking when I bought some for you. They know I don't smoke. And as for gin, if I bought it in the village, tongues'd be wagging from here to Gloucester.'

Venetia dug into the pocket of her tunic and held up a one-pound note. 'Don't you want this?'

Mrs Crisp stared at it. She said nothing. It was a small fortune to her, and Venetia knew it.

'Well? What do you say?'

'It's my half-day on Saturday,' she said slowly. 'If I took the bus into Gloucester, I could get some cigarettes. But not the gin. As for sweets, you'll have to wait and see.'

'All right. Better than nothing, I suppose.' Venetia held out the banknote. 'As many cigarettes as you can, OK? And not gaspers, either. Players if you can find any. Or Craven A. You'd better get matches as well.'

'I'd need money for the bus fare,' Mrs Crisp said. 'And . . . and something for my time.'

Venetia waved a hand dismissively. 'Take what you need. But get the cigarettes at least.'

She turned on her heel and passed through the kitchen without glancing at Stephen. I'll say one thing for Venetia. She wasn't mean. She had the careless generosity of those who have never had to think about money.

It started to rain as the afternoon went on. After lessons, Shaw came into the staffroom. Enid was making tea with the electric kettle. I had been enjoying being alone with her and he broke the spell. She offered him a cup. He put his briefcase on the floor and sank into the armchair that used to be mine.

'I hope this blasted rain will let up soon. Otherwise I'll have to make a run for it. I left my mac at the cottage.'

'I'm sure we can find you an umbrella.'

While the tea was brewing, they talked about work. She poured him a cup, and he gave her a cigarette in return, cupping his hands around the match when he lit it for her. It was all very pally, and I didn't like it.

'By the way,' he said, leaning back in the chair. 'There's something I wanted to ask you.'

'Oh?'

'Do you remember, we were talking about the Gothick Walk the other day?'

'Of course. You were wondering whether you could use it in your book.'

Shaw had the grace to look embarrassed. 'It's not exactly a book yet. Just a few pages so far. But yes.'

'Will you have a murder there?' Enid asked, and the absurd irony of the question amused me even as it made me wince.

'Perhaps. But I need to have a look at it first. See if it would work. Would you mind showing it to me sometime?'

There was a brief silence. Enid was cautious by nature, and she was weighing the implications of the invitation. In the end she said, 'Well – if you like, I suppose.'

125

'That would be awfully kind.'

'But I don't know very much about it. I've only been there once. Annabel – my friend – she'd found a way in, and she took me there. Did you know she was writing about its history? It was an essay – she was hoping to get it published. To be honest, it wasn't very inspiring. Then it started to rain, and anyway I was on duty for the girls' tea, so we had to get back.'

I noted with interest that Enid was talking too much, which she did when she felt ill at ease.

'It would be enormously helpful to explore the Gothick Walk,' he said smoothly. 'Once I know how to get in there, I expect I can find my own way around.'

'Annabel had all her notes about it in an exercise book,' she went on. 'She . . . she must have taken it with her when she went. But I think she said the Walk was mentioned in the *Country Life* article. That might help you.'

Shaw looked blank. 'What article?'

'They did a feature on Monkshill before the war, when the last people were living here. Mainly about the house, but there was something about the grounds as well.' Enid gave him one of her rare, impish smiles. 'Miss Pryce-Morgan makes sure to mention the *Country Life* article to new parents. And she quotes chunks of it in the prospectus. It adds *tone*, apparently.'

This time they exchanged smiles, complicit in their amusement. I didn't like it. I really didn't like it at all.

The park itself was partly remodelled by the Dowager Lady Ruispidge in the 1860s. Some of the woodland to the north and west was removed, and extensive shrubberies were planted near the house and elsewhere. The lake was extended to the south, and the stream that drains it was diverted and widened. At the same time, the South Drive was realigned to pass over a bridge across the stream at a point visible from the house. She also rebuilt the North and South Lodges.

To the east, however, little was done to alter the character of the steep, wooded slopes that descend to the river gorge. The features of the once celebrated Gothick Walk were suffered to decay, a neglect that has continued into the first quarter of the twentieth century; though there must still remain much to delight the student of such things. Equally regrettable was Lady Ruispidge's decision to 'restore' the fragmentary ruins of a small monastic grange east of the lake, thereby causing irreparable damage to Monkshill's sole remaining mediaeval feature above ground.

Country Life, 26 June 1937

That evening I saw Mrs Crisp walking in the park. It was late – well after eleven o'clock. In the half-dark of a midsummer night, her angular figure was outlined against the sky, a stick in motion.

She made her way on a course parallel to the line of the drive, walking along one side of a field where Mr Lewis's cows raised their weary heads to watch her pass. What was she doing out so late? Her duties at the school had finished hours earlier. And why wasn't she on the drive, a far easier surface to negotiate in this light?

She was going north, in the general direction of her home. I drew nearer. Her breathing was rapid and laboured, and every now and then she gave a muffled, rasping cough. There was a bag slung over her shoulder, the strap across her body.

Onward she went, with me trailing after her, a silent shadow. I was with her when she opened her garden gate and closed it behind her, when she walked up the path, fumbling in her pocket for a key. I was with her when she unlocked her door.

But I couldn't follow her inside. A moment later a muddy yellow glow appeared around the borders of the closed curtains, faint at first but growing steadily stronger. She had lit a lamp.

She unlocked her door.

Few people locked their door in this part of the world. Apart from Tosser and now Shaw. No one else bothered. Why should they? Not unless they feared that someone might steal something, or that someone might leave a turd as a visiting card. Not unless—

Not unless they had something to hide.

Then I saw what might have happened, in all its alluring simplicity. In that moment I knew why I had been murdered. And I knew the name of my killer.

16

When I came back to myself the following morning, the blinding certainty of the previous evening had ebbed away. The revelation (for that was what it had seemed like) had lost its force. But it still remained a plausible theory to solve the mystery of my murder. Something more than a possibility: something that felt like the next best thing to a probability.

I went over it in my mind, step by step.

Almost everyone knew about Mrs Crisp's trouble. Everyone knew but nobody talked about it – unless, like Mrs Broadwell the other day, they couldn't contain their curiosity or had a malicious desire to turn the knife in the wound and make it bleed again.

Mrs Crisp had a son. His name was Sam. According to staffroom gossip, the boy's father had been an Irish labourer working for a builder in Newport. He had married Mrs Crisp – or so she said anyway – and it was certainly true that, when Sam was five, the father had taken him home to County Carlow to stay at the family farm. But he brought the boy back after a fortnight and left him with his mother. That was the last anyone had seen of him.

Mrs Crisp's mother had lived at North Lodge since the turn of the century, and after her death the previous owners of Monkshill had allowed Mrs Crisp to stay there, as they had done with Tosser in East Cottage, in return for cleaning work at the big house. Sam attended the village school. He was always slow, people said, not quite right in the head, but gentle enough if he didn't feel threatened. But if he did feel threatened, he lashed out.

But that didn't happen often because everyone knew him. In a place like Flaxern Parva, people were broad-minded when it came to defining what was normal and what was not. Sam had managed well enough on the whole. When he left school aged fourteen, able to sign his name and read simple, clearly printed words if given enough time, he did odd jobs around the village, on the farm and even at Monkshill Park.

He was a large, clumsy youth, Maggie Squires had told me, liable to break things, but he could be trusted with straightforward tasks that involved physical strength, as long as they were carefully explained beforehand, and as long as you kept an eye on him while he did them. He was kept well away from the schoolgirls. His minute earnings were a welcome addition to the household budget at North Lodge.

Early in 1944 Sam Crisp had turned eighteen and his life was ripped apart. The army called him up to serve his country. Somehow he was passed fit for service and off he went to war. Except he never got there. He survived the first few months of training and then he simply vanished. He walked out of his barracks and he never came back.

All this happened before I joined the school. Of course,

Monkshill had been the first place where the authorities looked for their lost soldier. The Military Police tramped all over the village, questioning everyone. They even interviewed Miss Pryce-Morgan about the boy. ('I heard they were most disrespectful. Quite rude,' Little Covey confided to me, her eyes wide with wonder.) They searched the grounds. The local constabulary were still liable to turn up unannounced at North Lodge, as PC Fowles had done the other day. In the absence of any evidence to the contrary, people believed that he must have gone to ground elsewhere – even in Ireland, perhaps, with his father's people. Either that or he was dead.

To me, however, it now seemed probable that Sam was lying low at Monkshill Park after all. In the last day or two, the circumstantial evidence in favour of the theory had been steadily piling up. It explained why Mrs Crisp needed to run the risk of stealing from the school kitchen. It made sense if she had two mouths to feed and only one ration book and one modest wage coming in. She desperately needed more money – for only desperation could explain why she would run the enormous risk of accepting a bribe from someone as blatantly unreliable as Venetia.

I also remembered Tuesday morning, when a curtain had twitched at North Lodge just after she left for work. It might have been a draught. Or it might not. If it wasn't a draught, if her son had been inside, then it was now understandable why she habitually locked her door.

I reasoned that Sam could not be staying at the lodge itself. It would be too dangerous, though he must visit to have a proper wash or to warm himself in the winter. I ruled out somewhere in the village as a hiding place, because everyone knew everyone else's business; and too many people were coming and going; too many people who knew that Sam was a deserter on the run.

But Monkshill was different. Apart from the house and the gardens around the house, the rest of the park and its hinterland were empty of people for most of the time. Sam had grown up here. He must know its secret places with the intimate knowledge of a child.

Where more secret, where better to hide, than in Bleeding Yew Wood, isolated behind its apparently impenetrable fence? I had the evidence to support that. The footsteps at night. The brown button underneath the bleeding yew and the fence. The missing billhook at the Maiden's Leap. The flare of a match. The sighting of the Bear.

The jigsaw was nearly complete. A triumph of reason and deduction. It would remind Miss Marple of something that had once happened to her housemaid's nephew. Lord Peter Wimsey would offer me a celebratory glass of port. Hercule Poirot would twirl his moustaches and tell me he had known all along.

I should have felt pleased. Or even angry. Instead I felt sad. Sam was so young, so defenceless. It didn't take much effort to imagine what he would have felt if he had seen a stranger poking about his hiding place. The terror. The desperate, instinctive reaction.

A quick shove, and the danger was gone for ever.

'Well?' Sylvia said. 'What happened on Tuesday? Did you go to Tosser's?'

'Yes.'

'And?'

Stephen moved to one side so he could look through the crack between the jamb and the door. They were in the old stables by the drive, in what had once been a tack room before the army came. It was after lunch and before the bell rang for afternoon school. They were taking a risk meeting so close to the school. The stables were out of bounds. They were now the domain of Mr Lewis and his workers, who used them mainly for storage. Their visits were frequent but unpredictable.

'Nothing,' he said. 'The door was locked.'

'No one locks their door around here.'

'Tosser does. Anyway, I looked through the windows. I went right round the cottage – looked in the pigsty, the shed, even the privy.'

'No trace of her? Or her things? You're sure?'

He shook his head. 'I told you there wouldn't be. But I don't know for sure – I couldn't get inside. Anyway, if it was Tosser, he would have had plenty of time to get rid of her stuff.'

'It was always a long shot,' Sylvia said. She chewed her lower lip.

'You definitely think she was murdered?'

'I don't *know*. But I don't believe she'd give me some holiday prep and then go away. For ever. And people don't just vanish like that, do they? I heard Runty telling your aunt that her things are still up in her room. So yes, I think someone might have murdered her. It's the only thing that makes sense.'

Sylvia stopped suddenly. She was breathing hard as if she had climbed a hill too fast. *Good kid*, I thought, *you're trying to think this through, wherever it leads.*

Stephen said sharply, 'But why did you want me to scout round Tosser's place? Why him? Why would he murder her?'

'Because he had a motive. Warnie could have got him sacked.'

'You never told me that. What was it?'

Sylvia's face turned red. 'It doesn't matter.'

133

'Of course it does,' Stephen said. 'Tell me.'

The blush darkened. 'She saw him somewhere he shouldn't have been.'

'Where?'

Sylvia capitulated. 'He was looking at girls in the showers. Warnie saw him. He's a Peeping Tom. I heard her telling Archie. She said she put the fear of God in him. Threatened him with the police, and turning him out of his cottage.'

Now it was my turn to feel embarrassed. You'd think that after all these years as a teacher I'd have learned to be more discreet.

Stephen was embarrassed too, much more so, and for a different reason. He looked away and took out his penknife. It was one of those horn-handled ones with a spike for taking stones out of horses' hooves. He opened the spike and began to scratch his initials in the crumbling plaster on the wall. His cheeks were pink.

'Well?' Sylvia prompted. 'What do you think?'

'Yes, well. I can see he's a suspect. But maybe there are others.' He turned to face her. 'You know that book?'

'What book?'

'The one you lent me – *Peril at End House*. There's a bit where Poirot talks about motives. About the different sorts. One of them's gain – you know, money and stuff. Then there's love.' He cleared his throat again, embarrassed by the risk of sounding soppy. 'When . . . when you want someone so much you don't mind killing someone else to get them. And there's jealousy, when you don't like someone having something. So you kill them. And there's fear. Tosser's motive would be fear, wouldn't it? If he did kill her, I mean. Because he was afraid that she'd tell everyone what he was doing.'

Sylvia looked thoughtful. 'If it isn't Tosser, we should think of other people with reasons to harm her. And then try and find evidence. I don't think—'

The distant jangling of the bell interrupted her.

'Oh golly, I'm going to be late. It's Geog with Hampers.' She glanced at Stephen. 'Stay here for a few minutes. They mustn't see us together.'

He nodded. 'Think about motives,' he said. 'Think hard. That's what Poirot would do.'

I was living inside a whodunnit. I really didn't like it, and I wasn't exactly living, either. Nevertheless, all the ingredients of a typical detective yarn were here. The country house. The murder. The more or less closed circle of suspects. The clues. Except it wasn't a real country house, it was just a third-rate boarding school in the middle of nowhere in particular; somewhere for parents to park their daughters.

Believe me, it was no fun being the victim. What made it worse was that no one even knew that I was murdered, apart from the person who killed me.

Had it really been Sam? The evidence no longer seemed so persuasive. It was only circumstantial, after all – I couldn't be sure one way or the other. Not unless at some point in the future I happened to be there when he confessed the murder to someone else – and why on earth would he do that?

People come up with endless theories about how Dickens planned to end *The Mystery of Edwin Drood* – but no one can ever know for sure what was in his mind. There's nothing worse than a whodunnit with a missing ending. Especially if you were the victim.

* * *

Sylvia ran back to the house in time for her first lesson of the afternoon, Geography with Vera Hampson. She took the shortcut through the shrubbery. I trailed after her, having nothing better to do.

Runty was coming down the main stairs as Sylvia was passing through the hall. She gave the poor girl an order mark for being untidy and another one for running in the house. When the classroom door had closed behind Sylvia, Runty glanced up the stairs, then down the passage toward the green baize door to the back of the house. Finally she peered into the lobby leading to the side door.

At that moment, Shaw came out of the staffroom. He was in a hurry, but he paused when he saw Runty. I expected her to look at her watch in a meaningful way or even to point out that he was late for the third form's history lesson. But she just looked at him. And he looked at her.

For a moment I thought he was about to say something. But she turned away, pretending an interest in the noticeboard. He opened the door of his classroom, and there was the familiar stampede as the girls stood up. I barely had time to register the oddness of the encounter because Runty went directly into the study. I followed.

PM wasn't in the room. Runty went straight to the desk, opened the middle drawer and took out a key. She unlocked the closet door and went in. I hovered, expecting her to open the safe. Instead, she turned to face the shelves opposite the window.

My view was limited and through the doorway, because while I was alive I hadn't gone closer to the closet than PM's desk in the study. But I knew that this was where PM kept past copies of *The Times*, her cherished and entirely useless backfile.

Runty put on a pair of dusting gloves and, puffing with effort, lowered a slab of newsprint to the floor, where she crouched over it like a creature of the night mantling its prey and flicked through the pile.

It took her less than a minute to find the copy she wanted. She spread it on the floor and turned the pages, scanning each one. She paused and then, after a moment, removed the entire sheet from the newspaper. Folding it once, she slipped it out of the closet and onto the carpet in the gap between the desk and the study wall.

That was a stroke of luck. One item on the page caught my eye immediately.

HOME NEWS

PREP SCHOOL MASTERS FOUND GUILTY

TWO YEARS PENAL SERVITUDE

TWO MONTHS FOR ACCOMPLICE

Charles Warrender-Jones, a 45-year-old prep school master, was sentenced to two years penal servitude at the Hertford Assizes yesterday for embezzling funds from the school where he worked over a period of years. However, the judge accepted the defence's plea that his accomplice, George Shaw, had only . . .

I looked up as Runty left the closet. With swift, deft movements, she folded the sheet of newspaper and tucked it in the waistband of her skirt at the back. Her cardigan was long enough to conceal it. The key went back in the drawer.

In the hall, she met PM coming down the stairs.

'You're earlier than usual,' she said. 'How was your nap?'

'I couldn't sleep,' PM said. 'Too tiresome.'

'Oh dear.'

'And I think I've the beginnings of a headache.'

'You poor thing. Why don't I make us a nice cup of tea and find you a couple of aspirins? Oh – and Mrs Broadwell said she'd made us some scones.'

I couldn't help admiring the aplomb with which Runty carried off the unexpected appearance of PM. I followed her as she marched through the green baize door. Rather than the kitchen, however, she went into her office, formerly the housekeeper's sitting room.

She shut the door behind her and took a bunch of keys from her pocket. (She was a great one for keys.) She unlocked the top right-hand drawer in her desk, slid the square of newspaper under her account books. She relocked the drawer. A moment later she was in the kitchen and putting the kettle on.

I didn't know what to make of this. Were George Shaw and Alec Shaw one and the same? And why had Runty been looking for this particular story in *The Times?* What had tipped her off? Perhaps, I thought, meeting Shaw had jogged something loose in her memory, and it was only now that she had remembered reading a story about an embezzling prep school master.

There was also the point that Runty hadn't mentioned her discovery to PM. It was possible that she wanted to investigate further before telling the headmistress that her visiting tutor was probably an ex-convict.

The alternative explanation was that she wanted to keep the information to herself. Because she was planning to blackmail Alec Shaw.

17

'Have you got anywhere?' Prissy asked.
  'What with?' Sylvia said.
'You know. The investigation.'
'Not really.'

Sylvia was pouring herself a cup of tea. At four thirty every afternoon, the tea monitors brought a vast enamel teapot into each of the house dining rooms, along with milk and a tray of cups and saucers. Cup in hand, she edged away. Prissy followed.

'You should do what Monsieur Poirot does,' she suggested. 'Build a house of cards. It helps him think.'

Sylvia shrugged. 'Perhaps we were wrong about the Christie thing. *The Body in the Library*. Anyway, it was only a mouse. Probably it was just someone having a joke.'

'Not a very funny one,' Prissy said primly. Her German accent was more pronounced, usually an indication that she was feeling anxious or scared. 'Why don't we think—'

'Thinking's not much use without something to think about.'

Prissy stared. 'What?'

'We need more evidence,' Sylvia said. 'More to go on.'

A few yards away, Rosemary Lawson-Smith was sniggering with her current group of allies. They were too far away to hear what Prissy and Sylvia were saying, but it was clear that the two older girls were the objects of their amusement.

'How can we get it?' Prissy said.

'We can't.' Her mouth twisted. 'What we really need is another murder. That's what happens in books.'

'Prissy's got a fearful pash on her,' Rosemary said in a loud whisper. 'Just imagine – she kisses her pillow every night – ugh!'

The little girls dissolved into loud giggles. Sylvia and Prissy turned away, pretending they hadn't heard.

'She writes poems about her blue, blue eyes and her rose-pink lips,' Rosemary hissed, and the giggles redoubled.

Venetia happened to be passing. She paused beside Rosemary and took her ear between the thumb and finger of her free hand. Rosemary squealed.

'You beastly little toe-rag,' Venetia said in a conversational tone as if commenting on the weather. 'I'm going to pour my tea all over you.'

Rosemary went rigid with fear. That was the thing with Venetia – the normal rules didn't apply; you could never tell how far she would go if the spirit took her. At last she relaxed her grip. Rosemary scuttled away, leaving her allies shocked and silent.

Venetia ignored everyone. Tea in hand, she wandered out of the room, which incidentally was forbidden – Cavendish girls were supposed to drink their tea in the servants' hall and nowhere else.

The episode left me wondering whether Venetia had intervened because Rosemary was jeering at Sylvia and Prissy?

Or because she had decided that she didn't care for Rosemary? Or had she merely acted on a whim?

With Venetia you simply couldn't tell. Perhaps she couldn't either.

I was beginning to realise that my murder investigation was foundering because it was impossible to distinguish between what was relevant and what was not. There was too much going on at Monkshill. Too many secrets, too many contradictory emotions, too many mysteries.

This, I was learning, was the problem with being dead. When I had been alive, I hadn't noticed the ridiculous confusion of daily existence. Like everyone else, I had followed the lines laid down by habit and routine. Like a horse with blinkers, I had tended not to notice what was going on unless it was in front of my nose.

But now, being dead – or at least in a transitional phase between the animate and the inanimate – I glimpsed the private places of other people's lives. Not everything – and many of these chosen not by me but purely by chance; and all of them restricted to places I had known in life. Rather than help the investigation, my newfound ability seemed to make matters more complicated.

After Venetia had put a stop to Rosemary's sniggers, I wandered along to the hall and out of the front door. I wasn't going anywhere in particular. I wanted to think, and I thought there would be fewer distractions outside.

I turned left and followed the path that led along the front of the house and past the colonnade that linked it to the roofless East Pavilion. I heard raised voices ahead, growing steadily louder.

Around the corner of the pavilion, Little Covey was in her garden. She was waving a trowel at Tosser, who was facing her with a sickle in his hand. They looked like a pair of horticultural gladiators, squaring up for a duel to the death.

It was a ridiculous spectacle. But there was nothing amusing about it. Both were red-faced, and tears were streaming down Miss Covey's wrinkled cheeks.

Everyone knew that her garden was her pride and joy. It was a patch of ground about six yards wide by two deep against the east wall of the pavilion. She would tell anyone who would listen how she had dug it over, cleared away the stones, and fed the soil with manure from Home Farm. With tender care, she had planted seeds and cuttings, and nursed them into maturity. All this had taken nearly two years.

She loved her garden as if it were her child, which in a sense it was. Each plant, each flower, was an occasion for rejoicing, something to be talked about at length in the staffroom. Truth to tell, she could become rather tiresome on the subject.

At this time of year, with summer just around the corner, the tiny garden should have been full of flowers in all the glory and freshness of spring. But Tosser had laid waste to it with his sickle, cutting a swathe of destruction along the entire length of the bed. Blossoms and fresh green shoots lay dying, crushed underfoot. He had ripped the clematis off the wall. He had torn the climbing rose from its supports and methodically slashed it to pieces.

'You old bitch,' he was saying, spraying spittle in her direction. 'That'll learn you.'

Miss Covey backed away. She tripped over her trug, which was on the ground beside her, its contents scattered over the grass. She sprawled inelegantly on the ground, partly on the path and partly on her own flowerbed, giving her adversary an extensive view of her underclothing.

'Oh,' she cried. 'Oh!' and the misery in her voice would have drawn pity from a stone. 'I'll report you to—'

'You tell who you want, and I'll tell them you're a bloody thief.'

'What the hell's going on?'

It was Shaw. He had come up behind me, walking on the grass rather than on the path so none of us had heard his approach. He didn't wait for an answer but went directly to Miss Covey, put his arm around her and helped her to her feet. She twittered at him like an agitated fledgling. The tears were still running down her cheeks. Beside him, she looked smaller, older and more fragile than she actually was.

'I never laid a finger on her,' Tosser said, with an unconvincing attempt at innocence. 'She tripped over that bloody basket of hers.'

Shaw ignored him. 'Here.'

He produced a none too clean handkerchief from his pocket and gave it to Miss Covey. She dabbed at her eyes. I'd never thought about how old she was before. For all I knew, she was in her seventies, clinging to her job and accepting a pittance for it because she had nowhere else to go. Monkshill was the only home she had, and her garden was perhaps her only real pleasure. Death was making me sentimental.

'He . . . he did *that*.' Miss Covey waved the trowel at her murdered darlings. 'He's mad.'

Tosser glowered at her and edged away.

'Look here,' Shaw said to him. 'You've got some explaining to do. Why did you do this?'

'She stole my weedkiller.'

'I did *not*!'

'Like gold dust that stuff is.'

'I didn't steal anything.'

'Then how did this get there?' Tosser delved in his pocket and took out a small leather glove. He waved it at her. 'See? You dropped it in my shed. And look.' He gestured with it towards the trug. 'There's the other one.' He peeled back the glove to reveal a label sewn onto the lining. 'It's even got your bloody name in it.' He pointed a dirty finger at Shaw. 'And he's a witness to that.'

I craned to look over Tosser's shoulder. Sure enough, *E. COVEY* had been written on the label in indelible ink. He tossed the glove onto the ground.

Little Covey tore herself away from Shaw and staggered off. He took a few steps after her but she waved him away. She disappeared around the corner of the pavilion.

'Ground elder,' Tosser said darkly.

Shaw glanced at him. 'What?'

The old man pointed at the far end of the flowerbed. Nothing grew here. The earth had been freshly turned. 'That's why she needed the weedkiller.'

'Ground elder?'

'Yes. Best dig it out, get every last bloody root. But the old bat wanted to do it the easy way. Like I said, it's gold dust, weedkiller is.' He spat again. 'It's the bloody war, innit?'

Shaw clearly felt he had lost ground. 'Look, I don't know the rights and wrongs of it, but you shouldn't have done this to an old lady. You know the garden's her pride and joy.'

'Oh bugger that. Eye for an eye. That's what the Bible says.'

'Oh for God's sake. You're not an Old Testament prophet.'

'And a tooth for a tooth.'

144

I could see that Shaw was trying to rein back his temper. When he next spoke, it was in a quieter voice: 'Was it you, by the way? Who thought it would be amusing to treat my cottage as a public lavatory?'

'What? What you on about now?'

'Did you take a shit in my fireplace because I wouldn't buy your bloody rabbit?'

Tosser grinned, displaying bright pink gums and the occasional stump of tooth. 'Maybe. Maybe not. I know what I know.'

'What's that supposed to mean?'

'It means you'd better be careful what you say to me. Nice bike you got down at the cottage, eh? With them green saddlebags. They kind of stick in the mind, don't they, once you've seen them? Don't often see green saddlebags. Must have cost a bob or two, I reckon.'

There was a silence, sudden and expected. What the hell was this about Shaw's bicycle? At first I had thought Tosser must be threatening to damage it – to slash the tyres, perhaps, or scratch the paintwork. But why the emphasis on green saddlebags?

Shaw stared at Tosser, and Tosser stared at his handiwork, the ruined flowerbed. Then Shaw stooped, swept up Miss Covey's trug and its contents, and walked away.

The wasp was a sprightly young thing with quick, decisive movements. The window was only open about two inches, but that was quite enough. It darted through the gap, dropped sharply down and settled without any hesitation at all on the dazzlingly white square of linen that protected Miss Pryce-Morgan's ample lap. Under cover of the table, it dug its proboscis into a jewel-like blob of last year's raspberry jam in the shallow valley between her thighs.

'It's a problem,' Runty said, who sat facing PM with the teapot at her elbow. 'There's no denying that.'

'His bill's extortionate. Just for replacing a few pieces of rotten wood. I suppose we have to pay him what he asks?'

'I'm afraid so. If we make a fuss, it won't do us any good in the village. We depend on credit to keep things going until next term's fees come in. And that's three months away at least. What makes it worse is the late payers.'

The wasp dug more deeply into the jam. Meanwhile its human hosts chattered above its head. I knew what they were talking about. There was a domed skylight in the cupola over the main staircase. At the start of the war it had been blacked out with tarpaulins. Last month, the last of the blackout regulations had been lifted and there had no longer been any need for tarpaulins. A man from the village had gone onto the roof to remove them. Unfortunately, in doing so, he had discovered that the wooden frame of the skylight was in poor condition. Part of it needed to be replaced as a matter of urgency. A carpenter had been brought in. His bill had arrived by the afternoon post.

'The horrid little man wouldn't have got away with overcharging before the war,' PM said. Which was probably true.

'Perhaps the bank will let us have another loan,' Runty said. 'Or we could sell something else.'

'Or find a tenant for Mr Shaw's cottage after he's left.'

'We can't wait that long. We can't turn him out – we need him for the time being.'

Miss Pryce-Morgan sighed heavily. She took another scone and covered it with a liberal coating of butter. She stretched out a hand for the bowl containing the jam. Her movements were clumsy, and the spoon fell out of the bowl and clattered on her saucer. Disturbed by the noise, the wasp rose from her lap and hovered over the table. PM cried out. She struggled to her feet, spilling her tea in the process. The wasp swooped on the jam bowl.

'Pammy!'

Runty was already out of her chair. She flung up the central sash in the bow window, picked up today's copy of *The Times*, and tried to sweep the wasp outside. The wasp took this as an invitation to a game of Catch-Me-If-You-Can. Meanwhile, Miss Pryce-Morgan continued to back away, her hands held up like a traffic policeman as if ordering the wasp to go no further. She shuffled around the desk and edged towards the far side of the room.

At this moment there was a knock at the door.

'Oh, go away!' PM cried.

The door opened. Little Covey came in, oblivious to the drama unfolding in the study. Presumably she had interpreted the distraught cry as permission to enter. You could still see traces of tears, especially around her pink-rimmed eyes, but she had made an effort to tidy herself. Her hair was brushed, and she had washed her face and reapplied its usual layer of powder.

'What is it?' PM said, her eyes still on the wasp, which was outmanoeuvring Runty's attempts to deal with it with insulting ease. 'It's not convenient.'

Miss Covey wasn't listening. She plunged immediately into speech, the words tumbling over each other in their haste to get out. 'I really must complain . . . the strongest possible terms . . . that dreadful man . . . you know, the one who smells . . . but it wasn't his, it was from that nice Luigi, Mr Lewis's prisoner . . .

and how my glove got in there, I simply cannot say . . . I really must insist he's forbidden anywhere near the school . . . can you evict him? If it hadn't been for that nice Mr Shaw coming along, I do believe he was going to *murder* me . . . I was so shaken I had to—'

'Go away, you silly woman!' PM said, waving her hand as if she too were brushing away a troublesome wasp. 'Go away! Out! Out!'

18

*T*hink *about motives.*

That's what Stephen had said to Sylvia this afternoon. The boy was right. I already knew that I had given Tosser a compelling reason to kill me. And then I had handed him the opportunity to do it on a plate. On that last morning, he might have been in the woods already. Or he might well have followed me there, curious to see what I was up to.

Finally I had presented him with the perfect means of getting rid of me. I'd been standing with my back to him at the Maiden's Leap, looking out over the gorge. Asking to be killed. All it had needed was a quick, firm push.

Tosser's nastiness was not in dispute – and he'd given ample evidence of it this afternoon with Miss Covey. The trouble was, if he had killed me, he had succeeded in committing the next best thing to an undetectable crime. It was as easy to build a case against him as against Sam Crisp, assuming I was right about the Bear.

If it had been Tosser, my one hope of bringing the crime home to him was my ability to influence Shaw when he was writing his novel, together with the fact that I had told Enid about my threat to expose him after the Peeping Tom episode. If Shaw knew about that, it would give him the motive.

After poor Covey had been expelled from the headmistress's study, I stayed at the school for a few more hours. Enid was taking prep that evening. She looked tired and she was unusually snappy with the girls.

Evening prayers came and went. Enid went up to her room rather than linger with the other teachers over cups of cocoa and last cigarettes. She did some more marking and glanced over the lessons she planned for Friday. All very boring, but I found it restful. I used to be such a restless creature. I was calmer now.

Before I left her to herself, I allowed myself the pleasure of watching her getting ready for bed. I wished I could have done the same when I was alive – watched her like this, I mean, when she didn't know I was watching. Perhaps Tosser wasn't the only one who was a Peeping Tom.

Once in bed, Enid took up a book and began to read. Not *Peter Abelard* this time but one I had lent her last term: Virginia Woolf's *Orlando*. I was pleased to see that she wasn't using the lock of the boyfriend's hair to mark her page.

After a few minutes she laid the book on the chair beside her bed and tugged the cord that switched off the overhead light. It wasn't long before her breathing slowed into the soft regularity of sleep, and so I went away.

As I was passing across the landing, I heard someone nearby talking in a low voice, too low for me to distinguish the words.

The only door with a light underneath was Little Covey's. I slipped inside – I had been in her bedroom a couple of times before I died, once to change a lightbulb, and once to help her close her window on a stormy evening. She was kneeling by her bed, her eyes screwed shut and her hands clasped in prayer.

She looked older without the protective covering in which she faced the daytime world. She was wearing an elaborate cotton nightdress large enough to serve as a tent for at least three Boy Scouts. On her head was a cap secured by a pale blue ribbon. She looked like the poor relation in a Victorian novel. There were tear tracks on her face.

'. . . erred, and strayed from thy ways like lost sheep,' she was saying as I came in. 'We have followed too much the devices and desires of our own hearts. We have offended against thy holy laws. We have left undone those things which we ought to have done; and we have done those things which we ought not to have done; and there is no health in us.'

I stayed there, listening to her recite the rest of the General Confession. After that, she offered an extempore prayer begging forgiveness for offending Tosser and commending his eternal soul to God's mercy. She asked particular pardon for cherishing unchristian thoughts about Runty and Miss Pryce-Morgan. She finished with the Lord's Prayer, after which she climbed slowly and painfully to her feet and got under the covers.

But Miss Covey wasn't finished with the pursuit of holiness. She took up a small volume bound in black leather from the bedside table. It was *The Imitation of Christ* by Thomas à Kempis. Her lips moved silently as she read.

The old me, the living version of myself, would probably have sniggered up my sleeve if I had witnessed this pious scene. The new me felt – well, what exactly? Confused? Envious? Uncomfortable? Guilty? None of the words were quite right. I needed something else without a name.

* * *

151

The clock in PM's study chimed half-past ten as I left the house. I took the path that led to East Cottage.

I was increasingly curious about Shaw after seeing that story in *The Times*. Ignoring for a moment Runty's strange behaviour, I wasn't sure what to make of the revelation that he, or at least someone with the same surname, had been the accomplice of a prep school master imprisoned for embezzlement. Had he really spent two months in prison? I was pretty sure that he really had been a schoolmaster. You could tell he knew what he was doing by the way he handled the girls and how he taught. He was familiar with the examination system too.

But what was he doing at Monkshill Park?

There was still a light downstairs. I went inside. Shaw was at the table, typing by the light of a hurricane lamp. I looked over his shoulder and saw through a swirling mist of pipe smoke that he was writing his detective story again. That was a good omen. Tired though I was, it was worth having a shot at getting through to him.

. . . table in the library. The family solicitor, Mr Covey, sat at the head, with Roderick on his left and Cynthia on his right. Sir Giles sat at the foot of the table, with his wife on one side and his daughter on the other. The Squires, the poor cousins from London, were in the middle. Mrs Pryce-Morgan, the housekeeper, and Hampson were also in the room, standing in a huddle just inside the door.

'I say,' Roderick said, nodding in the direction of the servants. 'Why are they here?'

Cynthia kicked him under the table.

He rounded on her. 'Stop it, Cyn, it's a perfectly reasonable question.'

He paused for a moment and stared at the shadowy ceiling, no doubt looking for inspiration. I noted with interest that he had begun to give many of his characters surnames from Monkshill. Even the butler, formerly Frampton, had mutated into Hampson. No mention of an Enid Archer, though.

He bent over the typewriter again, and I gathered my flagging strength:

'You're such a dreadful snob. Why shouldn't they be here?'

Mr Covey cleared his throat. 'They are here because His Lordship ask Enid what Tosser did, and who told her.

Shaw reacted more calmly to my insertion than he had done before. *ask Enid what Tosser did, and who told her.* It was almost as if he had been expecting it. He stopped typing and sat back in the chair. The only sign of agitation was that he struck a match to relight the pipe, though it was still smouldering away quite happily, the tobacco glowing in the bowl. He lifted the lamp and held it closer to the typewriter so he could study the words more closely.

'I am not mad, you know,' he said to the empty room. 'I am perfectly sane.'

Was he talking to himself or me? He scrabbled among the papers scattered on the table and picked out the sheet on which he had written the earlier messages. He reread the list:

Help me. Help me.
Maiden's Leap. Maiden's Leap.
Gothick Walk. Look there.
The rucksack, the exercise book.
Find the bleeding yew.
The yew.

I wished I could edit that list to make myself clearer. The trouble was, it had emerged in fits and starts and, at the beginning, with little or no premeditation.

Shaw pulled the sheet from the typewriter and replaced it with the list, turning the platen until he had reached the end. Very carefully he typed the next line: ask Enid what Tosser did, and who told her.

Then he looked up, his fingers still poised over the keys of the machine, and said in a perfectly normal voice: 'Is anyone there?'

The bloody fool. Of course I was here. *Yes, yes, yes.*

Nothing happened. The words didn't flow from his fingers as before. I knew the reason. His transcript of my messages was in the typewriter, not a page from his wretched novel.

I didn't try again. The effort had exhausted me. It seemed to have exhausted him as well. He put away the typewriter, gathered up the scattered sheets of paper and went outside to water the brambles and the nettles by the light of the stars.

19

Mrs Crisp's behaviour with the basket alerted me.

It was Friday morning, and I was making a circuit of the park. When I started, it was still very early. The air was full of birdsong, and the grass was silvered with dew. Death hadn't given me many reasons to like it so far, but at least it had heightened my appreciation of living things, whether animate or inanimate. Since I no longer felt hunger or cold, since I no longer had anything I needed to do, I had the leisure to enjoy them as long as I wanted.

The sun was rising higher, burning off the dew. But the world was waking up. Carried on the wind came the chimes of the village clock striking seven. Closer by, a tractor rumbled into life. I made a circuit of the lake and climbed towards higher ground. In the distance the hunched figure of Tosser was walking towards the school. No doubt he was on his way to feed the boiler with coke.

I crossed the path that led to Flaxern Parva. After that, my route took me within view of North Lodge. I saw Mrs Crisp in the distance. She was closing her garden gate and setting off to the school, which meant it was probably around twenty to eight. The poor woman already looked weary. The prospect of the day's drudgery was unlikely to put a spring in her step. She had a heavy basket on her arm, which made her lopsided. When I was alive I had barely noticed her. It had taken death to make me realise how appalling her life must be.

She went off down the drive, ignoring the incurious stares of the cattle. I wandered down to the monastic ruin where the swallows were nesting below a ledge high in the stonework, and after that made for school.

As I drew nearer, I caught another glimpse of Mrs Crisp. This time she was on the path between the obelisk and the long wall of the kitchen gardens. She was walking more rapidly than before, perhaps because she was late, and she was swinging the basket as if to increase her momentum.

The basket. That's when it struck me. When I was alive, I used to hate those moments in films when a character carried bags or suitcases. Nine times out of ten, you could tell by the way they moved that the bags or cases were empty. It marred the precious illusion that the improbable monochrome story unfolding on the screen was somehow real.

Mrs Crisp had been carrying a heavy basket when she left the North Lodge. But now as she approached the school, the basket seemed to weigh almost nothing at all. Had the contents been for Sam?

I veered away from the school and went back to the bleeding yew. Nothing seemed to have changed since I myself had slipped through the fence a few hours earlier. I found no trace of Sam or of anything left for him. The brambles seemed undisturbed. Maybe there was another way into the wood to the north, where the ground was rougher. Or maybe the Crisps had found a spot where you could pass items through the fence.

Of course I only had circumstantial evidence that Sam was hiding in the wood at all. But I *wanted* it to be him. I felt almost possessive about him, as if I had willed him into existence.

Besides, along with Tosser, he was my main suspect.

There was a postbox in the hall at Monkshill, tucked away by the stairs. It was shaped like a pillar box you might see on a street corner. But it was much smaller and made of wood, covered with brown varnish rather than red paint. It had a brass letter flap and a brass-framed notice reminding you of letter rates. It was octagonal in cross section and had a jaunty acorn carved on top.

The people who had lived here before the war had left behind the postbox when they decamped to Canada. I supposed the family and their guests used to drop their letters inside for the postman to collect, rather than leave them on a tray in the hall where everyone could see whom they were writing to.

The door had a lock, just like a real pillar box, and Runty held the key. Only the staff were allowed to post their letters there. The girls' letters, both outgoing and incoming, were overseen by Miss Pryce-Morgan.

I had reached the school just after morning prayers and PM's daily lecture. I found Runty was in the hall with Maggie Squires. They were standing by the pillar box and pretending not to be quarrelling.

'It's too narrow, you see,' Maggie was saying. 'Asking for trouble. I had to stuff it in and it must have caught on something. I heard it tearing.'

'All I can say, it's the first time this has happened. Anyway, the bell's gone – shouldn't you be teaching?'

'Free period. Friday morning.'

Runty puffed out her chest like a fighting cock. 'I'm aware it's Friday morning, thank you. But I can't be expected to have the entire details of everyone's timetable at my fingertips.'

Maggie grunted. 'Well, anyway. Sorry to trouble you and all that. But what about my letter?'

Runty made a performance of searching through her bunch of keys until she found the one that fitted the pillar box. She unlocked the door and opened it. There were several letters inside. She took out the letter on top and handed it to Maggie.

'There you are.'

'Look at that – it must have snagged on that bit just inside the flap. Where the hinge is.'

'It's because it's too thick,' Runty said. 'That's the reason.'

'I'm sending my aunt some snapshots. That's why.'

'It's asking for trouble if it makes the envelope as bulky as that. In fact I don't know how you managed to force it through.'

'Oh blow – look, it's torn across the stamp. I'll have to find a new one as well as a new envelope.'

'You'd better hand it to the postman this time,' Runty said absently. 'Either that or put less inside.'

Her attention had moved away from the torn letter. She picked up the envelope that had been lying underneath it. It was an official brown one with OHMS at the corner, but it wasn't from some organ of the state. Someone had recycled it by glueing a square of white paper over the opening at the top, which also served as the address label.

Not that there was much of an address on the label. In fact

there was nothing at all, just two capital letters written in pencil: *PM*.

'Is that for the head?' Maggie said. 'I thought the box was only for outgoing letters.'

'I'll see she gets it,' Runty said. 'Now I've work to do.'

Maggie went off in search of a new envelope and another stamp. Runty walked briskly through the back hall and into the servants' passage. Once the green baize door had swung shut behind her, she paused to examine the envelope more carefully. She opened it with her forefinger and removed the single sheet of paper inside. It looked as if it had been torn from a school exercise book.

Five tiny rectangles had been glued to the paper. They had been neatly cut from an old book – you could tell that by the quality of the paper – and arranged to make three crookedly aligned words. But the letters were easy enough to read.

die – you – bit – Ch – es.

Runty pursed her lips. She folded the letter, returned it to the envelope and put it in her pocket. She walked briskly to her office and locked away the envelope in the drawer that contained the newspaper story about George Shaw.

Shaw had been here for less than a week but he was already developing habits. In the staffroom, for example, he almost always sat in the chair that I used to sit on, which happened to be next to Enid's. He had adopted it almost by right, and no one had challenged him. It was quite a comfortable chair, at least by comparison with others, and I suspected that both Vera Hampson and Maggie Squires had had designs on it. But they had surrendered it to him as if conceding a right of ownership, presumably for the pathetically inadequate reason that he was a man.

He and Enid were there together after the school's tea. At least they weren't alone. At the other end of the room, Miss Hampson was frowning at a crossword through her pince-nez, which were in danger of falling off her nose again. Technically Shaw shouldn't have been in the house at this time, but neither Runty nor PM had noticed that he was still on the premises.

They were talking about work, in particular about the School Cert class. But they didn't just have educational matters on their mind. You could always tell when two people were interested in each other, not just in the subject of their conversation. There was nothing overtly flirtatious about their behaviour. But still. Something else was going on beneath the words they were tossing to and fro between them.

I didn't like it but there was damn all I could do to stop it. How pleasant it would have been to whisper in Enid's ear: 'Oh by the way, did you know that man's been convicted for embezzlement?'

Shaw offered her a cigarette and took one himself. He lit them both with a single match, and for a moment their heads were very close together, and I could have sworn that Enid's hair brushed his hand. Her hair was exceptionally fine and soft, by the way. I definitely didn't want it touching his skin.

'I'm looking forward to our walk on Sunday,' he said in a lower voice than before, in a tone that I thought was the next best thing to seductive. 'When would be the best time?'

'After lunch? We could meet at the obelisk at about two thirty. Unless it's raining, that is.'

'It's awfully kind of you.'

'Not at all.' Enid paused to pick a shred of tobacco from her lower lip. 'I just hope you won't be disappointed – there's not much to see, and that wood is awfully hard going in places. I'd wear old clothes if I were you.'

'Thanks for the tip. By the way, did you hear about yesterday's fracas?'

'Miss Covey's garden?'

'That's it. Tosser was really unpleasant to her. And talking of Tosser, there's something I wanted to ask you. I—' He broke off. 'What on earth's that racket?'

For the last minute or so, a roaring, snarling sound had been steadily increasing in volume.

Miss Hampson raised her head. 'Would you listen to that? It's enough to make you permanently deaf.'

Shaw went to the open window and craned his head outside. He turned back into the room.

'It's a motorbike,' he said.

20

Apart from the postman and the tradespeople, almost any visitor was a rarity at Monkshill and therefore the object of intense curiosity. Enid, Shaw and Miss Hampson sauntered out of the staffroom into the hall. Shaw went to one of the windows. Enid and Miss Hampson were more subtle: they pretended to be consulting the noticeboard beside the door of the former library.

Almost immediately afterwards, Runty emerged from the PM's study with a tea tray. She noticed that Shaw was still in school and frowned at him. But he wasn't looking at her.

The noise outside grew louder. It reached a crescendo, then stopped abruptly. There was a pause, and then a small, broad man walked up the steps to the front door. The door had two leaves. It was half-glazed so we could see him clearly. He was wearing goggles with a flat cap attached to them. He looked like a toad in a raincoat. He gave the bell pull a vigorous tug.

Runty sighed and put down the tray on the table by the pillar box. The bell was still jangling in the servants' passage when she opened the door.

The man stripped off his goggles. 'Afternoon,' he said breezily. 'Your mistress in?'

Two things were immediately apparent. First, he was a she. And second, Runty did not care for this attack on her status, especially before witnesses.

'Miss Pryce-Morgan?' she said in an icy voice. 'Would you like to wait while I see if she's available? I'm Miss Runciman, by the way. I'm the matron here at Monkshill.'

'Excellent,' the woman said. 'Thought you were the housekeeper for a moment. One can never tell these days, can one? Would you let her know that Susan Vauden's here?'

'Oh.' Runty's manner underwent an abrupt change. 'Lady Susan! Of course – I'm sure Miss Pryce-Morgan will be delighted to see you.' She looked desperately around the hall. Her eyes fell on Enid. 'Miss Archer, would you be kind enough to take Lady Susan's things?'

She retreated into the study. Lady Susan handed her cap, goggles and gauntlets to Enid and then shrugged herself out of the raincoat that covered her from shoulder to knee. Underneath she wore a thick, ribbed jersey above a pair of tweed trousers attached with bicycle clips to scuffed riding boots.

'You wouldn't believe how damn chilly it gets on that bike,' she said.

The study door reopened and PM emerged in a flurry of agitation. Lady Susan turned towards her.

'Ah! Hello. Look here, I'm terribly sorry to barge in out of the blue. The Dower House phone is on the blink. And I'm only down here on a flying visit.'

Miss Pryce-Morgan burbled incoherently that she was only too glad – what a pleasure it was to see Lady Susan again – she hoped she was quite well – and how was the dear major?

'He's doing splendidly as far as I know. I just hope he never finds out I've stolen his motorbike.' She slapped her thigh. 'And his trousers. They're meant to be thornproof, stormproof and probably bulletproof too. But I haven't put that one to the test yet, ha ha.'

'Very practical, I'm sure. We'll let Venetia know you're here at once. Would you like some tea in the meantime? Miss Runciman, perhaps you would . . . ?'

Lady Susan seemed not to have heard the interruption. 'I came down the day before yesterday by train,' she was saying as she allowed herself to be shepherded into the study. 'Ghastly journey. Three hours late. And I have to be back in town by tomorrow morning. I couldn't face the train again, so I thought well why not go by motorbike instead? Handy to have the machine in London. Tom's bike has been lying idle since he went to Washington. Frank – he used to be our chauffeur at Fontenoy – he showed me what to do. I've never ridden one before but it turns out it's quite straightforward, if a little jerky and bumpy sometimes. All being well, I'll be back at the flat by ten.'

'Where would you like to sit?' Miss Pryce-Morgan asked with uncharacteristic timidity.

'Anywhere will do.' Lady Susan flung herself into PM's armchair, which groaned under the impact. She bent down and stripped off the bicycle clips. 'How's my niece? I haven't seen her since Christmas.'

'She's settled in very well, I think,' Miss Pryce-Morgan said cautiously. 'Venetia's a charming child. Well liked by staff and girls alike.'

'Really? I've always found her a bit of a nuisance. Just like her poor mother at that age.' Lady Susan glanced sharply at PM. 'No trouble of any sort, then?'

'Only the occasional burst of high spirits. Quite normal for her age.'

'That's a relief. I'm sure you know what you're doing, which is more than I can say for myself. None of my own, you see. Between ourselves she was quite a handful when she stayed with me in town. She sneaked off on her own one evening, and she didn't come back until nearly midnight. And I'm not at all sure she didn't help herself to my gin and top up the level with water. She definitely pinched a few cigarettes.'

Miss Pryce-Morgan smiled patronisingly. 'We don't permit that sort of behaviour here. That's one of the advantages of a school like Monkshill. We're very self-contained, you see, very tranquil. We are able to keep our girls well away from . . . unpleasant influences and temptations. And of course we keep a very strict eye on them.'

'I'm glad of that. It's what the child needs. Bit of discipline. Routine. Between ourselves, my sister and her husband led a terribly rackety life and they insisted on dragging Venetia around with them. And then Bobby fell off his horse and broke his neck, which in some ways was no bad thing, but after that things at home were even more unsettled. Her mother had some very strange friends. I shouldn't say it, but perhaps it was a blessing in disguise that she died when she did.'

There was a tap at the door. Runty entered with the tea tray. Venetia brought up the rear with a vast silver-plated teapot, which she was allowing to drip on the carpet. She set it down on the unprotected surface of the sofa table.

Lady Susan stood up. For an instant she and Venetia looked at one another, and it seemed to me that neither of them knew what was appropriate to the situation. In the end, Lady Susan bobbed her head, like a chicken pecking at a worm, and brushed her cheek against her niece's.

'Hello, dear,' she said. 'All well?'

Venetia did not reply.

'Shall we sit at the tea table?' Runty said brightly.

'Tea?' Lady Susan sounded surprised as if the notion of tea was foreign to her. 'Oh – that reminds me. I've brought something for you. For VE Day. I know it's a bit late, but it's still something to celebrate, isn't it?' She glanced at Runty. 'Would you bring us some glasses? Anything will do. Come and give me a hand outside, Venetia.'

She bustled away, with her niece trailing after her.

'Well!' said Runty. 'And I'd got out the best china too.'

'Lovely,' PM said vaguely.

Lady Susan and Venetia returned, carrying two bottles of champagne apiece, and placed them one by one on the hallowed surface of Miss Pryce-Morgan's desk.

'Roederer,' Lady Susan said. 'After all, the war in Europe doesn't end every day. Tom will be furious when he finds out. It's not as cold as it should be, I'm afraid. It was in the refrigerator at Fontenoy overnight, and they wrapped it in newspaper for me when I left. But it's been on the warm side today.'

PM gave a start. 'Oh – what? Now?'

'No time like the present. And I can't stay long.'

'Yes, yes, of course.' PM glanced apologetically at Runty. 'The glasses. Would you . . . ?'

'What about the rest of your people?' Lady Susan said. 'Plenty for everyone, and I'm sure they'd like to join us.'

Runty left to round up the staff and find the glasses. Enid and Shaw were the first to arrive, but the rest of the teachers weren't far behind. Maggie Squires, who was on duty this evening, murmured that she hoped it was all right but she'd left the head girl in charge. Nobody took any notice of her.

'A man!' Lady Susan said, seeming to notice Shaw for the first time. 'I didn't know you had men here. A teacher?'

'Mr Shaw isn't actually on the staff,' PM explained, frowning at him. 'He's our visiting tutor, a temporary appointment until the end of term. We had an unexpected teaching vacancy for our School Certificate class, and—'

Lady Susan had stopped listening. 'Jolly good. Well, Mr Shaw, make yourself useful and open a bottle or two. Ah – here's Miss Um with the glasses.'

The champagne had been shaken up on the way here, and the corks exploded like bullets. One of them hit the lampshade and made it rock like a mad thing. Another ricocheted off the wall, passed through my chest and broke a small china ornament. But this was soon forgotten. In a matter of minutes the air in the study had filled with smoke and chatter and even laughter.

Toasts were drunk, beginning with the king and Mr Churchill and Mr Attlee and ending with Major Vauden, Miss Pryce-Morgan and Monkshill. Little Covey became tiddly almost at once, and told Venetia all about the unpleasantness with Tosser yesterday afternoon. Venetia listened with interest and helped herself to champagne when no one was looking. On her third glass, Miss Hampson recited a splendidly filthy limerick about a young man from Cork, but fortunately only Enid and Shaw heard her.

Maggie Squires turned out to be unexpectedly knowledgeable about motorbikes. 'That's a Norton you've got there,' she informed Lady Susan. 'The ES2. Nice machine. My brother had one for a while. Used to get her up to eighty on the straight.'

She turned away abruptly, her face reddening, and blundered

towards the champagne. Her brother had gone missing after the Fall of Singapore. She didn't know whether he was dead or in a Japanese prisoner-of-war camp.

Meanwhile, PM became pink-faced and almost merry, while Runty drank steadily, looked sour and said little. As for me, I rather wished I were still alive. The last time I'd drunk Roederer was in a nightclub in Wardour Street with the muffled crumps of German bombs competing for our attention with the band. We had had to wait until the all-clear sounded, and in the interim there was nothing to do except drink.

When at last we had stumbled out into a summer dawn, the building opposite had vanished and the street was full of rubble. Bodies lay on stretchers and people in uniform scurried about being useful. The girl I was with was violently sick. I just stood there in my party finery and felt useless.

Shaw had just opened the fourth bottle when the chimes of Miss Pryce-Morgan's mantel clock cut through the hubbub. It was nine o'clock.

'Is that really the time?' Lady Susan said. 'Good lord. I'd better be off. I'll be lucky to reach London by midnight. Where's that niece of mine?'

Venetia had slipped out of the room twenty minutes earlier, around the time that Miss Covey had dozed off in an armchair. Judging by the girl's sudden pallor she needed to be sick.

'She will have realised it was her bedtime, I expect,' PM said, scenting an opportunity. 'Rules are important at Monkshill, and our girls rarely need to be reminded of them.'

'Say goodbye to her from me, will you? I don't want to disturb her if she's in bed.'

PM and Runty followed Lady Susan into the hall. Shaw topped up the glasses of those who were still on their feet, and they hastily drank what they could before filing outside to wave as the visitor departed down the south drive in a cloud of exhaust fumes. Once over the bridge, Lady Susan was out of sight, but the diminishing snarl of the motorbike hung in the air for another thirty seconds. Then that too was gone.

It was as if a spell had been broken. Everyone looked dazed and puzzled, as if they could not quite believe what had happened. For a few short hours, the outside world had breached the defences of Monkshill and laid waste to its routines and despoiled its holy places. But now the outside world was gone, leaving only a headache and a third of a bottle of champagne behind.

When she returned to the study, Miss Pryce-Morgan looked exhausted, and Runty made her sit in her armchair. She organised the rest of the troops with grim efficiency. Hampson was charged with helping Little Covey upstairs and laying her on top of her bed with a blanket over her. Maggie, Enid and Shaw were set to carrying the bottles, glasses and ashtrays into the scullery and washing them up, along with the unneeded tea things. ('Mind you save the tea leaves!')

A few minutes later, Runty followed. 'Thank you, Mr Shaw,' she said, taking the tea towel from his hand, 'we'll see you in the morning, as usual. Please do remember this has been an exceptional occasion. We don't normally expect to find you in the house after the end of lessons for the day.'

Once Shaw was safely out of the house, I left the rest of them to it and went upstairs to Birch dormitory. It wasn't dark – the long, summer evening shone a ghostly light through the uncurtained windows. I was hoping that Sylvia had left her notebook where I could read it again. But there was no sign of it.

With one exception, everyone was sound asleep. Venetia was curled on her side and facing the window. It took me a moment to realise that she was crying. She was doing it so quietly that at first I could hardly hear her. Her eyes were open and they glistened as though newly varnished.

I was worried about the girl. She was too young to drink. To make matters worse, she drank until she could drink no more. I'd seen direct evidence of this.

Her people had left her to spend most of the Easter holidays at school with no one to check her movements. A day or two before my death, I'd been on my way to the Gothick Walk. Not far from the entrance into Bleeding Yew Wood, there was an ancient oak, still living but hollow inside. I had found her inside it, completely squiffy on sherry with the empty bottle lying uncorked on her lap. I shook her awake and somehow got her back to school without anyone seeing us.

I'd threatened to tell PM about the episode, which in theory would have led to Venetia's expulsion. To my surprise, the prospect had seemed to terrify her. Perhaps Monkshill was preferable to any available alternatives. I'd let the threat linger in her mind, hoping it would be enough to restrain her in future.

Clearly it hadn't been enough. But for the first time it occurred to me that the threat might have had another consequence: Venetia was such a wild, impetuous child she might have taken advantage of a heaven-sent chance to push me off the Maiden's Leap.

Now here she was, tipsy and crying. I waited beside her until her eyes closed and her breathing steadied.

In the hall, there was a light under the study door.

Since I had last been there, Runty had wrought a miracle

and erased all traces of the party. She had even lit a small fire, and its flames flickered over the hearthrug and threw a ruddy glow over the faces of the two women. The only other light came from the shaded standard lamp behind the desk.

PM was in her armchair with a cup of cocoa at her elbow. Runty was sitting on the floor at the headmistress's feet, leaning against her legs and cradling her cup. Her face looked softer and younger than usual. Neither of them seemed to feel the need to talk or even smoke.

Apart from the flames, the only moving thing in the room was PM's hand, which was stroking Runty's shoulder as you might stroke a cat on your lap — not consciously in order to please the animal, but automatically, because the cat was there, and that was what you did when the cat was on your lap.

Their closeness didn't come as a surprise to me. I had seen them together on another occasion when they must have thought they were quite alone. It had been during the Easter holidays, a few days before my death, when the school was almost empty. I suppose that was why they were careless.

They had been in the study one evening, and the door had been a few inches ajar. It was well after eleven o'clock. I was making my way across the hall to fetch some notes from the staffroom. I hadn't switched on the overhead lights because the glow from the study doorway was enough for me to see where I was going. I was wearing rubber-soled slippers that made no sound on the marble floor.

I didn't mean to snoop but, as I passed the door of the study, I'd glanced inside, and there they were, standing on the hearthrug with their arms around each other.

I saw them only for an instant, but it was enough. I hurried into the staffroom, making as little noise as I could. But the door creaked when I opened it, and the click of the light switch was a small explosion in the silence of the evening. A few seconds later I heard footsteps in the hall and Runty came into the room.

'I thought everyone was upstairs,' she said. 'I thought you might be a burglar.'

I held out my notes. 'Just fetching these.'

'You gave me quite a shock, you know. You shouldn't creep around like that. Especially at this time of night.'

'Sorry to disturb you.' I slid past her in the doorway. 'Good night.'

What I had glimpsed was unexpected but I wasn't at all shocked by it – given my own preferences, that would have been absurd and hypocritical. Perhaps, like myself, PM and Runty had always tended in that direction. Or the embrace might merely have been the physical manifestation of a warm but platonic friendship. There might even have been something maternal in PM's display of affection – Runty was just young enough to be her daughter.

In any case, I didn't know, and I really didn't want to know, how far their intimacy stretched. It was none of my business.

Except . . .

Now that I was dead, I couldn't help wondering whether that episode could have given one or both of them a motive for my murder. What if they were afraid that I might spread a rumour that the headmistress was in a lesbian relationship with the school matron? No school could survive that sort of scandal. A word in the wrong ear could have meant social and financial ruin for both of them.

Absurd? Perhaps. But once that sort of fear got hold of a person, it didn't let go. And when you were terrified, you didn't always act rationally.

Seeing them now with their cocoa by the fire, I was envious of their closeness. I wished it could have been Enid and me. What I missed most about the loneliness of death was the warmth of companionship.

But there was no point in being mean-spirited. *Good luck to you*, I thought, *enjoy it while you can*; and I left them to each other.

21

The next morning, I came into school during assembly to find Maggie Squires standing in PM's place on the stairs and leading the morning prayers in a voice that was probably audible halfway down the drive. There was no sign of Runty either.

To everyone's relief, Maggie didn't come up with a homily after the prayers and the closing hymn, which meant that everyone had longer to prepare for morning school. I followed Sylvia and Prissy into a stone-flagged passage near the kitchen, not far from the former servants' hall.

Set against the wall was the bank of lockers reserved for Cavendish House. The girls were meant to use them only for their schoolbooks, though in practice they sometimes kept other items there, particularly sweets. In theory you could lock the doors, but half the locks were broken; and in any case their mechanisms were so simple that a single key could often open several doors.

Sylvia and Prissy rummaged in their lockers, finding what they needed for the morning's lessons. The School Certificate class had Shaw first thing, and he had set them a Latin prose for prep.

'I heard Muriel say she could hear PM groaning upstairs,' Sylvia said with ghoulish relish. 'She said it sounded like she was dying.'

'Perhaps she is,' Prissy said in a tone of scholarly speculation. 'When you think about it, everyone has to die sometime.'

Prissy pulled out her copy of *The Revised Latin Primer*, which had been retitled *The Revised Eating Primer* by a past owner. The movement dislodged a folded piece of paper from under the book. It fluttered clumsily to the floor like a bird with a broken wing. She bent to retrieve it. Typically, she banged her head on the open door as she straightened. She drew in her breath sharply but didn't cry out. Prissy was a clumsy child and she had learned to greet these mishaps with commendable stoicism; the poor kid had known worse, much worse.

'Anyway, what's wrong with her?' she said.

'Don't know. For all we know, she really is dying. And Runty too.'

'Gosh. I expect they'd have to close the school. But where would we all go? Would we all stay together?'

These were good questions but Sylvia didn't try to answer them. She had lost interest in the subject and was glancing through her prose. I watched her making a last-minute alteration, which as it happened changed a correct preposition to a wrong one.

Something about Prissy's stillness alerted me that all was not well. She was staring at the paper she had picked up. It had been torn from an exercise book. I looked over her shoulder and was horrified by what I saw. The letters, cut from a book, had been

175

pasted in a wobbly line in the middle of the page. This time they made three words.

I felt anger rising inside me like a tidal wave. For an instant it obliterated everything. I could have cheerfully murdered whoever had done this.

J – ew – GIRL – out.

Sylvia slammed her locker door. Prissy slipped the letter into the *Revised Eating Primer* and followed suit. They joined the stream of girls hurrying along the passage to the green baize door and the classrooms beyond.

Prissy didn't contribute much to her lesson with Shaw. For most of the time she sat there, looking stunned and paler than usual. Shaw glanced at her once or twice. Her prose was riddled with errors but he treated her gently. It irritated me that he was not only a good teacher but, for a man, quite sensitive. It made it harder to dislike him completely. Not that I'd given up trying.

'Drunk,' Mrs Broadwell said as if pronouncing a verdict from which there could be no appeal. 'You'd think they'd know better at their age, wouldn't you?'

'Is there a lot of extra work?'

'You bet your life there is. They've both been sick on the carpet, and they've both had the runs. Mrs Hitler's still got them. Four bottles! What can you expect?'

Mrs Crisp stared at the empty champagne bottles lined up like witnesses for the prosecution on the kitchen table. I wondered who had drunk the rest of the fourth bottle last night. Runty had sent Shaw packing before the washing up was done so it couldn't have been him. I'd put my money on Vera Hampson. Despite the pince-nez and the prim, high collars, she had a remarkable capacity for alcohol. Since my death, I had learned that she usually had a nightcap before doing her teeth. She kept a bottle of cherry brandy in her bedside cupboard for the purpose.

School had started. I had calmed down a little since I had seen the second poison pen letter to Prissy.

'It's not right,' Mrs Crisp said. 'They should be setting an example.'

'Mrs Hitler will need a change of sheets. Maybe more if it went through to the mattress. And then there's the other one's rug. Their bathroom will need a good going over as well. It's bloody everywhere. Not just the W.C.'

I had come into the kitchen to find out more about PM's mystery illness. Mrs Broadwell made it her business to be well-informed about such things. I soon learned that PM and Runty had been struck down by gastric pains during the night, leading to still ongoing bursts of vomiting and diarrhoea.

'Food poisoning,' Mrs Broadwell went on. 'That's what Madam said. You can tell that to the marines.' A note of menace entered her voice. 'Still, I can't sit around chatting all day. I've got work to do.'

Mrs Crisp took the hint and picked up her bucket and mop. I followed her upstairs. When I was alive, I had never been inside these two bedrooms, which meant that I could only accompany her as far as the landing.

She knocked on the door of PM's room and went inside. The room was suffused with crepuscular gloom. I glimpsed a bed with a huddled shape under the quilt and a chamber pot beside it on the floor. Mrs Crisp wrinkled her nose, presumably because of the smell, and closed the door in my face.

Later that morning, a van sputtered up the drive and parked in the kitchen yard. I didn't recognise the vehicle so I went to see why it was there. (Nosy? Yes. Given my limited range of options, any novelty had its charm for me.) The van was an Austin Seven which at some point in its life had been requisitioned for the war effort. It was painted a drab olive-green and had the letters HG stencilled on the side.

Today, however, it was not on Home Guard duties. A wizened man in patched moleskin trousers climbed stiffly from the driver's seat and opened the back doors.

Mrs Broadwell emerged from the house. 'What's this then?'

'Miss Venetia's bike. They sent it over from Fontenoy.'

She pointed at the door of the former dairy. 'You'd better put it in there with the others.'

'Any chance of a cup of tea?'

Mrs Broadwell looked at him more closely and seemed to like what she saw. *Whoever said that women were mysterious creatures was quite right; and each of them is a different mystery from the others. I should know.* She jerked her head towards the kitchen. 'In there.'

During second lesson, there were increasing sounds of merriment behind the closed door of the second form classroom. With PM and Runty confined to bed, there was no one to intervene. Attracted by the noise, I went to see what was happening.

Miss Covey was standing at the blackboard, her back to the class. Behind her, the girls were chatting and giggling. Two of them were trying to pull each other's pigtails in the corner.

As I came in, Miss Covey finished writing and turned to peer at the children. 'Now, girls. Write this down in your exercise books. *The black lamb has lost his mother, who is standing near the hedge.* Who can tell me which words in the sentence are the subject and which are the predicate?'

Rosemary Lawson-Smith raised her hand. She was sitting

with her cronies, who giggled in anticipation of amusement to come. 'Please, Miss Covey, I can't read your writing. Does it say brother or mother?'

'Mother, dear. Mother.'

'Mother dear, mother dear, mother dear' was repeated in a series of whispers along the back rows of desks, leading to snorts of ill-concealed laughter.

'Please, miss, can "the" be the subject,' Rosemary asked, 'or is it the president?'

This time the giggles showed signs of breaking into laughter, as a wave breaks into foam.

'No, no – it's *predicate*, not president.'

'Oh I see. So "the" is the predicate.'

'Not exactly. "The" is an article. A definite article.'

Rosemary frowned. 'Definitely an article? But I thought an article was a thing. Or something in a magazine.'

At this point, the girl next to her jogged Rosemary's inkwell. A spray of drops spread across the floorboards next to the desk they shared. This gave an excuse for most of the class to leap to their feet under the pretence of helping to clear up the mess. Somehow, in the confusion, several books fell to the floor.

It was only then that I saw Stephen. He was sitting in a corner at the back. A space had been cleared around his desk as though he might be infectious. He was a year or two older than the second formers but PM had decreed that he was 'backward', which was why he was here and not in a higher class. Probably his presence was the reason that the girls were being even sillier than usual. Everyone liked an audience.

He was ignoring them all. He had written down Miss Covey's sentence in his exercise book. Now he was sitting there, his face empty of emotion or interest, and sharpening his pencil with his penknife. For the first time I noticed his eyes, which were very pale, neither blue nor grey. He was frowning slightly, as if at an intractable problem that no one else could see.

I wondered what he was thinking. Monkshill Park wasn't much of a school, but these silly, privileged girls were frittering away the few scraps of education it had to offer. It wouldn't matter for most of them, or they thought it wouldn't, because they were being bred for the marriage market.

But it did matter for Stephen. If I'd been able to take him to meet the headmaster of the local grammar school, his entire life might have changed. But death had put paid to that, as to so much else.

His plight frustrated me. There was nothing sadder than wasted intelligence. He was a bright boy who deserved to make something of himself. But he wouldn't in this place. He'd be better off reading detective stories than going to Miss Covey's English Grammar class. After all, there are worse places to find an education than crime fiction.

The door opened. Maggie Squires appeared in the doorway and glared impartially at everyone. The noise stopped as though someone had flipped a switch. The girls slid back to their desks as unobtrusively as they could. Stephen slipped the penknife under his exercise book.

'*The* is called a definite article,' Miss Covey said faintly. 'And *a* is known as the indefinite article.'

After Maggie Squires had restored order, I left Miss Covey to it. Enid had a free period before break. I was just in time to see her coming out of the staffroom.

She stood in the hall, her head cocked, listening. After a moment she tapped on the door of PM's study. There was no answer – Enid must have known there wouldn't be, because both PM and Runty were ill upstairs. After a moment, she opened the door, which wasn't locked.

Someone had already been in, because the curtains were drawn back. The ashes from last night had been tidied from the hearth and a fire laid in its place. Enid walked purposefully behind the desk and tried the drawers, one by one. Some of them were unlocked, but their contents were innocuous – stationery, copies of the prospectus, even a hot-water bottle.

To be honest, her behaviour surprised me – she was usually such a law-abiding woman, not given to dramatic transgressions. But was that actually true? I remembered how she had told me she loved me out of the blue, and what we had done next, which she had wanted as much as I had. If that wasn't a dramatic transgression in Monkshill terms, I don't know what was.

When Enid had exhausted the possibilities of the desk, she tried the door of the closet. It was locked. She muttered something under her breath and left the room. In the hall, she paused, looking up the stairs. The rattle of a bucket came from above. She glanced at her watch and walked briskly upstairs, despite the fact that the main staircase was reserved for the exclusive use of PM and Runty.

I followed, admiring her shapely calves with a melancholy, almost aesthetic interest. Mrs Crisp was on the landing, surrounded by a litter of cleaning equipment. She turned her head at the sound of footsteps.

'How are the invalids, Mrs Crisp?' Enid said in a low voice.

'Not so good,' Mrs Crisp whispered furtively. 'Still bringing stuff up. Or out the other end.'

'Better out than in, perhaps. You can't carry all that at once. Let me give you a hand.'

Mrs Crisp looked startled. Enid picked up the bucket, the mop, and the dustpans. Mrs Crisp was left with a basket containing dirty bedclothes and towels. Enid made some inane remarks about the weather as they walked along the back landing towards the servants' stairs.

'Oh – by the way,' she said as they clattered down the first flight, in a tone that was meant to be casual, 'do you know when you and Mrs Broadwell will sort out Miss Warnock's room?'

'No, miss.'

'I don't suppose you have the key?'

'Miss Runciman keeps all the keys.'

'Of course she does. I must ask her when she's better. The thing is, I lent Miss Warnock one or two books, and I'd like to get them back before the room's cleared. Otherwise I'm afraid I'll lose them. And I've got one of hers to give back as well.'

It was a flimsy excuse. Mrs Crisp said nothing. They reached the door at the bottom of the stairs.

'In fact, would you be a dear and let me know when you do the room – and then I can pop in and get them without bothering Miss Runciman?' Enid gave a most uncharacteristic laugh, almost a titter. 'To be honest, she's not best pleased with me at present, and I'd rather not trouble her if I can help it.'

'Yes, miss.'

It was impossible to tell whether Mrs Crisp had agreed to help Enid or whether she was merely acknowledging that she had heard what she said. The story seemed transparently false to me, but then I knew what Enid was up to, and Mrs Crisp didn't.

Mrs Crisp shouldered open the kitchen door and led the way inside. A burst of laughter greeted them. Mrs Broadwell was entertaining the man from Fontenoy Court – though perhaps it was the other way around: judging by the few words I overheard, he was regaling her with an anecdote about his employers.

Mrs Broadwell swung around to look at the newcomers. The smile left her face. 'You've changed the beds and done the bathroom?'

Mrs Crisp nodded.

Enid put down her burdens.

Mrs Broadwell's eyes flicked towards her. 'Thank you. Very kind of you, I'm sure.' She never liked to see a teacher in her kitchen. She turned back to Mrs Crisp. 'You'd better do the study next, as it's empty. Windows need cleaning.'

'It's my half-day . . . and I was hoping to leave a little early this morning. Just quarter of an hour – I'll make it up on Monday.'

Mrs Broadwell stared at her, savouring her power. 'Why?'

'I want to catch the bus to Gloucester. I need a few things.'

Ah, I thought. The errand for Venetia.

There was a pause. Just long enough to make Mrs Crisp feel uneasy. Until my death, I hadn't realised how the exercise of power ran like a dark vein through every relationship at Monkshill. In that respect there was no difference between the adults and the girls. Where there was power, there tended to be cruelty, often all the nastier when it was subtle; it left no visible bruises but festered in the mind, in the heart and in the memory.

'I suppose so,' Mrs Broadwell said at last, heaving a sigh and glancing at her guest, inviting him to sympathise with the crosses she had to bear. 'But I hope you won't make a habit of it.'

'I'll say goodbye then,' Enid said brightly. She had been ignored in all this.

The two women mumbled something in response but neither of them looked at her. The man took no notice at all.

The bell rang for morning break. Enid went out into the

hall, passing Venetia on the way, and followed Shaw into the staffroom. A tide of chattering girls flowed towards their lockers and their house rooms. Among them were Prissy and Sylvia.

'Sylvie – slow down. Something's happened.'

'What?'

'Not here . . .' Prissy hissed. 'It's secret.'

Sylvia allowed Prissy to steer her into an alcove where a statue had once stood. 'What is it?'

'I've had a letter,' Prissy whispered. 'A poison pen letter.'

22

After lunch, Maggie Squires caught Venetia in the act of taking her bicycle for an illicit spin. Venetia tried to bluff it out by saying that she had special permission from the headmistress on the grounds of health, but Maggie was having none of that.

In the absence of PM and Runty, Maggie was in charge, and she was clearly enjoying the experience. She gave Venetia a hundred lines – *I must ask permission each time I want to use my bicycle* – to be completed by Sunday teatime, and ordered her to join the Botany Society's outing that afternoon.

'That way we can keep you out of mischief for an hour or two,' Maggie said, which as it turned out was overoptimistic.

After lunch, the Botany Society assembled in the hall. They were going to Home Farm again. The girls fell into several camps – those press-ganged as a punishment; those who liked the walk as something to do; the Twisden twins, in a special category of their own, each of whom recorded their finds in a notebook and competed with each other to see who found more specimens; and those like Prissy, who went because they wanted to be with someone.

I fell into that group too. To my dismay, so did Shaw. When Enid told him what she was doing that afternoon, he said casually that he fancied a stroll, and would she mind if he came too?

Off they went down the south drive, and I floated along with them, sampling the conversations. Several girls were taking the opportunity to discuss which film star Mr Shaw most resembled. It seemed to be a tie between Robert Donat and Cary Grant, with Laurence Olivier winning a creditable third place. Wishful thinking. To my mind he had a closer resemblance to a particularly vicious Jack Russell that my grandmother used to have. But I admit I was prejudiced.

In the event I had no need to worry about Shaw murmuring sweet nothings to Enid. He was monopolised by two of the younger girls, who wanted to interrogate him about his alleged career as a spy. Meanwhile Muriel Fisher accosted Enid and engaged her in earnest conversation about the historical background of the Old Testament.

Venetia slouched along by herself, talking to nobody. In front of her, Prissy was whispering to Sylvia.

'. . . but what should we do?' she was saying. 'Do you think it's the same person?'

'The same that made Warnie . . . disappear?'

'And did the mouse. Don't forget the mouse.'

Sylvia grimaced. 'I don't *know*. I just don't know.'

'And the letter . . .'

'That was beastly,' Sylvia said. 'You should show it to someone. To PM.'

'No,' Prissy said, colouring. 'Definitely not her. Or Runty.'

Prissy was many things, but she wasn't stupid.

They walked in silence for the rest of the way. Home Farm was bordered by a small river, and the Botany Society was going to look for wild flowers in the water meadows that bordered it. On the way, they passed a field containing cows. There was a bull among them. Enid glanced in its direction and began to walk faster.

'Come on, girls,' she called. 'Don't dawdle.'

Venetia touched Sylvia's arm. 'Look at that.' She nodded towards the bull, which was in the act of mounting a cow.

'What's it doing?' Sylvia said, turning to watch. 'Are they fighting? Why's the big one being such a bully?'

Prissy slowed down because Sylvia had. The cow was staggering under the weight of the bull. The three girls stared.

'What's that thing it's got underneath?' Prissy asked. 'Is it ill or something?'

'No – it's just doing it to the cow,' Venetia said. 'That's how they do it.'

'Do what?'

'Make babies. Calves.'

Prissy made a face and looked away. The bull withdrew. The cow wandered a few paces away and took a mouthful of grass.

'It's awfully big,' Sylvia said faintly. 'That thing it's got. How do you think it can squeeze inside?'

'Men's go like that too,' Venetia said. 'Not quite as big, of course, as they're smaller than bulls. And when they're not doing it, their thing goes soft and little and flabby.' She wrinkled her nose. 'They look like uncooked sausages normally. But sometimes they get big and hard and stiff and sort of stand up. That's when men do it to ladies like that bull did. Or ladies do things to their things.'

'It's not true,' Sylvia said. 'You're making it up. It's disgusting.'

'I'm not making it up. You don't know anything, do you? And I bet you didn't know that sometimes ladies put men's things in their mouths.'

'Ugh,' Sylvia said. 'That's *horrible*. Stop it.'

Prissy's face was white. 'I don't believe you. It can't be true. You're lying.'

'No one cares what you think,' Venetia said in a voice like the flick of a whip. 'So you might as well shut up.'

After the girls' tea that evening, Maggie Squires reported to the rest of the staff that PM was still poorly, but a little better than she had been. Runty was much improved, however, and hoped to come downstairs tomorrow morning. The news was greeted with a marked lack of enthusiasm.

I went down to East Cottage. Shaw was at work on his book again.

> . . . jolly rotten,' Roddy said. 'I'm beginning to wonder if Uncle wasn't in his right mind when he signed it.'
>
> Cynthia shook her head. 'We've no grounds to contest the will. Mr Covey made that quite clear.'
>
> 'It's so unfair. I've a good mind to get a second opinion. I was counting on that blasted money. I've had a run of bad luck lately.'
>
> 'Not the horses again? Oh, Rod – why haven't you asked Enid about Tosser yet?

My words rattled across the page. Shaw slammed the carriage return. *Ping!* His hands dropped away from the typewriter. He raised his head, turning it to his right. I had the odd sensation that he was looking straight at me.

'You're back,' he said to the empty air. 'If it's any of your damned business, I haven't asked her because I haven't had an opportunity. Maybe tomorrow. We're going for a walk.' He hesitated, and I sensed his anxiety. 'Can you hear me speak?' He waited a moment, then: 'Anyway, who are you? You're not inside my head, are you? You're outside. Are you . . . some sort of ghost?'

I couldn't answer unless he went back to his wretched story. He looked away, his hand reaching towards his cigarettes.

Before he could pick them up, there was a knock at the door. He leapt to his feet as if he really had seen a ghost, as if I had suddenly materialised in front of him. He snatched the page from the typewriter, put it with the others and turned the whole pile of paper facedown. He took a deep breath and opened the door.

Tosser was standing outside with a rabbit dangling from his hand.

'I don't think we have anything to say to each other,' Shaw said stiffly.

Tosser sniffed. 'I got something to say to you.'

'Your behaviour to Miss Covey the other day was intolerable. She's told Miss Pryce-Morgan what happened, and I'm sure you'll be hearing more about this. And I'll be more than happy to back Miss Covey up.'

'I saw you,' Tosser said. 'And I saw your posh bike with them green saddlebags.'

'So?'

'Back in *March*.'

'Nonsense.'

'And you was talking to—'

'Listen,' Shaw interrupted. 'All right. I don't want to be hasty about Miss Covey. There's . . . there's two sides to every argument, and I'm sure we can sort this one out to everyone's satisfaction.'

Tosser sucked his teeth. He held out the rabbit. 'Thought you might like this. Fresh as you like – snared it last night.'

Shaw looked uncertainly at it. 'Well, I suppose . . .'

'I'll do it in a nice little stew for you. Very tasty. And it'll only cost you twelve shillings. Now I call that a bargain, eh?'

After Tosser left, Shaw abandoned his detective story and got out the whisky. He was going to need another bottle soon. Tosser had insisted on payment in advance for the rabbit, which would probably turn out to be inedible if he bothered to cook it. They both knew that twelve shillings was a ridiculous price to pay, four times the price of the rabbit that had greeted Shaw on his arrival a week ago.

I went back to the school. Only a week since Shaw came, and yet so much had happened in that time. Most of the ingredients were already at Monkshill wrapped up and ready like a firework: and then he had arrived with the box of matches and lit the touchpaper.

Tosser had said he had seen Shaw in *March* – in other words, weeks before I was killed, several weeks before PM could have started her search to find a temporary replacement for me. When he was interrupted, he had been about to mention the name of the person Shaw had been talking to.

My mind scurried to and fro, trying to make sense of it, trying to work out the implications. I had the frustrating feeling that if only I could look at it from the right angle, I should be able to understand everything.

I went into the house and up to the second floor. Enid was writing to her friend in Germany again. She posted a letter almost every week, writing a paragraph here and the paragraph there when she had the time. They showed a different side of Enid from the one I had known – jokey, satirical and brittle; a side I had never known in life.

> . . . on Christian name terms – he's Alec – and (don't laugh) he says he's writing a detective novel. I don't think he's got very far with it yet. I was right about the army, by the way. He was invalided out in '42, and then went back to schoolmastering. But for some reason the girls all think he's a retired spy! They say he looks like a cross between Robert Donat and Cary Grant! (I don't agree!)

I was glad about that, but less glad that Enid was filling so much of her letter with news of Shaw. Particularly now. When it came down to it, what did I really know about his past? That story in *The Times* was enough to worry anyone. And now this other thing. If he had paid a clandestine visit in March, wasn't it possible that he had paid another one in April?

Someone had killed me in April.

Enid added another light-hearted paragraph about Lady Susan's visit and the effects of the champagne on everyone. She put the letter away in her writing case. The case had several pockets – for your writing pad, stamps, envelopes and so on. What I hadn't realised until now was that it also had a compartment tucked in the lining. It wasn't exactly secret but it wasn't obvious either. She slid her fingers into it and extracted a letter, turning away to read it by the light of the lamp.

She hunched over sheets of paper, as if hiding them away from the world. I didn't recognise the handwriting. But that was all I could find out about it. I couldn't read a word of it – the angle was wrong, and her body blocked it from me.

But my jealous heart told me what it was. A love letter from the boyfriend who had given her that lock of hair. She must have asked for the hair – it wasn't the sort of thing a man would offer of his own accord. Perhaps he was going on active service. Perhaps he was now dead.

What did that matter? The thing that hurt me was that Enid cared for him now I was dead, and she must have cared for him when I was alive.

Her shoulders quivered. She took a deep, ragged breath. She began to cry softly.

I couldn't bear it any more. I went away.

I prowled through the dormitories in search of distraction. Most girls were asleep by now, but not all. Two or three were reading under the bedclothes, the glow of their torches oozing into the pale darkness of a summer night. Some of the seniors in Howard were heating a tin of baked beans over a candle, while giggling and gossiping in whispers. I heard Shaw's name, accompanied by smothered laughter, and I moved on at once. I'd had enough of Shaw for one evening.

In Birch, everyone was asleep. Sylvia hadn't left her exercise book where I could see it. But there was a restless muttering near the window, the words indistinct. Venetia was talking in her sleep. I drew closer.

'Please, Mummy,' she whimpered. 'I don't want to. No, no. *Please.*'

Oh for Christ's sake, I thought.

23

On Sunday morning, I saw the Bear again, and this time by daylight. To be strictly accurate, I saw only part of him, for he was screened by a pair of yew trees. But I saw enough to recognise the bulky silhouette I had glimpsed during the flare of a match on Tuesday night.

It was early, just after dawn. He was on the Gothick Path beyond the Monks' Arches, a few yards further on from where I had seen him last time. He wore a heavy, dun-coloured overcoat or perhaps cloak, together with a beret crammed low over his skull.

I had only just come to myself and my reactions were slower than they might have been. By the time I followed him, he was gone. All I knew was that he wasn't on the path any longer. He must have found cover in the sloping woodland to the left. I had never explored that area in life, which meant of course that I was unable to go there now.

I wondered whether he had been coming back from spending the night with his mother in the relative comfort of North Lodge. What did he miss most about the life he had lost when he walked out of his barracks and never came back? Sleeping in a bed? Warmth? Dry clothes? Hot food? The society of other people?

If he was the one who killed me, I found it strangely difficult to feel angry with him. In his place I might well have killed me too.

At school, Miss Pryce-Morgan was still confined to her bedroom but Runty had come downstairs. She looked paler than usual. Her movements were slow and careful as if she was fearful she might break something.

PM, she said, was out of the woods, but Runty judged it wise to keep her in bed for another day. After all, the headmistress was not as young as she had been. While she was convalescing she would relay her commands through Runty.

'While the cat's away,' Vera Hampson murmured to Enid, 'the big bad rat can have it all her own way.'

It wasn't particularly funny but Enid giggled and so in my own way did I.

Runty was well enough to inspect the school before it marched off to church. She herself stayed in the house. The place was empty apart from PM in bed upstairs and Mrs Broadwell and Stephen, who were either in the kitchen or in their own quarters.

Runty went into PM's closet, opened the safe and removed a bunch of labelled keys. She relocked the safe and the closet, and went upstairs, pausing four times on the way to get her breath back.

In her terms, this was an opportunity not to be ignored, despite her convalescent condition. She had almost the whole house to herself. On the second-floor landing, she went from one room to another. She opened drawers and pried in cupboards. She found Vera Hampson's cherry brandy and Little Covey's *Imitation of Christ*. She read Enid's letter to her friend and looked in her underwear drawer to see if anything was hidden there.

It shouldn't have come as a surprise to me but it did. After all, I had known for months that Runty pried. I knew that she was obsessively determined to control her little world at Monkshill Park. But it was quite another thing to see her at work, picking her way among other people's possessions with the unhurried precision of an experienced burglar.

Last of all, she came to the room that had been mine. No one had packed my things yet. Though she must have seen them all before, she looked at the books on my shelves and examined the folder of lesson notes on the table as if making sure that they were still as she had left them. She opened the wardrobe. Lips pursed, she rubbed between finger and thumb the material of a pre-war silk dress that I had never worn at school.

Then she surprised me. She took the dress from the wardrobe and removed it from the hanger. She held it against her body, and turned to face the long mirror inside the wardrobe door. There was something practised about her movements, as if it wasn't the first time she had done this.

She swayed from side to side, and the material rippled around her, a cloud of soft blue and soft orange. It lent a spurious elegance even to Runty's sturdy little body, and it was also a glimpse of an unexpected weakness, a yearning for something soft and feminine.

She smoothed the silk over her breast. For an instant I feared that she would go the whole hog and try on the dress. At that moment, the wardrobe door began to close of its own volition,

195

a habit it had acquired with age and decrepitude. She moved sideways, trying to preserve her reflection in the mirror, which by an unlucky chance brought her onto the rug in front of the washstand. The floor creaked.

The sound distracted her. It was enough to break the spell that the rippling silk had cast. She shook herself like a wet dog, as though shaking the enchantment away. She put the dress on its hanger and returned it to the wardrobe.

As she moved away, the floor creaked again. Once again, Runty had managed to tread on the site of the botched repair to the floorboard. To her credit, she took her housekeeping responsibilities seriously. She lifted a flap of the rug and exposed the source of the creak. She probed the inadequate pine insertion with the toe of her immaculately polished brogue. The board wobbled slightly under her touch and creaked again.

By this time, I was cursing myself for failing to find a more secure hiding place for our valuables. Frowning, Runty lowered herself to her knees and examined the board more closely. She hooked a couple of fingers underneath one end of the insertion, and lifted the whole thing out. She peered into the cavity as far as she could. She sniffed. I held my breath (a figure of speech, I know, but the dead must use the language of the living) in case she produced a torch from somewhere and looked further between the joists.

But all she did was click her tongue against the roof of her mouth. She replaced the board, stood up and folded the rug back to its original position. She took her notebook and pencil and jotted down a few words. I was instantly at her shoulder to read them.

Replace board in Warnock's room? Rot? Def. some woodworm.

She put away the notebook and left the room, locking the door behind her. I didn't move. I was negotiating with a God in whose existence I did not believe.

Here's what I propose, I said to him, her, it, whatever pronoun they preferred. *If I stop making a fuss, if I stop trying to find my murderer, if I promise to believe in you, will you do this for me, please: let Enid get hold of our things under the floorboard first, and let her somehow be happy as well?*

Well, what do you think? Is it a bargain?

At one thirty, Mrs Broadwell emerged from her kitchen and sought out Miss Runciman. She found her in the former servants' hall where the girls of Cavendish House had just rounded off their lunch with a dish of tepid frogspawn and cat sick, which was the school's name for tapioca and custard. Most girls had finished, and had been allowed to leave, but not all. Runty was standing over Prissy Knecht and berating her for trying to hide some of her serving under the spoon.

'You won't want to hear this,' Mrs Broadwell said to her, accurately as it turned out, 'but there's no hot water.'

'Why ever not?'

'Boiler's out. I went and had a look. It wasn't made up this morning. No wonder it's out.'

'Well, send someone to find Tosser,' Runty said irritably. 'Tell him to come and light it at once. And I'll want to see him afterwards. What does he think he's playing at?'

Prissy took advantage of the diversion by scooping up a spoonful of tapioca and tossing it under the table in the general direction of Rosemary's Sunday shoes. She missed, and it landed in clear sight on the other side of the table.

197

'How should I know?' Mrs Broadwell said with a touch of belligerence. 'I'm not his keeper, am I? Anyway, Stephen went over this morning, but he's not answering the door. Maybe he's down the pub. Or off somewhere.'

'There must be someone else who can light the boiler.'

'Not on a Sunday. Besides, it's a brute, that thing. Needs careful handling. All them dials and things. Tosser says if you get it wrong, the tank explodes.'

'Nonsense,' Miss Runciman said, without a great deal of conviction. 'He's trying to frighten you. Well, we'll just have to find him. Have Stephen run over to the village and see if—'

'Stephen ain't here. He's gone off somewhere.'

'It's not a bad afternoon. I'd walk over there myself but I'm still a little off colour . . . Perhaps you might like a—'

'It's a half-day.' Mrs Broadwell's tone left no room for hope. 'Anyway, it's not my job, is it?'

'I suppose not,' Miss Runciman said listlessly. If she had been her usual self, she would have fought her corner more vigorously. 'I suppose we shall just have to grin and bear it until that man can be found.'

Mrs Broadwell nodded and made for the door. The frogspawn defaulters had taken advantage of the diversion and slipped away, leaving little mounds of tapioca underneath the tables for the rodents to devour at their leisure. On the way she trod in Prissy's spoonful of tapioca.

Rosemary was by the door, smiling in the unpleasant way she had.

'What's so funny then?' Mrs Broadwell demanded.

Rosemary sniggered. 'Nothing.' But her eyes gave the game away by dropping down to the cook's tapioca-fringed shoe.

Mrs Broadwell bent down and hissed in Rosemary's ear:

'You're a horrid little squirt, aren't you? Your ma should have strangled you at birth.'

'I'll tell Miss Runciman you said that.'

'Just you try, young lady. Who's she going to believe? You or me?'

While I was waiting for Enid and Shaw to have their walk to Bleeding Yew Wood, I noticed Sylvia sneaking into the old stables. I went over there and found her in the tack room discussing the novels of Margery Allingham with Stephen.

'The trouble is, most of them are not really detective stories,' Sylvia was saying. 'They're sort of mysteries. Adventures. Not like Sayers' books. But they are good. So the library still doesn't have *Busman's Honeymoon*?'

'I couldn't find it,' Stephen said, beginning to sound aggrieved. 'I did look yesterday. Maybe the library doesn't have it. Anyhow, I got you this instead, and I thought you'd be *pleased*.'

'Oh I am,' Sylvia said quickly, turning the book over in her hands. It was *The Case of the Late Pig*. 'And it's one I haven't read, so thanks awfully . . . funny title, isn't it?'

'Have you got one for me?' Stephen demanded.

She took a grubby paperback from her pocket and held it out to him. It was a Christie novel, *The Mysterious Affair at Styles*. 'You'll like it. It's a Poirot. The first one ever.'

But Stephen wasn't listening. He was staring out of the unglazed window. 'Look,' he said.

I looked too. Shaw and Enid were walking towards the obelisk.

'Where are they off to?' Sylvia said.

Stephen shrugged. 'Maybe they're sweet on one another.' He blushed and looked away.

Sylvia gave the suggestion serious consideration. 'You could be right. They spend a lot of time talking to each other, and sometimes their heads are really close together. But maybe they're just going for a walk. After all, there's not much else to do on Sunday afternoons.'

Stephen said, 'We could follow them.' His casual tone didn't deceive me. 'If you like.'

'All right.' Sylvia was pretending to be casual too. 'If you want.'

There was nothing surreptitious about Enid and Shaw. They walked along the north drive as if they had a perfect right to be together and they didn't care who saw them. Sylvia and Stephen followed at a distance, moving separately and trying without much success to cling to the available cover.

As for me, I accompanied them all, slipping from one person to another. As far as I knew, this would be the first time that anyone apart from the Bear and perhaps Tosser had been to Bleeding Yew Wood since my death. I nursed a foolish hope that they would explore areas that were inaccessible to me and come across some clue, some scrap of evidence that I had been in the wood on my last living day. If only they could find something, anything, that would tell Enid that I hadn't abandoned her of my own free will.

The two adults turned off the drive and worked their way down to the fence.

'I think they want to get into the wood,' Stephen whispered.

'Why?' Sylvia said.

'How do I know?'

'Warnie was researching its history. Archie might be carrying on with it.'

I drew closer to Enid and Shaw.

'When was that put up?' he was saying.

'The fence? A few years ago. I think the army did it when they were here.'

'Why?'

'Heaven knows. I expect they were practising something.'

Shaw grunted. 'Do you know what really annoys me about this blasted war? All the time and money spent on doing things that achieve nothing. It's such a waste.'

'Look – it's here,' Enid said. They both seemed relieved at the change of subject. 'See that yew? There's a way you can get in there. It's a bit of a scramble. Would that be OK for you?'

He gave her a puzzled look. 'Yes, of course. Oh – I see.' He patted his left leg. 'You mean because of this? No, it's fine. After the quacks had finished with me, I was almost as good as new, apart from the limp.'

'I'm glad,' she said. Then, after the slightest of pauses. 'How did it happen?'

'I was at Dieppe. Three Commando. I was hit on the landing craft, right at the start of the raid. Believe it or not, I've never even fired a bullet in anger. So all that training was in vain.'

'It must have been beastly. I'm so sorry.'

'Don't be.' He grinned at her. 'I'm still alive. That's what counts.'

I watched them push their way through the bushes and struggle under the fence. For a moment, Enid looked about her, trying to get her bearings. She saw the vestigial path and pointed it out to Shaw.

'Shall I lead the way?' he asked. 'Looks a bit of a tangle.'

Enid grinned at him. 'I'll go first – I know the way. And I'm not that fragile.'

I lingered, waiting for Stephen and Sylvia. A few minutes later, he scrambled through the bushes around the yew. 'There's a way under the fence,' he whispered to her. 'I'm going after them. Coming?'

Sylvia hesitated. 'I'd better not. I don't want to get messed up.' She was still in her slime-green Sunday dress, and there would be trouble if it had mud stains or tears. 'Besides ... it's ... sort of snooping, isn't it?'

'Suit yourself. I'm going anyway. It's what detectives have to do.'

He wriggled under the fence. Sylvia hesitated, perhaps wondering whether to follow. Then she turned and set off back to school.

I went into the wood. After a few yards, the track widened. It descended in a series of irregular zigzags to the Maiden's Leap. By the time I reached it, Stephen had vanished. Enid and Shaw were standing in front of the bench. It was unsettling to see two living people in a place I'd come to think of as my own.

'Quite a view,' Shaw said, advancing to the low wall.

'Careful. It's a long way to fall.'

He peered over the edge. 'It certainly is. And those stones down there ...'

'According to Annabel, this is the Maiden's Leap,' Enid said. 'And if you look up there – see those projecting rocks? – that's the Monks' Arches. The path goes underneath.'

'And the Gothick Walk goes on from there?'

'Yes – and the other way too, though that's even more overgrown. But this is the only part I've seen. Annabel went the whole length of the path, but she said it was awfully hard going and she couldn't find any trace of at least half the original features.'

'What an odd idea it is – spending your spare cash on

ridiculous ornamental flourishes that hardly anyone will ever see. Even in their prime.'

'I suppose it's no odder than having a plaster gnome in your back garden. They were just thinking on a grander scale.'

Shaw laughed. He patted his pockets and found his cigarettes. 'Smoke?'

They sat down on the stone bench and smoked for a moment in a regrettably comfortable silence. Enid was becoming easier in his company, even when they were alone, which meant she was more assertive with him than she had been at first.

'Well?' she said at last. 'Will it be any use?'

'What?'

'For your book. Are you going to have a murder here?'

He laughed. 'I can't think why not. It's a jolly good spot for it. And there's no reason why I shouldn't have a Gothick Walk of my own.'

'Do you know who you're going to kill?'

'I've already poisoned one chap – a peer of the realm, no less. But any decent detective novel needs at least two murders, so I'll have to murder someone else.' He squinted at her through the smoke. 'Someone like Tosser perhaps.'

'There'd be worse choices,' Enid said.

'He was beastly to Miss Covey the other day. Really unpleasant.' He looked sharply at her. 'But is there something else about him?'

She looked at him for a moment. 'There's no reason you shouldn't know. At the end of last term, Annabel caught him watching the girls in the shower block. Peeping at them in the showers.'

'What happened?'

'She put the fear of God in him.' Enid smiled, and in my own

203

way so did I. 'She was good at that. She said if she caught him near the school or near the girls, she'd report him to the police and get him sacked. He'd probably lose his cottage as well. And she would have done too.'

'Annabel sounds rather formidable.'

'She has a softer side. So are you going to murder Tosser?'

'The ideal candidate.' Shaw ground out his cigarette and flicked the stub over the edge. 'I suppose I should be making notes.'

'What are you looking for?' Enid said.

'I'm not quite sure. Inspiration?'

Shaw strolled over to the parapet, choosing a spot where the railing had vanished completely. He knelt down and craned over the edge. 'I could push him over here.'

'Careful,' Enid said again.

'Hello,' he said. 'There's something down there. At the base of the wall.'

He stretched out his arm. On its outer side the wall was only about eighteen inches above the rock platform on which it was built. Enid stood up, as if worried about his safety. But he pulled back almost at once. He stood up and turned towards her. In his hand was a pencil, one of the plain, unpainted ones that were used at school.

'Do you think it belonged to your friend? It's not been there that long.'

'I – I suppose it might have done,' Enid said. 'I don't think anyone else comes here.'

'Hang on – there's a name on it.'

I knew what he was going to say next.

'*Rosemary LS.*'

'Rosemary Lawson-Smith,' Enid said. 'Horrid child.'

24

They didn't stay much longer in Bleeding Yew Wood. Enid was subdued, and Shaw seemed preoccupied. I suppose it was the discovery of the pencil. Until then there had almost been a holiday atmosphere about the outing. But now the fun had oozed away from their afternoon.

Enid must have realised that it was almost certainly me who had dropped the pencil, though she couldn't have known when.

I hadn't forgotten about Stephen. I spotted him peering at Enid and Shaw as they began to climb the path back to the fence. He had done a good job of concealing himself. He wasn't far away from the Maiden's Leap. He'd taken cover behind one of the large rocks that littered the ground above it. They didn't notice him – they were too busy watching where they put their feet on the path.

He was near enough to have heard at least some of their conversation. Which meant that he could have heard about Tosser's taste for naked schoolgirls, as well as Rosemary Lawson-Smith's pencil.

Enid scrambled beneath the fence, and Shaw followed. His

jacket caught on the lowest strand of barbed wire. Something ripped, and he swore under his breath.

He wriggled awkwardly out of the jacket and turned back to unhook it from the barbs. A piece of paper fell from the inside pocket, along with his wallet. Enid picked them up. She glanced automatically at the words typed on the paper.

Help me. Help me.
Maiden's Leap. Maiden's Leap.
Gothick Walk. Look there.
The rucksack, the exercise book.
Find the bleeding yew.
The yew.
ask Enid what Tosser did, and who told her

Underneath the list Shaw had written by hand the words I had dictated to him yesterday evening.

why haven't you asked Enid about Tosser yet

'What on . . .' She looked at him. 'I don't understand.'

He was examining the tear in his jacket. As she spoke, he glanced up and his eyes widened when he saw what was in her hand. 'Just a few notes for the book,' he said easily. 'About having a Gothick Walk and so on.'

'But how did you know about the yew?'

'What?'

'I didn't tell you there was a yew at the spot where you can get into the wood.'

He shrugged. To my admittedly prejudiced eyes he looked downright shifty. 'Just a coincidence, that's all,' he said. 'I

206

thought I might have corpse number three entangled in the branches of a yew tree growing out of the cliff. You know – make it more atmospheric.'

Enid brushed aside his explanation. 'And I definitely didn't mention that it was a bleeding yew.'

There was something relentlessly forensic about her in this mood. Shaw was quailing under her questioning.

'They're not *that* uncommon.'

She ignored that too. 'And what's all this about asking me what Tosser did?' she went on. 'That's exactly what you did just now, isn't it? A rucksack and an exercise book? How do they come into it?'

He shuffled his feet, like a naughty schoolboy caught out in a lie. 'Listen, I know it seems odd, but honestly I—'

'What are you? Some sort of detective?'

'No – of course not.'

'This bit' – she tapped the paper – '*Why haven't you asked Enid about Tosser yet.* That's what I really don't understand.'

'I was just talking to myself, I'm afraid,' Shaw said. 'Bad habit. I told you I was thinking of inventing a Tosser character and having him as a victim. I was reminding myself to research his background, what he used to do – all that sort of thing. So I was going to ask you about him.'

His explanation sounded almost plausible – certainly more plausible than the truth would have been.

Enid looked gravely at him. 'I see.' She paused and then added, 'In that case I'm sorry I got the wrong end of the stick.' But she didn't sound sorry.

'Easily done,' Shaw said magnanimously. 'I'd have done the same myself.'

He put on his jacket, and she handed him the paper. They

walked back to the obelisk, keeping their distance from each other. There was no sign of Stephen. He must be still in the wood, too far away to have heard this latest exchange.

'Shall we chance Matron's disapproval and have a cup of tea in the staffroom?' Shaw suggested.

'I'd better not,' Enid said without looking at him. 'I've some work to do.'

At the obelisk, however, she stopped and turned towards him. 'I'm sorry but I still don't understand. That first line. *Help me. Help me.* It's as if someone's talking to you. Is someone coming into your cottage and leaving you typed messages? Was someone asking for help, someone real?'

'Don't be absurd.' He hesitated. Enid was still looking at him, waiting for more. 'It's just how writers work,' he went on. 'We're a strange breed, eh?'

'Evidently,' she said.

Without another word she set off towards the school. He stared after her for a moment and then walked away in the direction of East Cottage.

I looked about me. There was still no sign of Stephen. I lingered by the obelisk, wondering whether to follow Shaw or Enid or neither of them.

A movement caught my eye. Venetia Canford was running towards the school from the direction of the lake.

I don't think I'd ever seen her run before. Her usual mode of locomotion was a languid saunter. She tended to treat anything that smacked of exercise as beneath contempt. She reached the side door a couple of minutes before Enid and vanished inside the house.

Coming back from a smoke, I guessed, probably at the lake. Perhaps she had met Mrs Crisp at the boathouse with the cigarettes from Gloucester and was in a hurry to hide her booty. On impulse I turned around and went up the drive towards North Lodge. I was just in time to see Mrs Crisp walking very quickly towards her garden gate. A moment later she had vanished into her cottage.

I felt smug. I'd had a theory. I'd tested it. And here was supporting evidence to confirm it.

Later that afternoon, I saw Stephen again. He left the kitchen yard and walked past the walled gardens and turned down towards East Cottage. He knocked on the door with a clenched fist. A moment later, Shaw opened it, pipe in hand.

'Yes – what is it? I'm busy.'

It was unusual for Shaw to show irritation. His cheeks were flushed, and I wondered if he had consoled himself with whisky for his unsatisfactory afternoon.

'Please, sir, Miss Runciman says would you come up to the house?'

'Why?'

Stephen shrugged. 'She says it's urgent.'

Shaw scowled. But he put on his jacket, smoothed his hair and walked up to the house with Stephen. Neither of them tried to make conversation.

Runty was waiting in the study, sitting behind the headmistress's desk. When he came in, the first thing she said was to make sure he closed the door. He slammed it shut. She raised her eyebrows but didn't comment.

'There's a problem,' she said. 'The boiler.'

'What about it?'

'It's gone out, so we've no hot water. That horrid little man's gone off somewhere and simply left it.'

'There're worse things in life than cold water. I suppose he'll turn up tomorrow morning with a hangover.'

'I wondered if perhaps you could . . .'

Shaw shook his head. 'These big boilers are awfully complicated. I wouldn't know where to start.'

It wasn't so much what they said that alerted me as the way they were saying it. They tended to speak warily to each other. But this was different. There was a sort of ease about their manner.

'Can't you at least try? There's no one else I can ask. Please.'

'Oh all right,' he said.

'Bless you. I'm sure you'll get it going. You'll need the key to the boiler room. I won't be a moment.'

Runty went into the closet. Shaw flung himself into an armchair and whistled tunelessly under his breath. A moment later she came out with the box of keys. She rummaged among them until she found the key for the boiler room. She slid it across the desk. 'You know where it is? Turn left out of the back door and there's another door down a flight of steps. If you need another pair of hands, you can always find Stephen.'

I followed Shaw to the kitchen yard. He unlocked the boiler room door and brushed the switch on the wall. The boiler itself was a black monster squatting on a brick plinth, with pipes sprouting from it.

The boiler heated the tanks that supplied the hot water for the whole house, and it required feeding with inordinate amounts of coke. Runty was always grumbling about the expense; she ferociously monitored the school's usage of hot water.

Shaw hung up his jacket on a nail behind the door. There was a scrape as he opened the door of the monster. He peered inside, then straightened and looked about him. He found kindling and a stack of old newspapers. He raked out the ashes and laid a fire. He found it easy enough to light the paper, but the flames went out before the kindling caught. He tried again, fiddling with levers that I assumed controlled the draught.

Despite his disclaimers, he seemed to know what he was doing. On his fourth try he managed to produce a sickly yellow flame, which he nourished with larger and larger pieces of kindling until it was hot enough to add pieces of coke.

At one point Stephen came to watch. He stood there for a moment, frowning slightly. Shaw, who had his back to the boy, wasn't aware he was there. After a moment, a noise from the house startled Stephen and he scuttled off like a frightened rabbit.

He was only just in time. There were brisk footsteps in the yard. Runty appeared at the top of the steps. 'Well done. I knew you'd do it.'

Shaw looked over his shoulder. His face was red and sweaty from the heat. 'Don't count your chickens. It'll probably go out in a moment. I've no idea what these gauges mean or how to adjust the air flow.'

'I expect you'll work it out.'

'I'm not making a habit of this,' he said sharply.

'Of course not.'

He nodded. 'As long as that's clear.'

'But if he doesn't turn up, will you come and do it in the morning? Please? Just in case. I promise I'll find someone else by tomorrow evening.'

'OK. But that's it. Understood?'

She smiled at him. 'Perfectly.'

He pointed upwards. 'By the way, how's her ladyship doing?'

'Much better, thank you. Weak as a kitten though. All being well, she'll come downstairs tomorrow.'

A door banged, and Mrs Broadwell emerged from the flat she shared with Stephen. She was wearing a hat and gloves. She was wearing lipstick too, and what looked like nylon stockings.

Runty took a step back and raised her voice. 'Thank you so much, Mr Shaw. Tell me when you've finished, and I'll make you a cup of tea.'

She went back into the house, nodding graciously at Mrs Broadwell, who pretended not to see her.

I had plenty to think about before the girls' supper. Had Shaw and Runty had a relationship of some kind before he came here? Had they been lovers? Or did he know something shameful about her past? Perhaps he was blackmailing her.

A little after six o'clock, I dropped into the old servants' hall, where the girls of Cavendish House were having their evening meal. Sunday supper was always a dreary affair, even worse than lunch. It usually consisted of leftovers together with two-day-old bread.

Enid was looking more cheerful than she had been when I had last seen her. Over supper, she made polite conversation with the girls around her about their holidays and their pets.

Sylvia and Prissy were further down the table. Sylvia was describing the life she would lead when she reached Oxford, while Prissy was looking confused and worried. They were talking in whispers to prevent Rosemary Lawson-Smith from eavesdropping.

'But can I write to you when you're there?' Prissy asked.

'Of course you can,' Sylvia said magnanimously. 'And if I've time, I'll write back. But I expect I'll be frightfully busy. You know – writing essays. Going to lectures and tutorials. And . . . and having cocoa with my friends.'

Prissy looked more miserable than before.

When the meal ended, the senior girl said or rather gabbled grace: '*Benedicto benedicatur, per Iesum Christum Dominum Nostrum.*' (Miss Pryce-Morgan insisted on a Latin grace before and after meals on the grounds that it added 'tone'; a difficult word to define but one that held immense significance for her.) The girls poured out of the room in a chattering and oddly joyful stream, almost as if the poor little beggars had something pleasant waiting for them.

'Rosemary,' Enid said. 'One moment.' She held out the pencil. 'I think this is yours.'

The girl took it. 'Thank you, Miss Archer.' She looked down at it, at the name she had inscribed so laboriously at the unsharpened end. 'Yes – it's mine. I lost it ages ago.'

The girls waited as Enid left the room, and then the flow began again. But Sylvia and Prissy hung back.

'It's queer,' Sylvia said. 'The pencil, I mean. I found a pencil belonging to Rosemary during the hols. I gave it to Warnie on her last morning when she was going off.'

'Perhaps it fell out of her bag when she was walking,' Prissy said. 'And Archie has only just found it. Or perhaps it was another pencil of hers. She must have more than one, and she puts her name on everything.'

Sylvia shrugged. 'I expect you're right.'

Prissy went pink with pleasure, for Sylvia rarely conceded anything to her.

'Even so,' Sylvia said. 'It might a clue. The trouble is, almost anything might be a clue. That's the problem.'

I could have burst with frustration. Of course the blasted

pencil was a clue to what happened to me. But it was in two halves. Sylvia knew that she had given me the pencil on the morning of my death. Enid knew that it had been dropped at the Maiden's Leap. But unless they could put the halves together, it was useless.

25

Tosser turned up shortly after dawn on Monday morning. Not that I was aware of it until later, when I went up to school.

First lesson had already started. Little Covey was having even more difficulty than usual in keeping her first formers quiet. Maggie Squires was bellowing at the third form.

I heard voices in the headmistress's study, one of them a man's. PM was dressed and sitting behind her desk. She looked paler and more fragile than usual. Runty was standing beside her.

In front of the desk, with his back to me, was the village constable, PC Fowles. His stiff collar bit into the back of his neck, and the skin above it was red and sweaty. He was rotating his helmet in his hands. His trousers were wet from the knees down, and a series of small puddles had formed around his boots.

'. . . got him out, miss, and the doctor's there now.'

'You don't think . . .' PM faltered, cleared her throat and went on: 'Are you *sure* he's . . . ?'

'That he's dead? Oh yes. If you ask me, he'd been there for a while.'

'He must have come here on Saturday morning,' Runty said, 'because the boiler was done. He should have come back again in the evening, but he didn't.'

Fowles put his helmet on the floor, took out his notebook and made a note. 'So he could have been in the lake for thirty-six hours at least. But if that's the case, it's odd no one noticed him.'

'Not necessarily,' Runty said. 'The lake's out of bounds. No one from school ever goes there, and we have no responsibility for it. Yesterday was Sunday so none of Mr Lewis's men would have been about. What do you think happened?'

'Well, miss, it's not really for me to say.'

She fixed him with her steely glare. 'But you must have an idea, surely? A man of your experience.'

'As a matter of fact I saw him in the Ruispidge Arms on Saturday night – he was still there when I left.' Fowles cleared his throat. 'He usually walked back to his cottage. The landlady said he didn't mind the dark, even in winter – he had a torch, and in any case he knew the park like the back of his hand, night or day. His quickest route would have taken him down to the lake and over that jetty by the boathouse and then up to his cottage.'

'And he fell in?'

'That's what it looks like, miss. He was crossing the jetty, you see, and the timbers are rotting away in places. It's safe enough if you go carefully and you know where to tread. But it would have been dark, and he'd probably had a few, and maybe he was a bit unsteady on his feet.'

'Drunk as a lord more likely,' Runty said.

Fowles didn't deny the possibility. He shuffled his feet and his boots made a squelching sound. 'Could have banged his head. Maybe his coat snagged on something. We're not sure exactly what happened yet.'

'Who found him?'

'Mr Lewis's Eyetie' – Fowles cleared his throat – 'his Italian POW labourer. When he was on his way to work this morning.'

'Oh dear,' Miss Pryce-Morgan said. 'This is all very unfortunate.'

'Anyway, miss, Inspector Williamson told me to come up to the house and put you in the picture. And to ask you to make sure that no one goes near the lake for the time being.'

Runty stared menacingly at him. 'We'll rely on you to keep us informed of further developments. Above all, we mustn't let this . . . this unfortunate incident upset our girls.'

'Exactly,' said PM, straightening in her chair. 'Their well-being is paramount.' Which was a direct quotation from the prospectus.

'Thank you, officer,' Runty said. 'Good morning.'

When the door closed behind Fowles, PM moaned softly like a wounded animal. 'The scandal. What if the parents should hear? And what are we going to do about the boiler? Perhaps Stephen could . . .'

'Take over from Tosser? I think it would be better if we spoke to Lewis. Find out if he'll let us have Senhouse for an hour or so a day.'

'But the cost of the man's wages. Oh dear, oh dear . . .'

In palmier days before the war, Senhouse had worked at Monkshill and managed the hot-water boiler and the now disused central-heating system. He was a Lowland Scot who knew his own value and expected to be paid accordingly. Lewis had tempted him away with higher wages.

Runty patted the headmistress's shoulder as if she were a dog. 'Don't worry, Kitty. We'll find a way. We always do, don't we?'

Tosser was lying on his back on the verandah in front of the boathouse. His eyes and mouth were open, and there was a smudge of grey stubble on his cheeks.

He was wearing a mud-stained raincoat with a piece of cord in place of a belt. Someone had untied the cord and opened the coat, which now spread out like grubby brown wings on either side of his body. Underneath he wore patched corduroys and an old tweed jacket over a collarless shirt. One of his boots, the left, had a hole in its sole.

Someone had already been through his pockets, and the contents lay on a rickety wicker table from the boathouse. There was a beer bottle, a third full and stoppered with a cork. A mound of coins weighed down several banknotes, a door key and a ration book. Other possessions included a blackened briar pipe, a sodden matchbox, an oilskin tobacco pouch and a filthy handkerchief. He must have had a hat but there was no sign of it. I couldn't see a torch either.

I had assumed I would feel nothing at the sight of Tosser's corpse. After all, I was dead myself so death lacked novelty value. Anyway I had disliked him.

As it happened, I was wrong. It was partly because he looked so bedraggled and shrunken, so pathetic. So *dead*. There was nothing left of him, not really, in the heap of rags and decaying meat on the jetty. His possessions had lost their meaning without him.

218

The doctor was kneeling beside him. I recognised him – he was the GP who attended the school. On the other side of the body was the stout figure of Inspector Williamson. He was the detective who had looked into my disappearance.

'How long do you reckon he's been there?'

'Difficult to say. The rigor's gone.'

'Could he have gone in on Saturday evening?'

'Quite possibly.'

'And no other injuries, sir?'

The doctor shook his head. 'Nothing obvious apart from a few grazes. I wonder what condition his heart was in. Anyway, we'll have to see if the coroner wants an autopsy. How are you getting the body out of here?'

'Mr Lewis is letting us use a tractor and a trailer to get him up to the drive. There's an ambulance on the way to collect him.'

'Well, there's nothing more I can do. Let me know what happens, won't you?'

Before he stood up, the doctor stretched out his hand and closed Tosser's eyes. They refused to remain entirely shut. The effect was unpleasant: it was as if he were determined to peep at us even in death.

On his way back to his car, the doctor met Fowles hurrying down from the school. 'Are they all right up there?'

'A bit shaken, sir, especially the older lady. But coping.'

The doctor grunted. 'I'll give them a ring later.'

Death did shake you up. I remembered Venetia yesterday afternoon, running towards the school. Had she seen Tosser's body in the water? Was she running away from him, not towards the school? Perhaps Mrs Crisp had seen him too.

Inspector Williamson had his notebook out when Fowles reached him. He was copying information from the soggy but still legible ration book. Without looking up he said, 'Where's West Cottage?'

'Just up there, sir. Other side of the trees.'

'Any family?'

Fowles shook his head. 'And what did Mr Smith do for a living?'

'Mr Smith?'

Williamson pointed at the body. 'Albert J. Smith. That's what it says here.'

'Everyone calls him Tosser. He helps out a bit in the kitchen garden. Used to be a gamekeeper, I think.'

'There's nearly ten quid down there. Lot of money for a man like him.'

Fowles was looking awkward again. 'I heard he used to do a bit of poaching on the side. Salmon, pheasant – maybe venison occasionally.' His colour rose. 'Not that I saw any evidence of that myself.'

'Of course not.' Williamson took pity on him and produced a packet of cigarettes. 'Smoke?'

They lit up, and Williamson continued with his notes.

'What's in the bottle? Have a sniff, will you?'

Fowles uncorked it. He made a face. 'Cider. He made his own.'

Williamson reached out an arm for the bottle. He wrinkled his nose. 'Christ.' He gave the bottle back, turned a page and licked his pencil. 'How deep is the water he was in? Find a stick.'

The boathouse had been built at the top of a small inlet. The path along the bank used the jetty in front as a footbridge. Underneath the planking the water was a couple of feet deep. But depth didn't matter. If you were drunk enough you could drown in a puddle.

I was looking about while listening to the conversation with half an ear. The jetty was safe enough to bear a man's weight if you were careful where you trod. I couldn't swear to it, but it seemed to me that some of the boards weren't quite as I had last seen them. There were gaps where I thought there had not been gaps before. One board, partly rotten already, had actually snapped in two.

Perhaps Tosser had done that. Or perhaps not.

It occurred to me that it would have been such a safe and easy way to create an apparent accident that would cause a ducking. Once you were in the water, though, it might not be easy to get yourself out – particularly if it was dark and you'd spent the last few hours in the Ruispidge Arms. Particularly if you were unlucky.

In the normal course of things, few people came to the lake, and even fewer walked along this side of it. By daylight, the poor condition of the jetty was obvious. Things would be very different by night, particularly if you were stinking drunk.

The only person who regularly crossed the jetty after dark was Tosser, when he was passing to and from the village. Had someone come here during the day on Saturday and adjusted the boards to make them more unsafe than they had been before?

'Please, sir,' Fowles said. 'Can I cover his face?'

26

I didn't linger by the lake to watch the removal of Tosser's body. I made my way back to the obelisk. An engine was revving in the distance, probably the tractor negotiating the muddy path down to the lake.

An unpleasant question drifted into my mind. Where exactly was Tosser now? Was it possible that in some sense he was still here at Monkshill Park, just as I was? The alarming prospect of bumping into him in the afterlife gave me a chill. Solitude was bad enough, but the company of Tosser would be far worse.

On the other hand, hundreds, probably thousands, of people must have died at Monkshill Park over the centuries, and I had come across no trace of them since my own death. Was I uniquely cursed to endure a form of existence that was neither one nor the other? Or did we all end up like this, trapped in our individual solitudes until the end of time? Dear God, there could be millions of us floating about together yet never bumping into one another. Think of it: a sea filled with swarm upon swarm of dead souls, squirming like tadpoles, invisible to both the living and the dead.

To distract myself from this depressing possibility I went back to school. As soon as I went inside, it was obvious that the news of Tosser's death had spread far beyond the headmistress's study.

It was the mid-morning break. In the girls' part of the house, there was a buzz of chatter, much of it in whispers. In the old servants' hall, Venetia was perched on the windowsill, quite alone, and looking out at the yard below. No one came near her. She had the power to create her own solitude.

Sylvia was in a huddle with Prissy. They were convinced that Tosser had been murdered, and they were excitedly speculating about who might have wished him dead. Little Covey was on their list, so they must have heard something about the desecrated garden and the stolen weedkiller. Also on the list, to my surprise, was Enid.

'Warnie told her about him looking at girls in the showers, you see,' Sylvia said. 'Perhaps she saw him doing it again and pushed him into the lake to make him stop?'

'But she could have just told someone instead,' Prissy objected. 'Anyway, I don't think Archie's the sort of person who kills people. She's too nice.'

'That's where you're wrong. It's often the least likely ones. The last people anyone would suspect.'

Prissy looked unconvinced but wisely said nothing. As for me, I had another suspect in mind: Alec Shaw. Tosser had seen him and his bicycle at Monkshill in March – long before he should have even heard of the place. The old man had been using the knowledge as a lever for blackmail, and it was a fair assumption that he wouldn't have stopped at an overpriced rabbit. I already had grounds to suspect, thanks to Runty's newspaper cutting, that Shaw was a bad lot. Bad enough to kill someone if he felt threatened? It also struck me that if Runty were in some way collaborating with Shaw, then she might have a motive to wish Tosser out of the picture as well.

Venetia's shoulders twitched, distracting me from my speculations. I drew closer. Her face was expressionless. In the kitchen yard below the window, Stephen was kicking an old mounting block near the gateway – not hard, just for something to do. It was a fine morning, and Mrs Broadwell and Mrs Crisp had brought out kitchen chairs and were drinking their mid-morning tea. Their heads were close together. I guessed they were talking about Tosser too.

Stephen had his hands in his pockets and his shirt was too tight under the armpits. He looked bored. I remembered the unpleasant scene between him and Tosser that I had witnessed in the kitchen garden. The old man had delighted in upsetting people.

Venetia took a piece of paper from the pocket of her tunic. She read it, and so did I. My heart sank at the sight of the familiar letters straggling across the paper.

What were – You – do – ing – at – THE – la – k – e – on – SATURDAY.

The jangling of the bell cut through the noise in the room, signalling the end of break. Venetia screwed up the letter and stuffed it back in her pocket. She sauntered out of the room with her usual awkward, insolent grace.

After lunch, Sylvia and Stephen met once again in the old stables. They must have arranged the rendezvous during the morning, as it hadn't been mentioned the previous afternoon.

'What is it?' Sylvia said. 'Are you OK?'

'Yes.' He darted a glance at her. 'Why?'

'You looked really pale when I saw you earlier. Are you upset about Tosser?'

'No – why should I be?'

'You know. I know he wasn't very nice but it's strange when someone dies.'

'Doesn't bother me. I had a bit of a tummy ache this morning, that's all. I'm OK now. I'm fine.'

Sylvia lowered her voice. 'Do you think he was murdered?'

'No,' Stephen said sharply. 'Of course not. Don't talk rot. He was drunk, wasn't he, and he fell in and drowned. Stupid old man.'

There was an awkward silence. Sylvia cleared her throat. 'Well,' she said, 'did you find out anything yesterday? What happened when Archie and Mr Shaw went into the wood?'

'Not much. They just walked down to a place where there's a stone seat. And they talked for a while and then they came back. Do you think they're . . . ?' He looked at the ground. 'You know. Keen on each other?'

Sylvia screwed up her face as if the notion mildly disgusted her. 'I suppose they might be.'

'I bet the old cows wouldn't like that.'

He meant PM and Runty. Sylvia didn't comment. She looked uncomfortable. She was a nicely brought-up child. Perhaps she was also remembering the bull at Home Farm and Venetia's human biology lecture.

She said quickly, trying to change the subject, 'Someone's had a poison pen letter.'

'Who?'

'It was Prissy actually.'

'What did it say?'

Sylvia hesitated. 'Just something nasty. It doesn't matter.'

225

The poor child was looking dreadfully worried. 'It's so awfully queer. All these horrible things. Warnie going away without any warning. That beastly letter. The mouse with the string round its neck. And now Tosser. Are you really sure . . . ?'

'What?'

She stared at Stephen with wide, frightened eyes. 'Are you really sure he wasn't murdered?'

27

After lunch, Miss Pryce-Morgan went upstairs to rest. Runty stayed in the study. So did I. She phoned Home Farm and negotiated with Mr Lewis for the loan of Senhouse to keep the boiler going on a temporary basis. She had her way in the end, though Lewis made her pay dearly for it.

'Tell him to come to the front door when he arrives and ask for me,' she said before she rang off. 'I'll need to give him the key.'

It was only then that I noticed that Runty hadn't returned the box of keys to the safe. It was on the side table near the desk where they would sometimes put a tea tray or their drinks. I presumed the keys had been there since yesterday when she had needed the one for the boiler room. The box was partly concealed by one of PM's shawls.

Runty opened the school chequebook. Breathing heavily, she began to balance the figures against the latest bank statement, much of which was printed in red ink.

There was a knock on the door. Runty sighed, laid down her pen and called out 'Yes?'

Enid came in with a sheet of paper in her hand. She had a free period first thing on Monday afternoons. 'Oh – I thought the head was here.'

'She's resting.' Runty slid the bank statement under the desk blotter and gave her a hostile stare. 'She's still convalescing, you know.'

'Of course. Could I leave this for her? She asked me to outline some suggestions for this year's Sports Day.'

Runty, still seated behind the desk, stretched out her hand. 'I'll see she gets it.'

Enid advanced into the room and gave Runty the paper.

'Running races on the drive?' Runty said. 'That's a little unusual, isn't it?'

'There's no alternative, I'm afraid. Mr Lewis has ploughed up the lower meadow so we can't have them there again.'

'That man's a menace.' She lowered her head over the chequebook. 'Thank you, Miss Archer.'

I followed Enid when she left the study. She stood for a moment in the hall, thinking. Then she took a deep breath and knocked on the study door again. Without waiting for Runty to answer, she put her head into the room. 'I think the head's calling – would you like me to go up and see what she wants?'

Runty pushed back her chair at once. For an instant her face was unguarded, and I saw a flash of anxiety. Ignoring Enid, she crossed the hall and took the shallow steps of the stairs two at a time.

As soon as she was out of sight, Enid slipped into the study. It was a sign of Runty's haste that she hadn't covered up the bank statement before she went. Enid ignored it and made straight for the keys. There must have been thirty or forty of them in the box, and they were of all sizes and shapes. It took her an age to find the one she wanted. But at last she dug out the one with *Warnock* on its label, slipped it into the pocket of her cardigan and retreated into the hall.

She was only just in time. Runty was coming down the stairs. 'She was perfectly all right – fast asleep.' Her voice modulated into restrained outrage. 'And thanks to you I woke her up.'

'Oh I'm so sorry,' Enid said. She was surprisingly good at looking helpless and slightly stupid. 'It must have been from one of the classrooms. You know how the sound carries in this house. I suppose it's all the high ceilings and hard surfaces. I do hope she'll be able to settle again.'

'So do I, Miss Archer,' Runty said. The study door closed behind her.

. . . pushed the door of the old boathouse. It swung back with a creak. She gasped as a cobweb brushed her face. The room inside was full of shadows tinged with green from the leaves of bushes that tapped on the windows. Mrs Pryce-Morgan was slumped in an old wicker chair which had its back to the door.

I had heard the clatter of the typewriter through the open window of the cottage. In the living room, I found Shaw hammering the keys of his machine as if they were personal enemies. His school duties were over for the day.

He knew now that this was when I could reach him. It was as if he were consciously trying to summon me, to conjure my spirit from the dead. It was all so absurdly gothic that I wanted simultaneously to giggle, cry and run away.

Cynthia touched the shoulder of the old housekeeper. 'Well? What is it? What did you want to tell me?'

There was no reply. Suddenly Mrs Pryce-Morgan's arm fell from the chair and dangled beside it.

Cynthia gave a shriek. 'What is it? Are you ill?'

No, you silly man, I told him, I'm as dead as a doornail.

My contribution appeared on the paper in a staccato burst. Shaw looked up, and then from side to side, and finally behind him. He took a cigarette and tried to light it. I was pleased to see that his hands were trembling, so much so that he dropped the flaming match. He struck a second match and inhaled a mouthful of smoke before turning back to the keyboard.

He typed: Who are you? Ping.

I felt a rush of relief followed by a surge of energy. At last I had a direct connection to someone who was alive. But I didn't want to answer his question, not yet. I dictated: Just out of interest, did you kill Tosser?

His fingers pounded the keys at my bidding. But they were clumsier than usual. Afterwards he paused, looking at his hands with distaste, even with a kind of fear. That was understandable. They had betrayed him. I had stolen their loyalty. Then he replied to my question: No. Of course I didn't. Ping.

But you had a motive. He was blackmailing you.

'Nonsense,' he said aloud. He didn't realise that I could hear him so he also typed: Nonsense.

You and I both know that's not true.

You're not real, Shaw wrote, so it doesn't matter what I say, does it?

Then say the truth, I countered. I waited but all he did was sit back and smoke. Please don't be childish, I went on. I know he was blackmailing you. Did you kill him?

Shaw snorted. No. I did not. As for the other, it's none of your business. As I said, you're not real.

And yet we're having this conversation.

I don't believe this is happening. Are you inside my head?

Not as far as I know. You paid a visit to Monkshill in March, didn't you? Before the teaching post was vacant. Why?

'This is stupid,' he said aloud. 'I'm going to stop.' But he stayed in his chair with the typewriter in front of him.

I was tiring rapidly now. I summoned all my strength and took a leap in the dark. Was that just after you came out of prison?

He muttered something under his breath. For a moment I almost felt sorry for him. 'How do you know about that?' he blurted out. 'You . . . you *must* be in my head. Am I going mad?'

I was tiring, but this chance was too good to lose. I forced myself to set his fingers in motion again: You're not going mad. I'm outside you. I can only make you type my words when you're writing your story. That's the only time I can reach you. But I can see you whenever I want. I can hear what you say. Say something now.

'I don't believe you. Prove it.'

You want proof? Very well. You've just dropped about half an inch of ash on your trousers. Left leg.

Shaw glanced down at his thigh. He brushed the ash away as if it were burning him. He looked up.

'You can't be dead. It isn't possible.' His cheeks had lost their colour. He picked up the cigarette from the ashtray and sucked on it like a teat. 'You have to tell me more.' He sighed out the smoke. 'Or I'll go mad. Please. *Please.*'

Fatigue covered me like a blanket. I went away.

28

When I returned to consciousness, the sun had gone down. The sky was still a soft, perfect blue, decorated with playful green, pink and orange streaks along the western horizon. I went up to the school. Most of the girls were now in bed. In the staffroom, Vera Hampson and Maggie Squires were trying to teach Miss Covey how to play poker.

'. . . but why's it called a Hot Flush?' Covey was saying as I came in.

'It's a *Royal* Flush,' Miss Hampson said, her Irish accent becoming more pronounced, as it did in moments of high emotion or tipsiness. 'Ace, King, Queen, Jack and Ten of the same suit. It's the highest you can get, and it beats every other combination.'

'But why's it called a *Flush*?' Covey asked plaintively.

'It doesn't matter,' Maggie said. 'All you need to know is that's what it's called, and that's what it is. And now the Straight Flush . . .'

I left them to it and went upstairs. Enid was in her room. She had lit a fire, which was strictly forbidden unless justified by exceptional circumstances and authorised by PM or Runty. It wasn't much of a fire – a few sticks of kindling and a couple of small logs.

Enid was on the hearthrug, her legs drawn up beneath her, with the hoard from under the floor of my old room spread out before her. She had emptied her cotton bag and my manila envelope: the letters, the diaries, the photographs and the pathetic scraps of jewellery were heaped in front of her and she was picking through them.

My first reaction was unadulterated relief. The danger that Runty might find them had haunted me ever since my death. As I watched Enid though, I saw that there were tears on her cheeks. My relief gave way to another emotion. I had been criminally stupid in not destroying some of my memorabilia while I was alive – almost everything, in fact, that predated my meeting Enid. Thanks to my carelessness, she was now discovering who I really was, or rather who I had been before I knew her. I desperately wanted to tell her that I wasn't like this now. She had made me better than I was before.

The photographs of other lovers, their letters, the comments I had made about them in my diaries: all these showed another side of me from the one she had known. I might be dead but I was still capable of hurting her. I could still feel shame.

For God's sake, don't read them. I'm different now. I love you.

However hard I tried, I couldn't reach her. On and on she went, combing out my cruelties and misdeeds from the tangled remains of my past. But I noticed she was also doing something else. The bulk of the material on the hearthrug was in front of her. To her side, however, concealed from me by her leg, was a smaller pile.

It included a Polyfoto I had given her a few days before my

death. I'd had it taken in a department store in Cheltenham during the February half-term holiday. On a single sheet, forty-eight versions of my tiny monochrome face stared at the ceiling. In some of them I was smiling or looking sad. Sometimes I was hatless. Or I was pouting. In one I was laughing. And in another I was sticking out my tongue at the camera.

Perhaps I had not entirely lost her.

Enid picked up a snapshot of a girl, a former pupil of mine before I'd come to Monkshill; she was on a beach somewhere and squinting at the camera, her features almost bleached out by the glare of the sun. She wore a bathing costume and a cap covered her hair like a helmet.

Alice.

I'd forgotten that photograph was there – I must have slipped it into an old diary. The poor kid. Such a waste.

Enid glanced at the back of the photograph, where there was the pencilled inscription *For Miss Warnock*, and then again at the front. I expected her to throw it away with the rest, but she put it on the pile to keep.

At last she finished sorting. She fed the fire, piece by piece, scrap by scrap, with the remains of the person I had once been. My old life flashed past me on the way to destruction – diaries, photos of past girlfriends, letters, even a theatre programme for a play I'd forgotten.

Her face reddened in the heat, and the tears glistened on her skin as if varnished. Pale flames flared above the logs. Blackened scraps of paper fled up the chimney, shedding trails of sparks. The fire died down. The kindling was long gone, but the two logs still glowed in their decay. She poked the shreds of paper that remained with the tongs, grinding them to dust.

When she had finished, she shovelled what was left on

the hearthrug into the envelope. Afterwards she stared as if hynotised at the dying fire. Everything was still. Everything was silent.

Now it was over, I was relieved – not just because our diaries and letters were safe from Runty and PM, but because Enid had been wise enough to burn almost everything that belonged to my old life before I came to Monkshill. Unlike me, my past had been cremated and safely disposed of.

There was a knock at the door. Enid hastily picked up the envelope and scrambled to her feet. Her legs were stiff after sitting for so long, and she staggered, almost losing her balance.

'Enid?' Maggie called. She rattled the door handle. 'Are you decent? Can I come in?'

'Just a minute.'

Enid reached the door. Maggie was already twisting the knob and pushing. The door was locked.

'I'm coming.' Enid turned the key and opened the door.

'Have you got a pack of cards?'

'Cards . . .'

'*Cards* – you know, playing cards. I say, are you all right? You look a bit – well, hot and bothered.' By now Maggie was in the room. 'Gosh, a fire, eh? Let's hope *Somebody* doesn't notice.'

'I think I've got a pack somewhere. Hang on.'

Enid opened a drawer and thrust the envelope inside. She tugged open another drawer.

Maggie cleared her throat. 'You've been crying, haven't you?' she said gently.

Enid turned to face her, the cards in her hand. She nodded but didn't speak.

'All of us feel a bit mis sometimes. Perfectly understandable.'

'Yes. You're right.'

'Come on, old thing,' Maggie said. 'Don't worry. Always darkest before dawn. What you need is a nice cup of tea with a bit of sugar in it.'

'I don't know. I—'

'We're playing poker downstairs, or at least trying to. That's what the cards are for. The staffroom pack has lost two aces and a king along the way.'

'Poker?'

'We can't play bridge any more without Annabel to make up a foursome. And you were never terribly keen on it either. But poker's quite different – it's rather jolly actually. Why don't you come and join us?'

'I've never played it,' Enid said. 'Isn't it terribly complicated?'

'Not at all. My brother taught me and he's the sort of chap who finds Snap rather too intellectual.'

Enid managed a smile for that.

'So what about it? It'll take your mind off things. We're going to play for pennies, which will make it much more fun. Little Covey's there, and if you come, she'll think it's OK. At present she's afraid we're tempting her to do the devil's work. So you'll be helping us do a good deed, too – we're trying to take her mind off what that nasty man did to her garden. I know we shouldn't speak ill of the dead, but in Tosser's case I can happily make an exception.'

'All right,' Enid said. 'I'll come.'

Maggie turned to go, her hand on the door. For an instant she hesitated, looking at the mantelpiece, where Enid had left the stolen key to my room. Maggie must have seen the key but she didn't comment.

'Perhaps wash your face before you come down,' she said. 'I'll go and put the kettle on.'

When Enid went downstairs, I was tempted to follow her and watch the game. Poker at Monkshill Park! How shocked PM would be if she found out. But I had had enough excitement for one day. Instead I went down the backstairs and followed the landing into the servants' part of the house.

After all the shocks and upsets of the day, wandering through the dormitories had a calming effect. Most girls were asleep, which meant that for a few hours all was well in their worlds. As usual, there were a few exceptions. Two fifth formers were having a whispered conversation about boys they had almost kissed in the holidays. A first former whimpered in her sleep but then fell silent. A third former was informing two round-eyed younger girls that Tosser's ghost was already prowling the grounds arm in arm with the drowned maidservant; they were looking for living victims.

In Birch, everyone was asleep. The moon shone through the uncurtained window on the six beds, three on each side. Clothes were neatly folded on chairs. Drawers were closed, and the ghostly white towels were regularly spaced on the rails by the door, each with a sponge bag hanging from a hook on its left. Vera Hampson had been on duty that evening, and she was a stickler for tidiness.

In the moonlight the scene had a stark, geometric quality like an architect's drawing. The only thing at odds with this lifeless perfection was the irregular shapes of the girls' bodies beneath their blankets, and the ragged outlines of heads on pillows. Venetia's long white hand trailed from the bed and dangled towards the floor.

Her fingertips almost touched something that was lying on the floor partly beside her bedside cupboard and partly under the bed. I drew closer. It was a playing card. But instead of the familiar symbols of diamonds, hearts, spades or clubs, it had a single letter, a capital Y, on a white background.

It was a Lexicon card. I had never much enjoyed the word game myself but I had known people who were obsessed by it, as other people are obsessed with bridge or chess, to the extent of competing in Lexicon Drives. Probably every other household in the land had a pack of Lexicon cards stowed away in a cupboard.

But what was it doing beside Venetia's bed? She was the last person I would have thought likely to take part in word games. I wondered if the letter Y was somehow significant to her.

The letter Y. The question *Why?*

29

Judging by the light, it was about half-past six. Below the Maiden's Leap, the mist was writhing above the river as the sun's warmth began to drive it away. The sky was clear. It was going to be another fine day.

Tosser was on my mind – to be more specific, the possibility that I might encounter him in our unexpected afterlife. I hoped I was alarming myself unnecessarily. The best thing to do, I thought, was to go to the lake and see if there was any trace of him. In the first day or two after my death, I stayed at the Maiden's Leap. I simply hadn't realised that I was free to roam further than that. Tosser might be the same.

I made my way in the direction of West Cottage. I met no one. On the way I took the path along the bank of the lake to the boathouse and its jetty, following the route that Tosser must have taken in the last few minutes of his life. There was nothing to show that he had died here apart from the tyre tracks left by Mr Lewis's tractor and trailer.

West Cottage had a forlorn air. Perhaps it was my imagination but the garden was not quite as tidy as it used to be. By the gate, the dead creatures that he had nailed to the board were now so old and decayed that even the crows were disinclined to breakfast on them.

To my relief, there was no sign of Tosser. Was it possible that whatever regulations governed the afterlife forbade fraternisation? Or that my ambiguous situation between life and death was peculiar to me? Either option would suit me.

Feeling more cheerful, I wandered towards the drive. It was such a beautiful morning that I was not in a hurry to reach the school. Hardly anyone would be up yet. As I drew nearer the drive, I heard voices. I couldn't see the speakers because they were masked by trees, but it sounded as if they were in the middle of an argument. I came out just beyond the bridge, and there they were: Venetia Canford and an elderly man I didn't recognise. Both had bicycles. Venetia's back tyre was flat.

'. . . no, I really *can* pay you,' Venetia was saying. 'Just say how much it will cost.'

'Not interested,' the man replied. 'I got a job to go to.'

He had a stern face and a mild Scottish accent. I guessed this must be Senhouse, Mr Lewis's man, who had been temporarily engaged to look after the school boiler.

'Please. I'm sure it would take you no time at all.' Venetia's voice started confidently but ended with a quaver. 'And . . . and I've got a kit for it and everything.'

She gestured towards the saddle, behind which hung the usual pouch containing a puncture kit.

'And I can give you some cigarettes too.'

'If you've got the kit, you can do the job yourself. All you need's a pump and maybe some water, so you'll have to go back to the house anyway. As for the fags, I don't smoke.'

Senhouse pushed his bike away and swung his leg over the

saddle in an ungainly movement that made the machine wobble dangerously. He rode away, leaving Venetia red in the face and clearly trying not to cry.

Then, from behind her, there was a third voice: 'Are you all right? What are you doing?'

Venetia and I turned towards the interruption. I was surprised to see Shaw walking up the drive from the road. He looked as though he'd spent the night under a hedge. His unbrushed hair stood up in spikes. He hadn't shaved. He had turned up the collar of his tweed jacket and he wasn't wearing a tie. His eyes were bloodshot and his skin was flushed. I suspected he'd had recourse to the whisky bottle again after our typewritten exchange yesterday evening.

'I . . . I was going for a ride, sir,' Venetia said.

'At this time?' He looked sternly at her. 'Did you have permission?'

She said nothing. He glanced at the bike.

'A puncture, eh? That's bad luck.'

He took in the bag crammed in the basket at the front of the bicycle, and the satchel strapped to the carrier at the back.

'What exactly are you trying to do, young lady?' he said. 'Run away?'

She didn't reply.

'Where were you thinking of going? London? To see your aunt?'

That earned a shake of the head. She still wouldn't look at him. 'The Dower House,' she mumbled. 'At Fontenoy.'

'Is that where you live when you're not here?'

She nodded. 'I want to see the horses.'

'What?'

'The horses.' For the first time she looked him in the face

242

and her voice sounded almost scornful, as if everyone ought to know how important the horses were. 'We've still got two. I ride them when I'm there. They . . . they know me. They need me. I was going to come back after I'd seen them.'

'You'll see them in the holidays,' Shaw said. 'But now you're going back to school. If you don't turn up at breakfast, there'll be hell to pay. They'll phone the police and you'll be hauled back here by morning break.'

Her lips trembled. 'Are you going to tell?'

'I'm not sure. But if you go back now, there's a sporting chance that no one else will see you. Who was that man by the way?'

Venetia shrugged. 'He said he's come to do the boiler.'

'All right. Get back to school as fast as you can, and keep your fingers crossed no one else notices you. Off you go.'

She hesitated and I wondered if she was going to thank him. But she swung the bike around towards the house and walked quickly away.

Before assembly, I went into the staffroom, where Miss Covey was reliving her triumphant introduction to poker the previous evening. 'I just kept pretending,' she told Shaw proudly, 'and for some reason they all believed me. It's not like lying, you know – it's part of the game. Afterwards, when we totted up, I found I'd won two shillings and fourpence!'

'Congratulations,' Shaw said. He'd smartened himself up since I had last seen him but he looked haggard.

'Enid said I must be a natural.'

'Then I'm sure you are.'

'But do you think it's all right for me to – to gamble?' Now she had grown used to Shaw, Miss Covey had a touching faith in his masculine wisdom and knowledge of the world. 'Mother used to say that gambling can be as bad as drink. She said it can tear homes apart and lead straight to hell.'

'I think that's only true in extreme cases,' he said, clearly making an effort to be agreeable. 'Otherwise it's just a harmless recreation. Like . . . like knitting.'

He managed to escape. Enid had come in, and he sidled up to her as she was sorting herself out for the next lesson. 'All well?' he said in an undertone.

'Yes.' She threw him a glance. 'Why shouldn't it be?'

'No reason . . . it's just I felt I hadn't explained myself very well on Sunday.'

'Oh that.' She gave the insulting impression that she had forgotten all about it until then. 'I suppose it was a bit odd.'

'Perhaps we could have a chat after lunch? Or after school if you'd rather.'

'Perhaps.' The bell rang for assembly. 'Saved by the bell, eh?' she said without smiling.

But he smiled at her. He knew then, as I did, that she was willing to give him a second chance.

A chance at what? That was the question.

It looked as if Venetia had got away with it.

I saw her in class as usual, looking remote and bored as Miss Hampson was describing Abraham's meticulous preparations to sacrifice Isaac. I wondered whether Venetia was thinking about her horses. On the evidence so far, they seemed her only reliable source of emotional support.

Her bicycle was in the kitchen yard. She hadn't wasted much time in sorting out the puncture repair. Stephen had already removed the inner tube from the back tyre. I followed him when he carried it into the kitchen, where Mrs Broadwell was making tea for Senhouse.

'Ah,' said Senhouse. 'She's got you mending her puncture, has she?'

'How much are you charging?' Mrs Broadwell said.

'Five bob,' Stephen said proudly.

'More money than sense, that girl.' She reached for the sugar bowl. 'And what was she up to on the drive so early?'

'Doing a bunk, I reckon,' Senhouse said.

'She'll catch it if Mrs Hitler finds out.'

'This chap came up as I was leaving. Packed her off back to school. So he's the one who's teaching them girls.'

'His name's Shaw,' Mrs Broadwell said. 'He's temporary. After the other one buggered off and left them in the lurch. He let her off, did he?'

'Looks like it. Bloody fool. Spare the rod, spoil the child, that's what I say.' Senhouse glanced at Stephen. 'Got everything you need, lad?'

Stephen removed the tin containing the John Bull puncture repair kit from his trouser pocket.

He put it on the table and flipped up the lid. 'I think so.'

'What's that then?' A blackened forefinger poked a roll of brown paper wedged inside the tin.

Stephen unfolded the paper, which turned out to be a small bag. He looked inside. 'A bit of sugar or something?'

Senhouse stretched a hand. 'Let's see.' He looked inside. He sniffed the powder. He moistened a finger and took out a few grains. He put one on his tongue and almost immediately spat it on to his jacket. 'That's not sugar. More like weedkiller. Or rat poison.'

'Plenty of rats in this house,' Mrs Broadwell said. 'I blame them girls throwing away good food. How many sugars is it, Mr Senhouse?'

'Three,' he said.

Enid avoided talking to Shaw after lunch by the simple expedient of going up to her room until the bell rang for afternoon school. Her first lesson was with the School Cert class. They were doing the French subjunctive and everyone was making heavy weather of it, Enid included.

Afterwards she told Sylvia to wait behind. When the other girls had left the room, she opened her desk and took out two blue hardbacks.

'These are for you.' She handed them to Sylvia. 'You should just have time to put them in your locker.'

The girl's face blazed with surprise and joy. 'But – it's *Gaudy Night.*'

'And *Busman's Honeymoon.*'

'Ooh, I really want to read that one. Thank you.'

'I'm afraid you'll find it rather sentimental and silly in places,' Enid said sternly, 'but it completes the series and it's not all bad.'

Sylvia flipped open the cover of *Gaudy Night* and glanced at the flyleaf. 'This is the one Miss Warnock lent me.'

'Yes. I know she would like you to have it. And the other one. But don't mention it to anyone, will you? Miss Warnock wouldn't want to play favourites. You can just say that I've lent them to you. A long loan.'

'Is she all right?'

'Miss Warnock? Yes, I'm sure she is.' Enid walked towards the door, saying over her shoulder: 'The last thing you need to do is worry about her.'

* * *

The second half of the afternoon was devoted to games, which in practice meant two sets of older girls playing rounders under Maggie's supervision, while Enid dragooned some of the younger ones into running heats along the drive, telling them it was practice for sports day. Everyone else sloped about the grounds, trying to avoid anyone with authority over them.

Rosemary Lawson-Smith was in the last category. I followed her when she sneaked back into school by the side door. She avoided the front of the house, where PM and Runty were in the study, and made her way to the kitchen.

The room was empty. Mrs Broadwell usually retired to her own quarters for much of the afternoon to recover from her exertions at lunchtime. Stephen had repaired the puncture. He could be seen through the window, wobbling round and round the yard on Venetia's bicycle.

Standing well back, Rosemary watched him. After a few seconds, she went over to the stove. Her face expressionless, she pulled down her knickers and crouched. It took her only a few seconds to defecate. She pulled up her knickers and walked rapidly from the room.

The whole business had taken little more than thirty seconds. Mrs Broadwell had insulted Rosemary after Sunday lunch, and my guess was that a misplaced turd was the little girl's way of taking revenge.

Similarly, Shaw had told her off at lunch on his first Sunday here, which would explain the appearance of the first turd in the empty hearth of the cottage.

As with the poison pen letters, it was perfectly possible there had been other episodes. Some people might have been too embarrassed to report it. The unfortunate child was profoundly disturbed, and there was nothing I could do to restrain her, let alone help her. I was powerless in this as in everything else.

Rosemary retraced her steps, leaving the house by the side door and taking care that she couldn't be observed from the bow window of the study. She made a beeline for Enid and asked which heat she would be in.

The girl was a sly little baggage; this was her attempt to construct a quasi-alibi. Soon she was whispering and giggling about Mr Shaw with her coterie of friends as if nothing had happened.

30

Shaw spent much of the afternoon pacing out the distances of the running races. There had once been a measuring tape for this in the staffroom, but it had mysteriously disappeared, as had the contraption for marking the lines between the lanes.

On sports day there would be ample opportunities for more unscrupulous girls to take short cuts without being observed. The 100 yards race would be run over a relatively straight stretch of the drive, but the 220 and the 440 would have to continue around a bend shielded from view by a line of trees and bushes.

It seemed to me that Shaw was jumpier than usual and more subdued. Normally I found him almost offensively cheerful. The coolness between him and Enid was still going on. Perhaps it was that. But sometimes he glanced over his shoulder as if sensing that someone was watching him.

Not just someone. Me. Yesterday afternoon, he had finally been forced to accept that I wasn't a figment of his imagination. That I was, in some sense, real. He must have feared that he was constantly under my observation. I almost felt sorry for him.

Since Enid was organising the heats, she could hardly avoid seeing Shaw, and he her. I noted that they avoided looking at each other, which was more of a giveaway than exchanging the odd word in passing would have been.

Afterwards he followed her into the staffroom to join the others for tea. Technically, he wasn't meant to be in the house after school, but by now it had tacitly been accepted that it would be inhumane to deprive a teacher of a cup of tea at the end of the teaching day purely on the grounds of his gender.

To my surprise, she was the one who approached him. 'Listen. You've still got some questions to answer.'

'I know. I'm sorry.'

'To be fair, I didn't give you much opportunity.'

'Can we talk now?'

'What's that?' said Maggie Squires, once again exercising her talent for blundering into other people's conversations.

'School Cert stuff,' Shaw said smoothly. 'I was telling her an idea of mine about the maths teaching. There was an article in *The Times Ed* a few weeks ago. But Enid wasn't convinced. Clearly I need to explain more about their approach to logarithms.' He flashed a smile at Maggie. 'That should do the trick.'

Long before he had finished, her expression had glazed over. Whatever else Shaw was, he wasn't a fool. He had grasped that it was a simple matter to blunt Maggie's curiosity by boring her.

'All right,' Enid said to him, 'when we've both got a moment, let's have a chat. But I'm afraid I'm too busy now.'

Vera Hampson came into the staffroom and had closed the door behind her. 'There's been ructions,' she said happily. 'Mrs

B. has just stormed out of the head's study looking like the wrath of God.'

In the study I found PM in her armchair and Runty was leaning over her. Their heads were very close together.

'. . . but how can we afford it?' PM wailed as I came in. 'An extra ten shillings a week! First Senhouse, and now this.'

'We've no choice, Kitty. You heard her. She was going to walk out on us. We had to do something.'

'It wouldn't have happened before the war.' This was PM's usual comment about a crisis of any sort. 'She wouldn't have dared be so rude.'

'Mrs Broadwell is a vulgar, domineering woman,' Runty said crisply. 'But on this occasion I can see her point. If we want to keep her, we have to pay her more. It's as simple as that. I just hope she keeps her mouth shut.'

'Poor you, having to clear it up.' PM passed a hand over her forehead. 'This term has been one thing after another, hasn't it? It's ruining my nerves. I thought things would be better after that Warnock woman went.'

'It won't always be like this. I promise.'

'But who would do such a disgusting thing?'

'I don't know,' Runty said. 'But I'm going to find out. But first I've got to clean up that mess in the kitchen.'

I missed the loss of my sense of smell. On the other hand, it did have its advantages. One of them was the pig bin. This stood in the corner of the kitchen yard furthest from the back door. The pail of scraps in the scullery was emptied into it several times a day.

Given the quality of school food and the parsimonious

251

regimen laid down by Miss Runciman, it was hard to believe
that there might be anything remaining that was nutritious to
man or beast, particularly when one bore in mind Mrs Crisp's
preliminary raids on the pail's contents. But they say pigs will
eat anything.

Emptying the pail into the bin once a day was the job of the
girls on the dining hall rota. The smell when you raised the lid
was so disgusting that it was usually delegated to the weakest
member of the team. In the warmer months of the year, the
smell was so powerful that it was almost visible. Moreover the
scraps attracted a wide variety of insect life and, despite the lid,
the occasional rat.

The contents of the bin were eventually fed to the pigs
at Home Farm. Every now and then, Mr Lewis would send
up a man with a tractor and trailer to collect them. Usually
it was the Italian POW, Luigi, but on this Tuesday Lewis
had given the job to Senhouse, presumably because he would
already be coming up to the kitchen yard to give the boiler
its evening feed.

When Senhouse arrived, I was loitering in the gateway of
the kitchen yard, waiting for Shaw to go back to East Cottage.
Enid was now upstairs in her room reading my diary. I couldn't
bear to be there with her so I'd decided to try my luck with
Shaw in the hope he would be working on his novel.

To pass the time, I watched Senhouse as he went about his
unpleasant work. I drew closer, taking a wry pleasure from the
fact I couldn't smell anything. I was there when he found the
book. His face was not designed to show emotion but, just for
an instant, a muscle twitched on either side of his mouth.

He fished out the book and brushed it with a filthy hand. I
looked over his shoulder. It was by L. T. Meade and was called

The Little School Mothers. I remembered seeing it in the school library. My guess was that it had once belonged to the juvenile Miss Pryce-Morgan.

Senhouse opened the novel and riffled through the pages. Several of them had been roughly torn out, either entirely or in part. That's when I really started to pay attention. The title page interested me especially. Someone had snipped out a strip parallel to the binding from the top to almost halfway down. As a result, the word *THE* was missing.

I remembered the letter Venetia had found yesterday: *What were – You – do – ing – at – THE – la – k – e – on – SATURDAY.*

THE. I was pretty sure that it was a similar font and a similar size to the one on the title page. Come to that, I'd have been willing to bet that *The Little School Mothers* had provided the raw material for all the poison pen letters.

If the book had come from the school library, did that suggest that one of the girls was responsible for the letters?

Senhouse shrugged. He tossed the book into the trailer with the rest of the bin's contents. Pigs will eat anything. Even a book?

At East Cottage, Shaw was at his typewriter, working on his novel. I interpreted this as a good sign. It suggested he was ready to talk.

. . . her eyes were wide open. Her features were contorted into a frightful mask. Cynthia could see at once that the old housekeeper was beyond the reach of any doctor's health. Death had come to the old woman with brutal haste. The question was I'm here now. And you mean HELP not HEALTH.

He stopped typing and looked around at the empty living room. I don't know what he was expecting to see. Perhaps an ectoplasmic version of his correspondent mingling in the air with the tobacco smoke.

His hand trembled. 'Can you hear me?' he said in a voice not much above a whisper.

Yes, his fingers replied. Automatically he added a carriage return. *Ping*.

'I can speak to you? As if . . . as if you were real?'

I am real. And yes, of course I can hear you. But you have to type what I say to you. For some reason it only works when you're writing your detective story. My words have to be part of it, even if you cross them out immediately afterwards.

There was a long pause. Emotion welled up within me. I felt absurdly happy. I was having a conversation with a living person. He knew I could hear what he said.

He said in a shaky voice, 'This is ridiculous, talking to you like this. Who are you?'

I'd expected this question, and I'd already thought long and hard about how to answer it. I decided that only the truth would serve: Annabel Warnock.

'The . . . the teacher I replaced?'

Yes.

'I thought you went away last holidays and never came back. Miss Pryce-Morgan said you were rather flighty.'

Did she indeed? The cow. I never left.

'What happened?'

Someone pushed me off the Maiden's Leap. That's when I dropped the pencil you found. I had a rucksack too, and a notebook. They've vanished.

Ping.

I watched the shock spreading over his face. 'Who did it?' he said.

I don't know. I want you to help me find out. But first I want to know more about you.

I watched the words clattering across the paper. *I want to know more about you.* It sounded almost as if we were in the early stages of courtship. *Tell me more about yourself.* But if he was going to be in some sense my ally, I needed to know who I was dealing with.

'No, wait,' he said. 'Tell me something first. Are you watching me all the time? Round the clock?'

No. You're really not that interesting. Typical man, I thought. Completely self-obsessed.

'How much of the time then?'

Not that much. I'd had enough of this. Tell me, is your real name George?

There was a pause. 'Yes,' he said. 'But my second name's Alexander. Before I came here, I decided to have a change. Hence Alec rather than George.'

When did you get out of prison?

He lowered his voice. 'February. It . . . it was all a damn silly mistake. I can't stop kicking myself. I was so stupid.'

What had you done? I asked.

'The bursar at my school asked me to countersign four or five cheques. Not at once – over about six months. He made it seem as if I was doing him a little favour each time – you know, something not quite according to Hoyle, but just making his life simpler, nothing actually wrong. Nothing that meant anything.' He hesitated. 'God, I sound like an idiot, don't I? What a fool I was.' He shrugged. 'And I feel a fool now, talking to empty air.'

255

But I had the feeling that he liked telling me all this – or rather that he was relieved at not having to pretend to me, as he did with everyone else. Perhaps he was glad to have a chance to explain himself with impunity. Talking to a ghost was like talking in a priest's confessional or on a psychoanalyst's couch. You could say anything.

After a while he blundered on: 'It wasn't as if I gained much by it. I was just helping a pal. He'd buy me a drink occasionally, and he gave me a bottle of whisky on my birthday. He let me touch him for a fiver to tide me over when I lost a bit of money on a horse.' He stopped and cleared his throat. 'And . . . well, it's true that I had a bit of a rise in salary around then, which was nice, and I was moved to a bigger bedroom around the same time – I suppose that could have been his doing. The prosecution said it was.' He paused again, chewing his lip. 'But at the time, none of it felt like a bribe or anything like that. It was just that I'd scratched his back, and he was scratching mine.'

In March you came here. Why?

'To see if I could get a job,' he said. 'I needed to find somewhere that would take me on without references. I thought maybe a fourth-rate girls' school might.'

Did he seriously think I'd swallow that one? I want the truth.

He flung back his head and laughed. 'There's no fooling you, is there?'

For an instant I almost liked him. Runty knows you were in prison.

'I decided it was only fair to tell her. She's the one who really runs this place after all. Luckily it turns out she's got a soft heart.'

256

A few weeks later she gave you a job. My job, which suddenly happened to become available. How convenient.

'Look – if you really want to know, that first time, I came here on spec. I happened to be passing the gates – I was on my bike, going to see a pal in Gloucester. I didn't even know there was a job – and of course at that time there wasn't one. But I thought, why not? I was desperate. And if you don't ask, you don't get.'

Tosser saw you. And your bike with the green saddlebags.

Shaw looked startled. 'Yes. You're right there. Hence the business with that bloody rabbit.'

And now he's dead, I commented, to see how Shaw would respond. Again, how fortunate.

'Yes, in a way,' he said, choosing not to understand what I was implying. 'Do you know about the – ah – calling card that was left in my fireplace?'

Yes.

'Was that Tosser as well?'

There was no harm in trading a little information. I'd put my money on Rosemary Lawson-Smith. She has form in that respect.

His face wrinkled. 'Why the hell does she do it?'

Something's messed her up.

Rosemary wasn't unique, and nor was Monkshill. In my years as a teacher, I had seen several instances of deeply disturbed behaviour, including a girl who smeared her menstrual blood on the wall of her dormitory and another who climbed fully-clothed into a bath full of cold water on a freezing winter day. Monkshill was woefully ill-equipped to deal with such things.

Shaw shrugged this uncomfortable subject aside. 'Anyway, a few weeks after my first visit, this job came up – your job, I mean – and Miss Runciman remembered me. She arranged for me to have it. Just for this term. Mind you I was doing her a favour as well as the other way round. She'd have found it hard to find anyone else so quickly.'

She's very trusting to take you on without a reference.

'I suppose she is.'

You must have left your address with her. Just in case she heard of something.

'Yes. That's right. Just in case.'

I do wish you'd stop lying. There's absolutely no point. How long have you known her? Why is she helping you?

Shaw hesitated. Then: 'All right. If you must know, she's my sister. The first time I came here, I wasn't looking for a job – I was hoping she'd lend me money.'

As soon as he said that, I knew he was telling the truth, at least about Runty. The very first time I'd seen him, on the day he turned up on his bicycle at the bottom of the south drive, he'd reminded me of someone. It had been something about his face – the cheekbones, perhaps, or maybe the eyes. At the time, I'd assumed that he had a vague resemblance to a minor film actor or someone like that. But now I realised that I'd glimpsed a fugitive trace of Runty in him, a similarity of expression, as much as of feature.

'She's my half-sister, to be precise,' he added. 'Older than me. We have the same mother.'

My frustration boiled over, and the next questions poured out of me in a rush: Do you think she loves you enough to kill me to give you a job and somewhere to live? Or was it you? You've got Commando training, so you must know

258

a thing or two about killing. Is this 'temporary visiting tutor' business just a way of easing you into a permanent post?

'For God's sake, I didn't kill you. I wanted a job but I wouldn't commit murder for it. And I know Pam's no pushover, but she'd never hurt anyone. Anyway, she doesn't love me that much.'

Shaw sounded sincere – and indeed outraged that I should think such things might be possible. On the other hand, even if he himself was telling the truth, his sister might be more ruthless than he knew. Besides, he didn't know that Runty had another reason to want me out of the way, a reason that had nothing to do with him: that I'd seen her and PM in an embrace that went beyond the normal bounds of friendship.

'It's more likely to be the other way round,' he went on.

What do you mean?

'That someone else is hurting people, including her. You know that she and PM were ill with some sort of stomach bug? And before that there was all the business about Tosser accusing Little Covey of pinching his weedkiller? That stuff's basically arsenic, isn't it? I know this will sound fanciful, but do you think it's possible that someone tried to poison them?'

Oh God.

'Exactly,' he said. 'It's barking mad. But this place is like that, isn't it? Here I am, apparently talking to a murdered woman about a possible poisoner on the loose. And then there's what happened to Tosser. Probably an accident but – well, who knows?'

You still don't know the half of it, I thought. The strangled mouse. The anonymous letters. The contents of Venetia's puncture kit. The Bear.

259

I felt weary. I had never made Shaw type so much for me before, and the expense of kinetic energy had exhausted me. I gathered what was left of my strength for one last effort.

Will you do something for me? Talk to Sylvia. She remembers lending me Rosemary's pencil on my last morning, the one you found at the Maiden's Leap. Doesn't that prove that I was there on my last day? And while you're at it, go back there yourself and see if you can find my rucksack and my notebook. If you can, that would prove I never left Monkshill. I might have dropped the pencil but I wouldn't have left the rucksack and notebook behind.

The words clattered across the page in the typewriter. Shaw looked up. He was saying something to me but I couldn't hear him. I was fading from everything, including myself, and slipping swiftly away from East Cottage towards the Maiden's Leap like water draining from a bathtub.

And then the familiar nothing.

31

When I came to myself in the morning, I was feeling happy; more than that — *excited*. Yesterday Shaw and I had talked, though the only spoken words had been Shaw's. He'd understood me. He now knew who I was and what had happened to me.

Slowly my excitement subsided and I took stock of my surroundings. It had rained in the night, though I hadn't been aware of it. I could tell by the light that it was later than usual. The rain had turned the earth at the Maiden's Leap into mud. Puddles reflected the sky.

That was when I noticed the footprint. It had been made by a large shoe or boot. The mud was too moist for the imprint to have much detail.

The previous day the ground had been hard, which meant that someone had come here in the night. I examined the area methodically, finding three more footprints, incomplete and with even less detail than the first.

For the last day or two, Mrs Crisp's son had retreated to the back of my mind. Now he returned in a rush. The Bear.

I followed the Gothick Walk a hundred yards or so both upstream and downstream from the platform. I found no other traces. But the earth here was still dry. At Monkshill, the rain usually came from the south-west, which meant that most of the path was shielded from the worst of it by the rising slope of Bleeding Yew Wood. At the Maiden's Leap, however, the stone platform projected above the river, which meant it had more exposure to the weather.

There was something stupidly plausible in the idea that Sam Crisp in a fit of panic had pushed me over the edge. He might even have been responsible for the apparent accident that had ended Tosser's life – it wasn't a huge leap of the imagination to suspect that Tosser had been blackmailing him or his mother.

But Sam couldn't have written those poison pen letters and (if Shaw was right about the arsenic) he couldn't have been the person who had poisoned Runty and PM with arsenic; nor could he have left the artistically strangled mouse in the library.

Who then? The field was wide open.

The postman came during morning break. Enid happened to be crossing the hall when he rang the bell and she answered the door to him. He presented her with the usual bundle of letters, tied together with string, and also with a parcel.

Parcels were something of an event at Monkshill, even for adults. As for the girls, they were desperate for contact with the outside world and parcels punctured the monotony of their humdrum lives. Above all, they held the promise of a delicious novelty: they might contain clothes or books or, best of all, sweets.

After she shut the door, Enid hesitated for a moment with the letters in her hand and the parcel in the crook of her arm. With her free hand she felt in the pocket of her skirt. She crossed the hall and knocked on the study door.

Inside, PM and Runty were having their elevenses. 'What is it, dear?' PM said. 'Oh the post. It's late again, isn't it? Give it to Miss Runciman.'

Enid handed her the parcel but somehow fumbled the letters, which fell to the floor, breaking loose from their retaining string. She murmured an apology and dropped to her knees to retrieve them.

'Who's the parcel for?' PM asked.

Runty glanced at the address. 'Venetia. It's from London.'

'Ah. From dear Lady Susan, no doubt.'

Enid rose to her feet with the letters in her hand. She held out a key in her other hand. 'I found this on the floor,' she said. 'At the corner of the desk.'

Runty almost snatched it from her.

'It's lost its label,' PM said. 'Is it somewhere down there?'

Enid pretended to search for it. 'I can't see it.'

'Oh dear. It'll be a nightmare to find out where it fits.'

'It looks like a room key from the main house,' Runty said. 'It shouldn't be too hard.'

She looked suspiciously at Enid, who avoided meeting her eye. Personally I thought Enid was being reckless. She should have left the key to my room somewhere neutral, like the library or even the front doormat; somewhere that had no connection with her.

Meanwhile PM sorted swiftly through the letters. She looked up. 'Nothing for you, I'm afraid, Miss Archer. I expect your cup of tea will be getting cold.'

By lunchtime it was all over school that Venetia Canford's parcel contained a large round tin, within which was a cake.

And not just any old cake. This was a chocolate cake of almost pre-war splendour. It must have cost somebody a small fortune.

Cakes were very high-value currency at school. The weak used them to curry favour with the strong. The strong ate them with a careless indifference to the cravings of lesser folk.

'No,' Venetia said as she displayed it to the favoured few in the relative privacy of the small classroom used by the School Cert set, 'I'm not going to cut it now. I might not cut it for days. I'll see how I feel.'

I saw from their faces how her audience were feeling: covetous and depressed. The cake had a thick layer of chocolate icing. Quite probably there was another layer of icing in the middle. It was making even me feel hungry.

'I tell you what,' she went on. 'If you promise not to breathe on it, I'll let one or two of you smell it.' She glanced at the knot of girls around her and nodded at Sylvia. 'You first.'

Sylvia bent reverently over it and sniffed. She straightened, a flush on her normally pale face. 'Golly,' she said. 'It's heaven.'

'One more,' Venetia said. She pointed a finger at Muriel Fisher, the tall earnest girl in the School Cert set. 'You.'

Muriel, despite her precocious interest in mathematics and theological speculation, abandoned her usual air of scholarly abstraction and gave way to sensory lust like the rest of them. After her prolonged bout of sniffing, there was a groan from the others when Venetia put the lid on the tin and shut away the cake in its box.

'When will you eat it?' Amanda Twisden asked.

Venetia's lips twisted. 'That would be telling, wouldn't it?'

The bell rang for the start of afternoon school.

* * *

When afternoon school was over, Shaw and Enid went for a walk, even though it had begun to rain again. They must have made the arrangement earlier in the day when I was elsewhere.

They weren't foolish enough to set out together, which would have caused a storm of prurient speculation and unhealthy excitement among the girls and at least some of the staff. Instead they met on the south drive at almost the exact spot where they had first encountered each other on the day of Shaw's arrival.

He was the first to reach the rendezvous. He waited under the shelter of a lime tree and lit a cigarette. When he saw her approaching he threw away the butt and went to meet her. He opened an umbrella and held it over her with a flourish. If he'd had a cloak I'm sure he would have flung it over the nearest puddle and invited her to step on it.

'Where did you get the brolly?' she asked.

'I stole it from the stand by the side door.'

'You do know it's PM's?'

'No.' He grinned at her. 'But she'll hardly be wanting it in the immediate future. The tea hour is sacred. Do you mind if we walk down to the postbox in the lane?'

'Why don't you use the one in the hall? It won't go out any earlier.'

'Ah but this letter is to my bookie. I don't want everyone knowing my business. Especially Runty.'

Enid raised her eyebrows. 'Any other vices you'd like to mention at this point?'

He laughed and shook his head. 'Anyway. Am I forgiven?'

'For what?'

'Our little misunderstanding on Sunday afternoon.'

She stopped abruptly, forcing him to stop as well. She was

tall enough for their eyes to be on a level. 'Look, Alec – you're obviously up to something you don't want to tell me about. On the other hand, you're good at your job, which makes my life easier, and you're sometimes quite amusing. Can you look me in the eye and promise me that you're not planning to do something truly awful, like hurt someone or steal something?'

'Of course I'm not!' Shaw sounded genuinely outraged. 'I'm no saint, I know, and there are things in my past that even I don't approve of. But that's all over. I'm just trying to jog along here. Earn an honest penny. And the funny thing is, I *like* teaching. When I wasn't able to do it for a while, I actually found myself missing it.'

Would that be when you were in prison? I wanted to ask. *Why don't you tell her the truth?*

Enid turned away and they started walking again. 'All right,' she said. 'I suppose I have to accept that.'

'Thank God,' he said, and he sounded as if he meant it.

She glanced at him. 'But don't expect me to trust you.'

He grinned at her. 'I'll settle for that.'

They walked in silence to the postbox in the lane, which was set in the wall of the park. Shaw dropped his letter in the slot.

'Let's go back and have tea,' he suggested. 'It's a bit too damp for walking.'

Enid nodded, and they turned back into the drive. 'Perhaps it's best if you go in the side door and I use the front.'

But Shaw wasn't listening. 'I was wondering about my predecessor.'

Enid gave him a sharp look. 'Annabel?'

'Yes. What was she like? I gather she was a splendid teacher.'

'She was. Especially with the bright girls, the ones who wanted to learn. She didn't stand any nonsense, though.'

'A bit hard?'

'Not really.' Enid was staring straight ahead and there was a tell-tale pink spot on each of her cheekbones. 'Only if she felt a girl deserved it. Heaven knows some of them do.'

Shaw grinned. 'Venetia? Rosemary Lawson-Smith?'

She ignored that. 'And she could be very kind if she thought you were unhappy.'

'You make her sound like a paragon. You must have been great friends.'

'Yes, she was a friend.' Enid sounded flustered. 'We had to work together, of course – especially with the School Cert work.'

Was that all she wanted to say about me? That I had been a good teacher, though on the strict side? A colleague as much as a friend? Why wouldn't she even admit that we had been 'great friends'?

Suddenly Enid pointed to the right. 'Isn't that Stephen?'

I sensed that she had seized on a distraction to change the subject. But she was right about Stephen – he was about two hundred yards away beyond the trees of the avenue. He was crossing a patch of rough, uneven ground at this end of the park. The soil here was very rocky. It had defeated even Mr Lewis's attempts to make it productive. The land sloped down towards the southern boundary, where there were a couple of Nissen huts abandoned by the army. As we watched, Stephen reached them. He slipped inside the nearer hut.

'He must be soaked,' Enid said. 'Why isn't he wearing a coat?'

'Children think they're waterproof.'

'No wonder he wants to get under cover.'

'More likely he just wants somewhere to have a quiet smoke.'

Enid winced. 'They start so young these days, don't they?'

'Just as they did when I was a lad,' Shaw said. 'Come on. The rain's getting heavier.'

They set off briskly in the direction of the house. I watched for a moment and then took a detour towards the huts. It was true that Stephen smoked whenever he could beg, borrow or steal a cigarette. But if he'd merely wanted to have a cigarette in private and under cover, he could have found somewhere considerably nearer to home than this. The stables, for example.

My hunch paid off. As I drew close to the hut I heard voices. The door was a few inches ajar. I couldn't see anything inside other than a strip of concrete floor and a long green tendril of ivy that had forced its way through a window frame or found a gap in the corrugated iron sheets of the roof.

I couldn't go inside because I'd never been there when I was alive. In the days when I had been prospecting for potential places to meet Enid, I had tried the door handle and found it locked.

'. . . something,' Stephen was saying. 'Are the teachers' rooms locked?'

'I don't think so.' That was Sylvia's voice.

'For a start we could search them. See if there are clues. Maybe we can find out who's writing those letters. Or find out who's poisoning people before they kill someone.'

'Don't talk rubbish. Anyway we *can't* do that. We can't sneak into their bedrooms and look at their things. It would be *prying*. It wouldn't be right.'

Stephen laughed. It was a harsh laugh for such a small, quiet boy. 'Don't you know anything? It's not prying when you're a detective. Now Tosser's dead, it's most likely one of them teachers that's doing everything. They're grown-ups, after all. They can do what they like.'

Sylvia said something I couldn't make out.

'But *why*?' Stephen burst out.

'Because we're just children,' Sylvia said. 'Come on. This is just a game. We can't really do anything, can we? Anyway they'd just laugh at us if we tried to tell them.'

'But – but we're *detectives*.' Stephen sounded close to tears. 'We can't just stop with the case unsolved.'

'But there isn't a case. I know we thought some things were queer, but we don't know everything and we're probably wrong. Anyway, I had a talk with Archie yesterday and she says Warnie's all right.' There was a pause. Then: 'Besides, I can't spare the time. I've got to work really, really hard if I'm going to get my School Cert. Especially Latin.'

'You're just a swot,' Stephen said. 'What's the point, anyway? Girls don't need Latin and stuff. They're just going to get married and have babies.'

'I'm not.'

'' Course you are.'

'Warnie says girls can do anything they want. Just like a man can.'

'That's just stupid. Anyway, Warnie's a busybody who likes telling everyone what to do.'

'No she's not.'

'Yes she is.'

A pause. Then Sylvia said sharply: 'So what did she want *you* to do?'

There was a long pause.

'Well?' Sylvia must have sensed she'd touched a sore spot. 'What was it?'

'Why don't you fuck off?' Stephen said in a thick voice I'd never heard him use before.

'What?'

Sylvia sounded puzzled rather than offended. I suddenly realised that she had probably not heard the word in her sheltered life or at least not registered it for the crude obscenity it was.

The door swung back and Stephen stormed out into the rain. His eyes were glassy with tears. I had no time to move aside. Half of his body walked straight through my ghostly outline, and I felt the muted tingle, mild yet unpleasant, of living flesh and blood passing through me.

I watched him running through the rain towards the drive, stumbling over the uneven ground. He had skinny little legs, and one of his long socks had puddled around his ankle.

Something irritated my mind, like a tiny stone in one's shoe.

Why, I thought, *he's just a little boy*. I wanted to put my arms around him and dry his tears.

32

It was no fun hearing what people had really thought of me. Stephen said I was a busybody, presumably because I'd tried to encourage him to think seriously about going to grammar school. I couldn't think of anything else it could have been.

A busybody.

It was as if he had shown me what I really looked like in a mirror. I'd fooled myself into believing I was doing my best for him, and that one day he would thank me for it. Dear God, there was nothing worse than a self-righteous do-gooder.

Perhaps it was as well that I could no longer interfere in his life or anyone else's. I couldn't stop caring about them entirely – particularly Sylvia and Prissy, and even Venetia – but my position was now, at best, that of a passive spectator. I was like the reader of a novel who had grown interested in the characters and wanted to find out what happened to them next. That was all now. That was all it could ever be.

But I still wanted to find out who had killed me. And, in the back of my mind, I was aware that something had hooked my attention when Stephen and Sylvia were talking, something I needed to think about. But I couldn't remember what it was now.

I made my way back to school, where nothing of interest was happening, and then carried on to East Cottage. If Sylvia meant what she had said to Stephen, she would no longer investigate what had happened to me. Even if Stephen continued, which was unlikely now, he could hardly do much on his own. Which meant that my one real hope of finding out the truth depended on Alec Shaw.

The great point in his favour was that I could communicate directly with him. But I was not convinced that he entirely believed that I was who I said I was, as opposed to some sort of mental disturbance in his own head. I couldn't blame him for that. It was not every day that somebody turned upside down your assumptions about life and death.

I went inside the cottage. I heard someone moving about upstairs. For an instant I thought Shaw must somehow have overtaken me, which was clearly nonsense. I was about to go up and investigate when heavy footsteps thundered down the stairs.

The door at the bottom burst open and Mrs Crisp appeared with a bundle of washing in her arms. I suddenly remembered that she cleaned Shaw's cottage and changed his sheets on Wednesdays.

She dumped the laundry on the armchair and went into the kitchen, where she attacked the pans and crockery in the sink as if they were her personal enemies. As she worked, she muttered under her breath, 'Bloody man, bloody man, bloody man.'

She was still at it when Shaw returned. He wasn't best pleased to see her. 'I thought you'd have finished by now.'

'So did I,' she said.

'It's inconvenient. I need to work.'

'I'll go now if you want. But I'll have to leave the dusting till next week.'

'That suits me.'

Mrs Crisp took him at his word. She flung the cloth in the sink, crammed her hat on her head and swept up the bundle of washing. He stood aside to let her pass. She paused, looming over him – she was taller than he was. Her gaunt face was unreadable. She was a physically powerful woman, and Shaw felt sufficiently uneasy to take a step backwards. She opened her mouth as if to say something, but snapped it shut and left the cottage without closing the door behind her. An orphan sock remained on the threshold.

Shaw threw his briefcase on the table, shut the door and went into the kitchen to put the kettle on the stove. He ignored the sock.

Mrs Crisp's uncharacteristic behaviour puzzled me – I had never seen her in such a state. Then it occurred to me that I had assumed the 'bloody man' referred to Shaw. But perhaps she'd meant Tosser. It was only two days since his body had been found. I had already considered the possibility that Sam Crisp might have been responsible for the old man's death. But there was an equally strong reason to suspect his mother, if she believed that he knew of her son's whereabouts and was bent on making mischief.

While Shaw was waiting for the water to boil, he stood in the kitchen doorway and glanced around the living room. It was as if he were looking for me. It was not a pleasant sensation.

'Annabel?' he said in a low voice. 'Are you here? You know, I still don't really know if you exist out there in some shape or form. Or if you're just inside my head.'

I was in fact about a foot away from his right shoulder. It was unexpectedly disagreeable to have him talking to me like this, to hear my name on his lips. Knowing the name of something – or someone – gives you a sort of power over them.

He crossed the room to the table and whipped the cover from his typewriter. He sat down. He had written nothing more since our conversation yesterday evening. Most of the page was filled with my side of the conversation. He picked up a pencil and crossed out everything I had made him write. He took a deep breath and began to type like a maniac, as if his life depended on it.

Cynthia took a deep breath, bent down and sniffed. The unmistakable odour of bitter almonds hung in the air. She recoiled with a cry. Cyanide!

As she stepped back, her heel collided with something small and metallic. She glanced down. A silver—

Shaw came to the end of the page. He tore it out of the typewriter, wound in a fresh sheet and began to type again in the same frenzied way.

—hip flask was on the floor. She picked it up and opened it. Brandy – yet underlying it there was a tell-tale hint of bitter almonds. So this was how the poison had been administered.

She turned the hip flask over. Engraved on the other side was the familiar outline of the family crest, a winged dragon displayed over a turtle. Heavens! Roddy had a flask just like this. He— This really won't do, Mr Shaw. Cliche after cliche. You'll have to rewrite this whole scene.

He raised both hands in a gesture of submission. 'I knew you were there. I could *feel* you.'

I doubt it, I said, and watched his fingers type like mad things. You're imagining things. But you're not imagining me. Ping.

'I talked to Enid about you.'

I know. I was there. She gave me a clean bill of health. As a teacher, at least.

He nodded. 'And I also had a word with Sylvia after lunch.'

And?

'She confirmed what you said. That she'd given you Rosemary Lawson-Smith's pencil on the day you disappeared.'

So that proves it, yes? I'm not a hallucination. I'm real.

Shaw grunted. The corners of his mouth turned down.

You might have the grace to look happier about it. Which would you rather: chat with me or discover you were mad?

'I just wish you'd shut up,' he said. 'And stop pestering me.'

I will. Once you've helped me. Then I'll let you get on with your awful detective novel in peace.

'All right.'

The first thing you need to know is that everything is more complicated than you think. I paused, wondering how much to tell him. First, there's Tosser's death.

'We talked about this yesterday,' he said with a touch of impatience. 'Everything says it was an accident. An accident waiting to happen. We'd have heard by now if the police thought it was anything else. It was dark, after all, and he was drunk as a lord.'

Perhaps. But he must have known the way blindfold. I think someone might have tampered with those planks.

'But you can't be sure, eh?' Shaw was growing used to this: he was talking to me as though I were sitting on the other side of the table. 'And even if they did, it wouldn't prove an intention to murder.'

He was right. I said: You mentioned the possibility that someone gave arsenic to PM and your sister. Luigi and Tosser both had access to arsenic. So did Miss Covey.

'Little Covey?' He threw back his head and laughed. 'You can't believe she'd wilfully poison anything. Even a rat.'

She was very distressed after the row with Tosser. Her garden was like a child to her. And when she came to tell PM and your sister what Tosser had done, they wouldn't even listen to her.

He was silent.

Yesterday morning, you stopped Venetia running away.

'What?' His head jerked up. 'So you saw that too?' When I made no comment, he went on, 'Anyway she wouldn't have got very far with a puncture.'

I thought you handled it rather well.

'Thank you,' he said drily.

She paid Stephen to mend the puncture. She had one of those John Bull puncture repair kits. Do you know what he found in the tin? A brown paper bag with a few grains of powder in it. Senhouse said it was weedkiller. Or rat poison. Arsenic, in other words.

Shaw moistened his lips. 'Why would Venetia want to poison them?'

I don't know. But I do know she follows her impulses and she's quite capable of being cruel for its own sake.

'For God's sake, she's just a child. Precocious in some ways, I grant you, and terribly spoilt. But I can't see her as a potential murderer.'

Then you're a fool. In the right circumstances, I'm sure we're all capable of killing.

Ping.

Shaw was beginning to irritate me. In any case, I was tired. I went away.

33

After supper, there was a great deal of whispered conversation among the School Cert set – Sylvia, Prissy, Muriel and the Twisden twins. This was unusual, because Muriel and the Twisdens were in Seymour House, whereas Sylvia and Prissy were in Cavendish. Apart from lessons, members of different houses tended not to mingle.

What made it odder was that sometimes Venetia took part in these conversations. Earlier in the day Venetia had tantalised the School Cert class with a glimpse and a sniff of her cake. Here she was again, talking to them. They were a very different sort of girl from her, both in character and background. I'd heard her dismiss them as 'the most ghastly swots'.

Something was in the wind, and it didn't take much to suspect that it was connected with the cake. Illicit feasts often took place after lights out, just as they did in the school stories that partly inspired them. Thanks to the war, 'feast' was hardly the appropriate word to describe a meal that typically consisted of a handful of stale biscuits or a tin of beans. But the imagination did wonderful things. As I said, names had power, and in more ways than one.

While they were doing their teeth, I heard Prissy whisper to Sylvia that she wasn't sure she could stop herself falling asleep. Sylvia told her not to worry, that Venetia never needed much sleep, and if necessary she would wake both of them at midnight.

'But she might leave me behind,' Prissy hissed. 'Anyway I don't know why she asked me in the first place.'

Sylvia spat out a mouthful of toothpaste and water. 'What does it matter if she gives us some of that cake? You didn't smell it. I did.'

Venetia came in and they both fell silent, no doubt fearing that an incautious word might jeopardise their invitations. Venetia didn't speak to anyone, but there was nothing unusual in that.

When they had finished brushing their hair, one by one the girls got into bed. Sylvia read *Busman's Honeymoon*. Prissy was trying to memorise French irregular verbs for Enid. Venetia methodically investigated the contents of her nostrils. (She was in many ways a disgusting child with few inhibitions and only a limited acquaintance with personal hygiene.) The other three girls in the dormitory chattered among themselves; they clearly had no idea that this was anything other than a normal night.

Little Covey arrived to take lights out. As luck would have it, she was on duty that night. She was by far the least observant teacher on the staff.

'Have we all said our prayers?' she asked, her fingers on the light switch.

There was an embarrassed mumble from five of the beds.

The exception was Venetia, who turned her head on the pillow to face the window.

'Nighty-night, then.'

Little Covey plunged the dormitory into darkness. I waited by the window. Prissy fell asleep almost at once and after a while began to mutter, which she often did at night, her words jumbled and anxious, as if she were having a conversation with someone only she could hear, someone she was afraid of. Sylvia continued to commune with Lord Peter and his bride for another twenty minutes by the light of her torch.

The girls dropped off, one by one, with the exception of Venetia, who lay on her bed with her face turned to the ceiling. In the pale light, she looked like the graven image of a saintly ancestor, eternally at rest on the top of a tomb.

I settled by the windowsill. It was wide enough for me to have sat there in the old days when I was taking lights out. I looked out over the park. The light was draining from the sky, and the trees were already reduced to cardboard silhouettes.

It was very peaceful. Had I been at the Maiden's Leap, I believe I would have drifted into the nightly absence. But every now and then I would jerk into full consciousness when Venetia stirred and brought up her arm to read the illuminated dial of her wristwatch.

At last she pushed back the covers and slipped out of bed. She pulled out a bag which had been under her pillow and removed a torch from it. She shook Sylvia's shoulder violently. Sylvia reared up in the bed, and Venetia clamped a hand over her mouth.

'It's time. Come on. Bring your torch. Wake Prissy.'

Yawning, Sylvia staggered over to Prissy's bed and pressed the temple in front of her right ear. Nothing happened.

'What are you doing?' Venetia hissed. 'Pinch her or something.'

'This is an old hunter's trick to wake someone so they don't make a noise. I think it was in a book by John Buchan.'

'Well, John Buchan doesn't know what he's talking about.'

Venetia pushed Sylvia aside and pinched Prissy's arm so hard that the unfortunate girl squealed.

'Ssh! Get up. We're going.'

'Dressing gowns,' Sylvia said. 'Slippers.'

Even Venetia saw the sense of this. The three of them crept from the dormitory, leaving the other three still asleep. Venetia opened a door on the other side of the passage, which led to the windowless closet where the dirty laundry was collected in large wicker baskets. She delved into a heap of dirty linen and brought out the cake tin.

'I'm tired,' Prissy whimpered. 'I want to go back to bed.'

'Wait.' Venetia prised off the lid of the tin. 'Smell this.'

Prissy obeyed. She moaned softly.

'Come on.'

Venetia passed the torch to Sylvia and led them along the landing, the cake tin clasped in both hands. They reached the door that marked the end of Cavendish territory. At a nod from Venetia, Sylvia opened it, and the three girls entered into the forbidden land of Seymour House.

Almost immediately they turned right and took the narrow flight of boxed-in stairs that led to the third floor. Unlike those in Cavendish House, the Seymour dormitories were arranged on both the second and third floors at the back of the school. There were three doors on the landing. The girls walked to the one at the end, on which was painted the word ETHELDREDA. (The headmistress had decreed that

Seymour dormitories should be named after notable Anglo-Saxon women rather than trees.)

Etheldreda was the smallest dormitory in the school. It had a sloping ceiling under the eaves. It was occupied by only three girls: Muriel Fisher and the Twisden twins.

Venetia opened the door and flashed her torch around the room. 'Wake them up,' she ordered Sylvia and Prissy. 'Quietly.'

She herself crossed to the wall opposite the door. There was another, smaller door here that butted against the slope of the ceiling. At its tallest point, it was no more than four feet high. It was supposed to be kept locked but the mechanism of the lock was so flimsy that you could open it with a hairpin. I had learned that from personal experience.

Tonight there was no need even for a hairpin. No doubt Venetia had already made sure that the door would not be locked. My respect for her staff work was increasing. She ducked through the opening.

'Wait here,' she said. 'Just a moment.'

The room beyond was roughly the same size as Etheldreda, and with the same sloping ceiling. There the resemblance ended. At least half the space was filled by an enormous cast-iron water tank covered with sheets of plywood and loose planks. The walls were unplastered. In the roof, the rafters and slates had never been decently masked with lathe and plaster. Everything was grey with dust and crumbling mortar.

Last winter, the ballcock that controlled the flow of water into the tank had jammed in the open position. The overflow cascaded into the dormitory below. Even Runty had been close to panic. I volunteered to see what the problem was. It had taken me five minutes to free the ballcock, which earned me the short-lived admiration of the school and a glass of watered-down sherry from PM.

From Venetia's point of view, I realised, the advantages of the tank room were the lack of windows and the absence of neighbours. You could show a light here. Indeed you could do almost anything you wanted without the risk of being seen or heard by night or day. For the first time I felt a hint of unease, like a draught of cold air on the back of your neck. Venetia was going to a great deal of trouble to arrange her little party.

She placed the cake tin on the cover of the tank. She delved into the bag on her shoulder and took out three candles and a box of matches. She lit candles and fixed them with drops of their own wax on the cover of the tank. She arranged them like sentinels around the tin.

Whispering broke out in the dormitory behind. Venetia quelled it by crouching in the tank room doorway and hissing, 'Who wants cake?'

There was an instant of silence followed by furtive scuffling. One by one, the other girls squeezed through the doorway. The candles and the two torches spread a soft, uncertain light through the room, illuminating discarded furniture and other rubbish that had been piled beyond the tank at the far end. There were more cobwebs than even I felt comfortable with. They hung like decaying wedding veils from the ceiling and the walls.

'I say, it's jolly cold in here,' Amanda Twisden whined.

'No it isn't,' her sister snapped. 'You're just scared.'

'I'm not.'

'You are.'

'I can see a spider.'

'If you two don't belt up,' Venetia interrupted, 'neither of you is getting any cake. And shut up about spiders or I'll put you both in the tank. There won't be any spiders in there, will there? Or cake.'

The twins gasped and fell silent. It was a completely absurd threat but Venetia sounded so recklessly confident in her ability to fulfil it that neither of them was willing to put it to the test.

Venetia tugged out a small, square table from the lumber and set it up in the open space beside the tank. She brushed the dust from the top with the sleeve of her dressing gown.

'What's that for?' Muriel Fisher asked.

'You'll see.'

'Why don't we just have the cake?'

'Shut up. We need six seats to go round – doesn't matter what. That big old chair will do for two of you. Keep the noise down.'

'It's a bit like a tea party,' Miranda said brightly. 'Without the tea.'

'We're doing something more interesting than have tea.'

I assumed that Venetia was referring to the cake. So did the others. Despite some muttered grumble, the lure of cake was still strong and her guests obeyed her.

'Why here?' Muriel said as she sat down on a backless kitchen chair. 'Wouldn't we be comfier in the dorm? We could sit on the beds. It'd be cleaner, too.'

'There's no windows here, so we can have lights,' Venetia said. 'And there's a special reason why we need a table.'

'To put the cake on,' Miranda said. 'Goody.'

Venetia ignored that. She dug into her bag again and took out a glass – one of the water glasses that the girls used every day at meals. She set it in the middle of the table. My heart sank.

She put her hand in the bag again. But instead of a bottle of spirits, as I had feared, she produced a pack of cards.

Prissy was surprised into speech. 'Are we going to play a game?'

Venetia ignored her. She dealt twenty-six cards face upward in a rough circle around the edge of the table. They were Lexicon cards. Venetia had already sorted them into alphabetical order.

'We've got Lexicon at home,' Amanda said. 'I'm best at it. I even beat Daddy in the hols.'

Venetia withered her with a glare. She upturned the glass and put it in the middle of the table with a crisp tap, as if calling the meeting to order. 'We're going to talk to the spirits.'

'I don't understand,' Prissy said. Under cover of the table, her hand crept out to take Sylvia's.

'You mean a seance?' Muriel said, betraying a certain scholarly excitement. 'Talking to dead souls? I've often wondered if there was anything in that.'

'But what about the cake?' Miranda said.

'Afterwards,' Venetia said. 'This is what we have to do. It's very easy, and it won't take long. We all rest a finger on the top of the glass. Just lightly, and at the same time. Don't press down hard. And then each of us asks the spirit a question. Usually just one spirit comes to talk to you.'

'Is it safe?' Sylvia said. 'I mean, you don't know who might answer. You might get someone like Hitler talking to you.'

'Of course it's safe. It's never someone like that – it's just ordinary people. I used to see Mother and her friends doing it loads of times. She said the spirits are just lost souls who have to answer the questions of the living. But they can't harm them.'

That bloody mother of hers, I thought. Better off dead.

'This is how it works. Once we've all got a finger on the

glass, someone asks the spirit a question. The glass moves to the letters, one by one, and spells out what the answer is. The best questions are the ones that can have the answer yes or no, because that just means the glass can go to Y or N. Otherwise we could be here all night.'

'But are the answers *right?*' Muriel said.

'Always. But sometimes it won't answer if it thinks you've asked the wrong question.'

'Is it . . .' Prissy said, 'is it dangerous?'

'Not if you know what you're doing,' Venetia said. 'And I do. And then afterwards we cut the cake.'

'Couldn't we do it the other way round?' Amanda suggested.

Venetia stared down her nose at the other girl. 'No.'

'How long does this go on for?' Sylvia asked.

'We'll go round the table, and we'll each ask a question. Five minutes or so. That's it. Unless the spirit we're talking to says goodbye before that.'

There was a silence. 'I'm scared,' Prissy said.

I think the others were scared too, even Muriel. The occasion hung in the balance. Venetia must have sensed it, for she picked up the tin and put it on the table. She removed the lid, and the six heads craned towards its contents.

'And then we have this.'

'All right,' Muriel said. 'Who begins?'

'You can if you want, as you're on my left.' Venetia rested her forefinger on the glass. 'Come on. I'll see if there's someone there. Then if there is, Muriel can ask her question and we'll go round the table till we come back to me.'

One by one, the others placed their fingers on the glass.

Venetia took a deep breath. 'Is there anyone there?'

The glass twitched. Then it juddered into movement, covering a couple of inches towards the letter A. Someone gasped. The glass stopped. It changed direction and scraped in fits and starts in the general direction of the other side of the table. Towards the letter N.

But it stopped six inches away from the card. Even I was on edge now. Not because of the nonsense unfolding on the table but because of its possible effect on the girls.

Sylvia said, 'But if there's no one there, they can't answer at all, can they? So someone must be there.'

The glass moved once more. This time it described a neat arc across the table and came to rest at the letter Y. There was a collective intake of breath.

'Your turn,' Venetia said, in an uncertain voice very unlike her usual tone. For the first time I wondered whether she actually believed in this claptrap.

Muriel cleared her throat. 'Is God real?'

Trust her to go for the theological equivalent of the jugular. One of the Twisden twins giggled nervously. It was difficult to know which because they were squeezed together on an old dining chair with a sagging upholstered seat.

The glass took its time thinking about that one. In fits and starts it zigzagged around the circle of cards until it at last came to rest against the N.

'My arm's aching,' Sylvia said. 'Can we have a rest?'

'No. The spirit will go away if we don't talk to him.'

'How do you know it's a man?' Sylvia asked.

Venetia shrugged. 'I don't. Maybe it's a woman. But who cares?'

The Twisdens were whispering to each other, probably discussing the questions they would ask.

'Come on. Fingers on the glass.' Venetia pointed at Miranda, who was sitting on the far side of Muriel. 'Your turn, Amanda.'

'I'm Miranda actually.'

'Whoever. Just ask your question.'

There were more giggles. Then Miranda said: 'Is Mr Shaw really a spy?'

The glass scraped across the table and came to rest beside the letter N.

Miranda made a face. 'I still think he is.'

'That was a silly question,' Amanda said. 'Everyone knows he isn't. That sort of thing only happens in films. My turn? This is my question: when will the war end?'

'That's not a yes or no question,' her sister hissed.

But the glass was already in stuttering motion. By now the occasion had lost the undercurrent of giggling it had previously had. The six girls watched the glass with morbid fascination.

The glass reached the letter S, nudging the edge of the card. It paused for a moment and then took a roundabout route to the O.

'So . . . ?' Miranda whispered.

Venetia gave her a savage look. 'Shut up.'

As if annoyed with the interruption, the glass didn't move for a good thirty seconds. There was an audible sigh of relief around the table when at last it came to life again. It wandered around the table and at length returned to the letter O. Then it moved briskly on to N.

Soon? We'd be lucky. Germany might have surrendered, but Japan wasn't going to give up easily.

The girls didn't seem overjoyed by the news, assuming they believed it. They were all so young, and six years is a long time at their age. The peace would be unknown territory for them, something to be longed for and also, because it was unknown, something to be feared.

'Me next?' Sylvia said. At Venetia's nod, she went on: 'Is Warnie all right?'

I could feel the words aching to come out of me: *Of course I'm not all right. I'm bloody dead.*

It then occurred to me that if I could reach Shaw through his novel, perhaps I might be able to interrupt the proceedings now. I concentrated very hard on the glass, trying to make it move to the N. Instead it moved to the Y.

'That's good,' Sylvia said. 'But I wish I'd asked what happened to her instead.'

'You should have thought of that first. Anyway, it doesn't mean she's alive, does it? For all we know it could mean she's all right because she's dead and gone to heaven.' Venetia glanced upwards with mock piety and then nodded to Prissy. 'Your go.'

Prissy swallowed. 'I can ask anything?' Her accent was more pronounced than usual. 'And will it really know the answer?'

Venetia raised her eyebrows as if surprised by the naivety of the question. 'The spirits know everything.'

Prissy leaned forward, the reflected lights flickering in her eyes. She blurted out: 'Is my mother alive?'

There was an intake of breath around the table. No one moved. All eyes were fixed on the six fingers resting on the upturned glass. Nothing happened for what seemed like minutes. Then the glass glided without hesitation to the letter N.

Prissy gave a single sob.

'My turn,' Venetia said. 'Then cake. Concentrate, everyone. Tell us, dear spirit: who killed Warnie?'

Prissy's chair scraped back. She pushed between the Twisdens and the wall. Amanda's arm jogged the table leg, tilting it up, so the cards began to slide and the glass toppled over. Prissy blundered through the doorway. Her slippered feet pattered over the bare boards of Etheldreda.

Sylvia stood up suddenly. 'This is stupid,' she said. 'And . . . and it's wrong.' She snatched her torch and followed Prissy.

Venetia laughed. It was the sort of artificial, tinkling laugh that adults use when they are trying, not very hard, to defuse an awkward social situation. She glanced at Muriel and the Twisden twins, each of whom was avoiding looking at anyone else.

'I'm afraid the spirit's left us,' she said, 'so we'll never know who killed Warnie. Let's cut the cake instead.'

I wasn't there to see Venetia do it. I was with Prissy and Sylvia as they padded along the shadowed landings and down the dark stairs.

I had followed Sylvia and Prissy back to their dormitory. Which was silly of me, because there was nothing I could do to help them. But the instinct to protect goes deep, and if anyone needed protection, Prissy did.

The girls were exhausted, both physically and emotionally, and as far as I could tell they were asleep by the time Venetia slipped into the room. Her face was smudged with chocolate cake.

By now I was very tired but my mind was whirring so quickly that I knew I wouldn't settle for a while. The seance business had been profoundly disturbing. But there was an almost comic irony that I, genuinely as dead as a doornail, should have eavesdropped on what purported to be a question-and-answer session with a dead person.

It had been nothing of the sort. I'd observed Venetia's

290

forefinger on the glass. She had been the first to touch it and it had been quite clear that she was exerting pressure. But the lights were so dim and uncertain that it was unsurprising that the others had been fooled. Besides, part of them would have wanted to believe that what they were seeing was what it was said to be. We all want to believe in something, and often it doesn't much matter what it is.

The thing that puzzled me was why Venetia had gone to such elaborate lengths to stage the charade – even at the cost of wasting her chocolate cake on people for whom she seemed to have so little liking.

I also thought about the last three questions that had been asked. I was touched by the fact that Sylvia had wanted to find out if I was all right. Children lived mainly in the present, so it was nice to know that she still cared enough about me to wonder how I was.

Prissy's question, on the other hand, had been raw and revealing. The fact she had even dared put it into words, and in such company, showed how desperate she was. No one knew what had happened to her mother but she must have heard something of the terrible news coming out of Germany. She was suffering, and there would be more suffering to come. Yet Venetia had lacked the compassion not to answer the question, let alone to give Prissy a shred of false hope as a temporary comfort.

But Venetia's own question, the one that remained unanswered, was the one that had really disconcerted me: *Who killed Warnie?*

Shocking people was one of Venetia's principal pleasures. Had she simply tossed it into the seance on a whim, a wilful desire to see the effect of a verbal hand grenade?

It was also possible that she really knew something about how I had died. That she really knew I had been murdered, rather than made the question up on the spur of the moment to shock the others.

Leading on from that was the darkest possibility of all: that Venetia had murdered me herself, probably on impulse as she feared I would tell PM about her drinking herself senseless. It would have been so entirely in character for her to tease the other girls about it.

34

When I came to myself the following morning, I saw a man.

The rising sun was in front of him, reducing him to a silhouette. He had a bag or something slung over his shoulder, which gave him the appearance of having a hunchback. A jolt ran through me like an electric shock.

I snapped fully awake. The man was standing beside the retaining wall with its ragged fringe of rusting railings. His head was bent. He was looking down the face of the cliff to the jumble of rocks and the brown river below, as sluggish as an overfed snake.

I was horribly afraid he was going to kill himself. But he straightened. A cloud of tobacco smoke dissolved into the air around his head. He fumbled in the pocket of the overcoat he was wearing and dragged out a beret, which he crammed on his head, drawing it down to his ears. Ragged tendrils of hair escaped from underneath it.

The man turned his head and for the first time I saw his face in profile. He had a thick, bushy beard below a long nose and a receding forehead. The cheekbones were wide and the ears prominent. The coat disguised his body, but I was willing to bet that underneath it he had a big, raw-boned frame.

The Floor Mop – the likeness was striking. Here at last was Sam Crisp.

He stubbed out the cigarette half-smoked and put it away in a tin. He plodded off, shoulders bowed, going north along the Gothick Walk.

I went after him as far as I could but I lost him somewhere beyond the Monks' Arches. He plunged deeper and deeper into the woods where I could not follow, climbing up through the scattered rocks and trees until I could no longer see or hear him.

He must have found a place to go to ground there, somewhere barred to me because I had not been there in life. Some of the features of the Gothick Walk were set back from the path itself. Perhaps, unlike me, he had discovered the Hermit's Cave.

My theory about the Bear's identity had now been confirmed beyond all doubt. The other point was the bag on his shoulder. It was olive-green, quite large and very familiar. It was my missing rucksack.

On my way up to school, I thought about the implications of what I had seen. The Bear really was Sam Crisp. And he had my rucksack. Didn't that mean I had found my killer?

By the time I reached the obelisk, however, my certainty was fraying. Did it necessarily follow from the rucksack that Sam had killed me? Yes, he was a deserter, a fugitive, who faced a military prison if he was caught. But wouldn't killing me have made it more likely he would be discovered, not less? He couldn't have known that my body wouldn't be found, that the spring tide would wash it down the estuary and deposit what was left of it in the sea beyond.

Moreover, if he had killed me, wouldn't he have got rid of my rucksack? After all, it was the one piece of evidence that connected him to me. It was far more likely that the real murderer had failed to notice the rucksack, that Sam had come across it later and decided to find a use for it. If he didn't know I had been murdered, he wouldn't know it was evidence.

Breakfast was over by the time I reached the house. The passages were filled with chattering girls. The lazy were finishing their prep. The housekeeping teams were going grim-faced about their duties.

Sylvia was in the Cavendish dining room. She was on table-clearing duty that week. Her face was pale and drawn. Blue shadows smudged her eyes.

She carried a tray laden with crockery into the kitchen. No one was in the room but Stephen, who was standing by the back door with his hands in his pockets. He turned and saw her. At once he began to open the door.

'Wait,' she said. 'Please. I need to talk to you.'

His left hand was on the doorknob. 'Why? There's nothing to say now.'

'Yes there is. I'm sorry. I shouldn't have said all that.'

He grunted and stared at his feet.

'And I've changed my mind.'

'What about?'

'The investigation. I want to carry on with it.'

He shrugged and opened the door more widely.

'Please,' she said. 'I made a mistake, all right? I'm sorry. And the thing is, something's happened.'

He looked at her at last. 'About the case?'

'Yes. And there's something I need to tell you about Venetia.'

'I can tell you something about her too. You didn't give me a chance yesterday.'

There was a rattle of crockery in the passage. Sylvia glanced over her shoulder.

'Stables after lunch? The tack room?'

Miranda Twisden burst into the room. She was carrying a stack of Seymour plates. Stephen slid out of the kitchen into the yard.

'I say,' Miranda said. 'Why did you shoot off last night? That cake was *heaven*. We ate it *all*, just the four of us. Amanda was sick afterwards but she said it was worth it.' Miranda licked her lips ostentatiously. 'Yum yum. You are stupid.'

Shaw had a free period after morning break. Halfway through, he abandoned the exercise books he was marking and went in search of Runty. He found her in her office near the kitchen.

When Shaw came in she slid the blotter over the letter she was reading. But not before I'd seen what it was: the poison pen letter addressed to PM.

die — you — bit — Ch — es.

Shaw shut the door behind him. 'Could I have a word?'

'I'm rather busy.'

'Come on, Pam. You can spare a moment for me.'

She frowned at him. 'Please don't call me that. You never know who might be listening. And I really am busy.'

He flung himself into an armchair. 'I won't be long.'

'You're getting careless,' she said quietly. 'You're not out of the woods yet. I found yet another cutting in *The Times* the other day. A report about you and that awful man being sentenced. I think I've got the lot now. But all it would take is for someone who knows the school to look at an old newspaper when they're laying a fire . . .'

'Don't fuss. You always did worry too much.'

'That's because you don't worry enough. And look where it's got you.'

He grimaced. 'All right. Point taken. I'll try and be more careful.'

Mollified, Runty left her desk and took the other armchair. 'Anyway. What was it you wanted to talk about?'

'I'd like to know about Annabel Warnock.'

'Why on earth do you want to do that?'

'Her name keeps cropping up.' Shaw grinned at her. 'Enid said she was a good teacher.'

'There were no complaints in that department,' Runty said. 'Quite the reverse in fact, though some girls found her rather brusque. She could be very sharp. It was the same in the staffroom. Popular on the whole, but she was sometimes a little too forthright and strong-willed for her own good.'

'And then she left? Just like that?'

'Yes – no warning. She went off on holiday and she never came back. The police looked into it but really there was nothing to investigate. There may be a war on, but it's still a free country. She was perfectly at liberty to go wherever she wanted.' Runty tightened her lips and then added, 'Of course she may have had her reasons.'

'What do you mean?'

Runty took a cigarette from the packet on the desk. She tapped it on the blotter but made no move to light it. 'Did you know she was at Worcester Ladies' College before she came here?'

'I heard something.'

297

'It's not common knowledge, but she had to leave rather suddenly at the end of the summer term last year. I know one of the matrons there and she filled me in about what had really happened. There's no point in raking over the coals but Miss Warnock resigned. I suspect they'd have sacked her if she tried to stay. Anyway, we had to fill a post, and she was desperate for a job.'

'So you got her cheap?' Shaw said.

They certainly had. Beggars can't be choosers, and I had been a beggar.

Runty steamed on, ignoring the question. 'There was no doubt about her qualifications – in fact we've never had a teacher like her. First-class Honours degree. She'd taught at two leading schools. And her Worcester references were passable, despite everything. Once she was here, she started the School Cert class off her own bat, and it turned out that some of the parents are actually quite keen on the idea.'

Shaw raised his eyebrows and mimed shock and disbelief. 'Fancy that.'

'Don't be childish, George. Times are changing, and we have to adapt.'

'Has PM grasped that yet?'

'Not entirely. But I'm working on her.'

'OK.' He grinned at her, and for an instant he looked like an impish child, not a grown man and an ex-jailbird. 'So on the whole, Miss Warnock was a good thing for you?'

'Yes. All in all, we were quite happy with her. But then she left us in the lurch. Just like that. No consideration.'

'You can't leave it like that. Why did she have to leave Worcester in a hurry?'

Runty sighed. 'It was all rather unfortunate. A girl died.

Very sad – she drowned herself in the river. My friend told me all about it – she was actually the poor child's house matron. She was a very nervy little thing apparently, very emotional. At the inquest it turned out she was particularly upset about doing badly in her exams. She was running a fever at the time too. But from the school's point of view, the worst thing was that she'd developed an unhealthy attachment to Miss Warnock, and she felt she'd let her down. The silly child kept a diary, and it was all there in black and white. It was hard to tell where to draw the line between fact and fantasy. Luckily the full story didn't come out at the inquest. No one wanted to cause unnecessary scandal, least of all the coroner – he had two girls at the school himself.'

'Had Miss Warnock encouraged the . . . the attachment?'

'Well. It's hard to tell in these cases. It does happen sometimes. There was no suggestion that Miss Warnock was at fault. Not officially. But the school thought it would be best for all concerned if they parted company with her. People were talking. You know how it is.'

'Yes,' Shaw said. 'I certainly do. I—'

There was a knock at the door, and Mrs Broadwell came in. 'Some of them potatoes are rotten,' she said without preamble, ignoring Shaw. 'We've got enough to last until Friday if they don't make pigs of themselves, but we'll need more for the weekend.'

'Thank you, Mrs Broadwell,' Runty said at her most stately. 'I'll telephone Mr Lewis and see what he can do.'

Mrs Broadwell sniffed. 'All I can say is he better do it quickly.'

The bell rang for the end of the lesson.

'I'd better be off,' Shaw said. He held open the door for Mrs

Broadwell and turned back to Runty. 'History with the third form. Wish me luck.'

After lunch, Stephen was first to arrive at the stables. Once he was safely in the tack room he lit a cigarette, which he smoked in rapid furtive puffs.

Sylvia turned up a few minutes later. She looked disapprovingly at what was left of the cigarette but made no comment. I was fairly sure that he hadn't smoked in front of her before. It was a declaration of independence on his part.

'Well?' Stephen said. 'Why did you change your mind?'

'Something queer happened last night. Venetia had a seance.'

'A what?'

'It's like spiritualism or something. It was at midnight. We had to sit round a table, with a glass on it, and Lexicon cards, and ask a spirit questions.'

'Could you see it?' Stephen fluttered his fingers, miming ghostly draperies. 'Was it sort of hanging in the air and groaning?'

'No it wasn't like that at all – we all had to touch the glass and it moved to letters when you asked it a question. Y for yes. N for no. Or it could spell out words.'

'Sounds stupid.' But Stephen was interested, I could tell, and perhaps unsettled too. 'Only girls would believe in something like that.'

'Now you're being stupid.'

They glared at each other. The fragile truce was at risk.

'Listen,' Sylvia said, pulling back from the edge. 'Just listen, will you? There were six of us there. People asked things like when the war would end. Venetia was last. She asked who murdered Warnie.'

Stephen coughed and spluttered. He dropped the butt of the cigarette. 'She thinks Warnie's been murdered?'

'Yes. Maybe. It's hard to tell with her whether she means something or not.'

'What did this thing say? What was the answer?'

'There wasn't one. The . . . the table was jogged, and we all stopped.'

He let out an almost silent whistle. 'I've got something to tell you about Venetia too. She had a puncture on Tuesday and she got me to mend it. I found a little bag in her repair kit. It had white powder inside. Mr Senhouse said it was weedkiller or something. Arsenic.'

'What are you saying?'

'Maybe,' he said, 'just maybe, she's planning to poison someone. If she hasn't already.'

'But – but that's horrid.' Sylvia backed away from him. 'She wouldn't do something like that.' But her voice was uncertain. 'Stephen, we have to tell someone.'

'No.'

'We have to. I'm scared.'

'That's because you're a girl.'

'Don't be silly,' she snapped. 'It's because I'm not stupid.'

'Now you shut your—'

'*Listen*. There's another thing. You know that pencil Archie and Mr Shaw found on Sunday? It's a clue. It belonged to Rosemary Lawson-Smith. I know it was that one because Mr Shaw asked me about it yesterday. But the thing is, I'd found it lying around the house during the hols. And I lent it to Warnie on the day she left.'

Stephen saw the point at once. 'You mean it was the very same morning?'

'Yes. Just as she was leaving. She needed a pencil to write down something about my holiday prep.'

'But that means . . .'

'Yes.' Sylvia stared at him with wide, frightened eyes. 'It means that she went into that wood on the day she disappeared.'

'But we don't know . . .'

'. . . if she ever came out of it.'

35

It was absurd to think that he would poison dear old PM. Besides, wasn't he still in Uncle George's study going through his priceless collection of pornographic postcards . . .

S haw stopped typing and looked up. 'There you are. Pornographic postcards, eh? It's meant to be Ming dynasty jade.'

Boring. This is much better. Ping.

He laughed. Not much of a laugh. Just a polite chuckle. But something had shifted in our relationship. He was no longer hostile or fearful. He was relaxed. It was as if he'd accepted that he was stuck with me and he'd made up his mind that he might as well make the best of the situation.

'I wasn't planning to work on the book this afternoon. But I thought I'd give it a try just to see if you'd turn up.'

Any news?

'I talked to Sylvia about the pencil. She confirmed she gave it to you on the morning you left.'

I know.

He cast his eyes towards the ceiling. 'Of course you do. And do you also know I had a chat with my sister about you?'

Yes. I was there.

There was an awkward pause. Shaw rubbed his forehead vigorously as if trying to erase an unwanted memory. 'Sorry about that girl who died.' He waited, but I said nothing. 'And rather bloody for you too. Being forced out of a job for something that wasn't your fault. What was she like?'

An only child. Bright – university material, I thought, perhaps even Oxbridge. A nice kid too, rather like Sylvia in many ways, but more sensitive. Too sensitive.

'What went wrong?' he said.

She was coming up to her School Cert. At the beginning of the summer term, we had mock exams. She didn't do badly but she didn't do nearly as well as expected. I paused, wishing I could find better words, magic words that would make everything all right again. When the results came out, she was very upset and she told me that her life was ruined and she wished she were dead. I tried to reassure her that she'd be fine when it came to the real thing. But she didn't believe me. That night she slipped out of her boarding house and drowned herself in the river.

'But that wasn't your fault, surely?'

The problem was, she had a pash on me. A really bad one. Afterwards, when they looked through her things, they found a diary and at least a dozen poems. She'd torn out a photo of me in the school magazine and covered it in kisses. She'd even made up conversations we'd never had. I told the head all this but I'm not sure she

304

believed me. Anyway, she decided that I'd encouraged an unhealthy degree of intimacy, and the governors agreed. So they asked me to leave. Bitterness rose like nausea within me. I think it made them feel better. The head gave me a reference that was lukewarm, nothing more. That's how I ended up here.

'What about the girl's parents?'

I almost wished I had shut down this line of conversation at the start. On the other hand, it was a relief to talk about it to someone, to put my side of the case. I hoped Shaw would believe me. After all, why would I bother to lie now? The dead have no need for lies.

The mother was very ill. Cancer. I think that was partly why the child was so unsettled, coping with that and with the onslaught of puberty as well. The father was at the inquest, poor man. He must have been at least sixty. I went to the girl's funeral but he turned his back when I tried to talk to him. They're both dead now.

Shaw made a performance of lighting his pipe. Afterwards he looked up as if he could see me in front of him, though in fact I was at his shoulder.

'Well,' he said. 'All very sad. But what now? There's not much more I can do, is there?'

We still haven't found out who killed me.

He shrugged. 'We've given it a damn good try. But now I think that you just have to accept that you'll never find out. Anyway, what does it matter in the long run? You're dead. Nothing's going to change that.'

If I'd had the billhook in my hand at that moment, I believe I would have hit his head with it. What you don't realise is that this may still be going on.

305

'What do you mean?'

There was a pause. He had come to the end of the page. He pulled it out of the typewriter and wound a fresh sheet in its place.

The arsenic for a start, I went on. Attempted murder of your sister and PM? Tosser's death, of course. And there are other things you don't know. For example, someone's been writing poison pen letters. I know of at least three. Your sister's got one which she keeps in her desk. It was addressed to PM but meant for them both. Prissy had another. So has Venetia. They're nasty little things. Letters pasted on bits of paper – just like in the stories. Senhouse found a book when he was emptying the pig bin. It had letters cut out of it. The pigs have probably eaten it now.

Shaw laughed. His frivolity was grating on me. 'Who's sending them?'

I don't know.

'What else?' he demanded.

I hesitated, debating what to tell him. He was my only ally but I didn't trust him. I was still grappling with the knowledge that Sam Crisp had my rucksack. I wanted time to digest it, time to learn more about him, time to make up my mind. If I did decide to throw him and his mother to the wolves in the shape of Shaw and the authorities, there was no going back.

So I told Shaw about something else instead. The body in the library.

'What are you talking about?'

Prissy and Sylvia found a dead mouse in the library classroom. It was on a shelf near the window. It had string around its neck as if it had been strangled.

Shaw snorted. He struck a match to relight his pipe. 'Unpleasant, I grant you. Sounds like the sort of thing Venetia might find amusing.'

It's not just unpleasant. Can't you see, it's a sort of joke? The body in the library. Strangled.

'Why's that a joke?'

There's a well-known detective story by Agatha Christie called The Body in the Library. It starts when a woman's found strangled in the library of a country house.

'Never read it,' Shaw said, blowing out smoke. 'In fact, I'm not sure I've read many of her books. To tell the truth, I don't usually read detective stories.'

And yet you're trying to write one. No wonder it's so awful. Ping.

His lips tightened but he said nothing.

I'll tell you what, Mr Shaw: you help me and I'll help you. I'm a good editor, and I've read lots of crime novels.

That raised a smile. 'Perhaps I'll take you up on that.'

Then you'll have to help me find my murderer.

'All right.' He glanced out of the window. 'But not now. Look at that rain.'

I didn't want to outstay my welcome, so I left Shaw to his novel and went back to school. Enid was in her bedroom. She was sitting by the window and looking out over the rain-washed park and the estuary and the endless sky.

I watched her, marvelling at the elegance of the long neck and the perfection of the small, delicate head. I wondered whether I was the only person in this world or the next who found her so astonishingly beautiful, so desirable.

After a while the rain stopped. She got up and combed her hair and powdered her face. It was almost time for the girls' supper. We went downstairs to find a small drama unfolding in the staffroom.

'He forgot to bolt it, you see,' Miss Covey was saying, her voice high and tremulous.

'Easy to do, especially when you're bursting to go,' Maggie Squires said.

'And there he was! He *looked* at me!'

Vera Hampson giggled. 'Was he enthroned and waiting for you? How priceless!'

'It was horrid!' Little Covey's face was shiny with embarrassment. 'I knew this would happen sooner or later if we had a man using the staff lavatory.'

'It really doesn't matter,' Enid said, grasping the situation with commendable speed. 'I'm sure Mr Shaw quite understood.'

'But *was* he enthroned?' put in Vera Hampson, who was inclined to find her own witticisms so amusing that she liked to repeat them with minor variations. 'Or standing?'

'Standing.'

'Did you *see* anything when he turned to look at you?'

I wondered if Vera had already been at the cherry brandy.

'No – I closed my eyes.'

'Worse things happen at sea, eh?' Maggie Squires said. 'My brother used to come in all the time when we were kids. Mother wouldn't let us bolt the door. I told him to use the garden if he couldn't wait. I threw the soap at him once. Hit him slap bang in the mouth.'

She pulled out her handkerchief and blew her nose vigorously. She dropped her brother into the conversation so often that perhaps it was in the hope of somehow keeping him alive, wherever he was. Even if the best that life had to offer him at present was a Japanese prisoner-of-war camp. Because the alternative was that he was dead.

The door opened and Shaw came in. There was an instant hush. He must have guessed that everyone had been talking about him, and why, but he chose to ignore it.

'I've come to fetch my marking,' he said. 'Forgotten it yet again. Anyone would think I didn't want to do it.'

'I had to move it,' Maggie said. 'It's on the table by the window.'

He turned away to pick up the exercise books and wedge them in the crook of his arm. Miss Covey left the room in a flurry of agitation while he was distracted. The bell rang for the girls' supper.

Shaw followed Enid from the staffroom. He said quietly, 'Something to ask you.'

She stopped, letting the others go on ahead. 'Yes?'

'How would you like a trip to Gloucester after school on Saturday?'

'What do you mean?'

'I thought we might catch the bus after lunch, go to a flick, have some tea and then perhaps a drink or two. Maybe even a spot of dinner. My treat.'

Enid bit back a laugh. 'What's brought this on?'

'Well, why not? Wouldn't it be nice to get away from this place for a few hours?'

'I don't know. I'll have to think about it.'

'Go on. You know you want to.'

'People would talk.'

'Let them.'

'It's not that simple.'

He shrugged. 'If you turn me down I'll just have to take Miss Covey instead.'

This time Enid did laugh. I hated the fact that he amused her. They weren't quite flirting, I decided, but this was the next best thing. I flounced away, insofar as someone in my condition could be said to flounce anywhere.

The sky was growing heavy and dark. People complained about the warmth and the stuffiness of the air. 'My sinuses are blocked,' Vera said, tapping her nose. 'That always means there's a storm coming.'

I went back to the Maiden's Leap earlier than usual. Shaw's encounter with Enid had soured me, and for once I had no desire to spend the rest of the day eavesdropping at school or mooning after Enid. Nor did I want to haunt East Cottage in the hope of another barbed exchange with Shaw.

So I drifted down the path from the yew tree. To my surprise I saw Sam Crisp sitting on the stone bench and smoking a cigarette. My rucksack and his overcoat were beside him. *What cheek*, I thought. *Especially if you killed me.*

Just as he was stubbing out his cigarette, it started to rain. The wind had veered around. For once it was blowing hard from the east. It screamed over the flatlands that lined the estuary, shot up the face of the Monkshill cliffs and combed through the tangled branches of Bleeding Yew Wood.

The rain was nothing like the shower we had had earlier in the afternoon. It was hard and driving, as though it had a score to settle. The heavy drops pattered and puddled on the cracked paving stones of the Maiden's Leap.

Sam leapt to his feet, scooped up his coat and my rucksack, and hurried along the Gothick Walk. He turned off into the

310

shelter of the wood, into a steep, dense thicket strewn with rocks which I had never penetrated.

I stayed where I was, watching nature remind the living world of her power. The spectacle suited my mood. The wind brought leaves and twigs, making them whirl like dervishes.

I glanced at the bench. There was something rectangular lying on it at the end where Sam had been sitting. As I watched, a gust of wind caught it up and sent it spinning and flapping in the air. It described an inelegant arc through the air and landed in a sodden heap beside the bench.

That was when I saw what it truly was: a Monkshill Park exercise book.

36

The exercise book was the first thing on my mind when I returned to myself on Friday morning. It was still there, albeit much wetter than before. Even if the pages could be peeled apart, I doubted whether much would still be legible. Sam Crisp had had it all the time, along with my rucksack.

I examined what I could see of the book more closely. It was lying open. I could still make out some smudged letters among the streaks and blobs of ink.

...adi...Los......othick W... ...kshil...ark. My title now struck me as unbearably pompous. *Paradise Lost: The Gothick Walk of Monkshill Park.*

Enid had known I was bringing it on our holiday. She'd even borrowed the old book about Monkshill that I'd found in Gloucester: she said she wanted to find out more about the background before she read my essay so she could ask intelligent questions. She was the only person who knew how precious it was to me, the pathetic piece of original research that connected me to the historian I had once wanted to be. In my vanity, I'd pictured evenings by the pub fire, just the two of us, with her reading my scholarly thoughts about the Gothick Walk and occasionally letting fall an admiring comment.

Before we went upstairs to bed.

I needed Shaw here as soon as possible, before the weather destroyed what was left of the exercise book or even blew it away. I would tell him to show it to Enid. It wouldn't absolutely prove to her that I had *died* at the Maiden's Leap. But she would realise that I must have been there on the last day of my life. She would also know that I wouldn't have abandoned it willingly.

I felt a wave of sadness. My work had been reduced to a slab of saturated paper, good only for making papier-mâché. I stared at the book, thinking how futile my efforts had been. That was when I noticed that something else about it had changed.

Rectangles of paper had been torn from the two outer corners of the page. Each measured roughly two inches by one. Several other pages had been similarly mutilated. But not the cover.

The soonest I could hope to communicate with Shaw was after school, assuming he kept to the usual time for writing his detective story. In the meantime, I made my way up to school as much for distraction as for any other reason.

In the kitchen, I watched Enid making one of Mr Lewis's hideously expensive eggs last as long as she could. I eavesdropped on Runty bullying Mrs Crisp. I spied on Rosemary Lawson-Smith skimping the dusting of the room used for dancing lessons and Physical Training. I found Venetia grim-faced in the shrubbery, smoking the first of the day's cigarettes as if it were a solitary penance not a stolen pleasure. By the Cavendish lockers, Prissy was trying to finish her maths prep and looking so woebegone that in the end Muriel noticed and condescended to explain equations to her.

But I didn't see Sylvia. Or Stephen. Their absence didn't strike me as odd, or not at first. The school was a big place after all, with nearly a hundred people milling about inside it.

Enid came into the staffroom, with Shaw strolling after her, pipe in mouth, hands in pockets. To me, at least, he gave the impression that he owned the place – and Enid as well. He was all sunshine and smiles. The women fussed over him, even Little Covey, who appeared to have put yesterday's embarrassment behind her. Enid said nothing, and it seemed to me that her silence spoke the sort of volumes I didn't want to read.

Since yesterday, since his invitation to Enid, my complicated feelings about Shaw had acquired a broad streak of hatred. Previously I'd disliked him sometimes and distrusted his morals. I'd mocked his efforts to write a novel. But I'd also respected his skills as a teacher and occasionally he'd amused me. Sometimes I'd even found myself liking him. Above all, he was the only person I could talk to in this world or the next, and for that reason alone I had to cherish him. But now Enid had taken his fancy, and it seemed to me that she was encouraging him. All right, hatred was the wrong word: I was jealous.

The bell rang for assembly. I joined the school in the hall. Sylvia was in her appointed place with the rest of Cavendish House. When all was ready, Vera Hampson struck the opening chords of 'My God, My King'. Attended by Runty, PM descended from the heaven of the first floor and the proceedings began.

After the usual prayers, PM addressed the school about the duties of a parlour maid, and in particular the importance of ensuring that she always washed the tea things in the right order: glasses (if any) first, then the silver and finally the china.

She made the subject last for seven and a half minutes with the help of a digression on the subject of why a man should never wear brown shoes with a blue suit. It was a bravura performance. She only stopped because Runty cleared her throat in a threatening way.

The headmistress moved on to announcements. Since the weather forecast was good, the afternoon lessons would end earlier than usual and the school would turn out en masse to prepare for sports day.

The day's lessons dragged on. Sylvia was unusually abstracted, earning reproofs from both Enid and Vera. After break there was the sound of an engine on the drive, which caused a frisson of excitement to run through the school. But it was only Luigi on the tractor with a sack of potatoes from the farm to avert the threatened famine.

Soon afterwards I wandered into the kitchen garden, where I found Luigi and Mrs Broadwell furtively sharing a cigarette in a secluded corner by the greenhouses. I was pretty sure they were either having an affair or about to begin one. I speculated that Mrs Broadwell had probably been going to meet him last Sunday afternoon when I'd seen her dolled up to the nines in the kitchen yard.

I left them to it and drifted down to Home Farm, where Mr Lewis was deep in conversation with two grim-faced men in raincoats from the Ministry of Agriculture and Fisheries. On I went, making a long circuit around the park, down to the lake, upto the North Lodge and at last, as if drawn by a gravitational pull, back to Bleeding Yew Wood.

Judging by the position of the sun, it was now the middle of the afternoon. The girls would probably be outside, with Enid, Maggie and Vera trying to organise them into heats and teams, while Little Covey fluttered about getting in the way and Shaw tried to do as little as possible.

I followed the path down to the Maiden's Leap. Just before the stone bench, I heard voices ahead. Stephen and Sylvia were down by the rusting railings at the edge of the precipice. They were crouching over my exercise book. Sylvia was in her games kit. She must have sneaked off as soon as she'd changed her clothes after the end of lessons.

Stephen prodded the book. 'It's like a sponge.'

'We could try and dry it out. Put blotting paper between the pages, if we could get enough. Or newspaper. Or put it on the hot-water pipe.'

Stephen wrinkled his nose and sat back on his heels. 'Probably wouldn't work. The pages would tear.'

'We've got to try something,' Sylvia said desperately. 'It must be Warnie's. Look – you can see a bit of writing on the cover, I'm sure that's hers.'

'What does it say?'

'I don't know,' Sylvia said. 'Why's it got those bits torn off the corners of the page? Why would anyone do that?'

Stephen glanced down at it. 'Fag papers?'

'What?'

'It's about the size you need to roll a fag. That's what people do if they run out. They tear off any old bit of paper and use that instead. You have to lick it, of course, and it doesn't always stay together. But it's better than nothing.'

Sylvia frowned. 'But who would want to do that here? Anyway, I'm going to take it back to school.'

'I don't think that's a good idea.'

'But it's *evidence*. It proves Warnie must have been here.'

'But she could have come here anytime,' Stephen said.

'No – don't forget Rosemary's pencil. That shows she came here the morning she left. If only we could find her rucksack too.'

'I wouldn't take the book up to the house if I were you,' he said, refusing to be deflected. 'Better to hide it down by the lake.'

'Not where Tosser . . . ?' Sylvia said.

'Why not? No one goes there now.'

'But . . .'

Stephen recovered his self-possession. 'What does it matter? He's not there, is he?' There was now a touch of scorn in his voice. 'Nothing to be scared of.'

'I'm *not* scared. It's damp and mouldy in the boathouse, it'll just make it harder to dry the book out.'

He shrugged and smiled at her in a way that made me want to kick him. 'It's the safest place. We could use the stables but the men from the farm might throw it away.'

Sylvia looked obstinate. 'I'm taking it up to school.'

'Ah, I see,' he said. 'You *are* scared, aren't you? Scared of seeing the old man's ghost.' He gave a theatrically scornful laugh. 'Just like a girl.'

The quarrel flared up as quickly as it had in the Nissen hut the other day.

'As a matter of fact, Warnie says that girls are just as brave as boys. More so, in fact.'

'Warnie this, Warnie that,' Stephen said in a sneering, sing-song voice. 'You've got *such* a pash on her, haven't you? Even though she left you in the lurch.'

'You're a beast, Stephen Broadwell. You should try and grow up. Warnie—'

'Shut up!' he shouted. 'You're just like her. Always telling people what to do. And I *won't*.'

Sylvia stared at him. I'd never seen her so angry, so focused on the object of her rage. 'So what did she tell *you* to do then?'

'Nothing.'

'Come on. What was it? Tell me.'

Stephen looked down at the ground. 'She was going to make me go to grammar school,' he muttered quickly. 'And wear a silly blazer and learn to talk all posh and la-di-da.'

'Well why not? Go away and learn something useful for once. Maybe you'd be able to get a good job afterwards. Earn lots of money.'

'That's what Auntie said,' Stephen mumbled. 'But I don't want to, all right? I don't want to go to bloody grammar school.'

'Oh *I* see,' Sylvia said. 'So you're the one who's scared.' There was a gloating note in her voice that I hadn't heard before. 'You're scared to go away from Monkshill.'

He straightened up, leaving her squatting beside the exercise book.

'You can just bugger off,' he said. But he was the one who went away.

Hell and damnation, I thought, watching him retreating up the path. I hadn't realised he hated the idea so much.

37

Besides, wasn't he still in Uncle George's study going through the old man's collection of Ming dynasty jade?

Cynthia slipped the flask into her pocket. She stood thinking for a moment and then left the summerhouse. She returned to the big house, hoping she would encounter no one.

On her way to the side door, however, she passed the motor sheds. As luck would have it, the chauffeur was polishing Roddy's Lagonda.

He looked up and touched his cap. 'Excuse me, my lady. I'm afraid I've mislaid my trousers.

Shaw muttered something under his breath. He looked up. 'Trust you to lower the tone.'

You do that quite nicely all by yourself. Ping.

At least he was ready to talk. That was obvious – otherwise he wouldn't be here and at work on the whodunnit.

His fingers tapped away at my command. Has something happened?

'Why do you say that?' he said.

Has it?

Shaw took a cigarette but didn't light it. 'Actually there is something. I found a letter in my pigeon hole after school. One of those poison pen things you mentioned. Usual sort of stuff – cut up letters on a page torn from an exercise book.'

What did it say?

'It made some rather silly, rather beastly insinuations.' He cleared his throat. 'About Enid and me.'

Rage welled up within me, as irrational as it was violent. It was nonsense to think that Shaw was responsible for the letter. But somehow I blamed him for making Enid vulnerable. I waited.

'Are you still there?' he said.

Yes. That's the fourth letter. And there may have been more, of course. What did you do with it?

He jerked his thumb towards the fireplace. 'Burned the wretched thing.'

That's a pity. I slid over to the fireplace. A few ashy fragments remained on the grate. I could decipher the ghostly trace of a single word. *You.*

'I know I should have hung onto it. But – I don't know – I just wanted to get rid of it.' He sniffed. 'Why do people write them? It's the malevolence I can't stand. All the planning. It's not just the letters, either. It's the little things like the mouse, and the big things like what happened to you. It's as if someone's playing with us.'

That's exactly what they're doing.

His hand trembled as he managed to light the cigarette at last. 'Then we've got to stop it. Before something else happens.'

My exercise book turned up yesterday during the storm.

'Where?'

At the Maiden's Leap.

'How come it just turned up out of the blue?'

I don't know. I wasn't going to tell him the truth. Or not yet. Perhaps it had been trapped in a bush or something.

'Do you want me to get it?'

Sylvia took it away.

'What was *she* doing there?' Shaw scratched his head, making his hair stand up in greasy spikes. 'When was this?'

About an hour ago. She was with Stephen but they had a quarrel. The writing's probably more or less illegible now. But Enid would recognise the book. And I saw where Sylvia hid it. On top of one of the bookcases in the library. The one just inside the door.

He pushed back his chair. 'I'll go and find it now.'

Better wait until the girls' supper. Less risk of meeting someone.

'There's over an hour until then. If there's nothing else, I might as well get on with this in the meantime.'

We've finished. Ping.

I watched him put a line of xxxs through my addition to his story. Then off he went again, setting his fingers dancing on the keys and studiously ignoring the possibility that I might be reading over his shoulder.

'Excuse me, my lady. There's something that Mr Roderick asked me to tell you – his lordship, I should say now – he said if you do want to use the car this evening, the keys are in . . .

321

I went away, thinking about Sam Crisp. I'd come within an ace of telling Shaw about him. But something had stopped me. I'd hurt a lot of people in my life. I didn't want to hurt another one now. Two, counting Sam's mother.

Not before I knew for certain that he had killed me.

Shaw had to climb on a chair to reach the exercise book. Even then he could only just reach. Sylvia must have had to balance precariously on the back of a chair to hide it up there. When he lifted the book down, it brought with it a shower of dust that speckled the shoulders of his jacket like clumps of grey dandruff, together with a few drops of dirty water.

Once he was back on the floor of the old library, he glanced about him, but not warily. It was almost as if he were looking for someone to share his achievement with. As if he were looking for me.

The fool hadn't brought a bag with him so he had to carry the exercise book in his hand. He opened the library door and set off across the hall towards the side door, leaving a trail of drips scattered behind him. That was when his luck ran out.

The study door opened. Runty was on the threshold. She saw him and froze.

'What are you doing here, Geor— Mr Shaw?'

She closed the door behind her.

'I . . . I had to pop back and fetch something.'

By now Runty had noticed the drops on the floor and what was in his hands. 'Is that an exercise book? What on earth's happened to it?'

'I dropped it in a puddle on the way here,' he said promptly. 'You always did call me Butterfingers. Sorry – made a bit of a mess.'

She scowled at him. 'It's a shame you had to bring it into the house in the first place.' She frowned. 'Anyway, what did you forget?'

'My fountain pen. I thought I'd left it in the library.' He really was a polished deceiver; I was quite impressed. 'And I was right.' He patted his pockets and gave her a distinctly roguish smile. 'See you tomorrow, Matron.'

I followed him outside into the evening, leaving behind both Runty and the distant clatter of the school eating its supper. As he was walking past the shrubbery, a figure slipped from between two overgrown rhododendrons. It was Venetia, probably on her way back from her most recent cigarette.

'Sir?'

He stopped and looked back. 'What?'

'You didn't tell.' It wasn't quite a question, but it wasn't a simple statement either.

It took him an instant to realise what she was talking about – her attempt to run away from school on Tuesday. 'No I didn't. No harm done, after all. Just don't do anything like that again.'

She blinked, looking at the exercise book dripping on Shaw's shoe. 'Thank you, sir.'

You could never tell with Venetia. Sometimes she was pitiless, even sadistic, as she had been at the seance. Sometimes she was a *fille fatale*, prematurely on the loose, searching for male prey. But today she was all awkwardness, chewed nails and pigtails.

'Why aren't you at supper with everyone else?'

'I wasn't hungry.'

'Don't be silly. Supper isn't voluntary, and well you know it. Off you go now or I really will have to report you.'

'Sir? Can I tell you something first?'

He looked warily at her. 'What?'

She ran the tip of her tongue between her lips. 'There's a man in the woods.'

'What do you mean?'

'A man. He's got a big beard.'

Oh lord. That's put paid to Sam Crisp whether he killed me or not.

Shaw made an impatient gesture. 'Which wood do you mean?'

She pointed in the general direction of Bleeding Yew Wood. 'That one. Along the river.'

He glanced over his shoulder. I guessed he was making sure that they couldn't be seen from the bow window of the study. He turned back to her.

'What's he doing there?' he said.

She took a step back. 'He's living there, sir.'

'What, camping?'

She nodded. 'But I don't know exactly where.'

'But what's he *doing* there? Is he a tramp or something?'

'It's Sam Crisp.' She realised that he was looking blankly at her. 'Mrs Crisp's son.'

'I didn't even know she had a son.' He shifted the exercise book into the other hand, releasing another drop of water on his shoe. It wasn't really surprising that no one had told Shaw about Sam. He'd only been at Monkshill a few weeks. 'But why's he living there and not with his mother?'

'Because he's a deserter. He ran off from the army. They've had police looking for him, and the Redcaps too. But they couldn't find him.'

'Then how do you know he's hiding there?'

'Because he came out over the Easter hols and stayed at North Lodge,' Venetia said calmly. 'I saw him at the window and I heard him and his mother talking one evening. He'd had flu or something. When term started again, and the weather was better, he was well enough to go back to the wood.'

'And you didn't tell anyone?'

She didn't reply. She stood there looking at him in the way only a child can, armoured in her own silence.

'Why?' he said. 'I want an answer.'

She stared at her feet. 'I didn't want to sneak, sir.'

Shaw stared at her. His face was expressionless but I knew his mind was racing. So was mine. First, if Sam had spent the Easter holidays being nursed by his mother at North Lodge, he couldn't have killed me. Second, here was the secret of Venetia's ability to manipulate Mrs Crisp. It wasn't the poor woman's need for money, as I'd assumed, or only in part. It was the fear that Venetia would tell someone where to find her son. The girl was a blackmailer as well as everything else.

Shaw wasn't stupid. 'Why are you telling me this? And why now?'

I'd never heard him speak so harshly. Venetia flinched as though he'd hit her.

'Because . . . because I thought someone should know.' She lifted her face to his, and now those blue vulnerable eyes were swimming with tears. 'Please, sir, I don't know what to do. Perhaps he's dangerous. I was scared to tell anyone before. But . . . but you're different.'

Venetia scared? She'd kept her mouth shut while Mrs Crisp was useful to her. But after last time, after Tosser's death, it looked as if Mrs Crisp had decided that enough was enough, and damn the consequences.

Shaw thought for a moment. 'All right. Leave it with me. You did right to tell me. But now cut along to supper or you'll be in serious trouble. Off you go.'

'Yes, sir. Thank you, sir.'

38

I went back to East Cottage with Shaw in the hope of talking to
him. When he came in, he put the exercise book on the slatted
shelf next to the pump in the back porch, presumably to dry out.
But his next move wasn't to take off the cover of the typewriter.
Instead he went into the kitchen and started clattering pans and
crockery.

In a few minutes he had the Primus going with a frying pan
on top heating up a slab of lard. He took a string of sausages
from the meat safe in the larder and started frying them. They
were proper sausages too, which suggested that he'd already
tapped into the black market that operated from the back room
of the Ruispidge Arms.

He left the sausages sizzling and popping and he turned aside
to open a tin of baked beans. There was a knock at the cottage
door. He swore and went to answer it. I was shocked to see Enid
on the doorstep.

'Come in,' he said. 'Do you want a spot of supper?'

'It smells heavenly, whatever it is. But—'

'It will be. Sausages. There's plenty for two.'

She gave him the shy, sideways smile that I'd once told her reminded me of Bambi. She hadn't liked that. 'I must admit it's very tempting,' she said.

'Yield to temptation, Miss Archer. I promise you won't regret it. We can drink whisky afterwards.'

'I don't like whisky.'

'It's not oblig— Oh my God, they're burning.'

He rushed back into the kitchen and lifted the frying pan off the stove. He howled with pain because the handle was hot.

Enid had followed him in. 'Put it under cold water,' she commanded, taking in the situation at a glance. 'I'll look after the sausages.'

He plunged the hand into the bucket of water he had pumped up from the well this morning. Enid took control of supper. Five minutes later he was cutting bread under her direction, then laying the table and filling the kettle.

It wasn't until they were eating supper that he remembered to ask why she had come.

She put down her fork. 'It's about tomorrow. About your suggestion.'

'Going to Gloucester? You're coming? That's splendid.'

'I didn't say I was coming, did I?' But she gave him another Bambi smile. 'Don't you think people will talk?'

'Let them.'

'Anyway, I've got tons of marking to do.'

'But you'll do it so much more efficiently on Sunday if you've had a chance to recharge your batteries.'

They argued the point to and fro while they finished the meal. Their conversation was an uncomfortable echo of the ones that she and I used to have when we were arranging to go away together. It had been clear to me from the start that Enid

328

would allow herself to be persuaded. In our case we had decided to go separately and taken elaborate precautions to avoid people knowing. But Shaw was having none of that.

'Nonsense,' he said. 'No need to be cloak and dagger about it. Vera tells me there's a very good second-hand bookshop in Gloucester. We can say we need English set books for the School Cert class. Simple as that. If anyone asks, we're going on school business.'

Her silence was consent. Such a flimsy excuse wouldn't stop the gossip for a moment. They both knew it and neither of them cared.

'We can skip lunch,' he went on swiftly, 'and nip off as soon as school's over.'

'I don't know what Matron's going to say about that.'

'Don't you worry about that. If necessary I'll square it with her. I think we should find somewhere really decent for dinner.'

'I want to pay my share.'

'I wouldn't dream of it.'

For the rest of the meal they chatted about their projected outing like a pair of excited children. Meanwhile I nursed my jealousy of Shaw. If he had had any decency, I thought, he should have said something about me to Enid by now. I so desperately wanted her to know that I hadn't left her voluntarily. But of course he couldn't. If he told her he had been talking to my ghost, she would very reasonably assume that he was round the bend.

Afterwards they cleared away, at Enid's insistence. Shaw made tea and carried the tray into the sitting room. He fetched the whisky too and lit the lamp, which to me seemed an unnecessarily cosy and romantic touch.

'It's later than I thought,' Enid said. 'The light's beginning to go.'

'Have some tea first, and I'll walk back with you. Do me good to stretch my legs.' He offered her whisky but she shook her head. But she did take one of his cigarettes. 'Actually, there's something I want to ask you about,' he went on. 'Venetia told me something rather odd today. She says there's a man living in the wood – in Bleeding Yew Wood, that is.'

'What?' Enid's face was blank with surprise. 'Who?'

'She says he's Sam Crisp.' Shaw poured her tea and pushed the milk bottle across the table to her. 'Mrs Crisp's son. Do you want sugar?'

'Oh dear. No sugar, thanks.'

'You know him?'

'I know of him.' Enid sipped her tea and went on, 'He used to work for Mr Lewis until he was called up. But he couldn't cope with the army and he ran away. The police came looking for him but they couldn't find any trace. Everyone assumed he'd got to Ireland somehow – the father's Irish, apparently. He must be very young – he can't be more than about nineteen. They say he's a bit simple.'

Shaw leaned back in his chair. 'His mother had him at North Lodge over the Easter holidays, and since then he's been lying low in the wood. Do I have to tell someone? The authorities, I mean. It's a bit of a poser.'

Enid looked gravely at him. 'I can't decide that for you. But I suppose you could talk to his mother.'

'So she could warn him, give him a chance to move on?'

Enid compressed her lips. 'I didn't say that.'

'I need to think it over for a day or two. I daresay the school could do without another dose of scandal.'

'And then of course there's the question of Venetia,' she said. 'You'll have to think about her too.'

'You mean she might tell someone before I do? Or even after.'

The light was changing. Despite the lamp on the table, Shaw and Enid looked less substantial that they had done an hour earlier. Elsewhere the shadows were gathering. The colours were draining away, and the sharp outlines were blurring.

'Well, yes,' she said. 'That could be awkward. But the other question is whether you can take what she said at face value. You see, she does so like making mischief.'

It was eight thirty by the time Enid and Shaw left the cottage and walked back to the house. He left her at the side door and strolled on, pipe in mouth and hands in pockets, looking as if he owned the place.

Enid went into the staffroom, where she put up with Maggie and Vera's banter about where she had been for the last hour or so. Shaw's name did not come up. Enid deflected this line of conversation by suggesting another poker session after all the girls were in bed, a proposal enthusiastically endorsed by Miss Covey.

I went upstairs and immersed myself in the familiar sights and sounds of the girls settling for the night. In Birch dormitory, Venetia was reclining on her bed propped on an elbow and looking like a juvenile Roman empress in a bad temper. She was doing her best to conduct a poll to establish who among the adults at school, servants as well as teachers, was the ugliest of them all.

The other five girls participated in a half-hearted way, largely because that was the easy way out. Most of them mentioned either PM or Runty. But Venetia swept aside their votes.

'No, no, no,' she said. She cupped her hands to make a pretend megaphone and switched from empress to racing commentator.

'And the winner is Floor Mop, and by at least six and a half lengths. None of the other runners is even coming close. The crowd's going wild!'

Sylvia picked up her book. She was still reading *Busman's Honeymoon*.

Prissy perched on the side of her own bed. 'Is it any better yet?' she said, nodding towards the book.

Sylvia turned a page. 'No,' she said without looking up. 'They still won't stop talking, and it's all lovey-dovey stuff that doesn't make any sense. I don't care who the murderer is, and I don't think Dorothy Sayers did either.'

Venetia left the room to use the lavatory, and the atmosphere in the dormitory perceptibly relaxed.

'How's the investigation going?' Prissy whispered.

Sylvia put down the book. 'I went into the wood with Stephen. Right down to the Maiden's Leap.'

'You are brave.'

'We found Warnie's exercise book. The one she was always writing in.'

Prissy's eyes became round. 'So she really was there.'

'It's all soggy after the rain, but there's bits of her writing on the cover so it must be hers. I've hidden it in the library. We know about the pencil too, so we can prove she was there on the morning she died. I'm going back to look for other clues.'

'I'm scared.'

'Why?' Sylvia sounded irritated. 'It's not as if you're putting yourself at risk or doing anything to help.' She didn't notice Prissy's face crumpling like paper. She carried on: 'But I had a frightful quarrel with Stephen while we were there. He was being so stupid. Do you know what? Warnie thought he was bright enough to go to grammar school. But he wouldn't even try. He's too scared to leave Monkshill.'

'Boys are such babies,' Prissy said with the invincible certainty of ignorance.

In the dark depths of my mind something stirred, something shapeless and sinister like a blind sea creature that never saw the light. Boys could be more than babies.

The door opened and Venetia came back. The conversation ended and the creature fled.

The sky was still light when I came down the back stairs, went through the kitchen and passed into the yard. The windows of the Broadwells' flat were open but the radio wasn't on and there was no sign of life inside. Perhaps Stephen was already asleep. I wondered whether Mrs Broadwell had nipped out for a romantic tryst with Luigi.

I set out for the Maiden's Leap. I hadn't gone far when a movement to the left caught my eye. Someone was walking down the path that led to the lake, too far away for me to make out who it was. But the figure was small, too small for an adult.

I went in pursuit. As I drew nearer, I saw that my quarry was wearing a dressing gown and sandals. Maybe one of the children was sleep-walking. I drew close as we entered the woodland that fringed the lake.

The child glanced back, as if sensing pursuit. It was Stephen. He had a towel around his neck. Surely he couldn't be planning to swim in those muddy, weed-infested waters? He could drown himself if he wasn't careful.

When we reached the side of the lake, he turned left along the path that led to the boathouse. The water was a darkening mirror, smooth as silk. At the jetty, the boy stopped and took something from the pocket of the dressing gown. Suddenly there was a circle of light dancing to and fro over the path, the rough grass and the planking.

He was looking for something. That was clear enough. But whatever it was, he didn't find it. He straightened up and untied the dressing gown. He removed it and draped it over the rail of the verandah. Underneath he was wearing pyjamas. Soon they too were folded over the rail and he was standing pale and shivering, looking down at the black water. His body was thin and bony. It looked too frail to house a living person.

Holding on to the side of the jetty, he lowered himself into the water. I heard him gasp as the cold hit him. Whimpering, he pulled himself under the jetty. I heard him splashing around under there. I couldn't see him clearly but it looked as if he was bobbing under the water and then coming up for air, like a duck. Sometimes I heard him muttering to himself but I couldn't make out the words.

I don't know how long Stephen was down there. It felt like hours to me and it must have seemed far longer to him. At last he reappeared in front of the jetty. He hauled himself out of the water with difficulty. The first thing he did was drop something on the path beside him. Whatever it was landed with a dull thud.

His teeth were chattering and he was shivering violently. He rubbed himself briefly with the towel and pulled on his pyjamas over skin that was clearly still wet. Next came the dressing gown and the sandals.

The torch was in the pocket of the dressing gown. He switched it on and shone the beam on the path. It slid from side to side and at last came to rest.

Lying there in the pool of light was a horn-handled penknife with a spike for taking stones out of horses' hooves.

39

A nother dawn, another day. No sign of Sam Crisp.
I returned to myself with a heaviness in my mind,
the neurological equivalent of the leaden atmosphere before a
storm. I was terribly afraid. Sylvia didn't realise how dangerous
her relentless pursuit of clues had become. For her, playing
detectives was a game, albeit one with sinister undertones. But
this was no game – a fact that had been thrown into stark relief
by the disturbing behaviour of Stephen yesterday evening.

Two people had died already, and I was increasingly fearful
that there might be more. We had already come close with the
poisoning of PM and Runty.

The possibilities chased through my mind. My murder wasn't a
jigsaw puzzle, where you could take it for granted that all the pieces
would fit together and make a picture enclosed in a tidy rectangle.
It wasn't like a detective story either, where you could pause near
the end, weigh up the suspects without much caring one way or the
other, and then make a wild guess who the murderer was.

The world was waking. I set off for school. Halfway up
the path to the Bleeding Yew, I remembered something I had

overheard. It gave me another idea, another possibility to join the others. An increasingly plausible one. *But it's absurd*, I told myself. *It must be.*

A robin chose that moment to fly through my chest and out the other side, leaving behind it the usual unpleasant tingle of a living thing passing through my non-existent body. It looped back and perched on a branch above my head, where it sang its song. Robins looked sweet, full of perky, bright-eyed friendliness. But they were said to be ruthless birds, viciously territorial.

It just showed, didn't it? You shouldn't let yourself make cosy assumptions about anyone or anything. And you really should never take anyone on the basis of their appearance. Even robins.

I drifted up to school, where the girls were filing out of breakfast. Runty was marshalling her housekeeping teams. Everything seemed normal for a Saturday, when the fact that there would be no lessons in the afternoon, and none at all on Sunday, made the girls more cheerful than usual. It was a triumph of hope over experience.

I went up to Enid's room. Her best dress was laid out on the bed. Beside it was the blue cardigan that I had once told her brought out the colour of her eyes. Her jewellery box was open on the desk. When I came in, she was stooping over the mirror on the dressing table and applying what little make-up she wore with more than usual care.

She must be in a quandary. If she looked too smart, it would be noticed by the girls as well as colleagues. On the other hand, if she and Shaw left to catch the bus as soon as morning school was over, she wouldn't have much time to make herself look presentable for him. It was clear that vanity was winning the battle.

I stood behind her, looking over her shoulder at her face in the mirror. The absence of my own reflection beside hers always brought home to me the reality of my situation. Instead of me I saw the reflection of a monochrome engraving on the wall above her bed. It showed Sir Galahad kneeling in prayer before the Holy Grail.

I left Enid to Sir Galahad and went downstairs. The girls were scurrying about trying to finish their jobs and prepare for the morning's lessons. Prissy and Sylvia were deep in a conversation conducted largely in whispers. This was not exceptional in itself. It was an established sociological fact that schoolgirls often whispered together, even when they weren't sharing secrets. I settled beside them.

'. . . it's just that . . .' Prissy was saying.

'I know why it is,' Sylvia interrupted. 'You don't have to say anything. You can't help being scared, I suppose.'

Prissy stared at her shoes, which needed cleaning. 'I wish, I wish . . .'

'Don't bother.'

Sylvia turned on her heel and walked off. Prissy turned away to hide her face behind the end of the row of lockers. It wasn't obvious to the rest of the world that she was crying, but I knew. She had mastered the art of silent tears.

The bell rang for assembly. I followed the flow into the hall. Shaw was already there. Enid came in and he made a place for her beside him. She was wearing the brooch I had given her.

'I say, you do look jolly,' he murmured.

She flashed a smile at him but said nothing.

'Slight change of plan. I've just had a word with Matron. I'm afraid she's dead set against us going before lunch.'

'Oh no – why?'

'Vera and Maggie are down to take games this afternoon, and she says it wouldn't be fair if we didn't do our bit at lunchtime. But it's fine. We can get the next bus. There'll be plenty of time.' He lowered his voice to a murmur. 'By the way, I had a word with Mrs Crisp.'

'You made up your mind then?'

He grinned at her but didn't reply.

PM and Runty appeared at the head of the main staircase. I slipped down the passage to the kitchen.

Mrs Broadwell was adding up her accounts at the table. Mrs Crisp was at work on a mountain of potatoes at the scullery sink.

Stephen came in from the pantry. Last night's adventure had left no trace on him. He was carrying a trap. He held it out, obviously hoping for a reaction from his aunt. But she didn't look up. He set down the trap on the table with a clatter.

'It's a rat,' he announced proudly. 'Quite a big one.'

At last Mrs Broadwell responded. She leaned across from her chair and hit him, a casual backhanded blow that sent him sprawling on the flagged floor. 'Get that thing off the table and out of my kitchen.'

He scrambled to his feet. He didn't look at her. He was trying not to cry.

'A rat's a rat, dead or alive,' she said. 'I don't want it in here. Put it in the pig bin.' She bowed her head over the account book. 'And now you've made me lose my place.'

He picked up the trap and carried it into the yard. He squatted on his haunches and removed the rat. Carrying it by its tail, he walked towards the pig bin.

The little corpse swung to and fro. Its pink paws looked as if they were waving at someone.

40

I waited for Enid and Shaw by the obelisk, where the path from the house merged with the north drive. I planned to go with them as far as I could, in other words as far as I had walked in life: which meant to the village bus stop.

I was watching the path that ran between the house and the shrubbery, and then along the kitchen garden wall. But a movement further to the left caught my eye. It was on the far side of the kitchen garden, nearer the gorge and the river, where there was another path. It was narrow and almost always muddy whatever the weather, and therefore rarely used.

A girl had just emerged from the cover afforded by the wall. She was crouching as she ran along the path, as though trying to shrink her body.

The girl was Sylvia. I couldn't see her face clearly but I recognised how she ran – her chest flung forward and her arms pumping up and down.

I guessed that she was going back to the Maiden's Leap to look for clues – specifically to look for my rucksack. This must have been the reason for her spat with Prissy this morning; she had invited Prissy to come with her in the absence of Stephen, and Prissy had been too reluctant to break the rules, too afraid of what might be lurking in the wood.

Sylvia left the path and, still running, charted a diagonal course down the rough grassland sloping towards the boundary of Bleeding Yew Wood. She climbed the gate of a fenced enclosure that blocked her way. Adult sheep scattered before her in the leisurely manner of their kind. The lambs delayed, crying plaintively for their mothers, and then cantered awkwardly after them.

I wanted to go after Sylvia. But I was still obsessed with Enid and Shaw. It made no sense that on some level I should hunger for the pain of seeing them together. But I did.

In the end I compromised. I left the path and slipped among the sheep, who took absolutely no notice of me. But I stayed further up the slope of the field than Sylvia, which meant that I could keep an eye on her while remaining in sight of the drive from the obelisk to the North Lodge.

The minutes passed, each longer than they had any right to be. Then three things happened.

Sylvia reached the bleeding yew. She wriggled into the bushes that concealed the gap under the fence. Within seconds she was out of sight.

Almost simultaneously Shaw and Enid appeared on the drive at last: they were walking rapidly in the direction of the village, and they had already passed the obelisk and the chestnut tree. Enid was wearing the hat and coat she kept for Sunday best. She glanced over her shoulder like an escaping criminal fearing pursuit.

Almost at once, Shaw stopped suddenly and patted his jacket. Enid wheeled around to face him. They were too far away for me to hear what they were saying. I went up the slope to the drive as quickly as I could. As I reached it, Shaw turned away from Enid and limped briskly away.

'I won't be a moment,' he called over his shoulder. 'Just wait there.'

She stared after him. She didn't look best pleased. Soon he was out of sight beyond the obelisk and the big chestnut.

But then there was a distraction: Stephen turned up – not on the drive but on the lower path, the one that Sylvia had taken. Clearly he was following her. He was carrying something, but I couldn't make out what it was.

Enid caught sight of him too. She began to walk slowly along the drive, keeping him in sight. Because of the lie of the land, she couldn't see the yew from where she was. But she must have guessed his destination.

As Sylvia had done, Stephen left the path and went down the slope towards the fence along the boundary of the wood. He climbed the gate into the enclosure, and the sheep reenacted their scene of panic in slow motion. He crossed the field and scrambled over the gate on the other side.

Enid veered off the drive. She watched as Stephen disappeared into the bushes by the bleeding yew.

I felt a jolt of fear when Stephen went in there, a strangely physical sensation like a blow to my non-existent chest. I followed the children, leaving Enid to take care of herself. But when I reached the yew, I couldn't help looking back.

She was walking rapidly down the slope towards the fence, towards me. Her face was pale and grim. There was still no sign of Shaw.

As Enid drew near – if I'd had a hand I could have touched her – first one bramble sucker entangled her and then another.

She struggled to escape. Her hat fell off, and she dropped her best handbag. She swore under her breath. Thorns tore at her stockings. They drew blood from her hand and her cheek.

I slipped past her, went under the fence and rushed down the familiar path. As in a nightmare, everything took much longer than usual. As in a nightmare, that bloody robin was there, perched on the drooping branch of a sweet chestnut sapling and chirping merrily away.

I burst into the open space at the Maiden's Leap. And stopped.

Sylvia was standing with her back to the low wall at the edge of the precipice, her body pressed against a section of the rusty railing. Her hands were in front of her, the palms facing Stephen as though trying to push him back. He was close to her – no more than two yards away. I couldn't see his face.

Stop!

My scream was so loud that I could hardly believe that no one in the living world heard it.

Stephen was dangling the dead rat by its tail. He held out the little corpse in front of him. He inched half a step closer to her.

Sylvia pressed herself harder against the railing. 'Please,' she said in a thin, desperate voice. 'Please don't.'

If only Enid would hurry. But negotiating the path down here would take her a good five minutes, probably more. And she might still be tangled up in the brambles.

Stephen swung the rat forward and backwards. He drew closer and closer to Sylvia. The rat's front paws brushed her hand. She screamed and tried even harder to push herself against the corroded iron of the railings.

'You really don't like it, do you?' He stood back, still swinging the rat. 'Shall I stuff it down your shirt?'

'I'm sorry about yesterday,' she gabbled. 'I didn't mean it, really. Let's forget it, shall we? Let's start—'

The railing creaked behind her. Sylvia lost her voice. She stared open-mouthed at him.

'I don't want to do anything with you again,' he said. 'Ever. You think you're like Hercule Poirot, don't you, and I'm your stupid friend. Your Captain Hastings. The one who makes you look clever. That's a joke, isn't it? You think you can solve crimes, but you can't, can you? You don't even know who put poor little mousy in the library.'

'What?' Then, more loudly: 'Stephen, *please* put that thing down.'

The rat dangled in front of her face. 'The mouse in the library. Remember? With the bit of string round its neck. *The Body in the Library*. You haven't solved that one yet, have you? Or who's writing the letters.'

'Have there been more than one?' Sylvia said before she could stop herself. She sounded younger than she really was, adrift in a world that had lost its certainties. 'But I thought . . .'

'Of course there's been more, you stupid cow.'

That was it – that was the tiny discrepancy I'd noticed earlier but failed to register: Stephen had known all along that there had been more than one letter. *Maybe we can find out who's writing those letters.* That's what he'd said to Sylvia just before their quarrel in the Nissen hut. And in the heat of the moment, I hadn't realised its significance.

'And I've found out lots of other stuff too, things you don't know about because you're too stupid. Like who poisoned Runty and the old cow.'

'And . . . what about Warnie?' Sylvia said.

343

Oh God, I thought. Oh Christ. Was it him? A child? Did I die because I wanted a boy to go to grammar school and make something of himself?

I'd have prayed if I'd known how to. I'd have died all over again if it would save Sylvia. Where the hell was Enid?

'Warnie?' Stephen said. 'Warnie? What about her? She was another one. Thought she was so clever she could tell everyone what to do. But she buggered off, didn't she? Just another fucking cow, like the rest of you.' Then his voice sharpened: 'Go on, you say it.'

Sylvia stared at him. 'Say what?'

'Go on,' Stephen shouted, his temper slipping away. He sounded like a spoilt child. 'Go on. Warnie's a fucking cow. Say it. Warnie's a fucking cow.'

'W-Warnie's a fucking cow,' Sylvia said in a voice not much above a whisper.

He took a step forward, swinging the rat towards her. 'Again. I can't hear you. Louder. Much louder.'

'Warnie's a—'

'Aah!'

Stephen howled with pain and staggered to his right. Something fell to the ground with a clatter. He put a hand to the left-hand side of his forehead. Blood welled from a cut. It oozed between his fingers and trickled down the side of his face. The trickle widened steadily, became a stream.

There was a rock at his feet. It was irregular in shape, roughly the size of a cricket ball, with jagged edges.

I glanced into the bushes. There was no one. No one visible.

Sylvia came to life. She darted to one side, away from the railing. Stephen moved swiftly back, blocking the path up to the bleeding yew. He held out the rat like a vampire hunter holding out a crucifix. She swerved and sprinted into the mouth of the Gothick Walk.

Stephen began to follow but, now half-blinded by the blood and perhaps concussed, he was unsteady on his feet. After a few steps, he gave up the pursuit. He tossed the rat over the railing and staggered to the stone bench. He took a filthy handkerchief from his pocket and dabbed ineffectually at his head.

Time passed. His breathing slowed. Somewhere in the distance, I heard Sylvia fighting her way through the wood. Then footsteps, much nearer.

'What on earth have you done to yourself? Who was that shouting?'

Enid was coming down the path towards the bench. She looked like a scarecrow. One of her stockings had come adrift and she'd failed to find her hat. But she'd retrieved her handbag.

Stephen stood up. Adrenaline revitalised him. 'Was it you?' he said, half angry, half incredulous. 'Chucked that bloody rock at me?'

'Of course I didn't,' she said. 'And don't swear.'

Stephen's anger swamped him. 'Or what?'

Enid looked shocked. So was I, though I felt an unwilling admiration for the boy's refusal to be cowed. Children simply didn't answer back to an adult at Monkshill, and especially not to a teacher. Even Little Covey. Nor did they use bad language, or at least not when there was a danger that grown-ups might hear.

'I shall have to tell your aunt about this. Go back to the house at once. You'd better see Matron right away and get something for that cut. And what do you think you're doing here anyway? You know this wood is strictly out of bounds to everyone.'

Stephen stuck his chin in the air. 'Then why do you keep coming here?'

'What do you mean?'

'I saw you. You and the other one came here, didn't you? The one that went off. You know. *Warnie*.'

Shock spread across Enid's face. The anger drained away, leaving wariness behind. She cleared her throat. 'I don't know what you're talking about, young man. And you should refer to her as Miss Warnock.'

Stephen sensed his advantage. 'She was writing in her notebook, remember? And telling you stuff. And afterwards you sat on the bench and cuddled each other like a pair of soppy school kids. Kissy, kissy, kissy.'

Enid stared at him, her mouth slightly open. At last she said: 'You . . . you're lying.'

He smiled slyly. 'And you came down here by yourself too. Remember? Last holidays. You were meant to be away. But you weren't, were you? You came back the next day. I saw you coming out of the wood by the yew tree. You must have been down here with her. But she didn't come out, did she? She didn't catch the bus. I'd have seen her.'

My mind filled with a white noise that made thought and feeling impossible, like static masking a radio broadcast.

Enid took a step back. She cleared her throat and stared at him. 'You talk such a lot of nonsense, Stephen, don't you?' She opened her handbag and took out her purse. She drew out a pound note and held it out. 'Do you want this?'

'OK,' he said warily.

'And then we'll forget all this. We'll pretend it never happened. Everything. All right?'

'OK.'

346

She took a step towards him. 'Here.'

He reached for the note. She clamped her hand around his wrist.

'Hey – let go – what you——?'

She dropped both handbag and banknote. She grabbed his other wrist and dragged him towards the low wall of the Maiden's Leap.

No, I shouted in a place where no one could hear me, *for God's sake, stop, stop.*

'Let go,' Stephen cried, his voice jagged with panic. 'Let me go.'

He kicked at her shins but she ignored it. He tried to bite her but she held him further away and he couldn't get his head close enough. He was a small boy and Enid was a strong, desperate woman.

Her face didn't look like hers. It belonged to a goddess, grave and calm, cruel and unforgiving.

They reached the wall. She pulled him along to where there was a gap in the railings.

There was a clatter. Another rock ricocheted off the wall and skated harmlessly away. Enid glanced towards the sound. So did Stephen. So did I.

The Bear was lumbering towards us, his overcoat flapping open. Time simultaneously slowed and speeded up.

Sam Crisp was a big, gaunt man, a mountain on legs. His eyes were startlingly blue. The sole of one of his boots was coming away. A grimy toenail, horny as a claw, poked through the gap. His hair was long and matted, and so was his beard. He looked like an Old Testament prophet on the rampage.

Stephen wrenched himself from Enid and ran towards him.

She threw a glance in their direction. She was white-faced

and breathing hard. Her mouth opened but no words came out. She and I watched as Sam wrapped his arm around the boy and led him away from the Maiden's Leap and into the Gothick Walk.

In thirty seconds they were out of sight. Enid and I listened to their stumbling footsteps diminishing into silence.

Thank God, I thought, *no one's been hurt.*

Gradually Enid's breathing slowed. She gave the ghost of a shrug, the merest twitch of her shoulders. Her lips moved. I thought she said *Alice*. That made no sense. But nothing made sense any more. She turned to face the river and stepped onto the low wall. Her movements were neat and precise as though rehearsed. She was usually a little clumsy like a long-legged puppy. But at that moment she was as graceful as a ballerina.

She looked up at the sky. Then she spread her arms and jumped.

41

I stayed inside Venetia's oak for the whole of Sunday and listened to the rain. I'd spent the previous night there too. I couldn't stay at the Maiden's Leap any longer, not after what had happened.

On Sunday morning I heard the faraway bells of the village church summoning the faithful. Later, and much nearer, there came the sound of men's voices, and again in the afternoon. I didn't bother to investigate.

There was only one thing in my mind: the frozen memory of what I had seen yesterday when I had looked over the wall and down at the river. It had been low tide, near enough. Enid's body had been on the foreshore, splayed on the rock-strewn shelf of mud that sloped down to the water. She was lying on her front, her legs and arms flung out, the skirts of her Sunday coat spread like dark wings. Everything was still, apart from the river.

Funny, really. If the tide had been high and on the ebb, as it was when she pushed me over, she might well have been

349

washed out to sea as I had been. As far as I knew, neither Sam nor Stephen had seen her jump. People would have believed that she had simply vanished. But the tide had been low. There were houses on the opposite bank and a footpath. Someone would soon have seen her lying there.

Time passed. Towards evening, the rain became even heavier and more relentless than before. Slowly the numbness receded from my mind and the pain flooded back.

I listened to the rustle of falling water until the blessed darkness took me into its arms again.

I couldn't stay inside the oak for ever. On Monday morning I went up to school. If nothing else, the place would be a distraction from the roundabout of my thoughts, which always brought me back to Enid's betrayal.

I wondered whether she had killed me because she couldn't bear to love me. She'd once told me that she was a clergyman's granddaughter. Perhaps she had thought that women who were in love with each other, women who went to bed with each other, were committing a mortal sin. But how could she have loved me if she killed me?

Near the obelisk I met four vehicles coming the other way. Two of them were police cars. The third was a plain van with men in overalls in the front. Last of all came Mr Lewis on his tractor with a trailer bumping along behind him. I wondered whether they intended a full search of the wood. I hoped that Sam was long gone by now.

When I arrived at the house, breakfast had finished, and the girls were rushing about before assembly. The school had become a place of whispers and sidelong glances.

I looked for Sylvia, and found her in a huddle with Prissy and Muriel by the Cavendish lockers. She must have been scared out of her wits on Saturday by Stephen's behaviour with the rat, but she seemed normal enough now.

There were scabbed scratches on her hands and legs. Brambles? I guessed that she had struggled through the wood and fought her way up to the bleeding yew. If she'd been lucky, she'd have made it back to school without anyone noticing that she had gone.

I moved on. In the staffroom PM was talking to Maggie, Vera, Shaw and Little Covey. Runty was just inside the doorway, which meant I had the unpleasant necessity of passing through her body in order to enter the room.

'I'll put up the emergency timetable,' PM was saying. 'I'm afraid we'll have to combine some of the classes. No free periods, of course.'

'But we will get someone soon, won't we?' Vera said, the words tumbling on top of each other. 'We can't manage like this for very long.'

'We'll need to find someone who can help with the School Cert as well,' Shaw said. His face was gaunt, and he had cut himself shaving.

PM passed a hand over her brow. 'Yes. Naturally. But . . . but it's early days yet. I really—'

'A pal of mine might be able to help,' Maggie interrupted. She looked as if she hadn't slept. 'I had a letter from her last week. She's been filling in at Newport High School. But the girl she replaced came back at the beginning of term, so she's out of a job.'

Little Covey, who had been sniffing quietly in the corner,

gave a sob. She wiped her eyes with a sodden lace-trimmed handkerchief.

'Has she taught at a boarding school before?' Runty asked, ignoring this. 'And could she help with the School Cert set?'

'Oh, I'm sure she'd be fine,' Maggie said, evading both questions. 'She *has* to be fine.'

'Anyway beggars can't be choosers, can they?' Vera pointed out.

PM's cheeks wobbled. 'I hardly think we're beggars, Miss Hampson.'

'It seems so wrong to be talking like this,' Miss Covey wailed, 'with poor, dear Enid so, so . . .'

So dead.

Her voice trailed into silence. Runty said, 'There's no harm in writing to your friend, I suppose, and asking if she would like to apply.'

The bell rang for assembly, and the crisis meeting broke up. I went along to the kitchen. The room was empty apart from Stephen, though Mrs Broadwell was talking to Luigi in the yard. He had brought her a tray of lettuces.

Stephen had just poured himself a cup of tea. But as I entered he stood up and glanced furtively out of the window at his aunt and Luigi. He crossed the room to the huge wooden dresser that filled most of one wall. He stood on tiptoe to reach Mrs Crisp's handbag, which she always deposited on one of the upper shelves when she arrived for work.

Anger flashed like lightning across my mind. How dare he? It was one thing to steal from his aunt, but quite another to steal from the person at Monkshill who could least afford it.

He opened the bag and took out a worn leather purse. He took something from his pocket. I drew closer. It was a piece of paper, folded several times into a square.

Dear God, not another poison pen letter?

But as he pushed the paper into the purse, I realised that it wasn't another letter after all. It was a pound note.

Enid's pound note.

During assembly, Miss Pryce-Morgan informed the school that Miss Archer had had an accident. It was clear that the girls already knew or at least suspected this, and the announcement stimulated speculation rather than suppressed it.

Everyone was confined to the house while the police came and went outside. The girls crowded to the windows whenever a vehicle was heard. After morning break, Inspector Williamson called on PM and demanded the key to Enid's bedroom.

I didn't go with them when he and his subordinate searched her room. I wanted nothing more to do with her. She tainted my memories. Instead I watched Shaw making a gallant attempt to cope with one of Enid's School Cert classes in the old library, while keeping the Second Form moderately quiet at the other end of the room. He didn't do badly in the circumstances.

The police were gone by lunchtime. They took the key with them and they didn't call on PM before they left, which made her grumble at their discourtesy.

They returned when the girls were at supper – a single car this time, containing Inspector Williamson and a colleague, a thin, balding man who was also in plain clothes. As they drove up the drive, PM and Runty were drinking gin and It. Runty had time to slip the glasses into a drawer before they reached the study.

PM looked dubiously at them, perhaps wondering whether the policemen should be offered a seat. Runty smoothly took control and waved them to the sofa, where they sat, squeezed together like menacing, oversized schoolboys.

'Well, ladies,' Williamson said. 'I thought you'd appreciate hearing what we've learned so far.'

'Such a tragic business,' PM murmured.

'Quite so. The evidence we have suggests that Miss Archer may have been in the habit of entering that piece of woodland by the river.'

'Really? But *why*? And how do you know?'

'She took your Mr Shaw there once, and she told him she'd been there before.'

Runty frowned. 'How did she manage to get in?' she asked. 'How did *they* get in?'

Williamson glanced at her. 'We found a place where you can scramble under the fence. It's well hidden. There was a hat just outside it with Miss Archer's name inside. Mr Shaw says it's the same hat she was wearing on Saturday. He says they were on their way to catch a bus from the village when he realised he'd left his wallet in his other jacket. He went back for it, leaving Miss Archer to wait. But when he got back she'd gone. The other lady confirmed it. Miss . . . ?'

The other detective glanced down at his notebook. 'Miss Squires.'

'Yes. Miss Squires met Shaw coming back from his cottage with his wallet. She was on her way to the shop in Flaxern Parva, and they walked together. They couldn't see Miss Archer so they assumed she'd gone on ahead. They didn't realise she hadn't until they reached the village.'

PM frowned. 'I still don't understand why Miss Archer

would want to go into that horrid wood. She knew it was out of bounds for everyone.'

Williamson shrugged. 'We don't know. Not yet. Once you get inside – and it's not an easy business, I can tell you – there's a path of sorts. It goes down to the cliff above the river, to the spot directly above where her body was. There's a stone seat down there. Her handbag was on it. Nothing had been taken as far as we could see. We looked for a note of course, but there was nothing.'

'A note?' PM was looking increasingly agitated. 'You mean a suicide note? You can't be suggesting that she killed herself, officer?'

'It's one possibility.' He scratched his neck. 'And we found evidence up in her room that might support that.' Runty raised her eyebrows and began to speak, but the inspector cut across her. 'I've had a team of men searching the wood, and they found no sign that anyone else was there.'

Runty leaned forward. 'You said there's another possibility, Inspector?'

'Yes. The railing and the wall in front of the drop are in very poor condition. You wouldn't want to trust it with your weight, so if she was leaning against it . . .'

'An accident, you mean?' PM said eagerly.

'Could be. And there's also the fact that she had an old book in her handbag. What's it called, George?'

The other officer consulted his notebook. '*Some Observations on the Pleasure Grounds of Monkshill Park.*'

Williamson grunted. 'There's something in it about an ornamental walk overlooking the river in the old days. Perhaps Miss Archer was looking for it. Did she have a taste for history and old things like that?'

'Oh yes, she did,' Runty said. 'And I suppose that would explain it.'

* * *

... was in a good mood when she parked the Lagonda on the gravel sweep outside Abbotsfield Court. The trip to town had been even more successful than she had hoped. Her plans were maturing nicely.

Shaw was working on his detective story as if nothing had happened, as if Enid were still alive and well. It was just as well that he was. I needed to talk to him.

Humming a gay dance tune, Cynthia ran up the steps to the front door. It opened before she reached it. Nanny's figure appeared in the doorway.

'Oh Miss,' she gasped. 'Come quick. Mr Roddy's talk to me

Ping.
Shaw glanced up, as if expecting to see me miraculously made flesh at his shoulder. 'I thought you might turn up,' he said. 'You know what happened on Saturday, don't you?'
I didn't answer.
'Of course you do. You could hardly avoid it. But did Enid kill herself?'
The police aren't sure. If she did, she didn't leave a note.
'Oh Christ. She wasn't murdered, was she?'
They searched the wood but they've found nothing to suggest that anyone else was there. In fact they're saying it's just possible it was an accident. There was

356

a book about Monkshill in the eighteenth century in Enid's handbag. It includes something on the Gothick Walk. The theory is, she might have been looking for traces of the path and she leaned over too far. Or some of the railings gave way.

He reached for the cigarette packet. 'But that's all nonsense. We were going to Gloucester, to a second-hand bookshop among other things. She was probably wondering if she could sell the book there. Was it worth anything?'

She might have got a few shillings for it. Ping.

Enid had asked to borrow the book when she was leaving for the holiday we had planned so carefully. She'd said she wanted to read it on the bus and be better equipped to appreciate my article when I finally let her read it. If Shaw was right, I thought, her interest in my research had been just another part of the pretence of loving me. It was another sour spoonful of truth to join the others I'd already forced down my throat.

I said: Your sister doesn't think it was suicide. Nor does PM. For the school's sake they'd much rather it was an accident. More to the point, the police are keeping an open mind.

'Perhaps she saw someone down there, someone going into the wood,' Shaw said. 'Otherwise it just doesn't make sense.' He got up and poured himself some whisky. When he sat down again, he went on: 'Do you know about Sam Crisp?'

Yes. Ping.

'You don't think . . . ?'

No. It wasn't him. The police don't think anyone else was involved. Best to leave it like that. Ping.

The smudgy letters stuttered across the paper in the

357

typewriter. Shaw took a sip of whisky. He said, 'I had a word with his mother today. He's moved on.'

What will you do if Venetia talks to the police?

'Deny she told me anything about him. But I don't think she will. Because they'd ask her why she kept her mouth shut so long.'

And now?

'Back to normal, I suppose. That's the thing about schools. Life moves on.'

Are you sure? An accident's bad enough. But a teacher committing suicide isn't going to do the school's reputation any good. Particularly if people remember my disappearance as well. Ping.

'It'll blow over. These things do.'

Not necessarily. And if the school has to close, you'd be out of a job, and so would your sister.

'I'll take my chances.' He lit the cigarette. 'What about you?' When I didn't reply, he went on, 'I mean what about the fact you were murdered? I'm assuming you've been telling me the truth. In which case the person who killed you could also have killed Enid. Are we sure it couldn't have been the Crisp boy?'

I don't see how he could have killed me if he was in bed with flu in North Lodge over the Easter holidays.

Shaw grunted. 'You've been eavesdropping again.'

I'm glad you decided to have a quiet word with his mother rather than reporting him.

'It seemed better for everyone, at least in the short term.' He shrugged. 'But they'll get him in the end.'

He was probably right but I hoped he was wrong. I changed the subject.

Anyway I've been doing a lot of thinking. I'm pretty sure now that it was Tosser who pushed me. Then he got blind drunk last week and managed to drown himself. Poetic justice in a way.

I'd decided that it was simpler all round to attribute both deaths to him, mine as well as his own. I didn't want to tell Shaw about Stephen's expedition to the lake on Friday evening and about his retrieving the horn-handled penknife from the water under the jetty. I had no proof but I was pretty sure that he'd lost it when he was tampering with the planking. Tosser had given him the rough side of his tongue in the kitchen garden. This had been Stephen's revenge.

The boy couldn't have known that the trick he played would turn out to be fatal, not in water that was only a foot or two deep. I thought he had merely intended to give Tosser an unpleasant ducking.

'But what about all the other things?' Shaw said at last. 'The letters? The arsenic? The mouse?'

I couldn't blame those on Tosser. It was Stephen playing nasty little games because he hasn't any other way to use his intelligence.

'But he's just a kid.'

Age has got nothing to do with it. He's a clever little kid with a mean streak and a very big chip on his shoulder.

'You're sure it's him? How do you know? Even the poisoning?'

All the questions. They were giving me what I could only describe as a headache.

I'm sure. I don't think he really meant to kill anyone with the arsenic. I think he was trying to pay people back for being nasty to him by being nasty to them in return. You'd find it impossible to prove anything. With luck it doesn't matter. He's had a very bad scare, and I think he'll stop now. Probably. But you really need to keep an eye on him. Someone has to. His aunt's not much use. Can't you get him away from Monkshill somehow? To the grammar school ideally.

'I can try.'

Promise me.

I remembered the pound note and Mrs Crisp's handbag. Stephen wasn't all bad.

Someone has to help him, and the best person to do it is you.

'All right.' Shaw reached for the whisky. Then: 'So that's it? But—'

That's it. Ping.

I went away before he could ask any more awkward questions.

42

I went back to school in the evening. The mood was subdued. Many of the girls had been crying – the public expression of grief was infectious in a girls' boarding school. Even if they weren't really that sad, it was a relief for them to weep with others. It channelled emotions that otherwise had too few outlets.

In Birch, Sylvia and Prissy were discussing ambitious plans to set up a collection to buy flowers for Enid's funeral. On top of that they were both worried about what her departure would mean for their School Certificate exams.

Even Venetia was affected, in her own way. She was sitting cross-legged on her bed, head bowed, wrapped in a sullen silence and picking dead skin from her feet.

Vera Hampson came in to turn off the light. She too looked grim-faced. When everyone had settled down, she glanced around the dormitory.

'Listen, girls,' she said. 'I know it's beastly about Miss Archer. But I'm sure she'd want us to pull together now and keep our chins up. And do our best for the school, of course. I'm sure you all agree.'

There was a hint of a question in the last sentence, a desire for confirmation. She waited but no one said anything. She wished the girls good night in her usual gruff voice and plunged them into darkness.

'It's like one of your stupid detective stories,' Venetia whispered. 'Someone's murdering the teachers one by one. Who's going to be next?'

Prissy gave a muffled sob. Sylvia said, rather bravely, 'Don't be such a mean pig. Anyway, Miss Warnock wasn't murdered, she just went away. And Archie had an accident.'

Venetia didn't answer. She allowed the possibility of a murderer on the prowl to fester quietly in the minds of the other five girls in the dormitory. After that, no one felt like talking. Sylvia took her book – she was still reading *Busman's Honeymoon* – and wriggled under the bedclothes with her torch.

I went downstairs. There was a light under the door of Runty's office and the sound of voices. Inside she was sitting in one of the armchairs drawn up to the empty fireplace. The other chair was occupied by Shaw.

'. . . it was worth trying,' she was saying. 'Luckily Lady Susan was in. Kitty explained what had happened, and what a problem it might pose for the school. It all depends on the coroner's verdict, you see. If it's death by misadventure, or whatever they call it, we can probably ride it out. But if it's anything else . . .'

'Nothing makes sense,' Shaw said wearily. He had been pursuing his own line of thought. 'Why did she go off so suddenly? I thought she was looking forward to going to Gloucester.'

She looked at him, her head on one side like an inquisitive bird. 'You rather liked her, didn't you?'

He turned his head away but didn't reply.

'Perhaps she didn't feel the same way about you.'

He looked at her. 'I'll never know now, will I?'

'What's done is done,' Runty said bracingly, choosing to ignore the sharpness of his tone. 'We have to decide where we go from here. Kitty explained to Lady Susan how upset we all were, especially Venetia, and how worried we are about whether the school will be able to continue. Anyway, the good news is that she said she'd see what she could do. It seems that the coroner's father used to be the land agent at Fontenoy, and her brother was at school with the chief constable. So there's a faint light at the end of that particular tunnel.'

'Two of them, by the sound of it,' Shaw muttered.

She took a cigarette and tossed the packet to him. They smoked in silence for a moment. Shaw stirred in his chair.

'Why aren't you with PM this evening?' he said.

'She's got a headache, poor dear, and gone up to bed. No wonder, really. Besides, I needed to look through the bills.' She gestured towards her desk. 'And now they've given me a headache.'

'Bad, are they?'

'Not good.'

'Who actually owns the school?' Shaw said after a pause. 'Is it just PM?'

'Mainly.' Runty's cheeks reddened. 'I put in a little money myself. Technically I'm a partner, but Kitty prefers not to have it mentioned.'

'What if I put something in?' he said.

She snorted with laughter. 'Don't be silly. You haven't got any money.'

'Not much. But I do have a couple of hundred put by

for a rainy day. When I was in prison, there weren't many opportunities to spend it.'

'Hush.' She winced at the mention of prison. 'I thought you were broke.'

'I never actually said I was.'

'It would certainly help with the more urgent bills.' Runty moistened her lips. 'But why would you want to put your money into the school?'

'Because I like teaching,' he said simply. 'And now I've got a criminal record, who's going to give me a permanent job at a halfway decent place? Also, I like a challenge, and Monkshill is certainly that.' He grinned unexpectedly. 'And I do have a few suggestions about how things could be run.'

I listened to them talking through the possibilities. Shaw argued that they needed to raise the academic standards of Monkshill to meet what he was sure would be the changing requirements of the postwar world. He wanted to have a say in the appointment of new staff, particularly Enid's replacement. He even suggested he be called the senior tutor and oversee the academic side of the teaching. Delusions of grandeur.

It sounded promising, nevertheless, even exciting. I found myself wishing I could be a part of it: trying to turn Monkshill into a decent school where the girls might actually learn something worth learning.

It was Runty who called a halt. 'I need to go up and see how Kitty is. We'll talk more tomorrow, shall we? And of course I'll have to discuss your suggestion with her.'

'Will you tell her?'

'That you're my half-brother?' She sighed. 'I don't know yet. It won't be an easy conversation. But it would make life easier in the long run.'

He nodded and stood up. 'I'd better get back to the cottage.'

As they were leaving the room, Runty said as her hand reached for the door knob, 'By the way, did Enid ever mention someone called Alice?'

'No. Why?'

'It's rather queer. When the police searched her room this morning, they found a little black notebook. They showed it me. She'd written the name Alice over and over again. She'd filled almost two-thirds of the book. Nothing else in it. Just the word Alice. But we don't have an Alice at present.'

Alice. My heart turned over.

43

By the time I left the house, the moon had risen. The obelisk was a dark needle against a steel blue sky. I passed Shaw walking slowly back to the cottage, his pipe clenched between his teeth and his shoulders slumped. I wondered if he was much more upset by Enid's death than he had seemed with Runty or indeed with me. That was the thing with Enid. She got under your skin without you noticing.

I had no choice but to go to the Maiden's Leap. She might be there or she might not. Even if she were, we might not be able to sense each other's presence. It depended on whether the dead were condemned to be eternally cut off from each other, even if two of you had died at precisely the same spot, if not at the same time, even if one of you used to love the other to distraction.

I slipped under the fence and into the shadows of Bleeding Yew Wood. The familiar path zigzagged ahead into the darkness. I followed its twists and turns more and more slowly, like a child reluctant to reach school.

The stone platform was bathed with moonlight. Beyond the

broken railings the silver landscape of England stretched away into the night. In the distance I heard the familiar drone of aircraft engines.

Enid was sitting at one end of the bench. I couldn't see her, or rather not in the way that I had seen Runty and Shaw less than an hour earlier. But she was there nevertheless, an indefinable shadow of a shadow. I didn't know whether to be glad or sorry.

She turned her head. 'Who's that?'

I sat at the far end of the bench. I didn't look at her.

'Annabel?' Desolation clung to her like a cloud. 'It is you, isn't it?'

'Yes.'

'I thought I was alone,' she said. 'For ever. What is this? What's happening?'

'I don't know. Perhaps this is just a staging post before we go somewhere else. Or perhaps this is all there is.'

'Are there others here . . . others like us, I mean?'

'If there are, I haven't met them.'

'I don't understand.'

'You get used to it.'

We didn't speak for a while. Another plane passed overhead, invisible like the others. An owl hooted, and I wondered idly if it was the one that had flown through me on the evening after Shaw's arrival at Monkshill.

Enid's shadow shifted on the bench. 'I'm sorry,' she said. 'I suppose I should have said that first. But I am sorry. Really.'

'So am I.' I waited, but when she didn't reply, something broke inside me and the angry questions poured out. 'Why the hell did you kill me? Why did you lie to me for all those months? Why did you pretend . . . ?'

But when it came to it, I couldn't bear to say the words to her: *Why did you pretend to love me?*

'I didn't pretend,' she said slowly. 'But there were other things.'

'Alice?'

She turned her head and stared over the Maiden's Leap. 'Would you tell me about her? Please.'

It took me a long moment to assemble the words. Then they flowed from me like a statement from the dock in a court of law. I told her what I had told Shaw, almost word for word. She whimpered, a tiny sound I felt rather than heard.

But I didn't mention that Alice filled her pockets with stones to make sure she sank. I wondered if someone had told the poor child that was how Virginia Woolf committed suicide.

'Two more things you should know,' I went on relentlessly and swiftly, as if I were ripping a sticking plaster from a raw wound. 'Her house matron said that she was running a temperature that evening – some sort of summer flu perhaps – and also that she'd just started her period. She wasn't herself.'

I paused, remembering. It had been a new moon the night Alice died.

'And the other thing,' Enid said harshly.

I couldn't put it off. 'Alice fancied herself in love with me, and me with her. There was a diary – she'd made up the most ridiculous things about us. I tried to defend myself but the headmistress and the governors decided I was at least partly to blame for what had happened. So they made me resign.'

I glanced at her. Enid was still staring at England, not at me.

'You don't have to believe me,' I said, 'but I did nothing wrong. I was the scapegoat.'

She said nothing.

'I know you killed me,' I went on. 'I didn't until Saturday. I suppose it must have been because you believed what they said about Alice and me, and you thought I was responsible for her death. But I don't understand why. Why you cared so much about her.'

At last she looked at me. I felt the heat of her anger. 'Because she was my daughter.'

For a moment I couldn't speak. The lock of fair hair, I thought, wrapped in muslin. I'd watched Enid kiss it one evening, and I'd been jealous. The words stumbled out of me. 'I . . . I thought you said—'

'When I was seventeen, I went to a party,' she interrupted. 'I didn't want to go, but my parents made me. The son of the house got drunk and raped me in the shrubbery. I didn't tell anyone, not then. I was ashamed.'

'And then you found you were pregnant?'

Enid hissed. That's what it sounded like. 'No one had ever told me about that sort of thing. I didn't know what was happening. I thought I must have some awful disease. In the end I told my mother. When she heard what had happened, she blamed me, she said he was a nice boy and I must have led him on. What really worried her was the scandal if it all came out. She packed me off to a nursing home. One of those places where you send embarrassing relations.'

She was crying now, weeping without tears in the way I had grown used to myself. I wanted to say something that might bring a shred of comfort or at least a sense that she wasn't alone in her grief. But I didn't. Because she was alone in her grief and there was nothing anyone could say that would bring comfort.

'Then Alice was born,' Enid said at last. 'She was a lovely

369

baby, quite perfect. Even the nurses said so. I had her for ten days, and she was all mine. Then one night they came and took her away. There was no warning. I just woke up and she wasn't there.'

'Where did she go?' I asked.

'No one would tell me. I only found out after she died. My mother had cousins in Northumberland who'd always wanted a child. They were quite old even then, in their forties. I don't think Alice ever knew she was adopted. I was her mother but I was nothing to her.'

Neither of us spoke for a while. There was no hurry, I thought. We had plenty of time.

Enid stirred beside me. 'Who was it? That man.'

It took me a moment to realise whom she meant. 'Sam Crisp.'

'Oh. I see.' She paused. Then: 'Of course.'

'He's gone now. But just as well he was there on Saturday. Were you really going to kill Stephen?'

A shiver ran through her. It wasn't exactly a shiver because a shiver needed a body for it to run through. But I couldn't find another way to describe it.

'Well?' I said, after the silence had lengthened.

'I don't know what would have happened. I wanted to frighten him, to stop him talking . . . I didn't really want to hurt him.'

'Not like me then?' Enid didn't answer. I went on, 'How did you find out what had happened to Alice?'

'After she drowned, the cousin wrote to my mother. But my mother was in hospital then – she's dead now – and it was me who opened the letter. After that I went through her things. There was an envelope in her bureau. It had three other letters about Alice inside. And a copy of the birth certificate. Even a photo of her on her fourth birthday.'

Something still puzzled me. My name hadn't been mentioned in the press reports or at the inquest. I said, 'How did you know about me?'

She shrugged. 'I went to Worcester. I wanted to see where Alice had lived, what the school was like – even where she died. I stayed there for a few days. I used to have tea in that cafe near the gate at the end of the College drive.'

'The Blue Bird,' I said. It was where the staff used to go. It was out of bounds for the girls.

'Yes. I got into conversation with one of the mistresses. She was a dreadful gossip and when I said wasn't there something in the paper about a girl drowning, she told me all about Alice's pash on a teacher, how you were pushing her too hard. How you'd had to resign because you were responsible for her suicide. She said you'd only been able to find another job at a dreadful school called Monkshill Park, and it served you right.'

'Sandy hair? A mole on her left cheek?'

Enid nodded.

Millicent Fisher. A malicious woman who looked like a dried prune. She'd hated me ever since I caught her pilfering bacon from the girls' meat ration.

'Anyway that's how I knew where to come,' Enid said. 'I wanted to find out what you were like, this woman who caused Alice's death.'

The unfairness stung me. 'That's simply not true. I tried to help her.'

She ignored me. 'I didn't even know your name at that point. But the teacher said Monkshill was the sort of place that always had vacancies because people were always leaving. She said she'd seen one that very day in *The Times Ed*. It seemed like fate. PM nearly bit my hand off when I applied. She liked me because I came cheap – I didn't have any teaching experience.'

Neither of us spoke. I looked anywhere but at Enid. The silence between us was a desert, desolate as the surface of the moon. She had come to Monkshill purely to find me, to kill me, for no other reason. She'd hated me before she even met me, before she even knew my name. Everything I'd thought good about us had been a lie from start to finish.

'I've been trying to work out who killed me,' I said. 'Plenty of people had motives to do it. And opportunities. But I never for a moment thought it was you. You weren't here for a start, and anyway I thought you . . .'

The silence returned. *I thought you loved me.*

'That's why I suggested travelling on different days when we were planning our holiday,' Enid said in a toneless voice. 'If I went first, it would give me a sort of alibi. You told me you were going to come here to check something for your article on the way to the bus. All I had to do was come back that day. It was very early – I caught the first bus – and I met no one. I walked the last few miles through the woods. Then I waited until you came.'

In my mind the words circled again and again. *I thought you loved me.*

'I was going to use the billhook behind the stone bench,' she said. 'But I didn't need to. I just pushed you, and that was better because if your body was found people would think it was an accident. You . . . you made it so easy for me.'

It was the tiny hesitation that made me look at her. I found she was looking at me.

'I thought . . .' I began. But again I couldn't go on.

There was a flurry of movement. Enid was kneeling at my feet. 'I'm sorry,' she said. 'I'm so, so sorry.'

'What?' I sat up sharply. 'How can you even say that? You murdered me, remember?'

'I didn't want to like you. I didn't at first. It sort of crept over me. I'd never even met someone like you. But you were kind. And then you began to excite me. I'd never felt that way about anyone. I didn't even know it was possible. That really scared me, you know, and it made me hate you more. It was as if I was betraying Alice.'

I didn't know whether what she was saying made me feel better or worse. I didn't know anything.

'You can feel two things at once,' she said. 'It's horrible. It's like being in hell. When you love the one you hate.'

Time passed. Enid's hand was resting on the bench. I looked at it. A cloud floated across the moon. It was like being in a cinema when they lower the lights before the film begins.

I laid my hand gently on hers. I curled my fingers around it. She felt warm and soft. Neither of us moved as the moments slipped by. She lifted my hand and kissed it.

A kiss is transformative in fairy tales, in life and in death. Even as I looked at our clasped hands, they began to blur.

Enid was looking at me. 'Annabel,' she said urgently. 'Annabel, what's happening?'

I sensed her growing despair. But I could see her less clearly than before. It wasn't just her. The railings of the Maiden's Leap were fading, and so was the stone bench. And at last I realised that it wasn't the world that was changing. It was me.

373

'Annabel, please,' Enid said. 'Don't leave me.'

Time had lost its meaning. Darkness was everywhere.

My sense of hearing was the last to go. 'Annabel,' I heard Enid say. 'Annabel, I love you.'

AFTERWORD

Novels are like landslides. First you get a couple of pebbles skittering down a slope. They dislodge a few larger ones that encourage more substantial stones to join in. Eventually half a mountain is on the move, inexorable as fate and crushing all that lies before it.

Monkshill Park began with a real place. It's called Piercefield. Three hundred years ago it consisted of a Welsh mansion surrounded by a substantial park to the north of Chepstow. It's bounded to the east by a precipitous descent to a loop of the River Wye. Beyond the river lies England.

During the eighteenth century, the grounds were extensively landscaped. Walks were laid out, linking a series of viewpoints and eyecatchers both in the park and overlooking the Wye. Piercefield became a tourist attraction. Later in the eighteenth century, the Tudor house was substantially rebuilt according to designs principally attributed to the collector and architect Sir John Soane. A Jane Austen heroine would have found the result most agreeable. She might even have married the proprietor.

For all its ambition and elegance, however, Piercefield was an unlucky place. During the eighteenth and nineteenth centuries, it changed hands frequently, usually because its owners could no longer afford to keep it up. One of them was Nathaniel Wells, a former slave who, in the absence of legitimate heirs, inherited his father's plantations in the Caribbean and settled down as a landed gentleman in Monmouthshire; he became a Justice of the Peace and High Sheriff of the county before the sugar money ran low and he had to sell.

In the twentieth century, the estate went into a steep decline. After World War II, the house's fittings were sold off, many of them to museums, and the shell left to decay.

Nowadays the park is reduced in size, and Chepstow racecourse occupies most of its western portion. The house is a roofless box of cracked stone and crumbling brick surrounded by a security fence. But there are still footpaths, and you can still visit the outside of the mansion and walk along the heavily wooded ridge above the river and find traces of those eighteenth-century viewpoints.

I have been visiting Piercefield for thirty years. At first it was possible to enter the ruined interior of the house and explore what remained of the extensive kitchen garden and the stables. That can no longer be done. Every year, the decay advances a little further. In another twenty years, despite Herculean efforts by local people, all that may be left of the Grade I house is a pile of rubble buried in weeds and scrub. If you want to find out more about Piercefield's history, I would recommend as a starting point 'Early Tourists in Wales' (https://sublimewales. wordpress.com/), a useful resource with many suggestions for further research.

Whatever happens to Piercefield, it will still exist in the

memory and flourish in the imagination. I created Monkshill Park, its fictional cousin, over twenty years ago. It's one of the main locations in my novel *The American Boy* (2003), which is set in 1819–20 and shows Monkshill in its splendid prime. But, as Piercefield itself continued its inexorable decline in the real world, I felt an increasing desire to go back to the fictional Monkshill and discover what had happened to it more than a century after the events in *The American Boy*.

Which is where the school came in. A few years ago, Averil Kear of the Forest of Dean Local History Society researched a girls' boarding school that was evacuated to Lydney Park, a mansion ten miles north of Chepstow, during part of World War II. My immediate thought was what a wonderful set-up for a murder mystery, a riff on the Golden Age country house whodunnit with a cast of schoolgirls and adults, incomers and locals. The mystery would be set at Monkshill Park. And – this idea came later, when I was halfway through the first draft – the mystery would operate on more than one level.

Two books were particularly useful for my research, and I have plundered them mercilessly. Gillian Avery's *The Best Type of Girl* (1991) is an authoritative historical survey of girls' boarding schools. Even more useful for my purposes was Ysenda Maxtone Graham's gloriously anecdotal *Terms & Conditions* (2016), which covers the eccentric sub-culture of girls' boarding schools from 1930 to 1970.

Many people have helped in different ways. I'm particularly grateful to Averil Kear, of course. I should also like to thank my crime-writing colleague Priscilla Masters, who gave me a photograph of a child called Sus Knecht, a little Jewish girl trapped in Nazi Germany. Priscilla's parents offered to adopt her and made arrangements to bring her to the UK. The photo arrived but the child didn't. I promised Cilla that one day I would put the lost girl in a novel. At last, in the form of Prissy, I have. This one at least has survived.

Daphne Wright, better known as the crime writer Natasha Cooper, gave me Mr Senhouse, the man who knows a thing or two about boilers. My brother-in-law Peter Wightman lent me his mother and her motorbike, the origin of Lady Susan. (In the dark days of World War II, Mrs Wightman borrowed her husband's motorbike and rode it from Gloucestershire to London. Unlike Lady Susan, she had never ridden a motorbike before and was five months pregnant with Peter.) Roger Deeks and my cousin Ian Kew identified the model of the Wightman motorbike from a photograph. Cheryl Paten and Sue Barker read the first draft and provided truly vital reassurance, perhaps more than they realise. Thank you all.

I doubt the novel would have seen the light of day without the enthusiasm and the rigorous editorial support of my editor, Julia Wisdom, and of Lizz Burrell and other colleagues at HarperCollins. Equally essential was my all-seeing, all-wise agent, Antony Topping.

Finally, this book is for my wife, Caroline, because it wouldn't have been written without her. As ever.